The Hardest Fall

The Hardest Fall

Ella Maise

SIMON & SCHUSTER

London · New York · Sydney · Toronto · New Delhi

First published by Ella Maise 2018

This paperback edition published by Simon and Schuster 2022

Copyright © Ella Maise, 2018

The right of Ella Maise to be identified as author of
this work has been asserted in accordance with the
Copyright, Designs and Patents Act, 1988.

1 3 5 7 9 10 8 6 4 2

Simon & Schuster UK Ltd
1st Floor
222 Gray's Inn Road
London WC1X 8HB

Simon & Schuster Australia, Sydney
Simon & Schuster India, New Delhi

www.simonandschuster.co.uk
www.simonandschuster.com.au
www.simonandschuster.co.in

A CIP catalogue record for this book
is available from the British Library

Paperback ISBN: 978-1-3985-2160-5
eBook ISBN: 978-1-3985-2161-2

Printed and bound in Great Britain by
CPI Group (UK) Ltd, Croydon, CR0 4YY

This book is for those of us who are a little shy with a little bit of weird mixed in (in the best possible way). I hope you have a Dylan in your life.

CHAPTER ONE

DYLAN

The first time Zoe Clarke saw me, my hand was wrapped around my dick.

Unfortunately, I wasn't jerking off. If that had been the case, she might have found it sexy—emphasis on the *might* since it isn't a turn-on for every girl, let alone the fact that it would've been weird as shit to be caught masturbating in a bathroom at a party.

I wish I could tell you something you'd love to hear, something exciting, like it was love at first sight instead of an unexpected and weird dick sighting at a random college party. Or that it was a romantic setup, like we crashed into each other while running to class on campus, her books flew out of her hands so I dropped to one knee to help her out and when our heads knocked together, we looked into each other's eyes and the rest was history.

I think you get what I mean, some kind of dreamy movie scene like that, but...fuck no. I know that sounds sweet, and it would melt hearts every time we told people about our meet cute, but, again, that's a no. On the contrary, like I said in the beginning, the first time my eyes landed on Zoe Clarke and hers landed on my dick, I was in a bathroom, in the middle of taking a piss while chatting with my friend.

"And why did you want to watch me take a piss again?" I asked JP, unsuccessfully trying to understand why I had a spectator.

The corner of his lip tipped up lazily and his gaze dropped low as I unzipped myself. "I see it enough in the locker room, man—haven't missed it. I was telling you about Isaac, and you're the one who couldn't hold it until I finished." I gave him a side-eyed look as he ignored me and continued. "Man, you should've been there. The way Coach laid it on him after you guys left—I'm not sure he'll come back to practice again. Hell, I'm not sure *I* wanna go back, and I didn't do shit." He paused for a second or two. "You wanna bet a fifty on it? You think he'll show up?"

I glanced at JP, who was leaning against the wall, eyes closed, face turned toward the ceiling, appearing completely harmless and relaxed. As a rule, JP was never harmless—not on the field, and especially not at a party.

The way Coach had been working us on the field lately, I didn't think any of the guys wanted to be there, at least not the ones who were sane. But, if you loved the game enough, you handled whatever it threw your way to get where you hoped to get one day. Basically, go big or go home. Always beast mode.

"Not betting. If he wants it enough, he'll be there."

Just as the words came out of my mouth, we heard someone open and slam the door. For a brief moment, the blasting music and shouts from the party downstairs drowned everything out. Sure, someone barging in on you wasn't anything alarming since it would be stupid to expect any kind of privacy at a college party. But when I looked over my shoulder to see who wasn't patient enough to wait a few minutes, I saw it was a girl hugging the door and did a double take.

"Be cool. Be cool. This is nothing. Easy peasy. I'm *never*

making new friends again. You can do this, just open your eyes and turn around, dammit."

The brunette still had her back to us, her head resting on the door as she muttered to herself.

Frozen on the spot, JP and I glanced at each other; he shrugged, and I watched his lips stretch into a slow, cocky smile. He looked like he had just been handed a shiny new toy. Giving me a chin lift with his distinct smirk in place, he pushed himself off the wall and headed for the poor girl.

"You can do anything you put your mind to, baby," he said, managing to spook her thoroughly.

As soon as JP spoke, she stopped muttering, spun around to face us, and proceeded to do a pretty damn good imitation of a deer caught in headlights.

"I..."

"You..." JP countered when nothing else came out of her mouth.

As I was getting ready to tuck myself back into my pants, her eyes jumped between JP and me a few times as if she suddenly found herself on the moon and didn't know exactly how she'd made it up there. Then her eyes dropped down to my hand—which was still very much around my dick. Her gaze flew right back up to my face then dropped back to my hand again.

I could tell she was fighting off a grin because her lips twitched. "Shit! Oh...that's a...penis—your penis. Shit." Her voice was barely audible over the muffled music as she repeated her little staring game a few more times and the color gradually drained from her already pale face.

"Do you mind?" I asked, amused by the way her eyes were getting bigger.

"I didn't..." She started then closed her mouth as she met my gaze. "Your penis...I didn't mean to...your penis? I just saw your penis. I'm still seeing your penis. I'm looking straight at it, and it's right the—"

I met JP's amused gaze and glanced back at the girl. "Don't tell me it's your first sighting." I turned around so I could tug my zipper back up and save the girl from having a full-on breakdown.

There was a loud groan behind me then a thump that sounded a lot like someone repeatedly hitting their forehead against a door; it made me smile.

"I haven't seen you around before. Freshman, I assume? You're fascinating, little freshman. Is it my turn now?" JP asked into the silence. "If my friend's dick makes you stammer like that, I wanna see your reaction when you check out mine. It needs to be said: mine looks a lot more handsome than his—bigger, too—and if you'd like to give it a taste tes—"

The groan got louder and sounded more like a growl. "Don't even finish that sentence!"

I chuckled.

It should be said that JP wasn't exactly the smoothest guy on the planet, but apparently that didn't mean shit to college girls. He was one of those guys who attracted girls no matter what he did or said. Compared to him, I was the opposite—I tried my best not to get distracted by girls. He'd say some crazy shit to them, yet they'd still hang on to his every word. He'd say jump and they'd ask, *Which bed?* Him being one hell of a running back didn't hurt his odds of getting laid regularly either.

Don't get me wrong, I had my fair share of girls who'd have loved to get my attention, but early on—around kindergarten—I found out that I'm a one-woman kind of guy. Interestingly, that seems to be another reason girls seem to flock to my side. Trust me, this is not me being vain or pretentious, it just seems to be the way life goes when you're a football player who has a shot at going pro. It has nothing to do with how I look; frankly, Chris, our starting quarterback, is the pretty boy on the team, not me.

Football players—we're practically catnip to college girls.

I turned on the tap to wash my hands and glanced at the girl to see her reaction. She still had her back to us, but at least she was no longer banging her head. If JP was about to get his dick out for a show and tell, I was out of there. Whipping out dicks with my teammates for girls was where I drew the line of friendship.

Sending me a quick grin and wink, JP clasped his hands behind his back and leaned down to her ear. "Booo!"

The girl flinched, turned around to face him, and did a little shuffle back when she realized he was standing a lot closer than he had been a few seconds before.

"Thank you for the offer, but I don't want to see any dicks at all," she stated, and then she started to back away from him as my friend stalked his new prey.

"Aww, but you'd really like mine."

When I couldn't find anything to dry my hands with, I wiped them off on my jeans as I watched their awkward interaction until her back hit my chest and she let out a squeak.

"That's my cue." I glanced down and saw that her head was tilted back and up. She was watching me intently. Even from that close, it was hard to tell what color her eyes were, maybe green with hazel specks around the rims of the pupils.

Realizing I was staring into her eyes and easily seeing how panicked she was, I frowned, took a step back, and glanced at JP. "Ease up on her, man. Come on, let's head out." Before I could step away, the girl faced me, grabbed my arm, and held on tight.

"No—you can't leave," she blurted out, surprising both JP and me. "I'm here for you."

I raised my brows and sent JP a confused look. He just shrugged. He was still wearing that *I'm so intrigued* smile on his face as he very openly checked out her ass.

"I mean, I'm not here for you," the girl explained, and my

gaze went back to her. "But I came *in* here for you." She squinted a little, her nose scrunching in the process. "You know what I mean? You probably don't. I followed you in here because I really need to ask you something." Her voice rose with panic, but she kept going. "When I say I followed you in here, I don't mean I'm stalking you or anything like that because that'd be crazy. I don't even know you, right?" She let out a nervous laugh, patted my arm awkwardly, and then seemed to realize she was actually touching me. She snatched her hand back and clasped them behind her as she took a step away. "Not that I'd stalk you if I knew you, but that's not the point right now. I just...really, really need to ask you something before I make a fool of myself out there, and I thought what better way to do that than when he is alone...and I thought you'd be alone in here, and..."

I didn't understand a thing she was saying, but before I could respond, JP jumped in. "So, you're sending me away, huh? And here I thought we had something special."

She looked over her shoulder at him. "Sorry. I didn't see you follow him in here, and I didn't realize this was the bathroom anyway. If I'd seen you, I would've waited outside. I had no idea guys did that going-to-bathroom-together thing. It's sweet that you do though." Her eyes met mine for a second before she quickly looked away and addressed JP again. "It'll just be a minute, really, then you can come back and have him all to yourself."

He arched a brow at her but otherwise stayed quiet.

She glanced at me, and whatever she saw on my face made her wince. "Sorry, that sounded bad, didn't it? Not that being gay is bad or anything. I shouldn't have assumed. My friend is gay, and I know how hard it is when people say the most stupid fucking things and how much he—"

JP laughed and shook his head. "You should stop while you're ahead, girl. My offer still stands if you want to come find me after you're done with my boy here."

After that, he opened the door and left me alone with her. Crossing my arms over my chest, I relaxed against the sink.

She turned back to me, let out a long breath, and smiled nervously. "That was bad, wasn't it?"

"The whole thing, or just the last part?" I couldn't help myself; I smiled back at her. I'd had some girls do crazy things to get my attention so they could get in my bed, but I didn't think that was what was happening here.

With a grimace on her face, she shook her head, eyes dropping to the floor. "I just assumed this was your room and you would be alone and then when I came in, you had your... ummm...and then he was in here with you..." She met my gaze then quickly looked away. "And your...thing was out, and then it all went to hell from there."

Yeah, she was not the type who chased after football players.

Another nervous laugh and she was backing away from me toward the door.

"So, I'm sorry? And...thank you?"

My smile grew bigger. "For what?"

She rubbed her hands on her jeans, shook her head, and just appeared miserable as she looked anywhere but at me.

"At this point? If I'm being honest, I really don't know. Thank you for talking to me? For not kicking me out? For letting me see your penis?" Her eyes closed on their own and she shook her head, took a couple steps back, and lifted her hands, palms out, pausing when her back hit the door. "I didn't mean it like that—I wasn't trying to see your penis or anything like that. I told you, I didn't even know this was the bathroom. I mean, I assume it wasn't your best moment, so why would I wanna see"—her hand gestured toward my crotch area—"your...that...but it looked like you're a shower instead of a grower so that must be...good for you? Congrats? Not that you'd want a stranger to congratulate you on something like that, but you're a football player, so maybe you like compliments?"

For a few seconds, the silence stretched between us and I was unable to hide my grin. Now that my dick wasn't out and JP wasn't with us to put the moves on her, I took in her features: straight brown hair that framed her face and reached just below her shoulders, pale skin, big doe eyes that were something between hazel and green—I still hadn't decided—slightly plumper bottom lip, flushed cheeks from what I assumed was embarrassment. And then there were other things, like her C-cup boobs trying their best to rip through her tight t-shirt—I did have eyes, after all—her hourglass figure, and great fucking legs—not too thin, not too thick, just perfect for my taste.

I made sure to look into her eyes and nowhere else as I ran my hand over my short hair. Considering where my mind was going, I didn't think it was smart to spend more time with her in a bathroom. "You remind me of my sister," I said, completely out of nowhere, shocking both of us. "You're a little shy, aren't you?" She did remind me of Amelia. When she was nervous, she talked endlessly, too, did a lot of rambling. Even though she knew she didn't make much sense, she couldn't stop it. Being shy was the only answer that made sense.

She laughed and seemed to sag against the door. "You seeing me as your sister doesn't bode well for me, especially if you knew what I was trying to ask—not that you should see me as someone who you would want to or could...just forget about that. What made you think I was shy? Wait. Wait." She raised her hand. "I take that one back too. Don't even answer that."

Another awkward silence stole our words as I stared at her and she stared at my chest until someone pushed on the door and made her lose her balance.

A head peered through the partly open door. "Ah, sorry,

dude! Didn't know this was occupied." He pushed the door open a few more inches to look around inside. "We'll come in after you two are done." After giving me a thumbs up, he slowly disappeared.

As soon as the door closed, my brunette—scratch that, *the* brunette let out a deep breath and focused her gaze on me. She appeared steadier, but based on the way she was tugging on her shirt—which had *Smile for me* written on it in big bold letters—I wouldn't have bet money on it. Curious as hell, I waited for her to continue.

"You know what, I already made a mess, so at this point, asking this won't—no, *can't* make things any worse."

Already intrigued by her, I gestured with my hand for her to go on. "I'm all ears."

As I tried my best to hide my smile, she took another deep breath. "I need to kiss you," she blurted out quickly. Closing her eyes, she groaned. "That wasn't the best way to break it to you. Let me try again."

I raised my brow. "You need to kiss me."

"Need to, have to—I mean they're all the same thing, right?" A quick nod. "I mean, I don't want to kiss you, not really. I didn't choose you."

"You didn't choose me."

"Nope, I didn't. It's not that you're not good-looking—you definitely are, in a rugged sort of way, which would work for me. I'd kiss you if I had to, but you weren't my first choice."

"You're doing wonders for my ego. Keep going."

"Okay, I'm thinking that *really* wasn't the best way to go about this. Let me start over and see how that goes. My room-mate, Lindsay, kind of dragged-slash-forced me to come here tonight, to the party I mean. She thinks I'm not living the 'college experience' to the fullest. We came, met her friends—it's my first year, and I'm meeting new people, so that's good, right?" Without waiting for me to give an answer, she took a deep breath and kept going. "Nope, not good. Her friends realized I'm not adventurous at all because I don't tend to talk very much when I'm in a big group and prefer to just stay back. I like to take things in at first, observe, you know? I don't like to have too many eyeballs on me. Anyway, you don't care about that, so blah blah blah, more talk, more cringing on my part."

She shut her eyes and shook her head. I just stood there, watching her, listening to her, waiting for her to finish her story. I couldn't really have moved even if I wanted to; she was...it was all too...*captivating*—that's the word I was looking for. She was all over the place and yet she was captivating as hell, a fresh breath of air, for some reason.

"Then they bet—kind of dared me that I couldn't kiss a random guy. I said sure I could just so they'd stop talking about me, because what are they gonna do? Expect me to follow through on that? Are we in kindergarten? Pffttt. And, okay, fine, I was a little offended, but they were kind of right. I'm not adventurous or spontaneous. Not into kissing random guys, either. I've never done it, but I figured it's easy enough. Anyway, they said I wouldn't have the balls to kiss the guy *they* wanted me to kiss, because apparently that's also a thing in college—daring, betting, kissing random people..."

"Wow," I said before she could go on, and she lifted her eyes to me. It was my lame attempt to make sure she took a breath before she passed out. "There seem to be a lot of things about college I didn't know about, and I'm not even a freshman anymore. I've never kissed a random girl before either—didn't even know it was a requirement." I actually had, but she didn't need to know that. I got kissed by random girls sometimes, especially after a good game when everyone's adrenaline was running high, but I never had the urge to go kiss a random girl just because. Maybe I just hadn't seen the right random girl because at that moment I could see the appeal.

"See!" she exclaimed, her body relaxing a bit more. "That's what I said. Anyway, we're coming to the painful part, so I'll just push forward. My roommate, Lindsay, grabbed this poor guy who was walking past with his buddies and told me to kiss him, so I did, just a quick peck—that's nothing, right? I didn't even touch the guy, just leaned up and pressed my lips against his. It was pretty anticlimactic, actually, and since I've had a little bit of beer..." She lifted three fingers, presumably indicating the number of beers she'd had, then tucked her hair behind her right ear. I studied her lips—all this talk about kissing, and she had those beautiful shiny pink lips... "I didn't even feel a thing," she continued. "No butterflies. No nothing. The guy didn't look all that upset about it since he tried for a second, longer kiss."

I bet he didn't, I thought. *I bet the lucky bastard wasn't upset about it at all.*

She started talking even faster, making it almost impossible to follow her thoughts.

"But then Lindsay's friend, Molly, randomly pointed at you. You were talking to some guys across the room, and she dared me to kiss *you*. What's so special about you, I have no idea." I opened my mouth, but she held up her hand and continued without a pause. "So, I had to say I could because I'm not good with dares and bets. I get a tad bit competitive. Since I got away with just a peck with the last guy, they dared me to go full out with you. Again, I don't know if you're some kind of hotshot or something, but I guess there is something about you that makes you special enough for them to insist that much. Maybe you're their type, I don't have a freaking clue. I asked them to give me a few minutes and followed you here so I could ask your permission before I attacked you in front of everyone or at least attempted to attack you in front of everyone to basically suck your face. Now, after what I've seen…just to make sure…you're not gay, are you? Because if that's why they insisted so much…that's cruel."

When she kept looking at me expectantly, I straightened up and rubbed the back of my neck.

"This is probably gonna sound like a lie to you, but…" *How to say this?* "As much as I'd love to help you out with your dare, I have a girlfriend." We'd only been out once, but still… "She's late getting here, but she's probably out there now, and I think I should—"

"Ah. Oh. Oh, of course. Okay."

I watched her eyes bounce all over the place, her gaze touching me only once or twice, and even then, only for a second. Then she blindly reached for the handle, opened the door, and stepped out.

"I'm really sorry, you know," she started, her voice slightly louder in an effort to be heard over the ruckus going on outside. Her eyes dropped down to my pants then came back up to my eyes. "About that…and everything else. This whole night has been weird…weird and stupid. I'm just gonna leave, and…" Another step away. "Yeah. Sorry," she repeated, her eyes focused on my shoulder instead of my eyes as she kept backing away.

That's when I realized her eyes were watering. Having a sister teaches you a thing or two about these things, and I knew this girl was seconds away from crying.

"Wait. Hey, wait!" I yelled, quickly walking after her before she could disappear.

She glanced back at me over her shoulder without stopping.

"What's your name?" I yelled louder.

She gave me a small smile, something between sad and horrified, just as I watched that first tear slide down. Then she was gone, disappearing into the crowd before I could reach her.

Why I wanted to know her name, why my eyes looked for her every now and then the entire night…back then, I didn't know.

CHAPTER TWO

ZOE

One year later

The second time Dylan Reed saw me, I was trying to disappear into thin air. If we didn't make eye contact, if I couldn't *see* him, he couldn't see me either, right?

Well...apparently, that's not how it works.

A year before, when I'd made a complete fool out of myself, I hadn't even known the guy's name, and that had made it easier to just forget about the whole thing. If he had been just a nameless guy I'd randomly come across at a college party—admittedly, a very very sexy one—it would've been fine, but no, it wasn't. Of course not—things were never that easy for me. The guy the mean girls from freshman year chose for me to kiss was one of the hotshots from the football team, the star wide receiver who was apparently one of the few players expected to make it into the NFL, and *that* made him pretty popular around campus. Sure, it's a big campus, but not big enough for me to avoid him forever.

After a long day filled with classes, I was on my way to the apartment when I saw him—well, more like *them*. He had three of his friends with him, and I knew at least one of them was a teammate: the quarterback, Christopher Wilson. Who the other two were, I had no idea. Christopher Wilson, though...he was the big man on campus, as most quarterbacks always seem to be. I knew that much, and maybe a little more about him. It wasn't as much as I'd have liked to know, but I knew a few bits. Even so, at that moment, seeing Chris didn't even register in my mind. The person walking next to him had all my attention.

Dylan Reed, all six feet three inches of him.

Laughing at something his friends were saying, he was maybe forty, forty-five feet away, coming straight toward me.

I stopped walking, just froze to watch him. Some girl bumped into me, apologized, and I couldn't even respond. Standing paralyzed in the middle of campus, my stomach dropped, and I felt the blood drain from my face.

No.

I didn't want him to see me just then. I had no makeup on, and I was running on three hours of sleep. My hair was in a very, very messy braid that didn't even really count as a braid anymore because it looked more like I'd been in a fight with an angry crow and lost, and my clothes...I couldn't even remember what the hell I was wearing and couldn't find it in me to look down and see. More than likely, I wasn't wearing anything spectacular, anyway. Hell, I really didn't want him to see me again, period.

Thirty feet.

Staring at him, I lost precious seconds I could've used to get away—I knew that because I'd managed to do it successfully before. That day, however, I was too dumbstruck to do anything but watch him come closer. Maybe it was the lack of sleep that had me stuck in my place, or maybe it was the way he walked, the way his shoulders moved and—

Snap out of it!

He still hadn't seen me, his face tipped down, listening to his friends.

Twenty-five feet.

I thought maybe if I just stood where I was, closed my eyes and made no quick movements, he'd walk around me and it would be over in a few seconds—yet one more of my brilliant ideas.

Or better yet, maybe he wouldn't recognize me at all. To be honest, that was a pretty strong possibility. After all, who knew how many girls threw themselves at his feet on a daily basis? Most likely, he had forgotten about that awkward girl from the bathroom at the house party—AKA me—the very next day.

Twenty feet.

He was wearing a long-sleeved gray Henley that showed how great his arms were, and I mean *great*—that was one of the things I specifically remembered from that night, which might have had something to do with the fact that I was a sucker for good, strong arms, but that's not the point. Those same arms were connected to some even greater shoulders. He had brown, short-cropped hair, which didn't work for everyone, but on Dylan Reed...on him, it worked wonders. He had strong, masculine features. I couldn't see his eyes, but I knew they were blue—to be more specific, dark blue like the ocean. A year before, I had looked into them for several long seconds. His jawline was sharp, cheekbones strong, lips so full you couldn't stop wondering how they would feel against your own.

Fifteen feet.

His nose must have been broken at some point, because I remembered thinking it was something that set him apart. You wouldn't be able to tell from afar, but like I said, I'd stood closer to him before, had looked up into his eyes for just a second or two and then focused on anywhere *but* his eyes. That slightly crooked nose added even more character to his already pretty perfect appearance.

I imagined it was fairly easy to get your nose broken as a football player, maybe even more than once. He wasn't pretty; I wouldn't have used that word specifically. You might not even call him traditionally handsome, but he was certainly striking. He had charisma, confidence. He looked strong and big and maybe a little rough, too, but more than anything, he looked solid. Yes, that was one way you could describe Dylan Reed. I'm not even talking about in a physical sense, though he was solid on that count too. He wasn't a guy you could forget easily.

He lifted his head and made eye contact with me. The big smile he was sporting slowly melted off his face.

Dead.

Just chock-full of brilliant ideas that day, I quietly gasped, spun around, and kinda started speed-walking while cursing myself—not my best moment, as you can imagine. My eyes were glued to the ground, and my stomach dropped for the second time.

Calm down, you drama queen.

"Hey! You! Wait a second! Hey!"

No. Nope. Not doing that.

Just in case he was yelling at me—and I was pretty sure he was—I closed my eyes as hard as I could—as if that would help make me invisible—and quickened my steps, which was how I walked smack into...people. People, as in multiple. Of course I did. What did you expect with my luck?

I didn't fall on my ass, and that was my only saving grace. When the group I'd...ummm...run into looked at me with bulging eyes, I swallowed my hasty apology.

"What have you done?" one of them whispered before looking at the ground.

Thinking maybe they were exaggerating a bit with the

whole *the world just ended* act, I followed his gaze and discovered that not only were my books scattered all over the place, there was also an architectural model lying on its side in the middle of the mess my stuff had made. It was not some simple cardboard thingy either—oh no. It looked like it was made of wood, and it was huge...huge enough that there was no way one person could carry it on their own...hence the four-person group.

Completely forgetting why I was in this mess in the first place, I dropped to my knees and reached for the scaled structure.

"I'm so sorry. Really, can I do—"

"Don't touch it!" yelled the same guy who had spoken a second before as he slapped my hand away—actually slapped it. Surprised, I cradled it against my chest. He hadn't hurt me or anything, but, I couldn't even remember the last time my mom had slapped my hand away for trying to steal food from the table.

As the other guys crouched down to help their friend—while grumbling, might I add—I quickly glanced around to see that we had an audience. How nice. Just *perfect*; I'd always thought a red face did wonders for my complexion. The silver lining was that Dylan Reed was nowhere to be seen, and I couldn't help but feel cold relief wash over me.

"Goddammit! You broke the door."

"I'm so sorry," I repeated, a little lower in volume this time, but the guys kept giving me angry looks. From what I could see, there was no real damage—other than said door, of course. When they chose to ignore me, I tried to focus on my own scattered notes and books on the ground. Thankfully, I had left my camera at the lab that day, otherwise I wasn't sure it'd have been as lucky as the model building.

"I really hope it didn't..." I noticed the guys straightening from their crouch, holding the building oh so gently between the four of them. I didn't get to finish my sentence as I received one last death glare before they walked around me to hurry away.

Still on my knees, I sighed. What a great end to my already crappy day.

"Here, don't forget this one," said someone to my right. I froze again, my heart picking up speed.

My eyes slowly followed the big hand that was holding one of my art history books upside down, and then they kept following the long arm up to those spectacular shoulders, finally making it up to Dylan Reed's amused gaze.

All the chitter-chatter of the passing students dulled. I closed my eyes in defeat and hung my head. So much for trying to run away.

"Hi," he said, so simple, easy, smooth.

While my heart was doing a weird stuttering thing in my chest, I tried to get up from the ground, only to lose my balance. Dylan caught my elbow and righted me before I could topple over.

"Thank you," I murmured, looking away from his face as he let go of my arm and took a much-appreciated step back. I cleared my throat, as if that would make any difference. "Hi."

God, I was so ashamed. Not only had I asked him if I could kiss him like a middle schooler when he had a girlfriend waiting for him outside just because I couldn't back out of a dare, I'd also seen his penis...although seeing a penis wasn't such a bad thing. Quite the opposite, really. I liked looking at a good penis; what girl doesn't? But, on top of all that, now he'd seen me bulldoze some architecture majors.

How many times was I gonna make a fool out of myself in front of this guy?

"Hi," he repeated, holding out my book again. I mumbled my thanks, grabbed it, and finally lifted my head up to see an infectious smile on his lips. It completely transformed his face. Those strong, sharp lines softened, and if he'd looked amazing before, when he smiled like that...it made me wanna be the reason for it, which only made him more irresistible. My own lips twitched in response, and I could feel my cheeks warm up under his piercing gaze.

"Uh, hey."

"You didn't tell me your name," he said, smile still going strong.

I forced my gaze away from his curious one. "Oh?" Slowly turning away, I decided it was best to act like I didn't know what he was talking about and simply started walking again.

"You remember me, right?"

I felt this was a good time to start on that power walk, burn some calories, get away from people. My escape wouldn't be that easy though—he followed me, walking backward, keeping pace, studying me.

"Last year? At the end of first semester, some Greek party, don't remember which one." I sent him a quick, panicked look then looked away just as quickly when I realized he was studying me intently. "You know, I was in the bathroom, then you came in and asked me if—"

"Ahhh, now I remember." *You little liar.* "Yeah. Yes, of course. Hi." My voice came out in a croak. I laughed, a little awkwardly. "So many parties that year, couldn't remember at first." Mentally, I rolled my eyes at myself. I'd been to three parties, *maybe*—and that was a big maybe. "How have you been?"

"I'm good—great actually, now that I finally saw you again."

Is he making fun of me? I quickened my pace. He was right there with me.

"I'm Dylan," he said when he caught on to the fact that I wasn't gonna say anything more. "That night, I tried to catch up to you, but you disappeared on me. You were right there, and then you weren't."

I sent him another look. I would've quickened my pace yet again, but I thought it would be even more embarrassing and just plain weird if I just started actually jogging, and it's not like he couldn't catch up to me without even breaking a sweat anyway.

I made a hybrid laughing-choking sound. "That's me," I said with mock cheerfulness. "I'm there and then I'm not. I exist, but I really don't."

Awkward. Awkward. Awkward.

"And, I know your name—everyone knows your name." I stopped speaking so I could breathe for just a second. "I was a little embarrassed, as you can imagine—a lot embarrassed, actually." If I didn't throw up on him in the next few minutes, I knew I'd be safe.

"If I'm not embarrassed that you saw—"

I sent him a panicked look.

"You have nothing to be embarrassed about from that night either," he continued quickly, and then he grinned. "I'm not embarrassed, just in case you were wondering."

His penis... I'd had the privilege of seeing his penis, the penis I could still visualize if I closed my eyes—not that I sat around and pictured penises in my mind or anything like that... If I wanted to see one, I could easily ask my boyfriend to take it out for me, though I had not done so as of yet.

His tone had me glancing at him. Did he have to bring that up? Why was he even talking to me? To make me feel even worse? And where the hell were his friends? Chris?

I gave him what I hoped was something close to a smile instead of a grimace and kept quiet.

"You're gonna tell me your name, right, Flash?" I watched him glance around then focus his gaze back on me. "I mean, it's crowded, and you proved you're fast, I'll give you that, but I'm pretty good on my feet, and this time, now that I know what to look out for, I'll catch you, no problem."

Hi Dylan, meet mortification in the flesh.

"Flash?" I asked, confused.

He smiled. "One second you're there, the next you're not?"

He was repeating my words.

Clearing my throat, I ignored the somersault of my heart. I had a nickname. He had given me a nickname.

"It's Zoe."

There went that smile again.

He tried my name on his lips. Fascinated, I watched him do it. "Zoe. Hmmm. Okay then, Zoe."

A grin.

Goodie.

"I'm a little late to...somewhere, so..."

No one ever died of a few white lies.

"Still a little shy, huh?" he said quietly, his smile a little smaller now, more intimate.

I moved my bird's nest of a braid from my left shoulder to my right, thinking that having a curtain between us wouldn't be the worst thing in the world.

"I'm afraid it's a permanent thing."

As if he knew I was trying to hide behind my hair, he chuckled. "I'll give you this round then. I need to head back to practice anyway—can't be late or Coach will have my ass."

I locked gazes with him and just like that forgot why the hell I would try to get away. Was I actually a little disappointed that he was leaving? How stupid of me.

Look away, Zoe. Don't look at those eyes.

He lifted his hand to rub his neck and broke our eye contact. "Yeah. Okay then. It was nice running into you, Zoe. Maybe we'll do it again sometime?"

I smiled at him a little miserably but kept my mouth shut. I didn't like lying to anyone—even a stranger—if I didn't have to.

The whole thing, our entire interaction was torture for me,

beginning to end. I'm sure you'd have felt the same way if you were watching it happen.

Then Dylan stopped walking next to me and I kept going. It was the end of the road for us, where our paths parted. I closed my eyes and took a long, much-needed breath to clear my mind. I was passing the small cafeteria so it smelled like bad cafeteria pizza and caffeine. My heart was still tripping over itself. Talk about shame. Why couldn't I not be so...*painfully* shy?

"Zoe?"

I groaned loudly, and the group of students walking next to me gave me strange looks. I stopped and turned around, a tad bit curious to hear what he was going to say.

He was about ten feet away, just standing in the middle of the busy road. College life—everyone was trying to get somewhere. How come *he* didn't bump into anyone and everyone just parted to go around him? His smile slowly grew bigger when he had my attention.

"How about that kiss?"

Frowning, I asked, "What about it?"

"How about we have that kiss now?"

My eyes bulged a little bit and my mouth dropped open, or maybe I choked; I'm not so sure on details. I didn't look pretty though, I can tell you that much.

I noticed eyes on me, heard low murmurs, and my face started to flush again. Hugging my books closer as if they could protect me or stop me from heading his way, I kinda yelled back at him. "Sorry, I...I...have a boyfriend."

"You think that would be lovely?" He took a step toward me.

Cheeky bastard.

"I said, I have a boyfriend!" And I did; I really did have a boyfriend. His name was Zack. Zoe and Zack—he thought it was fate. Me, not so much. He wasn't the love of my life or anything like that, but yeah, we'd been on a few dates, and I was pretty sure he wouldn't enjoy hearing about me kissing some random guy in the middle of campus.

Someone yelled, "Good for you!" Snickers arose from the crowd, and I flushed some more.

God? Hello? Please, do something. Smite me. Smite me right now.

"Ah...got it." Dylan wasn't yelling so much right then. He tucked his hands into his pockets, rocking in place, and I had to force myself not to drop my eyes down to what I already knew was a sizeable package. "We don't have the best timing in the world, huh, Flash?"

What could I say? I nodded and forced a small smile on my face. Was that disappointment I was seeing in his eyes? And were those butterflies taking flight somewhere in my stomach?

He started walking backward, his steps light and easy, his eyes still on me. "See you around, Zoe. Third time is the charm, so maybe next time we'll make it happen."

I wouldn't bet on that, I thought, but I didn't say it out loud. I just lifted my hand and gave him a small wave.

He smiled that smile—that big, careless, oh-so-beautiful one—gave me a quick salute, and then turned around to jog away. Yup, it had been smart of me to choose not to jog—he would have totally caught up with me in no time.

The first time I'd parted ways with him, I'd done so with tears running down my face from the humiliation and shame. This time...this time I had all the smiles in the world.

CHAPTER THREE

DYLAN

One year later

It was ten PM on a Friday night, and I was dead on my feet, as I was almost every day. I loved it that way, lived for it.

I'd woken up at six AM as I did every morning so I could get in my first workout of the day before a quick breakfast and a team meeting. Straight from the meeting, I ran to make it to my first class. Around twelve-thirty, I usually had an hour to grab some lunch and just be a normal college student instead of an athlete. After lunch, depending on the day, I either had another class or went straight to get in my second workout in the weight room. After that came three hours of practice, which sometimes went an extra hour or so. After a thirty-minute break that included a smoothie and a sandwich, I'd found myself in the library trying to finish an assignment that was due the next day. On my way over there, the busy day starting to slow me down, I had texted my girlfriend, Victoria, to see what the plan was for the night. Before I knew it, three hours had passed, and I still hadn't heard back from her.

I shared a house a few minutes away from campus with four of my teammates: Kyle, Maxwell, Benji, and Rip. If they hadn't decided to throw a last-minute party for Maxwell's birthday, I could've spent my night in peace in my room with Vicky, maybe watch some Netflix and fuck around in bed. After a long day of getting ready for the season, that was usually all the energy I had left in me. But, knowing that wasn't possible, I decided to check out Vicky's dorm room first to see if we could avoid the party altogether and chill in there instead, even though I knew it would mean she'd be pissed at me.

Unlike me, she always had an abundance of energy and time for parties, but I also knew how to convince her to stay in. As much as she loved drinking and dancing, she loved what I could do to her body even more.

We'd been dating for five months. Two months of that we'd spent apart, FaceTiming and texting non-stop over summer break, and everything seemed to be going well. She didn't mind that I had to spend most of my time out on the field or in the gym because her own time was filled with classes, sorority meetings, and an internship. She was supportive, caring, and, well, truth be told, she had been completely unplanned.

My original plan had always been that I wasn't going to date during my last year.

Focus on the game.

Sharpen your skills.

Be the best on the field.

Make the time to study.

Those were just a few of the things on my priority list, and a girlfriend wasn't one of them. My plate was already full—actually, it was more than full; it was overflowing. With all I had going on—and I had a lot going on—I just didn't have enough time left in the day to handle that kind of commitment. Eventually, despite my busy schedule, Vicky had managed to wiggle her way into my life, and to my complete surprise, I liked having her there. Seeing her after a long, tiring day wasn't the hardest thing, and as far as I knew, she liked being with me even more.

In the past, when I was late for one of our dates because practice ran long or couldn't go to a party because I had to sit my ass down and study, she never complained. She gave me calm (not always) and balance (again, not always), and I tried to give her whatever I had left to give of myself at the end of the day. To be fair, that might not sound like a lot, but she always told me I was more than enough, always said I made her happy and she couldn't imagine being with someone else. I believed her—why wouldn't I? She definitely didn't mind having a boyfriend who was expected to be drafted in the top twenty, and I'd have been lying if I said I didn't enjoy seeing her face light up with excitement and joy whenever the media talked about me. I wasn't exactly planning on asking her if she wanted to come with me if I did indeed manage to get drafted at the end of the year, but she had hinted rather heavily a few times that she was game to travel wherever after graduation. So, I was thinking maybe if things kept going the way they were, it wouldn't be the worst thing in the world to ask her.

After talking to Vicky's roommate and learning that she'd actually left for the party—hoping to find me there, I assumed—I finally left campus, mentally trying to prepare myself for the mess that was waiting for me at the house.

Surprisingly, the house didn't seem to be as crowded as I'd feared. Instead of inviting the whole school, they just had the entire team packed into our three-story house. It was the team, the girlfriends of those players who had one, and just to balance everything out, some of the cheerleaders. So, it was still a madhouse, but on a smaller scale. I would have bet the only reason they were keeping it relatively small was their fear of Coach hearing about it.

I found JP trying to sweet-talk his way into a girl's pants in the kitchen. "Have you seen Vicky around?" I asked as soon as I was close enough.

"Not yet. I'm sure she's around here somewhere. Where've you been, man? You missed the Madden tournament." Before I could escape, he slapped his hand on my back. "Meet Leila before you disappear somewhere. She is the girl of my dreams. Girl of my dreams, meet my main man."

I shook my head and watched the girl giggle into her red cup. "Hello, Dylan."

JP pulled her back against his front and rounded his arm around her collarbone. He leaned down, ran his nose against her neck. "Let me have a taste. Then you can tell me all about what you're planning to do to me." Absentmindedly handing me her plastic cup, he proceeded to attack her lips with enthusiasm.

Leaving them alone, I checked out the living room, picking my way through couples making out in the hallway, then went down to the basement where things were moving a bit faster, and finally headed out to the backyard. She was nowhere to be found, so I sent her another text as I headed over to Chris and a few of the other guys before I went back in the house.

"Chris? Have you seen Vicky around? She's supposed to be here, but I can't seem to find her."

"I just got here a few minutes ago. Have you checked inside?"

I sighed. "Yeah, not there. Didn't see you at practice today—everything all right?" I asked when the other guys started to argue about the upcoming game.

"Yeah, I was in the weight room, left before you guys were done." He saw the look on my face and continued, "Don't ask. I'll tell you about it later."

Chris was one of my closest friends. "Coach?" I was guessing it was another argument. Chris was the son of Mark Wilson, one of the greatest quarterbacks of all time and our coach. They argued—*all the time*. You'd think with his dad as the head coach, he'd have things easier, but no. Chris worked just as hard as the rest of us, if not harder. We spent long, extra hours practicing together, perfecting our game.

He let out a long breath. "Yeah. We'll talk later, okay? It's been a long day, so I'm gonna call it a night and head home. I don't want him on my ass. I'll find you tomorrow."

Before I could ask anything else, he said his goodbyes to our small group and left.

I checked my phone again: nothing from Vicky. Thinking maybe she wasn't getting the texts, I tried calling her a few times, but she never answered.

Starting to get worried, I excused myself and slowly made my way upstairs. My room was at the very end of the hallway on the second floor, and because the party had been a last-minute deal, I hadn't locked it before I'd left that morning. As I passed the first door next to the staircase, my steps faltered. The second and third floor were always a no-go when the guys threw parties. If I hadn't known Kyle—our best tight end—for as long as I had, I would've barged in and kicked everyone out. But, this was Kyle.

If the sounds coming through his door were anything to go by, it was more than likely that there was an orgy going on in there, and he was most definitely the star of that show. Which didn't bode well for my room. An eyeful of multiple naked bodies would teach me to lock my door next time. Hesitating in front of my door, I listened for any suspicious sounds. When I couldn't hear anything, I opened it and was relieved to find that no one had made it that far yet.

The bad news was that Vicky wasn't in there either. I called her again; no answer.

I tried her roommate, and she answered on the second ring.

"Dylan?"

"Jessie, Vicky isn't at my house. Has she come back there?"

"No. I told you, she said she was going to meet you at your place."

I sat down on the edge of my bed and rubbed my temple. Just because they weren't blasting the house with music didn't mean people weren't being loud to make up for it.

"She isn't here. She knew I was planning on studying in the library after practice, so why would she even come here to look for me?"

"I'm not sure what you want me to say, Dylan. We had a sorority meeting at eight and after that was over, she changed and said she was heading out to your place. That's all I know. She probably has her phone on silent. Try again."

I got up and started pacing back and forth in the confines of my small room.

"Look, I've tried ten times already and she isn't answering. It's not like her to ignore my texts, or any text for that matter. You know better than I do that her phone is always glued to her hand. I'm starting to get worried here."

Jessie's long sigh reached my ears. I could picture her rolling her eyes on the other end of the line, which was basically her default when she interacted with people for longer than a minute. "Do you want me to call one of the girls and see if she doubled back there instead?"

"I'd appreciate that, Jessie."

Without saying anything else, she hung up on me. Even though the shower was calling my name, I was still worried enough that I decided to check the house again and maybe ask a few more guys if they'd seen her around. If she'd made it to the party, someone must have seen her, and if not, I was ready to go out and search for her.

As I was passing Kyle's room, I noticed that the orgy was winding down, the moans and grunts quieter now. I tried the door and it opened.

Since I had no idea who was in there with him, I kept my eyes on the floor when I asked, "Hey Kyle, did you see Vicky downstairs tonight? Her roommate said she came here."

Even though I'd heard Kyle murmuring to someone just seconds before I opened the door, the sudden silence that came with my question had me looking up.

The last thing I remembered seeing was Vicky...in the middle of the bed...between a pair of dicks—Maxwell's and Kyle's, to be specific—on her hands and knees. I'm sure you get the picture I was staring at.

I remember Vicky screaming at us to stop. I also vaguely remember Maxwell trying to give me explanations. I must have skipped minutes in between because the next thing I knew JP and Benjamin—our right guard—were hauling me off of Kyle.

Breathing with difficulty, I tried my best to throw them off, but they weren't budging. "It's okay. It's okay and done with. Settle down!" JP shouted in my face as he held my head in his hands and tried to catch my eyes. Benji, a mountain of a man and another one of my close friends, was holding my arms at my back as he tried to shuffle us out of the room. Even if I could have gotten JP out of the way, there was no way I could shake Benji. JP was still pushing on my shoulders to stop me from going after Kyle. "We're just gonna get some air, okay, Dylan? Take it easy, man. It's not worth risking your future. Keep it locked down."

Before they could pull me out, I glanced around the room. Maxwell was holding his bloody nose but otherwise was fine from what I could see. At some point, he must have put his dick back into his pants after pulling it out of Victoria's mouth, but the buttons of his jeans were hanging open, and he was still shirtless. Kyle...Kyle was naked and squirming on the ground, the room now filled with a different kind of a moaning.

Victoria, my loving girlfriend...she was still kneeling on the bed, eyes big and scared, chest heaving as she clutched a jersey to her body to cover herself. Number twelve—she was holding *my* number...*my* jersey. She was letting them fuck her while wearing my number.

Our eyes met, and I watched her lips form my name. When she made a move to get down from the bed, I stopped trying to get to Kyle and stopped fighting my friends, who finally let me shrug them off. I strode out of the room and the house without a second glance.

"Coach, I know what you're gonna say, and it isn't necessary. I'm doing fine."

"Get inside and sit your ass down."

I did as he asked.

"Cut the crap. From what I'm seeing on the field, you're nowhere near fine, let alone your usual self. I gave you one week and nothing changed. You're out of time. Now, you'll do what I tell you to do and stop acting like her pussy was the last one on earth. Look around for God's sake—you've got plenty of replacements waiting on the sidelines if that's what you're after."

My hands clenched into fists as I surged up from my seat.

"You think this is about her? You think that's why I'm having trouble focusing? She is not the one who's affecting my game. I don't care about that, but how can you expect me to give my all to the game when I don't trust my teammates? They're supposed to have my back, both on the field and off. How would—"

Coach got up from his chair, silencing me with one simple but deadly look, and came to stand in front of me.

"Okay, Dylan, let's play this your way. Tell me what you want me to do. I already talked to the whole team. You were there —you know I don't approve. I tell you boys all the time that if you want to make it into the big leagues, you can't let distractions into your life. You got into it with Kyle right in the middle of the weight room and punched him in the face—again—and I gave that to you without repercussions. I can't have my boys brawling for everyone to see. What else would you like me to do? You want me to cut them from the team just because they slept with your willing girlfriend?"

I tried to cover up my flinch, but it was no use. Tired of everything, I sat back down and rested my forearms on my knees. At the end of the day, as much as his words were hitting a raw spot, he was right—there was nothing more I could do. Neither Kyle nor Maxwell seemed to be having a hard time on the field. Yeah, they avoided me, but it didn't seem like it was affecting their game. Maybe I was the one who wasn't open-minded enough. Either way, not one of them—Victoria included —was worth giving up the end game. I wanted to hear my name announced on draft day. It felt like I'd been working toward that goal my whole life. At night, in bed, after a long day of workouts, practice, and meetings on top of classes, when I closed my eyes, I could see it, could feel it in my bones. I knew I was good enough, knew if I made it to the big leagues, I'd work my ass off even harder. I'd put in the time, the sweat, the work. It was time to move on. I heard Coach let out a long sigh and focused on him.

"You're aggressive on the field, you're working yourself too hard, and you're not in sync with Chris like you usually are. You don't even want to know how many incomplete passes I've counted today. You're a mess, Dylan. You know it, I know it, the whole team knows it. Do you think you can afford to be reckless this season? This is your future you're playing with, kid, and for what? A girl you won't even remember a month from now, much less a year from now?"

With every word out of his mouth, I could feel my shoulders tense further and further. Football was my life. I was a damn good player, the best wide receiver out there. I worked hard to earn that.

"Do you think it's all fun and games in the NFL? You think they'll give a shit about you throwing a temper tantrum about your teammates? The NFL is a whole new level. If you can't settle your differences with a few of your teammates, forget about your differences and play as a team on that field in college, you should forget about the NFL. You're good. We both know you'll get there, but not everyone has what it takes to stay there. It won't matter who you play for if all you do is sit on a bench because you can't get along with your teammates for whatever reason. Unless you're out on that field, giving it all you got—"

"Sir, with all due—"

"Shut up, Dylan. Shut up and listen to me. This is it. This is your last year. Do you understand that? You either make it or you don't. You have eyes on you. You know it's not just the media either. You've had eyes on you since your second year here, and don't forget that you were the one who chose to finish school before moving on to the big-boy league. The season starts next week. You have a shot, but you know every game counts. Don't screw everything up, not for something stupid like this."

"Sir, I have no intention of screwing anything up. I'm working on it. I promise the next time you see me on the field you will—"

He straightened from the desk and walked back to his seat behind it. "The next time I see you on the field, you better have your shit together. If you don't, I'll assume you're itching to get benched." Pulling out a small key from the back pocket of his jeans, he unlocked the top drawer, took out another key, and tossed it to me.

My hand shot out, and I caught it in my palm before it could connect with my face.

"I know you take part-time jobs here and there whenever you

can find the time, especially during the off-season. I'm assuming you send whatever is left after your expenses to your family and you'll do the same this year, too?" I held the key tighter in my hand, felt the edges biting into my skin, and gave him a silent nod before he continued. "Then you can't afford your own place. It's too late to apply for campus housing, and I can't have one of my top players sleeping on the floor at one of his teammates' houses." Leaning back in his seat, he gave me a long look. "I have an apartment just off campus. I had a—it's empty now. You'll be staying there. I need you to get your head back in the game. We need you this season."

And I needed to have football in my life. I wouldn't cope well if he decided benching me was a better idea.

"I'll have my shit together for the game."

"That's what I want to hear. We're done. Now get up and get the hell out of my office. I'll text you the address by the end of the day."

I opened my palm and looked down at the key. I wasn't looking for a free handout—hell, I hated the fact that I was even considering it, but I was out of options since everyone I knew had gotten their housing figured out months ago. I still could bunk up with a teammate or classmate, but I wasn't sure it wouldn't affect my game or my classes. I needed a party-free, girlfriend-free last year of college if I was going to make my and my family's dreams come true. My decision already made, I got up to leave.

"Thanks, Coach," I mumbled, just loud enough that he could hear me.

"Dylan."

With my hand on the door handle, I stopped and looked back at him over my shoulder.

"I don't want Chris knowing about this apartment or my involvement in you getting it. Sometimes when it's too late to head back, I stay over, and his mom doesn't know about the apartment. I want it to stay that way. Do you get me? I'll be staying there from time to time so make sure I don't see any of your teammates around either. I already see enough of your ugly faces to last a lifetime."

So my coach would be my roommate for my last year, not a big deal. Truth be told, the longer I thought about it as I walked out of the building to head to my two-thirty class, the more I liked the idea. It would be just one more reason to focus on what was important and steer clear of everything else.

CHAPTER FOUR

ZOE

S ince I was stupid enough to leave my towel back in my room, I had to step out of the bathroom with nothing but my dead phone clutched in my hand, and that's when I heard the telltale creak of the apartment door opening. The unexpectedness of it caught me off guard, and I froze mid-step. It could have been Mark, I supposed, so I entertained that idea for about a second or two, but then again, it also couldn't be. If I hadn't magically skipped a few days while I was in the shower singing my ass off, it was still Monday, which meant it wasn't Thursday, the usual night he'd come around or call. Plus, he had no idea I was still living there and not in another apartment with Kayla. That being said, as far as I knew, only Mark and I had keys to this apartment. So, it shouldn't—*couldn't* have been anyone else either. It wasn't like he would go around and give out the keys to the apartment he rented for me. I was his dirty secret, after all.

As I stood there holding my breath, completely naked and utterly still for at least five seconds—waiting for God knows what —my heartbeat steadily got heavier. My mouth was as dry as sandpaper, and when I finished my internal countdown from ten, I started panicking at full tilt. If it had been Mark, he would have called out by then. I thought of calling out a greeting myself, but all the horror movies I used to force myself to sit through with my dad came to mind, and I decided I didn't want to get killed by a clown that day.

It was not my time, not my day, and for sure not my first choice of a killer.

I especially didn't want to get killed by a clown while I was stark naked with water dripping down from my wet hair and body. I heard footsteps and only then realized that whoever had broken in hadn't moved for those first few seconds. When he finally started to walk, his footsteps were the slow kind...you know those steps, right? Again, in the horror movies I'd watched, I'd learned an important lesson: if someone is moving in slow and deliberate steps, you turn around and run. Run, my friend, run as if you have hellhounds nipping at your heels, because you know what? Those slow-walking creepy bastards always kill the shrieking girls.

It was too bad for me because I didn't have anywhere to run. The two-bedroom apartment was L shaped, and I was standing just around the corner from my soon-to-be killer.

Did I mention I never watch horror movies anymore? Or any kind of movies that keep me up at night?

As I started to silently back away, I looked down at my phone and cursed myself for listening to Spotify and draining the battery. Then I realized how badly my hands were shaking and started panicking even more. Grabbing the wall for some much-needed support, I managed to back into the bathroom quietly, grab a big hand towel, and wrap it around me, which only managed to cover me to a certain degree. Half my ass and other parts were just...there, but that little towel felt like an extra level of protection.

I heard some more footsteps coming from the open living room area then a loud crash followed by a hissed curse. Having trouble swallowing, and generally functioning, I cupped both my hands over my mouth to hold back a gasp and just crouched behind the door. If I could make myself as small as possible, I would be invisible and safe, and in a few minutes, it would all be over, because why would a thief come into the bathroom where there was nothing to steal? Unless he came to check why the lights were on...then I was screwed anyway.

Another crash sounded loudly, and this time I squeaked. My breathing was irregular and louder than I would've liked. Since my knees were about to give out on me, I put my palm on the wall and gently pulled myself up, only to feel my legs go to jelly.

Spotting a rolling pin leaning against the wall underneath the sink—don't even ask what it was doing in the bathroom—I grabbed hold of it and closed my eyes, just in case I needed it.

I was probably going to die in a bathroom in Los Angeles—actually, there was no *probably* about it because it would either be from a heart attack or at the hands of a stranger, whichever happened first. Unfortunately, neither one sounded all that appealing to me.

I had no idea if mere minutes passed or an hour, but I couldn't hear a single sound anymore. When I was sure there was nothing, I started to weigh my options—not that I had many.

Even so, I was either going to suck it up and get out of the bathroom, or I was gonna stay in there indefinitely. Then I remembered that all my camera equipment was out in the open in the living room: lenses I'd borrowed from my professor, the beloved Sony camera my dad had gifted me, my laptop, and even more expensive equipment I had no way of buying again anytime soon. Still shaking and shivering, I decided to step out and at least take a look around the corner. Surely, if someone was still in the house—though I was hoping really hard that someone *wasn't* in the house—I'd either try to make a run for it, or I'd just drop dead on the spot, because I had a feeling my heart wasn't going to be able to hang in there much longer.

I was so scared, I forgot how to breathe. Forcing my body to move forward, I swallowed and opened the door so I could slowly peek around the wall.

Someone *was* definitely in the house. It wasn't exactly pitch black thanks to the street lights softly illuminating the living room, but other than that, none of the lights in the apartment were turned on. There weren't many pieces of furniture in the living room, just a big comfy couch, an armchair big enough to comfortably seat two people, and a coffee table. Seeing this awful stranger kneeling down right behind the couch and going through something in a big bag on the floor made my blood turn to ice.

He was stealing my equipment.

The rolling pin still securely held in my hands, I pulled myself back from the edge, then leaned against the wall. The apartment door was closed. I was trapped. Even if I ran for it, he'd hear me and catch me before I could make it out. With the size of him, I didn't want that to happen. My only chance—my only option, really—was to hit him in the head with the rolling pin while he still had his back to me, grab the key I was eighty percent sure I had left on the kitchen island, and *then* make a run for it—after grabbing the bag that held my camera equipment, of course. Considering my lack of clothing, getting to Ms. Hilda, who lived at the end of the hall, was my best shot. She was always home, so I wasn't worried about not finding anyone, but was it possible to even make it out there?

When I realized there were cold tears running down my cheeks from the fear and anxiety of the whole thing, I took a choppy, deep, but quiet breath and told myself I could do this. I repeated it over and over again in my mind.

Before I could talk myself out of it, I stepped out into the open, the rolling pin held high in my hand.

Here goes nothing.

I sucked in air and started tiptoeing on my weak, trembling legs toward the dark figure who still had his back to me.

When I was only a few steps away, I started shaking in the worst way, so I chose to run the last few steps and lifted the baking tool even higher to inflict maximum pain. I released what sounded like a war cry to my ears but was more likely a high-pitched shriek as I hit him right in the back. I was aiming for his head, so...maybe that didn't work out all that great for me. Probably not a Viking warrior in one of my past lives.

"What the hell—" my killer grunted.

In the amount of time it took me to lift the damn thing again, he'd already spun around and grabbed my wrists in a tight, painful grip that caused the rolling pin to slip out of my fingers as I started screaming.

My breath hitched and I whimpered because I couldn't get enough air into my lungs. I couldn't exactly wrap my mind around what was happening, but I fought his hold on me like the Viking warrior I was not until my legs gave out.

"Shit," the man barked, tightening his fingers around my wrists as I started to slide out of his grip and down to my knees. I was trying my best to rip myself out of his grasp.

Nothing worked.

My vision blurred. No air.

He was talking, and I *thought* what I was hearing was his voice, but it was so damn hard to hear anything through the building pounding pressure in my head, not to mention my poor, wild heart, which was in overdrive.

"Hey! Breathe. Please breathe. Breathe, goddamn it!" my angry killer shouted, and I flinched.

Warm hands cupped my cheeks, and he basically taught me how to breathe again as I sat crumpled on the floor.

Eyes closed.

Heart beating out of control.

"You're doing great. Just breathe. Yes, just like that. Easy. In, now out. In and out. Good. You're doing great."

"Who the hell are you?" I wheezed out when I could, but then I remembered that if he told me who he was, he'd have to kill me. First rule of the dark world of criminals: you see my face, you die. "No, no, don't tell me. I take that back." I didn't really think a thief would just drop everything to help me breathe and calm down...but I wasn't taking any chances. "You can take anything you want, please don't hurt me."

"What the hell are you talking about? I'm gonna ask you the same thing—who the hell are you?" he asked impatiently. "Hold on." His hands left my face and I felt him move away from me. I wiped the tears from my eyes just in time to see the lights turn on.

When he came to stand in front of me again, I just about lost it. I was both terrified and shocked, and also very much naked under my tiny towel. Unsure if I was hallucinating due to the lack of air, I just kept staring up at him from my spot on the floor.

"You...but...what in the actual freaking hell?" I stuttered, maybe a tad bit louder than a whisper.

The star of the football team, the wide receiver, Dylan Reed himself, looked down at me with a deep frown forming on his face as he offered me his right hand.

Dumbfounded, I looked at it for a few long seconds before I looked back up at his face again. "What in the actual freaking hell?" I repeated in the same tone, because I couldn't seem to remember any other words that would be useful for the situation. That was the only vocabulary I could muster up.

Using one hand to hold onto my towel and the other to push myself off the floor, I tried to scramble up on my own. He must've taken pity on my weak attempt because he grabbed my arm and pulled me up.

"Do I know..." he murmured when I was finally standing on my own two feet like a normal person, albeit a little shakily, but I was still up on my feet.

I could see recognition set in, and I wasn't sure if that was a good thing or a very bad thing. He asked, "I know you, right?" Before I could try to come up with more words, his mouth transformed and he was offering me a big smile, a smile I'd happened to find very attractive a year before.

"There you are," he said, finally breaking the awkward silence.

Not sure what that meant, I cleared my throat. "Uh, yeah...?" Moving very slowly, I tugged at my hand and managed absolutely nothing.

His smile only got bigger, and instead of letting me go, his grip tightened just a fraction, there then gone. "I thought I'd see you again, eventually—thought I'd get another shot."

What shot?

I tried to make my lips move and form words, wanted to ask him what he meant by that, but that was when my stupid itty-bitty towel decided to just unravel and drop to the floor. Time stood still, my breath whooshed right out of me, and I froze for the nth time that day. If there was *ever* a time for the earth to open up and swallow me, that was it. I could do nothing but stand there with my hand in his as we looked at each other for long agonizing seconds, both of us undecided on what to do next. I tried to beg him with my eyes to not look down, but I wasn't sure he understood what I was saying.

He made his choice, and his eyes started to drop.

I think he saw my boobs. Actually, he *definitely* saw my boobs, and still very much high on adrenaline, I panicked.

Before his gaze could make it all the way down to complete

the full trek, my hand tightened around his—*Why is he still holding on to my hand again?*—and I threw my body at him, plastering myself to his front, forcing him to take a step back to keep his balance. It was a poor excuse of a tackle, but it hid me from his open view, which was all I was after. The backs of his thighs hit the back of the leather couch and he wrapped an arm around my waist to keep us upright.

"Don't!" I yelled right in his face. "What are you doing?" I could already feel the burning heat in my cheeks—and when I say heat, I don't mean the cute *Oh, look at me, I'm all naturally blushed* kind, but more like the, *I'm impersonating a tomato right now* kind.

It was the third time I'd come face to face with this guy, and each and every time, I'd embarrassed myself beyond what could reasonably be called cute. Sure, in the last few years I had become less shy, going from painfully shy to just plain shy, so I didn't really care all that much about what had happened that first night I met him, but...him seeing me naked was just the cherry on top of everything, and it was too much.

He cleared his throat and looked down at me. "Hi."

Hi? That wasn't the answer I was looking for.

"This wasn't the welcome I was expecting, especially since I wasn't expecting any welcome at all."

I cleared my throat too, because he had done it and it was something to do. I tried to keep my eyes on his even though I was practically shaking with the need to run.

"Well, I wasn't expecting to welcome anyone." I managed to squeak out the words after some time. I swallowed and lowered my voice. "Please don't look at me."

That right arm tightened around my naked waist as he brought us to an upright position so I was no longer lying on him. Make no mistake, I was still plastered to his body, and I wasn't thinking of letting him go anytime soon either. My poor heart thundering, our eyes met for a very brief second.

One side of his mouth quirked up. "To be completely honest with you, I'm not sure if I can do that."

I wished I were the kind of girl who would offer him a light smirk, maybe a light slap on his chest, and then just turn around and walk away, maybe even give him a seductive wink over my shoulder before waltzing into my room as he watches my naked ass sway for him and act like I was completely fine being naked in front of strangers. Needless to say, I wasn't that kind of girl—never had been. So, instead, I frowned up at him. "Are you kidding me?" I asked in a whisper when I couldn't think of anything else to say. I needed at least a week to process what had happened in the last ten minutes.

He offered me a small smile. "I'm sorry, I didn't mean it to sound like... I just meant I'm not sure if I can look away from your face—never mind, you wouldn't understand. I won't look down." I couldn't return his gaze, so I looked at his lips when they moved. "Promise."

His palm, which was splayed open at the small of my back, slowly moved up a few inches, and I accidentally arched into him. Goose bumps were rising on my skin all over my body, and the drops of water falling from my wet hair onto my shoulders and back weren't helping matters. He was warm and I was freezing.

"I'm gonna need that towel," I said, looking away as I tried to ignore the fact that I was starting to feel my nipples getting hard. It wasn't because I could feel his abs contract against me or because that arm around me was doing things to me, too, but because it was getting chilly. Could he feel it too?

"Can you lean down with me so I can get it? Or can you look away so—"

Dylan took his hand off of my back, and the sudden loss of the warmth of his skin on mine caused a small shiver to go through my body. He tilted his head up toward the ceiling and gripped the edge of the leather couch. Keeping my eyes on him, on those bulging arms, I slowly let go of his shirt, peeled myself off of him, and had to open and close my hands a few times to get rid of the tingles in my fingers. Still keeping my eyes on him to make sure he wasn't looking, I quickly leaned down and grabbed the towel from the floor. Instead of wrapping it around me again, where it would cover practically nothing, I decided to hold it up horizontally to cover more area. At least that way, instead of dancing on the edge of flashing him my private parts, only my backside would be open, and I was counting on there being no more surprise guests.

Now that he was looking at the ceiling and not at me, I took my time to take in all of him. *Good Lord, Dylan Reed is standing right in front of me.* I noticed the jeans, the damp t-shirt that fit him a little too perfectly, the wide shoulders. His arms looked bigger than I'd remembered, and I got stuck looking at that part of his body a little longer. They'd been no matchsticks before, but still. He was all hard muscle, nothing extreme, just toned, hard perfection. Even his freaking forearms looked firm and perfect with a light dusting of hair.

"Your shirt is wet," I blurted out, not knowing what else to say.

He looked at himself, brushed a hand down his front. "That's okay." Then he focused on me.

I took a step back. "Are you planning on telling me what you're doing here?" I enquired as I started to back away and put some much-needed distance between us.

His eyes found mine, and I accidentally backed into a wall.

"Are you about to run away again?" Was that a grin he was trying to fight off? I couldn't find one single thing that was amusing about the situation. He held my gaze as if he himself was trying to figure out the answer to my question. I dropped my eyes to his throat and kept backing away...right into the tripod I had set up earlier.

Great, Zoe. You couldn't have acted more like an idiot if you tried.

I was either gonna go for the tripod and save it, or I was gonna hold on to my towel as if nothing could break us apart. I went with the latter and just let the tripod crash to the floor, wincing when the sound echoed in the room. Thank God my camera was no longer attached to it.

When my feet got tangled and I lost my balance for a second, he made a move toward me.

"No," I yelled, admittedly a little louder than necessary. "No —ah, you don't have to move. Just tell me what you're doing here."

"What are *you* doing here?" he asked instead of giving me an answer. His gaze dropped to my tripod on the floor then met my questioning gaze again.

Come again? His question stopped me in my backward shuffling.

"Could you, maybe, oh, I don't know—come up with an answer instead of more questions? I live here. You're the one who's in the wrong place, not me, buddy."

Another easy smile. "I don't think so."

"You don't think so. You don't think what, exactly?"

"I don't think I'm in the wrong apartment."

"I actually, *really* think you are."

He crossed his arms and just stood there...fully clothed, unlike me. "I don't think so." He stuffed his hand into his pocket and pulled out a key, shaking it in the air.

He had a key.

Goddammit, Zoe, use your brain! How else could he have gotten in?

"Look, uh..." I glanced back over my shoulder—I was only ten, twelve steps away from the corner that would take me to my room. If I could just throw on some clothes and stop with the uncontrollable shivering, I was pretty sure my mind would start working again. "Just give me a minute to get dressed and come back out here so we can..."

He nodded. "I'm not going anywhere."

Instead of saying *Yeah, buddy, you are*, I gave him an exasperated look, barely stopped myself from huffing, and disappeared down the hallway.

Not two minutes had passed before I was back in the living room, fully clothed this time. It had taken me exactly thirty seconds to get dressed, and the other minute and a half had been spent trying to make myself look...better. My heart did this weird jump at the sight of him. Adrenaline...I was sure it was the adrenaline still coursing through my body that made my stomach clench and my hands go ice cold. He was standing in the exact same spot where I'd left him; the only difference was that instead of looking right into my eyes, he was looking down at his shoes and talking on his phone.

"Yes, I understand, Coach. Of course. Okay, I will. Yes. Again, thank you."

Coach...of course. What was I even thinking?

I'd have loved to call him and talk to him myself, but if he was with his wife, I knew he wouldn't pick up my call, so why bother?

I leaned down and picked up my wounded tripod. After making sure it wasn't broken, I set it up closer to the wall where I couldn't trip on it again then walked toward the couch, the one that would take me farther away from Dylan Reed. Before my clothed ass hit the cushions, he was off his phone, and we were alone again.

"So...from the sound of things, I guess neither one of us is in the wrong place, then," I said, speaking to his back. Even though I was surprised, I could already guess what was going on.

He turned to face me, and his eyes did a sweep up and down. "It would seem so."

I felt like I was about to shrink under his stare, so I grabbed the nearest pillow and hugged it to my stomach. The way he looked at me... I was tempted to look down and see what he found so interesting, but I already knew I was wearing my black leggings and an old t-shirt that had the words *Pizzama Party* all over it in small print—nothing interesting whatsoever.

"So..." What the hell was I supposed to say? "You're here to pick something up for Mark?" That could be a possibility.

He lost the small smile on his lips.

"No."

That was what I was afraid of. "You're not just dropping by, by any chance?"

"I think I'm your new roommate," he announced, getting to the point.

And just like that, I started feeling sick again. I had been holding on to the hope that whatever he was doing there was temporary, but *roommate* didn't sound temporary.

"Coach didn't mention I was coming?" he asked, pulling me out of my little freak-out.

I tried my best to act like everything was okay. This wasn't my apartment, after all. It was Mark who was paying the rent, not me. "Nope. I'm guessing he didn't mention *I* was here, either."

"No." He sighed and ran his hand through his hair, drawing my attention to it. It was still short, pretty much the same length it had been the last time I'd seen him, so at least that hadn't changed. I kind of liked him with short hair. Walking around the couch, he chose to sit right across from me and dumped his phone on the expensive marble coffee table. I winced at the sound. "He said he wasn't aware that you'd be here, but it wouldn't be a problem since you're barely in the apartment. Don't worry, I'm not gonna be around much either, with football season starting and everything else going on. I won't bother you."

I sighed and rubbed my temple. "Sorry to crush your dreams, but I'm always here."

He smiled, not a big, easy one that did things to my heart, just a promise of one. "You're not crushing my dreams."

Not knowing what to say—or more like not knowing *how* to say it—I fussed with the pillow in my lap instead of meeting his eyes. There was something unnerving about the way he kept meeting my gaze. "Did he tell you who I am?" He wouldn't, of course he wouldn't. I knew that, but still...

"He said you're a family friend's daughter." There was a pause, so I looked up. "Are you not?"

I wanted to laugh. "Yeah, I am. Family friend. So, what's your deal?"

A little hardness seeped into his eyes, and he leaned back. "My living situation changed in these last few days, and apparently I need a place to stay. Coach insisted that this would be okay. If you're gonna be uncomfortable with me being around...if this is not okay, Zoe..."

With the speed I looked up I almost gave myself whiplash. His eyes were intent on me. *He remembers my name?* Sure, he would remember who I was—how could he forget that-weird-freshman-who-made-a-fool-of-herself—but he remembered my name? It had been a year since the last time I hadn't quite managed to hide away from him, and a year was a long time to remember a stranger's name.

"You remember my name?" I asked, genuinely surprised.

The smile came out again and his features visibly softened, now sincere, playful, and inviting. I forgot what I'd even asked. "Like I said back then, I had a feeling I'd get to see you again. I thought we'd get another shot. I didn't think it'd take a year to get that shot...but here we are."

There was that word again.

I gave up on the pillow, pulled my legs up and under me, and averted my eyes. Where was my phone when I needed it to hide behind? Instead, I sat up straighter and lightly grabbed the armrest with one hand. "What do you mean by another shot?"

"You know what I mean."

"Actually, I'm pretty sure I don't."

"The kiss." He tilted his head, and one of his eyebrows did this arching thing that made him look really attractive. "The last time we saw each other, we said maybe we'd make it happen next time. Ring any bells?"

That bell rang, all right. Turned out, I did know what he was talking about after all.

"See, the way I remember it, it was you who said that, and I'm pretty sure I was trying to get out of there as quickly as possible."

"Why is that?" he asked without missing a beat.

I let go of my death grip on the armrest and rubbed my hands on my thighs. Did we have to talk about this again?

"Why is what?"

"Why do you always try to get away from me as quickly as possible?"

"Could it be because I don't know you?"

"You told me you were going to kiss me the first time we met."

I kept my eyes on the general area of his face. "First, we never actually *met*"—I did quick air quotes—"that first time. I didn't give you my name, you didn't give me yours. So, we didn't actually meet, and I told you then that my friends...actually, not really *friends*, my roommate and *her* friends dared me to kiss you. I told you that, and just so you know, they already knew you were dating someone, apparently for quite some time, so they dared me to kiss you in front of everyone so I would make a fool out of myself and face your wrath. They thought it would be fun, thought I should loosen up a little. They didn't like your girl-friend and wanted to see the look on her face."

Fewer words, Zoe. Use fewer words, please.

He seemed to process what I had just blurted out and opened his mouth to answer, but before any words could come out, I sprang up from my seat in the hopes of ending the conversation. "You know what, none of this matters since it happened two years ago. I'd forgotten about it until you brought it up." I stopped talking. He was staring at me, seeing right through my lie. Closing my eyes, I rubbed the bridge of my nose. "Okay, I'm lying. I didn't forget about it, but I'd like to forget about it since it wasn't one of my finest moments, if that's okay with you. Now that we're going to be roommates, I think that's for the best. If you're staying here, I should show you your room."

Without looking at his face, I walked by him and toward the hallway that led to the extra room he would be staying in, right across from my room—two steps away from my room, if you want me to be absolutely exact.

My new roommate.

When life throws you a wide receiver out of nowhere, what are you supposed to do with him? Try your best not to look at him for too long, maybe? That'd be a good rule of thumb, I thought.

I heard his footsteps, so I knew he was following me. I opened the door and waited for him to step inside, all the while making sure not to look him in the eye. Like I said, I still needed time—alone. I needed time to calm down and process everything.

There wasn't much furniture in the room. Just like mine, it had a pretty comfortable twin bed, a small wardrobe, a night-stand, a window that overlooked the road...and that was pretty much it, just the bare necessities, which was still better than most student apartments.

He walked past me and dumped a duffel bag right next to the

bed, the same bag I'd thought he was using to stash my equipment in. I watched him quickly take everything in and then nod. "No desk, huh?"

"A desk?"

"You know, to study on?"

"Do you guys really study? I mean jocks, athletes—I always wondered. I thought you had other students do that for you."

Stupid, stupid me.

Facing me, he raised his brows, and this time there was no playful smile forming on his lips. "I hadn't pegged you as someone who would stereotype people."

His words sank in, and I felt another flush in my cheeks. He was right—I actually hated people who stereotyped everyone, people who judged before actually getting to know a person. I was making an ass of myself yet again. Maybe it was something about him that unsettled me? That triggered the word vomit? It was easier to put the blame on him instead of admitting I was acting like a bitch.

Letting go of the door handle, I shook my head and backed up. "I'm sorry. You're right. I don't know why I said that. I don't know you. I know a few people who play and just because they would rather die than open a book or take notes, that doesn't mean you're like that too. I'm sorry." I reached for my own door and broke our brief eye contact, mostly focusing on his ear and the window behind him—anywhere but his eyes. "This is my room." I pointed over my shoulder. "I'll let you get settled in and maybe see you around later." I opened the door and before disappearing inside, I turned back. "Oh, about the desk—I don't have one in my room either, so I bought one off of Craigslist last year. It's in the living room. I'm not sure if you saw it with everything else going on, but my camera equipment was on it. It's pretty small, but it gets the job done. I rarely use it anyway, mostly use the coffee table. I'll get my stuff off of it, so you're welcome to use it anytime you want."

Without waiting for an answer, I closed my door.

Alone—*finally*.

After resting my forehead against the door for a few seconds, I quietly banged my head on it and didn't even care that he could hear.

CHAPTER FIVE

DYLAN

Two hours had passed since I had settled into my new room and Zoe had disappeared into hers. So far, I had been attacked, and with a rolling pin, no less. I'd been flashed (granted, not voluntarily) and stereotyped, all by the same girl—the same girl who had intrigued me so much the two times we'd bumped into each other. I was still intrigued, maybe even more so, and I knew I shouldn't have been. I'd mistaken a few girls for her a handful of times, which meant my eyes had been searching for her ever since our last run-in and I wasn't even fully aware of it. That same girl was my new roommate.

Life was a tricky bitch sometimes.

Lightly knocking on her door three times, I relaxed against the frame and waited.

Zoe opened the door—only slightly—and her head peeked through the opening.

"Yes?"

"I thought we should talk."

"About?"

"About this whole thing. If we're going to live together, we should get to know each other. At the very least, I should know more about you than just your first name—your last name to start, perhaps?"

"What do you need my last name for?" She looked back over her shoulder. "It's eleven thirty, getting a little late—maybe we could do that tomorrow?"

I bet she'd have loved to just avoid me altogether. Unfortunately for her, I wasn't going anywhere.

"Are you going to bed?"

Holding on to the door, she worried her bottom lip with her teeth. For the first time since answering the door, she looked up at me as she grudgingly answered. "Not yet."

Taking my hands out of my pockets, I straightened. "Come on. I'll ask you a few questions, you'll ask me a few, then we'll both go to bed and rest a bit easier about our new situation." Already walking away from her, I added over my shoulder, "Not to mention, I'll be reassured that you're not going to try to attack me with a rolling pin in my sleep."

Hearing her mutter something under her breath, I let her follow me at her own pace. When I glanced back over my shoulder, she was pulling on the hem of her shirt, looking down at her feet.

"Clarke," she mumbled, her gaze still fixed on the hardwood floor as she stood in the middle of the living room. This time, she spoke loud enough for me to hear.

I turned back. "Sorry?"

"My last name...it's Clarke."

"See, that wasn't so bad, now, was it?" I gave her a quick grin, which she chose to ignore. "Mine is Reed."

"I know. Everybody knows your name."

"Oh? I remember you telling me that the second time we met. You a football fan? Come to any of our games?" Since she and her family were close to Coach—close enough that they shared an apartment, apparently—I thought maybe she'd attend the games with them.

"Not really."

Her gaze briefly met mine then darted around the room as she tried to decide where to move to.

I had to be quick before she rounded the couch and saw the object of my first official 'getting to know my roommate' question. "My first question is..." I reached down to grab the unexpected find and turned to face Zoe. "Should I prepare myself to find more stuff like this innocently laying around the place? Or is this the only one?" Her jaw slowly dropped open, and even though I was trying my best to sound as serious as I could, the horror on her face was too much. I lost it and laughed. "You should see your face, Zoe Clarke."

Her gaze was locked on the pink, ten-inch vibrator held loosely in my hand, which seemed to have all the bells and whistles. "Oh my God," she managed to say, all breathless. "Fuck."

"Yeah, I believe that's what it is generally used for." I was already having more fun than I'd expected to have on my first night with her. "So, I'm gonna take a wild guess and say you forgot you dropped it between the couch cushions and that's not your usual hiding place?"

"It's not mine," she croaked out, walking toward me in quick steps. The familiar pink had risen in her cheeks again. I handed her the embarrassing item before she could start a tug of war and watched her carefully pluck it from my hand with two fingers.

My smile grew bigger. "There is nothing to be ashamed of. Masturbating is healthy."

The light flush on her cheeks seemed to spread more by the second. After giving me a death glare, she walked away without a second glance.

I chuckled to myself. I wouldn't have put it past her to lock herself in her room and not come back out. It seemed plausible at the time since it was kind of our thing—her blushing and promptly running away. It didn't matter that I didn't know anything but her name. When she did actually emerge from her room—which I had not expected her to do—there were no vibrators in sight, but that pink flush was still clinging to her pale skin, making the bright green of her eyes stand out more.

"It's not mine," she repeated as she took a seat and tucked her hands under her thighs. "I'm an art major focused in photography. I take photos to make extra money. It's my job, and that was one of the five vibrators I had to take pictures of for a girl who has a blog. I have no idea how I managed to leave that one behind." I must have given her a look that pretty much conveyed what I was thinking—*bullshit*—because her eyes narrowed on me. "Don't look at me like that. Look around—there are no drapes in this place, so if that was mine, I'd have to...*use* it right where you are sitting. I'm not an exhibitionist. I'm not about to do it right in front of an open window—not that it's any of your business if or where I do it at all..." She sighed and rubbed her eyes with her fingers. "I'm just going to shut up now so you can ask whatever it is you want to ask to feel safe in your bed tonight. Then when it's over, I'll run back to my room so I can scream into my pillow and pretend tonight never happened."

Facing the windows was the big brown couch where I'd found the vibrator in question after it poked me in the thigh. There was another two-seater that was a dark mustard color to the right, where she was sitting, wary and pretty much ready to flee. I took my time taking a seat on the far end of the brown couch.

"I don't want you to do that," I said softly. When she mustered the courage to look up, I gave her a small smile. "I mean, I don't want you to run back to your room. I was serious when I said I wanted us to get to know each other." Her eyes connected with mine for just a second then she was looking at something behind my back. She was so shy, but it only made her more attractive and interesting in my eyes.

I cleared my throat. "Okay, this is good. See, I've already started to learn things about you. Your name is Zoe Clarke, and you're not an exhibitionist—noted. I will sleep easier knowing I'm safe from walking in on you doing God knows what. You're an art student and you're into photography. You make your own money —props to you on that one. This isn't so bad, is it?"

"Maybe for you it isn't."

"I'm going to ignore that because now it's your turn. Ask me whatever you want."

She let out a long breath and tucked her hands back under her thighs again. "I don't have a question right now."

"Come on. It could be something as simple as my favorite movie."

She shot me an exasperated look, and her expression said everything that needed to be said. I wasn't giving up though —not yet.

"What's your favorite movie, then?"

I leaned back in my seat and got comfortable. "Oh, I can't answer that. I have too many to choose just one. My turn."

She raised her brows and her lips parted in disbelief. "You just told me to ask you—"

I cut her off before she could finish her sentence. "No, you're gonna have to wait for your turn. Don't be a bad sport. Do you still have that boyfriend of yours?"

Her response came out as a squeak. "What?"

"You know, the boyfriend who prevented us from kissing that last time. Still seeing him?"

Her brows drew together and she turned her body toward me, finally pulling her hands out from under her thighs in the process. It was exactly what I wanted her to do—forget about being shy and just be herself around me. If we were going to live together for however long, it would make things easier for both of us. Getting her to actually look into my eyes when we were speaking would be a nice bonus too. If making her angry was necessary to achieve my goal, I was fine with that.

"I don't think that's something you need to know to sleep safe in your bed."

"I think it is, actually. I know we decided you're not an exhibitionist, but I could still come to your room to ask for a cup of sugar and end up walking in on you two and have it scar me for the rest of my life. If I know he'll be around, I'll make sure to not come knocking for sugar."

Her lips were twitching when she gave me an answer. "Don't worry, you're not going to walk in on anyone. Your delicate feelings are safe. Mark doesn't want me to have friends over, so you won't be seeing anyone around at all."

That perked me up, so I scooted forward and focused all my attention on her. "Mark?"

Looking away, she reached for a colorful pillow and started to strangle it. "Your coach...Mark. He's not my coach, so I can call him by his name."

"Sure you can. So you didn't really answer my question—do you have a boyfriend or not?"

"No."

I was in the process of trying to decide if that was a good or bad thing for me and was heavily leaning toward bad when she grunted and sighed.

"Okay, I lied. Let's say I have a boyfriend and it's complicated."

"You lied?" Was she telling the truth now? I couldn't tell, but if she was, I was guessing she wasn't good at keeping secrets and I'd end up learning everything about her complicated relationship either way. "That's actually okay, I think. It'll make things easier." I leaned back again. "I don't have a girlfriend at the moment, but I can behave."

She gave me a questioning look, eyes narrowing, head slightly tilting to the side. "I got you—I know that's a lie. Maybe you were right and this getting to know each other thing isn't a bad idea."

"I'm the liar?" I asked, pointing at myself as my brows drew together. "I believe you're the one who admitted to lying—twice, so far. What makes you think I'm lying to you? And about what?"

Copying my move, she scooted forward in her seat. "Because I happen to know you actually do have a girlfriend, and before you accuse me of stalking you, I'm not—I didn't. I saw your Snap on Campus Stories. After I saw the way you were kissing her, I'd say she is the definition of a girlfriend, but I guess with so many girls throwing themselves at you, you can't bother to label someone as your girlfriend and bind yourself to only one person. Why stay with one when you can sample so many more, right?"

"I don't use social media."

"Then it was her account, I guess."

"Huh." She was still looking at me expectantly, so sure she had me cornered. "Is this how you are to all people, or is it just me that brings out this side of you? First the desk comment and now this—do you have something against athletes?"

Her expression faltered. "What?"

I rubbed my neck and sighed. I was the one who had insisted we do an impromptu Q&A, but I hadn't thought she'd start with all the hard questions. "It's true, I did have a girlfriend a week ago, or maybe it's been longer...I haven't really kept track, but it doesn't matter. I walked in on her getting fucked by two of my teammates, so that was pretty much the end of our relationship, which is also why I need a new place to stay. By the way, not all athletes do what they do just so they can have their fill of girls. It doesn't work like that. You can't put everyone in the same box. Some of us choose to stay away from distractions at all costs, and some of us like the attention. You can't decide which category I fall into before you make an effort to know me. I'm not a liar, and I have a very hard time dealing with them. Me being an athlete doesn't make me any less than some guy you'd fall for." *Why did I have to put it like that? Fuck me...* Nobody was going to do any kind of falling. "Again, I'm a little disappointed. I didn't figure you to be judgmental. My bad."

Maybe this getting to know each other thing wasn't one of my best ideas. Maybe I should've kept my head down and just coexisted.

I stood up. "This wasn't a good idea. Good night, Zoe—"

"No," she burst out, jumping up. "No. Please, don't go. I'm sorry, Dylan. You're right. I'm not like this. I'm being a judgmental bitch, and I'm not like that, trust me. I have no idea what's wrong with me tonight. I think after what happened earlier, thinking I was about to be killed by a clown and then the shock of realizing you were the intruder...anyway, the reason doesn't matter anyway. Sometimes when I'm nervous I talk too much and it's just a bad case of word vomit." She gestured at herself with her hand. "See, I'm still talking, aren't I? I should stop, I know I should, yet I can still hear myself talking, but you know what? You're right—if we're going to share an apartment, we should at least know a few things about each other." She came to stand in front of me, rose up on her tiptoes to reach my shoulders, and pushed me back down on the couch.

Then she was off walking toward the kitchen area that overlooked the living room. "I'm gonna make us coffee and we're going to talk until you're sure you're in a safe place and not living with a bitchy lunatic who will attack you in your sleep." She looked at me over her shoulder. "Though, I have to point out, you did scare the living shit out of me by walking in unannounced and all creepy like, so I'm just putting it out there that the rolling pin thing shouldn't be on me. That one was all you."

Standing behind the island that separated the small kitchen area from the living room, she stopped speaking. When I just kept staring at her instead of answering, she tucked her hair behind her ear and waited expectantly.

I relaxed in my seat and threw my arm over the back of the couch so I could watch her do her thing. "I can't have coffee this late because I have an early practice, but I'll have milk if you have it."

"Just milk?"

I nodded.

"Okay, see, I'm not even gonna make fun of you for drinking milk, though from the size of you, I can tell you're not a growing boy anymore. Hell, you know what? I'll even drink some with you."

Unexpectedly, she drew a laugh out of me, and I won a smile from her. Just like that, it struck me that she would stand out no matter where she was, and I was stupid for mistaking other people for her. A few seconds passed as we smiled at each other.

"Right...milk." She lifted a finger and checked the fridge, her head disappearing from view completely. She shifted a few things around and leaned farther in until all I could see was her ass.

"It's fine if you don't have it. I don't need to have a drink to chat with you."

"Got it!" she yelled as she came out with a box of milk held high. "Just let me check the expiration date. And...we're good."

After filling two glasses, she offered me one and went back to her seat. Resting her glass on the armrest, she sat cross-legged and took a sip of milk with a shy little smile on her face. I just stared.

"Sorry, I don't have any of those fancy milks—soy milk, almond milk, oat milk, or whatever other new kind I don't know about. I make extra money to get by, but it's not that much." She nodded at my untouched glass. "It's okay if you're not used to cow milk or something. You don't have to drink it."

I settled back and drank half of it. "What makes you say that?" I asked as calmly as possible.

"I just assumed since you're a football player you drink healthier stuff like green juice, or other fancy milks..." She took a deep breath and blew out her cheeks, all the while keeping her eyes somewhere over my shoulder. "I'm doing it again, aren't I?"

I grinned at her and took another gulp from my glass.

She groaned and covered her face with her palm. "I think you should do all the talking for a while. I'm acting like a complete asshole. So, please, ask anything you want...please."

I drank the last of the milk and set the glass on the coffee table in front of me. She held her own glass between her palms and took a small sip. I watched her discreetly licking her upper lip to make sure she had no milk mustache.

"Let's start small—how many siblings?" I asked, deciding not to dwell on the fact that she was the first person to make me smile since that night.

"Ah, siblings, huh? None. You?"

My smile grew bigger and I relaxed. "I have two monsters that happen to be my brother and sister. Amelia is the middle child. She just turned fifteen this summer and she's the princess in the family, Daddy's girl through and through, shy and sweet as can be." I watched Zoe duck her head and take a few more sips of milk. "And then we have Mason. He's seven, and he is the main monster, the most inquisitive kid you could ever meet. If you think you talk too much, wait till you meet him."

Not that there would be an occasion where she would meet my brother, but...you never know.

"He's seven? That's a big age difference."

"He is the surprise baby. Can't imagine not having him around though. It was weird when Dad sat me down and told me

I'd have a baby brother, and to be completely honest, it's a little embarrassing for a fourteen-year-old to know his parents are still doing it, but they did good with him. Now I don't even know how we survived without that kid. He's the best."

I grinned and watched her lips slowly tip up as her gaze focused on my lips. I didn't want to ruin our moment, especially when she wasn't acting like she wanted to collapse in on herself, but I needed to know and this was the best time to ask.

"That first night..."

She groaned and let her head drop back on the couch. "You're killing me."

I chuckled. "No, listen—just one question. I need to know."

I couldn't identify the expression on her face, but I could tell saying anything about it was pretty much the last thing she wanted to do. I forged on anyway.

"Did you cry? I thought I saw you crying when you were trying to get away, but I wasn't sure." When she didn't lift her head up, I kept going. "I kinda looked for you that night, you know. I mean, I was seeing this girl at the time and it was new... but still, after the way you ran out, I guess I just wanted to make sure you were okay. Trust me, it wasn't about you. Any of the other guys would've taken you up on your offer, but—"

"Oh, please, *please*, let's just forget it happened, all right? Yes, I kind of started crying at the end because I was embarrassed and I do that sometimes, but it wasn't about you. I cry all the time. Okay, maybe I don't cry *all* the time, but it doesn't take much for me to shed a few tears. Show me a video where a dog reunites with its owner and I'm a goner. I'll cry all over you. Plus, it wasn't like I was bawling my eyes out because you didn't want a stranger to kiss you in the middle of a freaking party. I was just embarrassed. If you haven't noticed, I'm painfully shy. It happens. I cried today when you scared me out of my mind and I thought I was going to die." She lifted a shoulder in a shrug. "To be honest, it wasn't because you rejected me. I was pissed at my roommate for putting me in that position and pissed at myself for playing along. I was fine...mostly."

It was fun to watch her rambling. "Define mostly."

She slumped in her seat. "Oh man. Well...I might've walked the other way whenever I saw you around campus after that... which wasn't often, just a few times, but I still did it. Again, like I said, it was only because I was embarrassed. Now, you're right here and I don't have anywhere to run to, so I won't be doing that this time." She gulped down her milk and leaned forward to set it on the table between us, unknowingly giving me a brief view of the swell of her boobs. I looked away, because she was off limits. Any girl was off limits, but Zoe Clarke was even more off limits. I was sticking with my decision to be distraction-free for my last year.

It was the worst fucking timing to meet her.

"Let me save you and get back to easier questions," I said softly. She exhaled and soundlessly mouthed her thanks. "Favorite movie?"

"I'm not gonna be vague like you, but...there really are a ton of movies I enjoy watching. Shia LaBeouf's *Eagle Eye*—can't even count how many times I've watched that movie. *Speed*—I love Keanu Reeves, both on screen and in real life. What else...*Transformers, Lord of The Rings, Mean Girls*, 2012, and *The Holiday* because Jude Law and Cameron Diaz and Kate Winslet...just to name a few that come to mind."

I parted my lips, ready to get to my next question, but she jerked her hand up, stopping me.

"Oh! Also, I basically love all animated movies."

"A little bit of everything, huh? That's good. I'm like that, too. Not really into romance movies all that much, but if you have an action movie on, I won't say no."

"Noted."

Why did I get the feeling I wouldn't be at the top of her movie-buddy list?

"My turn. What do your parents do?" she asked, cutting into my thoughts. "I'm thinking your dad was...a pro athlete? Maybe?"

"Hmmm," I hummed, pinching my bottom lip between two fingers. "As far as I know, my dad never played football, at least not while he was in high school, so that rules out him being an athlete like you imagined. He is actually a plumber, and my mom is a kindergarten teacher."

"Wow," she said as she exhaled after a few seconds of awkward silence. "Wow, I really am an asshole, aren't I?"

"I wouldn't put it exactly like that."

She laughed, and I had to grip the back of the couch tighter. "I would. So you're not some rich kid, then? Not that being rich is bad or anything, I just assumed, you know, because...who the hell knows at this point—obviously not me."

That soft pink started to spread over her cheeks again, and this time it was me who was laughing.

"I'm not rich, no. My family isn't rich either, but we're not doing that bad. Like you, I try to make extra money whenever I have time. Plus, I have an athletic scholarship, so that helps."

She tucked her hair behind her ear and looked down at her lap.

"What do your parents do?" I continued so we could get back to how we'd been a few minutes earlier before she started to hide herself from me.

"My dad is an investigative journalist. He used to write for The New York Times, but after he married my mom, they moved to Phoenix. He writes for a local newspaper now. My mom..." She cleared her throat and averted her eyes. "My mom passed away a few months before I came to college. On top of everything that came with her sickness, we had other issues as well. We weren't the closest mother and daughter, but she was still my mom. So, crying at the drop of a hat when I was a freshman might have had something to do with that too. New city, new people, and when you add in everything else, it wasn't a good combination for me."

That wiped the smile off my face and I straightened up, shifting in my seat. "I'm sorry for your loss, Flash."

After a brief glance in my direction, she gave me a small smile and nodded. "She had breast cancer. We were too late."

"My last year in high school, we lost my grandpa," I started after a short period of silence. "We have a pretty close-knit family, pretty loud sometimes, and in each others' business pretty much always. He lived down the block from us so he was always in our lives, a built-in babysitter. I used to run to his house every evening so I could play catch with him while he told me stories from his old days...just random, unimportant stuff." Looking away from Zoe, I smiled. "I swear to you I was there every day. As soon as the clock hit five, I was at my grandpa's, and every time he opened that door his first words were, *You again, kid? What's a man gotta do to get some peace and quiet around here?*" Just picturing his easy smile had me chuckling to myself. "And then he'd reach for the football before I could even open my mouth. Don't tell anyone, but I think I was his favorite. He loved that I was around so much. The effect his presence had in my life..." I shook my head and lifted my eyes up to Zoe, who was listening, rapt, her eyes sad and understanding at the same time. "You lost your mom...I know that's different, harder, and I know nothing I can say would make it any easier, but I understand how hard it is to cope with loss. It sounds so fucking stupid and selfish since they can't even... I'd give anything to have him around so he could see where I'm heading, or just hang out and talk, you know."

I forced my gaze back at Zoe and caught her quickly brushing away a single tear that was running down her face.

"Yeah, I know." She tilted her head. "We're getting pretty deep here. You're serious about getting to know each other, huh?"

To be completely honest...I wasn't. Sure, I wanted to ask her a few questions, maybe get a feel for what to expect with her, but I hadn't planned to get so deep, so soon—or at all, really. The conversation had just led us where we were. To lighten the heavy mood, I tried to steer us in another direction.

"Let's do a rapid-fire Q&A."

"Oh, I'm gonna suck at that. I'm not good with one-word answers but hit me."

"Cat person or dog person?"

"Dog person. Cats...they kind of scare me, not the kittens or the cuddly ones, but I don't like how some of them focus on you like they're plotting ways to kill you. You know what I mean? It's not all of them, but still. I'm a dog person all the way. You?"

I couldn't hold back my smile. She was right, she wasn't the best person for short answers, but I wasn't complaining. "I'll say dogs, too. So, art and photography, huh?"

"Yeah. Your major?"

"Political science. Your favorite movie snack?"

Her lips stretched into a smile and she played with the edge of her shirt.

"Moving on to harder questions, huh? Peanut butter M&Ms, hands down, but I don't actually buy them—that would be dangerous. Same with chips. Usually, I have no self-control when it comes to food. Yours?"

"Popcorn. You gotta have popcorn when you're watching a movie. And not buying M&Ms...not sure what to say about that. What's your biggest weakness?"

"I thought it was my turn, but fine, I'll answer." She sighed and dropped her eyes before answering. "Pizza. It's pizza."

"What's up with the face?" I asked, laughing.

"It's bad," she answered, looking up at me through her

eyelashes. "Really bad. I can eat a big one all by myself even though I know I'll feel miserable and have trouble sleeping because of being so full, but I can't say no. I can never say no to pizza. I'm definitely not gonna start saying no any time soon, either. Ask me what food item I would choose to have for the rest of my life or if I was stranded on an island and I could only have one thing and—"

"Let me guess, you would say pizza."

"Yeah. It's a weakness. Carbs galore. I know it's not good for you and all that stuff, but it's *so* good. All that cheesy gooey goodness, and the sauce is just as important. So is the dough, and the toppings...God, the toppings. Every layer is important. So many choices. It's magical, a circle of love. What's your favorite topping?"

The more she talked, the more my smile grew.

"Pepperoni, or any kind of meat, really." I could've sworn I heard her groan softly as she licked her lips.

"What is *your* biggest weakness?" she asked.

"Not to sound like I'm copying you, but if we're talking about food here, it has to be cheeseburgers. Pizza would be a close second. Okay, next one. Tell me your biggest pet peeve."

"This shouldn't be a surprise, but I have more than a few. I'm fascinated by people, which is a big reason I love portrait photography, but...I hate fake people. Can't stand them, don't care to be around them. People who constantly talk over you as if your opinions don't matter—just nope. It gets my blood pumping in the worst way. Entitled people. Unflushed toilets. Saggy pants on guys. People who believe they're the shit and good at everything —they usually aren't, and even if they are, I'd love to be the one to comment on it, not hear it from them. I could go on and on, so please shut me up."

"Unflushed toilets and saggy pants, got it."

There was something about her. Maybe it was how open she

sounded, so honest and real, or maybe it was the way she talked like she couldn't get the words out fast enough...the way she quickly looked away every time our gazes clashed, the way her hands seemed to be constantly busy with something around her—the pillow, the olive green watch on her wrist, the hem of her t-shirt. I couldn't pinpoint exactly what it was, but *something* made me feel relaxed around her, like this wasn't the first time we'd ever sat down and enjoyed a pointless, simple conversation.

"I don't want you to shut up. I like this," I admitted without a second thought. Why lie when I was enjoying her so much? "I'm gonna have to agree on entitled people, but my biggest pet peeve is actually people who chew loudly, especially when they're chewing gum. I've come to blows with a few of the guys on the team because of it. Now they all chew gum whenever they wanna piss me off. The smacking sound...fuck no. I hope you're not one of them. If you are, stop it, or I can't promise it won't get ugly."

"Sir, yes sir," she deadpanned with a serious but amused expression on her face.

"Another one is when people play with their phone all the damn time, like it's glued to their hand or some shit."

"My dad is the same. We actually have a rule about that. If we're having dinner—and he always insists on eating together, whether it's in front of the TV or at the table—I can't touch my phone. The same thing goes if we're having a conversation. He hates when I stare down at my phone while I'm talking with him."

"I don't like people who lie," I said.

"I don't like liars either."

"People who don't love animals."

"Oh, yeah. I wouldn't trust them with anything. So basically it sounds like we don't like people very much."

"Well, we have that in common, so that's good."

Resting her wrists on her crossed legs, she fidgeted in her seat. "I believe it's my turn to ask something."

"Go ahead."

"Who do you wanna be?"

"I'll be a pro football player. You?"

"I'll be a professional photographer."

We smiled at each other. I liked that we were both so sure about our futures.

"What's your favorite spot?" I asked.

"As in, my favorite spot...to go to?"

"Yeah, and don't tell me it's the library or anywhere near campus."

She raised her eyebrow at me, pairing it with a little grin on her face. "Now who's being judgmental? It's not the library. It's actually the beach. I don't have a long list at all, but it's probably one of the few things I love about L.A., especially when it's a little deserted. A few people here and there is okay, but I hate when it's too crowded. Santa Monica can be a bit much. It's even better if it's closer to sunset. And yeah, fine, I do like the library, too. You?"

"The field."

That earned me an eye roll. "You're probably on the field all the time."

"And I wouldn't have it any other way. So you're from Phoenix?"

"Yep. You? L.A.?"

"Nope. San Francisco."

"You know, none of these questions have anything to do with us living together. If you'd asked me what my schedule looked like, if I was a loud roommate, or if I sleepwalked, or...I don't know, anything related to this situation, I'd get it, but..." She pointed a finger somewhere over my shoulder so I turned to look and saw she was pointing at the big clock hanging on the wall.

"It's past midnight, and something else you might want to learn about me is that I rarely stay up this late, so I better...skedaddle. This was—" She paused and seemed to be surprised at what she was about to say. "This was fun, and maybe not so bad, and hopefully you won't be scared to go to sleep now. I'm not planning on hurting you with my secret ninja skills or anything like that. I have an early class tomorrow, so..." She uncrossed her legs and pushed herself up.

I stood up, too, and went to stand right in front of her. She rubbed her forearms as if she was itchy because I was standing so close to her. That close, I could smell the faint scent of her perfume, something fresh and sweet, but not over the top. It suited her.

I held out my hand, and she looked at me as if I had sprouted a second head.

"What's that for?" she asked with a small frown on her face.

"We're gonna shake hands."

"Why?"

I reached out, gently grabbed her wrist, and put her hand in mine. "Now, we shake."

With my help, she shook my hand. "No one does this anymore, you know that, right?"

"I don't know what you mean, but I like that we have officially met after two years of skirting each other."

"You think you'll be able to sleep on your own?"

She didn't realize what she'd said before I raised an eyebrow and grinned at her.

"Shit. I didn't mean it like that. You're gonna be sleeping on your own either way—that wasn't me trying to say I'd like to sleep with you if you can't sleep on your own, or that I would. Not sleep sleep, as in sex, but just sleep next to each other...and why don't you just go ahead and kill me now? Please?"

She tried to pull her hand away, but I held on to it. "For you,

Flash, I'll pretend I didn't hear any of that. It was nice getting to know you, Zoe Clarke. This was good. We should do it again sometime."

"Sure," she agreed, but somehow made it sound like the opposite. I let her hand go. "This Flash thing, the nickname—that's gonna be a thing isn't it?"

Grinning, I nodded.

She had only managed to get a few steps away from me when I called after her.

"One last question." Reluctantly, she looked at me over her shoulder. "A year with no sex or a year without a smartphone?"

"Aaand good night to you too."

"Come on. It's the last question—you can't skip this one."

"Again, this has what to do with us being roommates?"

I sat back down. "It will tell me a few things about you. Come on."

She stood silent for a few seconds, looked at me, then looked away, probably trying to make sense of me. I couldn't blame her.

"I'm gonna have to go with a year without a smartphone, though not because I'm dying to have sex. It's not like I'm having tons of—" Her eyes grew slightly bigger as if she had just blurted out something I wasn't supposed to know. I leaned back and watched her try to save herself. "I didn't mean it like that. I'm really not dying to have sex, and I could go without having sex for a year, because that would be easy. I just think a year without a phone would actually be therapeutic. It's probably glued to my hand from the time I wake up to the time I go back to bed, and I think it would actually be nice to use it just for its original purpose, just to see how it goes, you know. Maybe socializing more would have a positive effect on my life, who knows. It'd definitely be good for my eyes, that's for sure." She let out another sigh. "I'm rambling again. All I'm saying is I wouldn't choose sex because I couldn't possibly go without it for a year."

I got up again and stalked toward her as I watched her hide her hands behind her back. "You don't have to explain your reasoning to me, but that doesn't mean I don't appreciate it. Your answer tells a lot about you. Thank you for humoring me and answering my questions. It looks like we're stuck together for the next few months if I can't find another place, and I should tell you I'm surprised as fuck that you're the new roommate. Shit, Zoe, I wouldn't have guessed it in a million years."

Keeping her eyes around my chest area, she nodded. "Good night, then, Dylan."

After a quick hair tuck behind her ear and giving me a small smile, she started walking.

I let her take a few more steps toward her room while I stayed put in my spot. "Flash." She faced me but kept taking small steps backward.

"Yes?"

I tucked my hands in my front pockets. "This is the strangest thing, but I think you're going to be my best friend, Zoe Clarke."

When she fled to her room and was no longer anywhere near me, I sat my ass down and leaned back against the couch. Now that I was alone, I looked up at the ceiling and grinned. She had no idea what kind of trouble she was in with me.

CHAPTER SIX

ZOE

"I think at some point, I said skedaddle. Who says that?" I heaved a sigh and face-palmed myself for probably the hundredth time since meeting up with Jared and Kayla. I'd forced them out of bed at an ungodly hour for coffee and a rundown of the events of the day before. Because I had never mentioned meeting Dylan that first time two years ago, I spent a good thirty minutes telling them all about it. Sucky friend? I didn't think so. I'd always been good at keeping secrets. When I was nine, I'd kept my first secret from my dad for an entire week before blurting out that Nathaniel from my class had kissed me at recess then told me to keep it a secret. Evidently, I had gotten better with time.

After Jared gave me hell for about five minutes as Kayla kept shaking her head at me as if she was disappointed, they finally gave me a break.

"This is just a thought, gorgeous—don't give me that look—but I think saying skedaddle is the last thing you should worry about, here. You actually attacked him with a rolling pin? Why the hell were you hiding a rolling pin in the bathroom to begin with? I'm still stuck on that, and I wish you had taken a picture of the actual attack, or maybe a selfie while you were jumping him. Could've been pure art. I can already see it—vividly." For good measure, he closed his eyes and hummed softly. "I'm gonna have to sketch that for you. You're welcome, of course."

I lightly smacked his shoulder with the back of my hand and shook my head. "Don't you dare. I wasn't hiding it in the bathroom, and that's not even the worst part of the story here, so can we please focus?" I'd met Jared at the end of my freshman year after we kept bumping into each other in the same classes since we were both majoring in art. He always said it was fate that brought us together and that was that. I couldn't imagine what I would've done if he hadn't sat next to me in that Art History 201 class, and whenever I needed his friendship the most, he always came through.

He sat next to me, rubbing his shoulder and chuckling lightly. He had his black hair styled into a messy bedhead look that always worked wonders for him when he was in the mood for making new friends. I would've called them lovers, but he didn't like the pressure of the word. Since he wasn't interested in having a serious relationship in college, just friends worked fine. He was only slightly taller than me, probably around five foot nine, tops. The dark brown of his eyes and his plump lips only added to his bad boy rocker looks. If he had any interest in girls at all, I'm pretty sure I'd have been a blubbering mess around him just as much as I seemed to be around Dylan. The day the professor had kicked us out of class for talking too much had marked the first day of our friendship.

"I didn't attack him just for fun. I thought he was a thief. What was I supposed to do, welcome him with open arms? While I was *naked*? I was trying to incapacitate him so I could get out. Anyway, I don't even remember half the things I said later on, but I do remember *skedaddle*. Ask me how many times I've used that word in my life—zero. I don't know if you guys under-stand the extent of how bad and painful the entire thing was."

"I think we got it," Jared deadpanned, bugging his eyes out to Kayla.

I ignored their looks and kept going. "Every time I opened my mouth, I dug a deeper hole for myself. From now on, I'm gonna need to keep my mouth shut when I'm around him. I'll use nods and as few words as possible."

"I don't think that's possible, but believing is half the battle, I guess," Kayla said wryly.

I forced the fakest smile I could muster. "Har har. Aren't you guys just rays of sunshine today? I can't get enough of you two."

Jared just smiled and kept breaking up pieces of his toast then popping them into his mouth. "As you shouldn't. Plus, you know I'm always moody before the clock hits twelve, so feel free to ignore me and focus on your second best friend."

I watched a piece of brownie fly toward Jared, which he caught in his mouth.

"You're the actual worst," muttered Kayla before fixing her gaze on me.

"So? Any advice? Real advice? The kind friends give each other?" I asked Kayla. "What the hell am I gonna do? How am I gonna go back there tonight?"

Her perfectly filled thick eyebrows rose higher on her fore-head and she gave me an innocent look. "Walk, maybe?"

I returned her look with my most bored stare.

"Okay, okay. Sheesh. Save that face for someone else. I think trying to keep a bit more quiet instead of going off on an endless rant might be a better idea. I support you on that."

While Jared was the most easygoing and confident one out of the three of us, Kayla—AKA KayKay, as Jared had dubbed her—was our mama bear. She was just the person you wanted to open up to, so nurturing, sweet, quiet, and everything I was not around guys. However, when it came to her actual relationships, her choices were a little skewed. Case in point, her on-again, off-again prick of a boyfriend Keith gave me the creepy chills almost every time he was around. I just wished—actually, both Jared and I wished—that one of the times when they broke up, it would actually be for good. There was always hope.

"Any other ideas? We're going to be living in the same apartment and I'm quietly freaking out about it. It's not like I can stay in my room and never come out, and trying to act all casual when he is around is a no-go because we all know how I get around guys I think are good-looking."

"How about you go with *being* casual and normal instead of acting?"

"I'm too itchy and nervous around him, Kayla. If you'd seen me last night, you would've winced every time I opened my mouth. He was being so nice, and I think I'd love to be his friend. I think I could maybe handle that."

"You can definitely do that. Just think of him as already taken. That should make it easier."

"He actually just broke up with his girlfriend."

"Dang it, you don't say." Jared whistled. "Maybe I should give you a visit one of these days, just to check things out, you know."

Feeling like I had some kind of a game plan I could focus on when I went back to the apartment, I leaned back in my seat and let out a huge breath. I was thankful for having Kayla and Jared as friends, more than they could ever imagine. They made coming to L.A.—the biggest risk of my life—worth it for me. God knows nothing else had gone the way I'd hoped it would.

Kayla cleared her throat and fidgeted in her seat before glancing at me and then at Jared, all the while shredding her empty paper cup into small pieces. "So, I think in light of this new development, I have to tell you guys something." Before either of us could open our mouths to say anything, she went ahead and continued, "I might have gone on a few dates with Dylan."

"Dylan who?" Jared asked, still chewing on a piece of toast as he eyed the rest of Kayla's brownie.

"My Dyl—ah, I mean the Dylan that's staying in my apartment? The wide receiver? Dylan Reed?"

"Yeah. That one."

Jared stopped eating.

Something weird settled in my stomach. "Huh?"

"Two dates, Zoe," she rushed out, lifting two of her fingers to emphasize her words. "It was just two times."

Some guy bumped my chair from behind, and I scooted myself a little forward as I took a few sips of my already cold coffee, my attention focused on the table. It was fine. It was a surprise, sure, but still completely fine. It wasn't like I was interested in Dylan in that way or anything like that. It would've also been completely fine if they had gone out more than two times. He was off limits anyway, wasn't he? Not just because he was my roommate and out of my league, but because he was one of Mark's players.

"It was freshman year, before I met you guys. I think it was a few months before actually. I was having this two-month hiatus kind of thing with Keith"—which meant he had broken up with her for some stupid reason—"and my dorm roommate was going out with this football player. She kind of forced me to go out with them because I was upset about Keith, and the guy was gonna bring a friend, so I was supposed to keep him occupied while also occupying myself. You know I didn't have any friends other than Keith my first year here, so I said fine." She grimaced and went back to shredding pieces. "He was really sweet actually, but you know how I am. I love Keith, and I just wasn't into getting to know anyone else. I barely talked the whole night, and the second time...my roommate happened again. That time I actually managed to chat with him for a little while. We talked about our families, how we both had big, loud ones and all that, but neither one of us was acting like it could turn into something more. It was just a friendly night out sort of thing. I think my roommate started seeing the other guy—his name was something weird like Rap or Rip or something—so she didn't need me to hold her hand after that second time. I barely saw Dylan again. Also, it was only double dates, never just the two of us. Plus, a few weeks after that I was back with Keith anyway. He would always say hi those rare few times we ran into each other on campus, but I don't think I've seen him in a year."

Jared hummed and drew my gaze back to him. "Those don't count as dates, KayKay, at least not in my book."

"I agree, but at the time I might have described it as if I went out on these big dates with a football player to Keith, just to make him jealous. I just wanted to mention it now in case Dylan saw me with Zoe and actually remembered and said something. I didn't want it to be a surprise."

"I wish I had my own little interaction with this Dylan guy. You girls have both met him one way or another, one of you in a much weirder setting, of course." He gave Kayla a wide-eyed look and gestured at me with his chin.

That earned him another smack on the shoulder, which he barely managed to escape. "Haha. So funny."

"And here I am, the guy who only watches...oh, I don't know, *all* his games, and I've never gotten the chance to meet him? You will fix this horrible wrong, Zoe."

It was the wad of paper hitting me in the face that brought me out of silence. I flung it right back at Jared and turned my head to look at Kayla.

"Nothing will happen between us, Kay. He is way out of my league. Trust me. So, even if you had dated for real, that would've been okay."

"Because you have Mark to think about, right? And of course you're paper bag ugly, can't forget about that," Jared piped up, his tone flatter than it had been just a few seconds before.

Yes, there was always Mark.

"I'm not saying I'm ugly at all. I happen to find myself beautiful at times, but he is still way out of my league. You'd know what I mean if you saw him up close."

Jared sighed and shook his head. "And Mark?"

"Yeah, there's him, too," I mumbled without looking either of them in the eye as I busied myself with finishing my coffee.

"And when are you gonna get shot of him, Zoe? I'd be lying if I said I'm exactly clear on what you're expecting to happen here, but I can tell you it's not gonna happen—I know that much. You need to get out of his apartment, too. He is treating you like a paid slut, only calling you when he wants to and only meeting you at that apartment or all the way across town in a random restaurant, never anywhere public."

"Hey, take it down a notch, would you?" Kayla snarled at Jared as I swallowed my coffee down the wrong pipe. "That was a little harsh, don't you think?"

"Geez," I coughed out when I could breathe again, taking the half-full water bottle and napkins Kayla offered me. "Thanks for making it sound creepy. He is not as bad as you're making him sound, and it's not like we can walk around campus together, at least not yet. I wanted to move out, remember?" I wasn't blaming Kayla for flaking on me in any way, but I was blaming Keith for being a needy bastard.

While my plan for my third year had been to move out of Mark's apartment and move in with Kayla, it hadn't exactly gone the way I wanted it to. We'd found the apartment and were days away from signing the lease when Keith had a fit about her moving in with me.

If she was moving out of the dorms, why wasn't she moving in with him? Why would two college girls wanna live together? Was she seeing someone else? It went on and on and on and on. Kayla would've never gone back on her word, but when I saw the toll it was taking on her, how scathing Keith's words were, I told her it wouldn't be a problem if she chose to move in with Keith instead of me. As long as she was happy, I'd be fine, though after the whole deal, I wasn't sure how anyone could be happy with Keith. But, that wasn't for me to say, at least not then.

Jared's home was close to campus, only a fifteen-minute walk, so he didn't need a new place or a closer one to rent. Considering he needed to be home to help his single mom raise his five-year-old half-sister, he couldn't afford to move out anyway. These little facts prevented me from moving in with either of my best friends. Unlike Kayla, who had enjoyed her two-year stint in the dorms, I hadn't enjoyed dorm life all that much, so back to Mark's apartment I'd gone. I'd thought maybe things would change, thought we'd get closer and he'd keep his promises for a change.

"I'm really sorry, Zoe," Kayla said, breaking into my thoughts. "I was looking forw—"

I reached out and rested my hand on her arm. "Don't apologize, please. You have nothing to apologize for anyway. I didn't mean it to sound that way. I've been saving money, yes, but I can't afford to move out on my own yet. I still need to save money for New York too, as lame as that sounds, and you know I went back because he kept promising me it would be different this year. If things don't change and I can manage to stash away the amount I need, I'm getting out of there around April or May. Also...you know what I want from him, Jared. Don't be like that."

"That's the time you're giving him? Almost another full year?" Shaking his head, Jared reached out and covered my hand with his long, thin fingers, his features hard. "Look, I know this hurts you, but he'll never tell them about you, Zoe, not his wife, and definitely not his son. He is a pig. You deserve better than that."

But Mark had promised, and I wanted nothing more than to believe him.

When I didn't say what I knew he was waiting to hear, what he wanted to hear, he sighed and drew his hand back. "If I can get that part-time job at that gallery next year, I'll move in with you. You *will* get out of there, right?"

I gave him a silent nod.

"It'll be great."

"Even though I couldn't leave the love of my life to come live with you guys, I'll come visit so much that it'll feel like I'm living there."

She'd come only if Keith let her, but she wouldn't say that. She'd been with Keith since she was sixteen and still loved him enough to believe he could and would change. I could see an intervention happening in our future.

I felt a little sick, both in my stomach and in my heart, as I did every time Mark was the subject of our conversation. Jared's statements were not news to me, but unfortunately, that didn't help lessen the pain. I managed to force a genuine smile on my face. "Thanks, guys."

"You still want advice on what to do with the hunk in your apartment?" Jared asked after a few moments of heavy silence.

I huffed out a breath and fell back in my seat. "Yeah. Hit me. God knows I could use all the help I can get."

His next question made me question that. "Are you attracted to him?"

"I mean...he is attractive, sure, and I have eyes. I like his smile too—I'll give you that much—but I don't know him well enough to say if I'm attracted to him. I don't have a crush on him...let's say that instead. I'm attracted to his looks, but I don't have a crush on him. He seems nice, so I like him as a person—that sounds even better. Even if I did like him and by some dumb luck he was interested in me too, though I doubt that—"

"Of course you'd doubt it, because you're paper bag ugly," Jared repeated again, slowly shaking his head to emphasize his disappointment in me.

"Annnyway," I drew out the word then, ignoring Jared, continued. "We'll be staying in the same apartment for crying out loud, and there is no way Mark wouldn't find out about it."

"So it all comes back to Mark."

Frowning, I lowered my voice and leaned forward. "No, it doesn't, Jared. I said he is hot, and yeah, he does sound like a good person, but just because he is those two things doesn't mean I'm gonna fall at his feet and confess my love—or lust, for that matter. I'm only acting all weird around him because of what happened freshman year and because...okay, yeah, I think he is good-looking, but that's about it. You know that's not a good combo for me. Don't you remember how I was when you first talked to me in that art history class? Was I in love with you? No. That's just who I am, how I am until I warm up to people, and what I also am is embarrassed around him. First I ask him if I can kiss him like some kindergarten kid, and then the next time he sees me, I knock over some guys' model building and get yelled at right in front of him and his friends, including Chris, as if things couldn't get any worse. If all that's not enough, another year passes and here I am dropping my towel and showing my tits and plastering myself to him. I'm not mentioning the part where I attacked him because I was right to do so."

"So, being his friend is the best idea here—we all agree on that, yes?" Kayla looked at Jared and then me. "You'll get used to having him around. If I know you as well as I think I do, there'll be a lot of nervous laughing and hiding out in your room in your future if you don't do something about it. So, actually try to be his friend since you're so adamant about not having a crush on him.

Jared is good-looking and you're not a blubbering mess around him anymore," Kayla offered, gesturing at our friend.

"If I was interested in girls, this one would be all over me by now, so I'm not sure if I'm a good example in this situation, KayKay," Jared chimed in.

I snorted. "Oh, please. As if. That's all I'm saying to you: as if. Also, you wish...*and* last but not least, in your dreams."

So, instead of acting casual—as Kayla had so nicely suggested—and hiding in my room whenever I could, I was going to become friends with Dylan Reed. Sounded easy enough.

It was around five in the evening when I managed to make it back to the apartment after spending several long hours in the photography lab. Before I got to turn my key and step inside, the door at the end of the hall opened and Ms. Hilda peeked out from behind the cracked door.

"Miss Clarke, is that you?"

She was eighty-five years old and her eyes worked better than mine—she knew perfectly well that it was me.

"Yes, Ms. Hilda, it's just me," I yelled over my shoulder, my movements urgent.

I turned the key and opened the door, hoping she wouldn't ask me anything else and I would get to throw myself face first on the couch for a few minutes and then maybe force myself to get up and make a quick sandwich for dinner afterward before Dyl—

"Could you be a lamb and—"

Oh, not the lamb. I never wanted to be a lamb.

Please don't say hang the curtains. Please don't say hang the curtains.

"—hang the curtains back up?"

Hanging my head in despair, I closed the door, cursing myself for completely forgetting about her and making enough noise to wake up the dead while walking up the stairs. I walked back to stand in front of her now fully open door. "Did you wash your curtains again, Ms. Hilda?"

She grunted and raised a brow at me as if to say, *What's your point?*

"I'm only asking because you've already washed them five times this month." I had been chosen as the worker bee who hung the clean curtains back up because she just couldn't manage to do it herself. It was fine, because she really couldn't, and it only took me ten minutes to hang them all back up anyway, but I always wondered who else she cornered to take them down every other day.

"I like a clean house, Miss Clarke."

Of course she liked a clean house. She roped me into vacuuming her apartment almost weekly, not to mention her never-ending list of other small tasks. If you weren't quiet enough and that door of hers opened, she had chores she wanted you to handle. If she had been one of those sweet old grandmas who gave you warm chocolate chip cookies for helping her, or maybe sometimes offered you a home-cooked meal because you were a student who missed having home-cooked meals, she would be so lovable. But, no. She was...I had no idea how to be polite about my choice of word, but she was basically a witch. As I said, if she caught you, she always roped you into helping her out with something, and on top of that she basically sucked all the energy right out of you while she was at it. That was why I always tiptoed when I reached our floor.

"I'm really tired and I haven't had anything to eat since this morning. I'll come after—"

"You young people... You should never leave today's work for tomorrow." The door opened all the way and she stood back. I would've agreed with her if it had been my own work I had to handle without leaving it for tomorrow. I hadn't even said I'd do it the next day. All I wanted to do was sit my ass down and eat something before I had to tackle her. Holding back a frustrated scream and gritting my teeth, I gave her a toothless smile and walked in.

Before I was even four steps into her apartment, she closed her door and started in on me. "Was that a young man I saw leaving the apartment this morning, Miss Clarke? Back in my time, we wouldn't get near boys. These things were frowned upon, but I guess times have changed. At least this one is closer to your age. Did you know the girl in 5B cheated on her boyfriend? I heard them arguing just this afternoon—"

I wasn't even sure who lived in 5B. Tuning her completely out, I did what she'd asked me to do and as soon as it was done, I almost ran back out before she could ask me to take Billy out for a walk. Billy was the cat from hell who hid every time someone other than Ms. Hilda was in the house, and when he was thrust into someone's hands (i.e., mine), his go-to course of action was to scratch the hell out of your arms for even daring to touch him.

As I practically jogged toward the door that would take me to safety, I could hear Ms. Hilda's quick footsteps following me. For an eighty-five-year-old woman, she moved surprisingly fast when she wanted to and caught up to me just as I opened her door.

"You have a nice evening now, Miss Clarke, and I'll let you know if I learn more about the girl in 5B. I bet we'll see her new boo—"

I took a step out and collided with the hard body of a wide receiver in my haste to escape. Dylan had apparently just walked up the last step of the stairs, and he grunted in surprise. I gasped and he went back down a step. Grabbing me right above the elbow, he steadied us both before I could fall on him and quite possibly break his neck on the way down the stairs.

"Zoe?"

"Oh, I'm so sorry," I apologized quickly as he let go of my arm.

This guy would forever remember me as 'the klutz I had to live with that one year and had seen around campus twice before that'.

Before I could explain anything to Dylan or warn him telepathically, Ms. Hilda cleared her throat behind me and I barely held back a groan. Closing my eyes, I took a deep breath. If I didn't wrap this up quickly, she would hold us hostage for who knew how long.

Here we go.

"Ah, Dylan, here you are," I exclaimed a little louder than necessary so Ms. Hilda would have no trouble hearing—though when it came to the old woman's hearing, it was always a crapshoot. I plastered the biggest smile on my face and tried to come up with something in the two seconds it took me to right myself and face my nosy neighbor. "We were just talking about you, weren't we Ms. Hilda?" Before the poor guy could understand what was happening, I grabbed him by the arm and pulled him up to stand next to me—or more accurately, I urged him to stand next to me, because with the way those muscles felt under my hand, I couldn't imagine anything my size could move him even an inch if he didn't want to be moved.

My next brilliant move was to pat his arm and discreetly squeeze it as a warning, but then I felt his muscles flex under my touch and I forgot what I was going to say.

Holy shit...

I looked up at Dylan and our gazes met. I had no freaking idea what he was thinking, but I quickly looked away and pried my fingers off of his arm.

If we both wanted to get away from Ms. Hilda's endless chatter, I had to focus on one thing at a time. I thought telling a little white lie wouldn't hurt anybody if it meant we'd get back to the apartment and I'd get to my dinner sooner.

"This is who you must've seen leaving this morning, Ms. Hilda. His name is Dylan Reed and he's my new roommate."

Both Dylan and I watched Ms. Hilda take him in from head to toe. Shamelessly, I did the same. He was wearing black and gray Nike shoes, light gray sweatpants—which killed me, because gray sweatpants on a guy was heaven on earth, especially when they wore them in the morning—and a white t-shirt that stretched across his impressive chest, the sleeves hugging those arms I had touched only seconds before. He was also toting a big-ass bag that hung low on his hip, the strap crossed over his chest.

Ms. Hilda must not have been impressed because she released another grunt. Excluding our old Hilda, if any living, breathing female wasn't impressed when they clapped eyes on Dylan Reed, I was ready to give up pizza—for a week—and that was the biggest commitment one could make.

"It's nice to meet you, Ms..." Dylan trailed off.

"Hilda," I jumped in before he got her started. "I forgot to mention her to you, didn't I? This is Ms. Hilda. I was just helping her out with something and she mentioned how she had seen a young man leave the apartment and was confused about who you were."

"Oh?" Dylan asked politely, glancing between me and our neighbor.

"I wasn't confused, Miss Clarke. I gave you my exact thoughts on how I felt about another boy living with you. This one"—she turned to look at Dylan as she pointed her thumb at me—"should've been a juggler in a circus instead of fiddling away with that camera she can't seem to part ways with."

"Oh, but, Ms. Hilda, you didn't hear the best part yet." I put my arm through Dylan's, stood a little bit closer to him, basically plastering my front to his side, and had to forcefully suppress the involuntary shiver caused by standing too close to him. I leaned toward Ms. Hilda as if I was about to give her the world's biggest secret. She leaned forward too—she lived for gossip. "I'm afraid he's not into us girls," I whispered loud enough that she could hear, which meant Dylan could hear me perfectly clearly, too. Ms. Hilda's eyebrows furrowed and she gave Dylan another long look.

"Uh, excuse me?" Dylan spoke up after a few seconds of silence.

I angled my body toward him and this time patted his chest area, completely ignoring his lined forehead and questioning gaze. I had no idea where I was going with the whole petting thing, but I couldn't seem to stop myself.

"Nothing to be sorry about," the old woman answered, mistaking Dylan's question as an apology.

"Yes, nothing to be sorry about, Dylan," I repeated.

Dylan's eyes jumped from me to Ms. Hilda. "I don't—"

Before Dylan could finish his sentence, I discreetly stepped on his foot with my heel and applied as much pressure as I could. Points to him for not even letting out a grunt. Slowly he turned his head toward me and raised an eyebrow. I gave him the sweetest smile I could come up with and pulled my foot away.

"Ms. Hilda is a very open-minded woman," I explained, gesturing toward her with my head. "Nothing like her peers, right Ms. Hilda?"

She stood a little taller. "Yes, yes, that I am. Those old farts are nothing like me. Keep your head high, young man. There is nothing wrong about love. Do you have a boyfriend?"

"Uh…"

"You can tell me."

"Come on, Dylan," I urged, lightly shaking his arm. The sooner he went along with it and appeased her, the sooner we could get away. "Don't be shy."

He turned his head toward me yet again and gave me a long look that melted the smile right off my face, not because his expression promised a violent retribution, but the opposite, actually. He looked amused, a little confused maybe, but still amused, which was weird and unexpected. I frowned up at him and his lips twitched.

Still keeping his eyes on me, he finally said, "Actually, I do have a boyfriend."

"Is he a nice boy?"

With an easy smile, he broke our eye contact and turned back to her. "He's really nice. I'm lucky to have him."

The old woman slightly tilted her head and gave him her signature narrow-eyed look, where one of her eyes always narrowed more than the other one, making her look anything *but* serious. "How long have you two been together?"

Dylan seemed to ignore the wonky-eyed expression; again, points for him. The first time I'd seen her do it, I'd barely kept in my snort.

"It's been two years."

"See, Miss Clarke. See? Maybe you can learn something from your roommate."

I let out a long breath through my nose and managed to keep the smile on my face. "I know. I'll make sure to ask him for tips. Have a good even—"

"Mr. Reed, your roommate has the worst taste in men. Please teach her a thing or two, 'cause it looks like nothing I'm saying is getting through to her."

You can't close the door on her face, Zoe. You absolutely cannot close the door on an old lady's face.

"Please call me Dylan, and I will definitely try my best to teach her a few things. I agree with you—she should be with someone better. I'll make her see reason, don't worry."

"Good." She gave me one last glance and started to close the door, only to stop halfway. "You know what Dylan? I like you. It's a shame you like boys, as Miss Clarke could've used a nice strong boy like yourself."

Anyone up there? God? You can kill me now.

Turning to me, she continued, "I like him. Be nice to this one."

I gritted my teeth. "Okay then." Remembering my arm was still wrapped up with Dylan's, I untangled myself as we finally turned toward our own apartment.

"Mr. Reed?"

Ah...just when we were so close to freedom.

I felt Dylan pause and turn back, but I just kept going. I already knew she was gonna bestow a chore on him, and I had no interest whatsoever in letting her pull me into it, too.

Unlocking the door, I went inside. After making sure to leave it ajar for Dylan, I walked into the living room and just collapsed on the couch. Pulling my crossbody bag away, I flung it somewhere over my shoulder. The door closed with a quiet click in time with me covering my face with my hands.

There was a loud thud followed by footsteps and then nothing. I could already feel him standing over me so I shouldn't have felt the urge to look up to see the expression on his face, but just to make sure, I peeked through my fingers and...yup, he was right there, those big strong arms crossed over his chest, an eyebrow raised...waiting. I should've gone straight to my room.

"Hello to you, too, Zoe," he said when he realized nothing was coming out of my mouth.

I groaned and hid my face again.

"Care to tell me what just happened?"

I sort of snorted and then couldn't keep it in any longer. First, my shoulders started shaking, then my quiet, private laughter grew louder. When I had it under control and my laughs had pretty much died down to snickers, I chanced another look at him.

Thank God he had a big grin on his face; it helped me feel like less of a fool.

I dropped my head back and stared at the ceiling. "You're not angry at me, are you? I'm really hoping that smile on your face means you're amused and not psychotic."

Feeling big hands curl around my ankles made me sit straight up with the unexpectedness of it. Not affected by my little jump, Dylan gently set my feet down and sat right next to me, in the middle of the couch. I scooted back a few inches more until my back hit the armrest and there was a little more space between us, more room to breathe—hopefully.

"I'm not sure. I'll decide after you tell me what happened back there."

"I know you said you hate liars last night, but this doesn't count, okay? You shouldn't hate your roommate." Clearing my throat, I gave him something between a smile and a grimace. "She is the landlord and the only person over twenty-five living in this building. She is nosy as hell. I swear to you she knows everything that goes on. She'd already talked my ear off before I bumped into you, which is why I bumped into you, really, because I was trying to get away, and she thought I was being a slut and was basically trying to save me from myself. It's not that I care, but again, she is nosy as hell, and once she gets going, it turns into an interrogation, but what am I supposed to do? She's old, so I can't snap at her. I had to tell her something."

Dylan stretched his arm across the back of the couch and leaned just a little bit forward, causing me to lean back—just in case.

"So the best thing you could come up with was telling her I was gay?"

Another snort escaped me and I blushed. "No harm, no foul,

right? It seemed like the best idea at the time. At least this way she won't camp out in front of our door."

"You couldn't tell her we were just friends?"

Right, I was gonna be friends with him.

"Her mind doesn't work like that. Boys and girls can't be friends. She thinks boys are after one thing and one thing only, and since you're a boy...she'd think you're after my..."

"After your..." He trailed off, waiting for me to fill the silence. I wasn't going to do that.

"I think you get the picture."

"Maybe I do get the picture." His lips tipped up. "Thanks, Zoe. Looks like we're gonna have a lot of fun."

As his eyes bored into mine, we sat there like two idiots, smiling at each other.

"Why are you smiling like that?" he asked with a chin lift. I stopped smiling and touched my lips with my fingertips. Was something wrong with my smile?

"Why are *you* smiling like that?" I shot back.

An eyebrow went up, and the lone eyebrow lift combined with that damn smile...it was enough to make my heart skip a beat.

"This is how I smile," Dylan answered.

"Well...it's...too big."

Zoe. Oh, Zoe. You poor poor child.

His dark blue eyes were sparkling with laughter and those lips tipped even higher. One second stretched into two, and then two seconds turned into a staring contest. What the hell was he thinking? I didn't know him well enough to make a good guess, and it got harder to keep my eyes locked on his with each passing second. I was such a sore loser, so there was no way I'd be the first one to look away.

After what felt like an hour of the weirdest staring contest—

which I won, thank you very much—he shook his head and rubbed his hand over his short hair.

"What?" I asked quietly, genuinely curious to hear what he was thinking.

He sighed and got up. "Nothing."

"No, tell me. What?"

Dylan hesitated.

"You remember those people we talked about?" I prompted. "The ones we don't like?" A quick nod. "I don't like people who don't finish their sentences either."

"I didn't start a sentence."

I tapped a finger to my temple. "You started it in here."

That earned me a warm chuckle. "You keep doing things I'm not expecting you to do. It throws me off, that's all."

"Is that a bad thing or a good thing?"

"Haven't decided yet."

"Let's not waste your time—let's agree that it's a good thing."

I caught the twitch of his lips as he leaned down to hook his bag over his shoulder. "You think so?"

"Oh yeah. I'll keep you on your toes." I pushed myself up from the couch to stand next to him. "So we're good? Buddies? You don't mind that I told her you're gay?"

"Buddies?"

If he wanted to focus on that... "Sure, buddies—best friends, pals, mates...I'll let you choose." I lightly punched his arm, and then immediately hated myself for it.

I, Zoe Clarke, was officially the weirdest girl alive.

Why didn't the ground open up and swallow me when I needed it the most? Couldn't be that hard.

Looking down at where I'd punched his arm then back at me, he gave me another one of his infectious smiles that stopped me in my tracks every single time. "Buddies it is then."

CHAPTER SEVEN

DYLAN

It was only a few days into my move when I started to get back into my routine—or more like a new routine. We had a home game in two days and I was more than ready to play. I was doing my third set of push-ups when I looked up and saw Zoe rubbing her eyes as she walked straight into a wall, missing the bathroom door by ten inches or so.

"Fuck!" she hissed out in a low voice, this time rubbing her shoulder.

I dropped my head and tried to keep in my laughter. When I looked back up, I saw her looking over her shoulder toward my room right before she hurried into the bathroom and gently closed the door.

Two hundred twenty-three.

Two hundred twenty-four.

Two hundred twenty-five.

I heard the door click open then careful footsteps followed. When there was a loud gasp, I lifted my head, my gaze slowly making its way up her long smooth legs. Her hand was clutched over her chest and she was doing that *deer in the headlights* thing again. I smiled.

"Good morning, Zoe."

Letting go of her chest, she pulled at the hem of her t-shirt and took a few side steps toward the kitchen. Her eyes though—they stayed put on my body.

"Hello to you too. You scared the shit out of me."

I ducked my head and chuckled quietly. "I can see that."

"Uh, what's going on here?" she asked in a rough voice still laced with sleep.

"Getting in my push-ups."

A few more steps to the right and she reached the island. Keeping her gaze on me, she held on to the edge of the counter as if it was helping her stay upright, skipped the two bar stools, and walked around until she stood over the sink.

"Isn't it a little early to do push-ups?"

Two hundred thirty-six.

"I always wake up at six AM and get them done."

"So, this is an everyday occurrence?"

"Yeah." I dropped my head down and ignored the slight tremor in my arm muscles.

"Weekends too?"

"Yeah."

"Oh, okay. That's...good to know." Zoe reached for the glass sitting next to the sink—eyes still on me—opened the fridge, took out a water bottle, unscrewed the cap, and poured it into the glass. After a second of hesitation, she grabbed it and took a few gulps.

I looked back down to hide my smile and kept counting.

Two hundred forty-five.

Two hundred forty-six.

Two hundred forty-seven.

"Uh, and good morning...buddy."

"Sorry?" I grunted and looked up.

"You said good morning and I didn't say it back. I'm not really awake yet...might also be dreaming, can't be sure completely about that. Just in case I'm not in a dream and you're really there doing push-ups...good morning to you, too, buddy."

"You're really getting into this buddy thing, huh?"

She lifted a small shoulder, causing her very oversized t-shirt to slip and give me a view of the smooth skin so innocently hiding underneath the fabric.

"I'm liking the idea more and more."

Keep counting, Dylan. Keep going.

Two hundred sixty-one.

Two hundred sixty-two.

Two hundred sixty-three.

When I reached three hundred, I grunted and jumped up. Grabbing the towel I'd left on the couch, I wiped my face. "What are you doing up this early anyway? I haven't seen you around in the mornings these last few days. I only see you in the evenings." Not that she was around all that much. Whenever I came in, she found somewhere to disappear to.

She was still standing behind the sink, holding the glass in both hands as she took small sips and kept her eyes on me.

"Because I'm a normal person? You know, one who doesn't get up at an ungodly hour? Today I'm meeting with a girl who's paying me to take a few shots of her for her fashion blog. She wanted the streets to be empty, and according to her, her skin looks best with the early sunrise. No sane person would get up this early in the morning, but...work."

"Yeah? A fashion shoot, huh? Sounds fun."

"As I can see with my own eyes, you're not a sane person either, so...your idea of fun might be a little skewed."

Tossing the towel back over the couch, I dropped my ass on the floor and started on my sit-ups.

"Okay, what's happening now?"

"Sit-ups."

I heard a little groan, but instead of glancing at her, I kept my eyes forward and kept going. Out of the corner of my eye, I could see her moving around, and even if I hadn't been able to, the sounds of cabinets opening and closing and flatware rattling reached me just fine.

Forty-one.

Forty-two.

Forty-three.

Forty-four.

When there was a long stretch of silence, I spoke up without breaking my focus.

"What's up, buddy?"

"What's up?" she returned back.

I could feel her eyes sweeping over my skin like the gentle touch of a feather. My dick stirred in my sweatpants. "You're staring."

"How do you know I'm staring? You're not even looking at me."

"I can feel your eyes on me," I grunted.

"You can feel my eyes—of course you can. Well, I'm not staring because there is something to stare at, I'm only *looking* toward you because...you're in the way of my view at the moment and I don't know where else to look."

Curious, I turned to see what she was doing. I tried to maintain my pace and keep counting in my head at the same time, but she was making it hard. She was standing in the exact same spot, only difference was this time she had a blue bowl in one hand and a spoon in the other. The dish was full of what I could only assume was the cereal that was heading toward her pink lips. I tried to meet her eyes, but her gaze seemed glued somewhere else —namely, my torso. So I was the breakfast entertainment. For some reason I couldn't quite articulate, I didn't mind her gaze on me, and trust me, if it had been anyone but her, I would've minded. Being gawked at usually broke my concentration, thus pissing me off, but I'd never had a set of eyes moving over my body feel like fucking feathers, of all things. My body heated, and I was pretty sure it wasn't because of my workout.

"You're having breakfast and still staring," I grumbled, sweat starting to pour off my forehead already as each rep got a bit harder and my dick did the same.

Her spoon paused midair, and then she was chewing again. "I think so. Yes." There was a loud clink when her spoon hit her bowl and she winced, but two seconds later the chewing started back up. "They always say breakfast is the most important meal of the day, and I think I'm becoming a believer."

One hundred.

Finishing my first set, I lay flat on the ground and shook my arms to relax my muscles as I slowly caught my breath.

"So do you always do this...half naked?"

I smiled up at the ceiling. "If it's bothering you, I can do it in my room from now on. I only came out here because I didn't think you'd be awake yet."

"Nope, it's fine. Just wanted to check."

There was a two-second pause before she spoke up again.

"Always at the same time?"

"Are you gonna come out every morning and keep me company?"

Taking a deep breath, I started on the second set.

A hundred and one.

A hundred and two.

A hundred and three.

"Nope."

"You sure? You thought about it for a second there."

"Yup. Nope."

A hundred and ten.

A hundred and eleven.

Feeling that addictive good burn in my stomach, I pushed through my second set in no time.

I heard loud coughing so I glanced her way. "More?" Zoe asked in a squeaky tone when I went for the next hundred sit-ups.

"Yeah," I puffed out. I miraculously managed to finish my last set with only a few glances thrown my curious observer's way. At least my dick was behaving. A few times when I looked, she quickly averted her eyes and became increasingly engrossed in her cereal bowl or the sink. Standing up, I wiped off my forehead, chest, and stomach. Throwing the small towel over my shoulder, I moved toward my intriguing roommate. Her eyes followed my every step.

Stopping when only two steps separated us, I leaned against the marble counter. "Hi. How is your morning going so far?"

She made a few vague noises then cleared her throat after swallowing a mouthful of cereal. "Just like any other morning, really. Nothing special is happening. Yours?"

It was hard holding back my grin, so I chose not to. "I'm really enjoying it so far. Thanks for keeping me company." It looked like she was still having trouble holding my gaze when we were standing close to each other. Oh, she tried, I'll give her that, but it only lasted a couple seconds before she shifted her focus to my ear. I'd noticed the chosen spot could also be my mouth if I was smiling or talking.

"You want cereal?" She stirred her spoon in what must have been very soggy cereal by that point then sipped a little milk from the edge of it.

"Nope."

"Coffee?"

"No."

"Cereal?"

I laughed. "I'll grab something with the boys."

"Water, then?"

"I wouldn't say no to that."

She shuffled back and reached up to grab a new glass from one of the cupboards to my left, and I had to grip the edge of the counter in a white-knuckle hold when my attention dropped low.

Eyes up, Dylan. Don't look at her ass, man.

I only saw a flash of light blue against her pale skin before she dropped back down on her heels and filled my glass with water before handing it to me.

"Thank you, Zoe."

There was that pink flush to her cheeks again.

I looked down and focused on her bare feet. She had painted her toenails a light purple, and it looked adorable on her. Then, she curled her toes and hid her right foot behind her left. Something about it made me smile.

I'd met shy girls before, but none of them had the effect Zoe was having on me. I'd met girls that almost made *me* feel shy, too —not too often, maybe once in a blue moon, but it had happened. Some jersey chasers could be a little more forward than you'd expect them to be, and you already expected them to be forward, hence their name. I'd learned that my freshman year while I was still trying to find my way around a new school and a new team.

Not including my freshman year, I didn't sleep around. After that first year, I realized it wasn't my thing. Compared to some of my teammates, I was an angel, but I did date from time to time. Finding that elusive connection was even harder than you'd expect it to be.

This weird thing I had going on with Zoe was new to me. I'd had girls I'd been strictly friends with, and I'd had girlfriends I'd had nothing but a healthy sexual attraction in common with. Yet, there I was, standing in a kitchen, staring at a girl's feet and finding it extremely adorable that she was shy enough to try to hide them from my view. I wasn't sure exactly what was going on between us or if there was anything going on at all, but I had a feeling it was going to take some time to find our footing.

Zoe was shy, that was a fact, but then all of a sudden she'd change the play on me. She'd say something unexpected—like owning up to the fact that she was staring at me—and it would throw me off big time, and this was coming from a guy whose job was to anticipate what the play was and adjust accordingly so he could run for the win. I was damn good at reading a player's next move, but with the way Zoe was playing, I had a hard time guessing where the ball would come rushing toward me from.

It looked like she had a whole different side of her hiding underneath that first layer. Maybe that was what was drawing me to her—the possibilities of Zoe. I wasn't a dumbass; I knew I was attracted to her—my dick had been happy to see her more than a few times that week—but it wasn't just the fact that she was beautiful that had moving me in that direction. I was being serious when I told her I had a feeling she was gonna be my best friend.

"Where do you wanna live after you graduate? Stay here?" I asked out of the blue, surprising the hell out of myself in the process.

She held my gaze for another two seconds—which seemed to be her max unless she was getting into a staring contest with me—then looked back into her bowl and kept squishing the cereal into the milk. Anywhere but my eyes worked, I supposed.

Why did she have so much trouble meeting my eyes when were standing close to each other when she'd had no trouble checking out my abs and occasionally my arms and shoulders just minutes before?

"New York. You?"

"I'll know after the draft is over."

"Makes sense." She nodded and flashed me a small, shy smile.

"I admire your confidence—you're sure you'll be picked. Any idea where you'll end up?"

I shrugged. "If I don't believe in myself, why would anybody else? I might not end up being a first-round pick, but that's fine. I'll just work harder to show everyone what a mistake they made by skipping me." Her smile grew bigger, and I frowned at her lips. "Just so you know, that's not me being a big-headed prick, I just know what I'm capable of out on that field. That being said, I could blow my knee in the next game—or hell, even at practice— and never be able to play again. Going pro is the plan *and* the dream, but it's too early to tell where, or anything really."

She raised her spoon-holding hand in surrender. "A healthy dose of self-confidence is always good. I could use some of it myself." She paused for a moment. "And I know you're not a big-headed prick, Dylan. Yeah, you say you're good on the field, but you're not being obnoxious about it. You just said you'll work harder to show them what a mistake they made by skipping you— you didn't give me a dirty grin and say they'd be lucky to have you play on their team. *That* would've been obnoxious." She narrowed her eyes in uncertainty. "Do you know what I mean?"

Instead of smiling back at her, or taking a step forward that would bring me closer to her, or saying thank you in a gruff voice, I asked a simple question. This time it was no surprise; I was completely aware of what I was about to ask her. "Do you wanna make a bet with me, Zoe?"

Her smile shrunk a little, and she finally put the spoon down in the bowl to try to understand where I was going with my question. After a few seconds of contemplating, she shifted her weight and leaned her hip against the counter. "Where did that come from? And what kind of bet are we talking about here?"

The sun sent the first shy rays of light through the windows and onto Zoe's face as I put my water down and faced her. I watched her squirm when my new stance brought me just a bit closer to her. I could see how much she wanted to back up in the way she shifted from foot to foot. If I took one big step, we'd breathe the same air. The glint, the sparkle I could see in her eyes told me she wouldn't be scared away that easily.

"Let's bet on a kiss," I said, deciding to end her misery. "I think we're gonna end up kissing one of these days, and I bet you'll be the first one to beg for it."

She froze. Her bowl was still suspended in air, so I reached forward and gently took it from her hand. When she didn't release her hold on the spoon, I pried her fingers off of it with my other hand and put her soggy breakfast on the counter—Honey Nut Cheerios from the looks of it. Not a bad choice.

"Correct me if I'm wrong, but did you say I'm going to *beg* you?"

"Yeah, that's what I'm thinking."

"I stand corrected—you *are* full of yourself," she marveled.

"You don't believe me? That's fine—means you'll win. Let's make the bet."

"Did you forget about the part where I told you I had a boyfriend?"

I hadn't, and I didn't like it, but I was still unsure about her dating situation. Hell, I wasn't even sure if she was telling the truth or not, if I was being honest. She'd said it was complicated, and complicated never boded well for a relationship. He was probably a douchebag anyway. "You said it was complicated. Things change, and again, the worst that can happen is you'll win the bet. What do you have to lose?"

"Not always. Sometimes things don't change."

"I have a feeling about this one."

"Oh yeah?" She crossed her arms, making her oversized t-shirt hike up a few more inches on those smooth legs. If I looked long enough, hard enough, could I see that hint of soft blue again? "Care to share that feeling with the rest of us?"

My gaze snapped back up, and I lifted my shoulder in a half shrug. "Scared to lose? If you're so sure of yourself, why not just take the bet?"

"I'm not gonna fall at your feet"—she wildly swung her hand in my direction—"just because I saw you half naked. A lot of guys work out. I've watched a lot of guys work out."

One side of my mouth quirked up. "If you think that's what makes me special—the fact that I have muscles—you're definitely in for a surprise. Come on, what do you have to lose? I'm not gonna try to seduce you, I promise. In fact, I promise I'm not even gonna mention this bet again. Just an innocent game between friends. We'll still be buddies, like you said."

She started tugging on her lower lip with her fingers, thinking over everything I was saying. "Then why make the bet in the first place? I'm not saying I'd want you to seduce me or anything, not that you could anyway since I'm not even affected by half-naked bodies"—her hands moved in the air to indicate said half-naked body before going back to her pink lips—"and clearly, I wouldn't want you to—"

"Clearly," I repeated right after her.

"So, why?" she shot back, ignoring my amused words.

"Why not?"

She huffed. "That's not an answer."

I pushed away from the counter and she took a step back. "It's okay. I understand if you don't trust yourself around me."

She raised her chin just a bit higher and gave me a flat look. "Cute. What do I get if I win?"

"Whatever you want?"

"That's a lot of rein you're giving me. What if I ask you to... okay forget about it, I'm not gonna give it away. I have to think about it some more."

I nodded. That was fair.

"What are the rules?" she asked, her fingers finally leaving her lips alone. "The time frame?"

"No rules. Nothing changes. It's just a harmless bet between two friends, nothing more, promise. As for the time frame...let's say before I graduate. I don't think you'll take that long, but, just in case."

A saccharine smile touched her lips, surprising a genuine grin out of me. I half expected her to flip me the bird while she was at it, but then she pressed her lips together, her expression turning serious. "What do you get out of this?"

Even though I hadn't thought that far ahead since kissing her would be a win all on its own, I realized I didn't even have to think about it. "If I win, I get to have a second kiss...and a third one. After all, three seems to be the magic number with us."

Instead of making their way up to her lips, her fingers tugged and twisted the tiny charm hanging at the end of her silver necklace, just a little above her breasts. If the color of her bra straps were anything to go by, she was wearing matching underwear, which was a thing that got me going. A sexy set of matching underwear kicked everything up a notch for me.

She squared her shoulders, and I forced myself to snap out of imagining what kind of underwear she had underneath that faded t-shirt before my dick could salute her. "I'm really good at bets, just so you know," she said eventually. "And I've never begged to kiss anyone in my life, Dylan."

"Are you just as good with them as you are with impromptu staring contests?" I gave her a half shrug and tried to keep my smile at a minimum. "It doesn't matter. I like the idea of being your first, Zoe."

One side of her lip quirked up. "Make fun all you want. Better watch out—that's all I'm saying."

"See, then you have nothing to worry about. You'll be safe from my lips."

Again, as we seemed to do, we stood there staring at each other for a few seconds, both of us sporting a small smile. This time around she was the one to look away first, and I was nice enough not to point it out.

I gripped the towel hanging on my shoulder. "I better get ready to head out. Don't wanna be late to practice."

"You know this means if you beg me for a kiss, you'll lose too, right?"

I did nothing but smile. I could've kissed her right then and there, but if she wasn't lying and really had a boyfriend, that wouldn't go over well, and I wasn't that guy. I wouldn't do what had been done to me. I would have bet money there was no actual boyfriend, but there was football, and it was very much real. I was living the most important year of my life so far, and I already had a brutal schedule ahead of me.

Zoe nodded, like it was decided. Then, suddenly, she had her fist extended between our bodies. I looked down at it.

"What's that?"

"Hit it."

I arched an eyebrow. "Hit it?"

"Yes. Come on, don't leave me hanging. Buddies occasionally do fist bumps."

When I wasn't fast enough because I was busy trying to figure out how she had come into my life out of nowhere and how I was going to survive her, she gave her little fist a shake and tilted her head, pointing at it with her eyes, urging me to...*hit it*.

So, I fist-bumped my new friend and laughed all the way through it.

What else could I have done?

———

AFTER I LEFT the apartment and met up with the guys, we

pushed through a three-hour practice. Not everyone on the team was happy about getting their asses kicked every day, but I wasn't one of them. At least fall camp was over; it had been...ruthless, to say the least.

More than a handful of times, I had come face to face with both Kyle and Maxwell and had managed to ignore them just fine. On the field, I had to be their teammate, but as soon as we stepped off that green turf, I didn't know them. I was getting better at compartmentalizing.

The second practice was over and we were walking to the showers, sweat literally dripping off of our bodies, JP started in on me. It went on for ten minutes, even during the showers, and by the time we made it into the locker room, he still hadn't stopped.

"Don't lie to me, man. Where are you staying?"

"For the hundredth time, I found a new roommate. I'm fine, chill out."

"Where did you find him?"

I looked up at the ceiling and let out a breath. "Online." No sense in telling him she was a, well...a she and not a he.

"You just went online and moved in with some random dude? Why? Are you too good for my air mattress?"

"I really can't tell if you're being serious or not, but just to let you know...you snore, man. It's okay when we're staying in a hotel for away games—I can handle it for a night or two, but for a year..."

His arms crossed over his chest and gave me one of the perfected *fuck you* looks he usually reserved for referees. He continued to stare down at me, trying his best to catch something from my expression. His damn mouth opened yet again, but I shook my head. "If you ask me one more time, I'm gonna make you regret it."

"What's going on?" Chris asked as he walked straight out of the showers and into our little huddle.

I yanked my sweatpants up and sat my ass back down on the bench.

JP turned all his attention to our starting quarterback. "Do you know? Because if you do and you're not telling me, I swear to God, Chris—"

Apparently getting his ass kicked out on the field hadn't been enough for him. He was asking for seconds.

Frowning, Chris looked at me and then at JP. "What the hell are you talking about? I just came in."

"Fighter boy over here has a mysterious new roommate and he's being all weird about it," JP announced.

Not even bothering to lift my head up, I reached for my shirt. "If anyone is being weird around here, trust me, it's you."

"He's not staying with you?" Chris broke in, ignoring my words. "I thought he was staying with you. Where are you staying, man?"

Groaning, I stood up and pulled my shirt down my stomach. "Are you two fucking kidding me right now? I swear to God, if either one of you asks me where I'm staying or if I'm doing okay again, I'm gonna beat your asses."

"Do you see how defensive he's getting?" JP asked Chris. "He's still..."

Tuning them out, I reached for my phone when it started vibrating in my pocket. Chris went to his own locker, two down to my right, and started to put on his clothes, all the while going back and forth with JP about my 'situation'.

I opened my text and saw it was from Victoria. I ignored it, just as I'd been doing with all her *I want to talk to you* texts, and pushed the phone back into my pocket. Tossing my bag over my shoulder, I walked away from the guys.

"I'm out of here. If you two ever end up finding your balls, you can find me at the food court. I skimped on breakfast so I'm starving." I turned around and kept walking backward, leveling a death stare at JP. "Don't even come near me if you're planning on asking more questions."

"Do you wanna go for In-N-Out?" Chris yelled before I could make it out.

It was always hard to be careful with my diet and especially to say no to cheeseburgers, but I didn't want to miss my class, so this time it was an easy choice. There was also the fact that I always had to be careful with money if I wanted to keep sending some back home. Not having to pay rent would help with that. "Can't today. I have a class at two then a study session around five. You two go on without me."

"We'll see you at Jack's place tonight?" JP yelled as I pushed open the door. Jack was our kicker.

"I'll text you if I can make it."

When I slammed the door shut and rounded the corner, I could still hear JP shouting after me.

I had taken only a few steps when I heard a loud thump echo in the quiet building.

A brunette caught my eye as she exited one of the meeting rooms at the other end of the hall. I only realized who it was when she whipped her hair back while holding the door open for someone. Coach walked out next, right on Zoe's heels. Both of their shoulders were stiff, and neither of them looked particularly happy as they moved as far away from each other as they could get. Coach's face turned toward her and I saw his lips move. Even though I was walking toward them, there was no way I could catch up before they made it to the lobby and exited the complex. I didn't notice Zoe replying to Coach, but I noticed her posture stiffen even more. He turned around and disappeared into the team viewing room. Zoe picked up her pace, passed the trophy displays without lifting her gaze from the ground, and walked out...unaware that I had stopped moving and was standing completely still, full of questions.

CHAPTER EIGHT

ZOE

The weekend after Dylan and I made the bet passed in the blink of an eye. His team won their second game, which I heard about from Jared, and the whole campus was buzzing with the sweet taste of victory. Me? Not so much.

I had watched the first half of the game before heading out to meet up with Jared, and even though I didn't know much about football—I had a hard time following where ball the was, who had the damn ball, who tackled who, who lost the ball, who caught the ball, etc.—even I could see that Dylan became a whole other person out on field. At least, with my limited football knowledge, I thought so. His movements were sharper. He seemed super focused, super attractive, super aggressive—in a hot way, not in a Hulk way. Did I mention super attractive? He was super strong, super fast—the guy could *run*—and again, just in case you weren't following, super attractive. I was very appreciative of it as a viewer. It was probably the uniform and those damn shoulder pads that made him look like a sexy beast. Even the black face paint under his eyes that was supposed make him look ridiculous did the exact opposite. He looked like a warrior out on that field.

Obviously...*obviously* it would be a lie if I said it wasn't hot as fuck to watch him play. When he made his first touchdown—a forty-five-yard run, according to the announcers—I was all caught up in the excitement and did a little jump in my seat with the biggest grin on my face. I laughed when all his teammates rushed over to him as he did a little dance with his hips and they bumped chests and fists—*see! Friends do fist bumps all the time.* Then I saw number five run toward him—Chris. He hooked an arm around his neck as they pushed each other around, and my heart warmed at the sight. When the camera panned to the face of their coach as he paced the sideline, I turned the TV off.

I could definitely understand how the rush of the game...oh, and the uniforms...and, ah, okay, specifically those shoulder pads...and maybe those tight, *tight* pants affected every girl on campus. I assumed it would be a hundred times worse if you were actually right there in the stadium. I wasn't about to give in completely and become one of his shrieking fans, but I didn't see a problem with just watching his games every now and then either...you know, because he and I were on track to become best friends, and best friends kept up with each other's interests. In fact, as he was rushing out one day, he'd even asked for my phone number, and then later I'd gotten a *Hello, roomie.* In my book, that meant we really were becoming friends.

Which was exactly what I wanted.

Exactly.

Speaking of friends, as the clock neared eight PM, I picked up my phone and called Kayla.

She answered on the fifth ring. "Hey, Zoe."

"Hey you. I'm starving. When are we meeting? Are you done with your study session?"

I was planning on begging her to go for pizza, but I wasn't

sure if she was in one of her dieting phases thanks to Keith making random comments about her weight. If that was the case, I knew it would be a no-go, but as I listened to her sigh on the other end of the line, all thoughts of food disappeared from my mind pretty quickly.

"What's going on?" I asked carefully, even though I could already take a wild guess.

"I can't make it tonight. I'm so sorry, Zoe. I've been looking forward to it, and I haven't seen you or Jared in *days*, but I think Keith is coming down with something so I'm gonna have to head home and check on him."

It was right on the tip of my tongue, but she beat me to it.

"And before you say anything, he actually wanted me to meet with you, but his voice sounded so bad when he called so even if we went out, my mind would be on him the entire time."

I sat my ass down on the couch and slipped off my shoes. Just minutes before, I'd been ready and excited to meet up with her.

"I wasn't gonna say anything," I grumbled. "And I understand, of course. You should take care of him—I'd do the same. Don't worry about us. I can meet you tomorrow—would that work? I think Jared is free of babysitting duties so maybe he could make it too. Might even work better. Lunch, maybe? My class isn't until four."

I could hear her quick footsteps as I waited for her answer.

"I have two classes tomorrow, one in the morning, the other around two. If Keith gets better by then, we'll go for coffee. That okay?"

"Anything will work. You say when and where, and we'll be there. I just wanna see your pretty face, KayKay."

I could almost feel her warm smile through the phone. At least her tone was warmer when she answered. "God, I miss you guys, too. I'm not even asking about Dylan because I need to hear the details of every single day and we can't do that over the phone

—and don't tell Jared everything without me. I'm feeling pretty left out as it is, and he'll lord it over me forever."

"Okay. My lips are sealed until I see you in the flesh but don't worry, you haven't missed all that much, although on Saturday after he came—"

"Nope. Nope. You're gonna tell me everything tomorrow, remember? This is not a conversation you have on the phone. We need coffee and carbs in the form of baked goods."

"It wasn't actually that—"

"Oh, Zoe, I'm sorry, Keith is calling. Gotta go. I'll text you tomorrow, okay? Love you."

"Okay! I love you—"

The line went dead. I groaned and threw myself flat on the couch. Of course Keith would be calling. If she had ignored him and gone out with me instead, he'd have kept calling her until he made her feel uncomfortable and guilty enough that she headed back. I hoped he was actually sick and in actual pain.

I sighed and quickly texted Jared.

Me: *Kayla can't make it. Apparently Keith is coming down with something.*

Jared: *Asshole!*

Jared: *Keith, not KayKay.*

Jared: *You can come here and let Becky give you a makeover if you want?*

Me: *Your mom has the night shift again?*

Jared: *Yeah. Are you in? I promise I won't post the results of the makeover on social media this time.*

Me: *No thank you. Getting a makeover from a five-year-old was a one-time thing. It's off my bucket list. I'll never make the mistake of falling asleep when she is in the same room as me again.*

Jared: *Oh but we worked so hard to make you pretty.*

Me: *I saw how hard you worked, and so did everyone else.*

Jared: *You coming?*

Me: *Sure, change the subject. I'll just stay in and get some studying done. Coffee tomorrow?*

Jared: *Yes to coffee. Give Dylan a goodnight kiss for me.*

I smirked. *That little shithead!*

I lifted my phone up high and took a quick shot of me giving him the middle finger with a sweet smile. A few seconds later, I got back one of him and his little sister as he scowled into the lens and covered her eyes with his hand.

Becky would make mincemeat out of him. Not only was she hyperactive, she didn't get that other people needed sleep to function. She was also a little she-devil with the face of an angel. At least he was going to suffer, and knowing that gave me a little satisfaction.

Kissing Dylan good night...I didn't think so. I was made of tougher stuff.

I knew Dylan had a team dinner and a study group because I'd overheard him talking to his friend on the phone. I wasn't sure whether it was Chris or not, and it wasn't like I could ask him either, but knowing he wouldn't be home any time soon, I got comfortable in the living room and brought my laptop with me to get some studying done. If I could squeeze in some retouching of the last shoot I'd done for Leah's fashion blog before I hit my bed, that would be even better. From the way things were going with my little photography job, I had a feeling saving up to move out at the end of the year wasn't going to be as big of a problem as I had expected.

Facing the windows, I sat down on the floor, spread everything out on the coffee table, and got to work. The only break I took was to grab a banana and a piece of slightly burnt toast leftover from breakfast. It was a big letdown after imagining having a delicious cheesy pizza, but what's a girl to do?

It was around nine o'clock when my eyes started to grow

heavy from the school work, so I put in my earbuds and switched over to Photoshop to work on editing the fashion shots. The loud music I put on woke me up pretty fast, and I was able to tune out everything other than Leah's photos on the screen.

This was what I loved to do. Sure, sometimes I spent more hours in front of my laptop than I did actually behind the lens, but that was how it worked. If everything went according to plan, I was hoping photography would be my future. It didn't have to be fashion photos per se, but as long as I was using a camera, capturing different faces, emotions, memories, moments...heartbeats I knew I'd be fine.

At one point, my Spotify radio started playing "Gorilla G-Mix" by Pharrell, and in no time, I was belting out the lyrics to my heart's content because it was one of my favorite sex songs. Everyone had those, right? I'd never had sex while it was playing —it'd be weird if nothing else—but whenever I listened to it, I could definitely see it happening if I closed my eyes.

At the very least, it always brought out my inner stripper. It was weirdly sexy, or maybe it was only sexy to me because I was weird? Might have been the latter, but I didn't care one bit either way. Only Jared and Kayla knew about my weird R&B-hip-hop-sex obsession. Still singing, still sitting on the floor, I dropped my head back on the couch cushions, spread my arms out, and closed my eyes.

My hips moving of their own accord, I sang the whole thing, even made the gorilla noises, as if the lyrics weren't enough. You can guess where I'm going with this, right? Because it's me we're talking about here.

When my eyes lazily opened, Dylan Reed was staring at me upside down. I closed my eyes, opened them again...tried it yet again for good measure...but he wasn't going anywhere. When I'd first seen him looking down at me, I'd thought and hoped I had just conjured him up because I was feeling...a certain way.

Watching Dylan Reed do push-ups and sit-ups was not something that was easy to erase from your mind, after all. Watching his muscles ripple under that smooth skin that begged you to touch, lick, and slurp, to...do all the things you couldn't and shouldn't and wouldn't do to a friend...

My eyes fixed on the ceiling, I let out a long breath. He still hadn't uttered a word. Reaching for my earbuds, I took them out, and the next song that had started playing slowly drifted away, taking Drake's voice with it. The apartment was completely quiet. You could've dropped a pin back in my bedroom and I would've heard it from where I was sitting.

The roar in my ears started low until it drowned out pretty much everything. It felt like my heart was pounding in my brain like an intense bass line. Feeling a little lightheaded from the embarrassment, I sat up and the world righted itself. Biting my bottom lip, I gripped the top of my laptop with clammy fingers, clicked it shut, and then gently placed the earbuds on it. My face must've turned every color in the rainbow by then.

"You can say it," I choked out in a low, low voice.

Eventually, he came into view and stood right next to the giant leather couch that was made for snuggling. I kept staring forward, out the window, but I could see his lips twitching in my peripheral vision.

He cleared his throat, and I bit my bottom lip harder.

Could I never win with this guy?

He sat down on the wide arm of the couch, and I shifted and pulled my legs underneath me, feeling vulnerable.

"I heard you when I was coming up the stairs," he admitted.

I nodded, still keeping my gaze away from his. I tended to forget my volume; the whole building had probably been listening. Dylan kept going.

"I came in and called out your name, but you seemed to be too engaged. I didn't want to scare you so I...waited."

"Were you...uh, have you been standing there for long?"

There was a long pause then his voice came out low and deep. "I think I heard...'pussy growl' at one point? That stuck for some reason. Let's say it was a little before that."

Yup. Okay, then. So he saw me squirm in my seat too.

Still avoiding his eyes, I nodded and stood up. I wanted to cry so badly. He stood up with me.

"I'm just gonna go jump off the building now," I mumbled, ducking my head and trying to shuffle past him.

I knew it wouldn't be that easy, but I wasn't expecting an electric current to go through my body when his big hand encircled my wrist in an attempt to stop me. Goose bumps prickled my skin where he was touching me and all the way up my arm. My hand flexed, but he got what he wanted. My body stilled, and I waited for him to start laughing or making fun of me at any second. Somewhere in the back of my mind, I knew he wasn't like that, knew he wouldn't want to embarrass me, but he'd still think it, would still tell his friends about his weird roommate. I wasn't mortified because he'd caught me singing, but singing *that* song?

"Can you look at me, Zoe?"

When nothing happened, my eyes flicked up to his forehead, and I watched his brows slowly form into a frown.

I blinked, and the next second he was pulling me toward the kitchen sink. Letting go of my wrist, he tore off a piece of paper towel and held it under water until it was soaked. When he moved toward me, I arched back and made sure my head was out of touching distance. His frown getting even deeper, he reached out and curled his hand around my neck to keep me in place. Apparently, I was still in touching distance.

"Stay still," he ordered, his tone practically bordering on anger. What had *I* done except make an ass of myself yet again? As his eyes wandered to mine, for a brief moment, I wished he could've been at least a little unattractive; it would've helped me act normal around him. Even his slightly crooked nose added to his allure. "Your lip is bleeding," he muttered, almost to himself.

Ah, so that was the bitter taste I had swallowed—and here I'd thought it was the bitter taste of humiliation.

"My lips get really dry sometimes."

When the wet cloth touched my bottom lip, I winced and reflexively curled my hand around his wrist to stop him—more like halfway around his wrist, since my hand was tiny next to his. Even though it shouldn't have worked, it did, and his hand stilled. I was so stupid that even his forearm looked sexy to me, the veins lining his skin. There were also those arm hairs I could still feel on my skin if closed my eyes and thought about the day I'd attacked him in the apartment, and then his big hand with its big, strong fingers gently touched my lip, bringing me out of my daydreams.

My eyes met his. "Sorry," he murmured, his voice low, so low that my heart went from zero to sixty in two seconds flat.

Don't look him in the eye, Zoe. Don't do it.

"I'm sorry," I muttered sheepishly as I pulled my hand down.

He turned his wrist once as if I had hurt him. I doubted it. He cleared his throat and resumed cleaning my lip. I let him, openly enjoying the attention I was getting. Okay, maybe not so openly, but at least I hadn't done anything stupid—yet. When he was done, he balled the paper and tossed it into the trash. My eyes followed it, and if they weren't failing me, there wasn't much of anything on it, just a hint of pink, so what was with the sudden first aid help?

"Why is it that you always see me at my worst?" I asked, hoping he'd have an answer for me because I was coming up blank. I struggled to find someplace to put my hands—across my chest? On the island? Behind my back? On him? "I mean, getting caught singing is never the best feeling since it's a private moment, but I was also semi-dancing, as I can imagine you saw, which I guess is weird when you're doing it while sitting, but it still counts. To top it all off, that song? Why didn't you walk in when I was singing to Ed Sheeran? I don't sound so bad when I'm singing one of his songs. Getting caught by you, during that song?" With each sentence, my voice came out like a squeak. "Never mind." I slowly walked around him and headed toward the hallway. "Any chance you won't make fun of me for this?"

"Zoe—" he started as I managed to make it almost to the entrance of the hallway, but before he could finish whatever he was about to say, the power went out, shrouding us in darkness.

"What the hell?"

What the hell, indeed. There was a long eight-second pause where we stayed frozen, waiting for the power to come back on. "Uh..." I moaned, already going into panic mode. "I'm gonna say something, but you can't laugh."

"What?" he asked distractedly. He had already pushed away from the kitchen sink and was heading toward the windows, at least that was where his voice came from.

I cleared my throat and hugged one arm across my stomach. "Could it be a thief, maybe? Or thieves, plural? More than one? More than three? I stayed here last semester, too, and there was a series of robberies in the neighborhood. They could've cut off the power or something to make it easier to break in. We're being robbed, I think. I saw this movie once with my dad where..." I trailed off.

It was looking like the few buildings around us had also lost their electricity, and the silver moonlight spilling into the apartment made it possible for me to see Dylan's silhouette turn to me.

Instead of answering, he opened a window to check out on the street. "Yeah, the whole block is down. It's fine, Zoe. I—"

"Actually, I'm not the biggest fan of—"

"I think you should ease up on the movies."

"What?" Was that amusement I was hearing in his voice? "Are you smiling right now?" I asked incredulously.

I heard a low chuckle, but before I could respond to it, the universe decided to wrap everything up with a little red bow. The room started spinning, and I glanced down at my feet in confusion. Was I getting dizzy? I wasn't *that* scared of the dark. Then the building started shaking, and my horrified gaze flew to the shadow of my roommate.

"Dylan," I choked out in panic, an intense tremor in my voice.

Two seconds.

"It's okay. It'll pass."

Three seconds.

I turned back and focused my gaze toward where the door was. *Run away or stay? Run away or stay?*

Four seconds.

"Dylan," I choked out again, this time louder and more urgently as I swayed forward. My feet were dying to run—to the door, to Dylan, anywhere, really—and take refuge, but at the same time, I couldn't seem to move an inch. I wrapped my shaking arms tighter around myself.

It would stop.

I heard footsteps.

I swear to God, if he runs away and leaves me behind, I will—

Five seconds.

Six seconds.

The earthquake stopped at the exact moment I felt Dylan's front at my back and his hand curled around my shoulder.

"That was weird, but it's over," Dylan said casually, keeping his hand on me.

My heart started doing this weird thing it had never done before, big powerful thumps in slow motion. I hadn't even realized I was holding my breath through the whole thing until I finally released it. My body started shaking as I pulled in deep breaths and let them go through my mouth.

That's when Dylan put his other hand on my left arm and started rubbing up and down.

"You're cold," he mumbled.

Yeah, the dead are usually cold, I thought, but kept it to myself.

I couldn't even give an answer as I struggled to get my breathing under control. Half an hour before, I would've said it was too hot when I was singing. Even the short-sleeved t-shirt I had on had felt like too much at some point, and that was L.A. for you. Now, as Dylan's hands moved on my naked arms, I felt nothing but cold seeping into my skin. His thumbs slid under my t-shirt every time he swept up.

"We need to get out. We need to get out, right now." I moved to run straight out the door, but his hands stopped me before I could take more than a few steps.

"Wait—wait a second." He gripped my elbows and turned me to face him.

"We need to get out," I repeated, breathing heavily.

Even standing so close to him, I couldn't see the details of his face, but from the way his head was tipped, I knew his gaze was on me.

"It's okay, Zoe. It wasn't a big one."

"Who says the next one won't be?"

His hands started moving again, from my wrists, over my elbows, and up, up, up, at a slower pace this time.

"We're fine right where we are."

Were we though? Really, were we? I didn't think so, not with the way the goose bumps prickled my skin where his hands were traveling up and down.

After a few seconds of staring up at the dark shape of his head, I dropped my head and sighed. There was magic in his hands, and slowly their warmth started to warm me up. They weren't soft, not like my last boyfriend's had been. He'd used more hand cream than me, which was fine, but Dylan's hands— they dragged on my skin in the best possible way. I knew I'd remember the feel of them. He was sort of unforgettable.

"I'm really scared of earthquakes," I whispered, just in case he hadn't noticed.

"It's over now. We're okay."

"I'm really, really scared of them, Dylan. Why is the power still not back on? Did it go out because of the earthquake?" I was still whispering. Unable to stop myself, I took a step toward him. I was maybe half a step away from actually standing on his feet, my face only inches away from his chest. Me shuffling closer wasn't a cry for a hug by any means, but when his hands dropped away from my arms and a chill took their place, I felt like a complete idiot, a complete idiot who knew she was an idiot yet still couldn't find it in her to back away from the safety of the big guy in the room. They always said you should take cover next to strong, sturdy things, right? Well, Dylan Reed was plenty strong and sturdy.

Then I felt a big palm at the base of my spine, which pulled a quiet gasp from somewhere deep within me and caused a very small shiver to work its way through my body. His hand slowly started inching up on my back as if he wasn't sure if holding me would be okay.

Uh...

That was enough of an answer to a question I wasn't even thinking of asking. I didn't wait for vocal confirmation, just buried my cheek in his rock-hard chest and held my breath. His other arm reached around me and rested on my back, a little higher than the other one, and I felt like it was okay to close my eyes. He'd make it okay.

"It was probably just a coincidence and has nothing to do with the earthquake."

My arms were still wrapped around my stomach so when Dylan gently pulled me even closer to his body, closing that little half-step gap between us, my arms fell apart and I lifted one to rest on his chest, right next to my face and gripped his shirt at his waist with the other.

It was a little unsure, a little awkward. Fine, maybe it wasn't so much awkward as the best hug I'd had in a while. Let's call it the best half hug, maybe, because it wasn't as if he was crushing the life out of me. That would've been the perfect hug. The embrace was pretty loose, but it was still a hug, and it was still appreciated.

And dear God, his touch was warm and strong. His cologne was different, dizzying, something warm and spicy, maybe a hint of cedar. Basically it was magic. How did he smell so good at that time of the night? Had he been on a date?

Was it too forward to hug a friend like this? If we were being honest, calling him my buddy or friend was stretching the truth a bit but was I gonna stop or back away? Nope, not a chance in hell. If this was the big one for California and the building was going to come down, I was going to be in the arms of this guy.

With our close proximity, I could hear his strong heartbeat. I tried to keep my focus on that rhythm and match my breathing to it, strong and steady.

When I had it mostly under control, I let out another deep breath. "You must think I'm crazy," I muttered into his chest.

There was a four-second aftershock right at the tail end of my words. It was smaller than before but still noticeable. I buried my forehead in his chest and groaned.

"Shhh, it's fine. You're fine. It's just a small one."

I swallowed the lump in my throat and closed my eyes tighter this time, my hand curling into a fist. His arms weren't moving anymore, but he hadn't let go of me either.

"And I don't think you're crazy. My mom is not a fan of earthquakes either."

"Yeah? Would she jump into a stranger's arms, too?"

His chest moved with silent laughter. "I thought we were friends. When did I turn from the best buddy to the stranger in this scenario? And to answer your question, she wouldn't get to jump into a stranger's arms because my dad would be right next to her, ready to catch her if she decided to faint or anything. She always clings to his hand for dear life."

His gravelly voice helped me relax further.

"She faints?"

"Thankfully it hasn't happened yet, but I wouldn't put it past her. She always threatens us with it though."

I waited a moment before I spoke again. "Scientists are expecting a mega-earthquake to hit California, right? The power is still out, and I feel like something bad is going to happen. What if this is it?"

He hummed for a few seconds, and I could feel the vibrations through his body. "Do you have any regrets? Maybe someone you'd want to ask for a kiss before an untimely demise?"

He surprised me enough that I tilted my head back to look up at him. Thanks to the new angle we were standing at, it was easier to make out his features in the dark, and I could definitely see the playful grin on his face.

"Yeah, nice try, but I don't think so. I told you I'm made of tougher stuff when it comes to bets. I won't back out that easily—though, if the building actually starts crumbling down, all bets are off and I'll probably try to crawl right into you."

This time his laughter was audible. "Okay, I'll make sure to be ready for it."

Thinking he must've been starting to feel weird or uncomfortable holding me, I dropped my hand from his chest and took that half step back again. As soon as his arms released me, my body temperature started to come down.

"How come you're so calm anyway? Have you never watched 2012 or *San Andreas*? I just rewatched them last week so I'm thinking that's not really helping at the moment."

It sucked that I could feel exactly where his hands had held on to my body; it made me too aware of the fact that they were no longer around me.

"Is that why you're so afraid of earthquakes? Because of the movies?"

"Who in the world wouldn't be afraid of earthquakes? How can I not freak out about getting smooshed under a building?"

All of a sudden, my hand was in Dylan's and he was staring down at them as if he wasn't sure how it had happened when he was the one who had reached for it. His hand squeezed mine once, twice, and my heart rate picked up.

Shit. Slowly, as if my hand had a mind of its own, I stretched my fingers and linked them around his. It seemed like exactly what he was waiting for because before I could even process the butterflies in my stomach, he was pulling me toward the couch.

"What are you doing?"

"I'm dead on my feet, Zoe. I had a long day, and then the study session went longer than I expected, and I had to hit the weight room before I came here. I'm wiped out, so we need to sit."

Oh.

"I'm sorry," I mumbled as he sank into the couch with a heavy sigh and pulled me down next to him.

"I should get up and look for a candle or something," I mumbled and tugged my hand.

Instead of letting me go as I expected him to, he turned my hand in his then threaded his fingers through mine, palm to palm.

Sitting at a weird angle, I stared at our hands, not sure what was happening. He lifted them and placed the back of my hand on his thigh. I tensed. Dropping his head to the back of the couch, he scooted a little lower.

"Stay. Let's relax for a minute. Keep me company. The power will come back any minute now."

Keep him company with his hand wrapped around mine? Sure, what the hell? What were friends for if not this? I already mentioned that I was an idiot, right? I was actually happy he hadn't decided to go back to his room to crash, so I shifted in my seat, leaned back, and got comfortable next to him.

"Oh, and Zoe, no more of those movies for a while, yeah? Maybe stick to something that won't scare you. You said you liked animated movies—those should be good."

"Those usually make me cry," I mumbled under my breath as I turned my eyes on him.

"I think…"

When I didn't go on, he rolled his head toward me. Our eyes met in the moonlight and I flicked my gaze back up at the ceiling again.

"I think…it has something to do with you. I don't act nearly this wacky around anyone else. Don't get me wrong, I might come close, but not back to back, not like this."

"So what you're saying is that I'm a special friend, huh?"

I glanced at him out of the corner of my eye and saw he was still looking at me. I gazed at his temple. I remained silent, and he finally turned his head away.

"I like that," he murmured in a low voice, and I thought it was safe to look again. His eyes were closed, so mine could roam every inch of his face to my heart's content.

He groaned and arched his back, getting more comfortable. I couldn't say the same for myself, but I didn't move from my spot either. The alternative wasn't appealing at all.

I felt something touch my leg and when I looked down, I saw Dylan's thigh—which had been nowhere near mine just seconds before—lightly resting against mine.

"Did you have a good day?" I asked when he stayed silent.

"Yeah. Long one, but it was good. You?"

"Same. I was working before you came in, so maybe I should go back to that until the power comes back on and let you sleep—though I'll have to wake you up if there's another earthquake."

A low chuckle. "Oh yeah?"

The rumble in his voice rendered me speechless. I closed my eyes and held back a moan.

"Just giving you a fair warning, that's all."

"Feel free to wake me up whenever you want. I won't mind."

I wasn't going to comment on that one.

"Hey, Zoe?" he asked, his voice somewhere between husky and sleepy, heavier on the husky side.

"Yeah?" I croaked, not sounding nearly as sexy as he did. I was still trying to recover from what his voice was doing to me.

"Where is your boyfriend right now?"

Oh.

I stiffened and tried to pull my hand away from his, but I couldn't break his hold.

"Why are you asking?"

"He'd know you're scared of earthquakes, right? If he is your boyfriend, he knows. I just thought he'd call to see how you are by now. If my girlfriend was afraid of earthquakes, I'd be there for her."

"I told you it was complicated."

You're such a little shit, Zoe.

"Okay. If you say so. I was just asking."

CHAPTER NINE

DYLAN

"Zoe? Can I ask you a big favor?"

She was sitting on the small rug in front of the coffee table, her favorite spot to sit when she was working on her laptop, it seemed. If she was watching a movie, her preference was different: snuggling up on the big leather couch.

"How big is it?" she asked, her gaze still focused on the screen and the photo she was working on.

At her words, my lips stretched into a full grin.

When I didn't answer quickly enough, she lifted her eyes to find mine. She must've understood the reason for my grin because her cheeks turned a rosy color and she huffed out a breath.

"How old are you again?" she mumbled.

I chuckled and opened the fridge to get some orange juice.

"It's big, but not so big that you can't handle it."

She faced her laptop. "I already saw it, remember? It's not *that* big. Sure, it looks impressive since you're a shower, and if I remember correctly, I already congratulated you on that. I don't think it'd get any bigger though, which takes me back to...not *that* big."

I was watching her in shocked silence with the box of OJ still in my hand. She usually had that effect on me, so it wasn't new, but it still got me every time.

"Not that I remember it vividly," she muttered as an afterthought. "What?" she snapped when she saw the look on my face.

"Uh, Zoe, I was talking about the favor I wanted to ask—as in, it's a big favor, but nothing you can't handle."

Her lips parted. "Oh." She cleared her throat. "You're going to ignore the word vomit. You didn't hear any of that."

"Of course. What are friends for?" I smiled and poured myself some juice. "Do you want some?"

"No, thanks. So what is this favor?"

In the days following her little earthquake freak-out, we'd gotten a little closer, a little more like actual friends—not buddies, exactly, but friends. She was still having trouble meeting my eyes, but the amount of time she spent looking at my chin or ear while talking to me had decreased. Plus, even though we only saw each other in passing, and some days not even for more than ten minutes, the more time passed, the more I learned about her.

It was great. I liked that she was opening up little by little every day—apart from the fact that I still wasn't sure about her boyfriend situation, that is. I was having trouble getting a read on her. She had secret phone calls, whispering to make sure I couldn't hear anything even when I wasn't in the same room with her, but it could've easily been one of her friends. Still, I had my suspicions, but that was all they were—suspicions—and I hoped some of them really were just that.

Until I knew for sure, I wouldn't get to steal the kiss she owed me, and from seeing how seriously she was taking our bet, I didn't think she'd cave any time soon either.

"I'm swamped today. I need to meet with one of my trainers to discuss if he can help me get ready for the combine. If it's a go, we need to make a schedule. After that, we have a team meeting, and then I have a class and another study group right after. I need to get a few things for the week, like pasta, chicken, and a few others, so if you have time, can you help me out with that? I'll owe you one."

"You want me to get you groceries?"

"If you have the time. I'm pretty much out of everything, and this week's already going to be crazy as it is with the game, so I don't think I'll get a chance to do it myself. I'll give you my debit card if you say you can do it."

She twisted at her waist to look at me. "I have photography lab at two-thirty, but I'm free between four and eight. I was planning on texting Jared and Kayla to see if they were free to hang out, but I can get what you want after my class."

"Are you sure? If you already made plans, I can ask one of the—"

"It's fine. I love grocery shopping. I can do my weekly shopping a little early—two birds with one stone. I also happen to love grocery lists. Do you have a list for me?"

"I do." I smiled at her and reached into my pocket so I could take out my debit card and the short list I'd made earlier. I placed them on the marble island right in front of me. "The pin is seven five three two."

Her face lit up with a playful smile. "Aren't you afraid I'll steal all your money and run away?"

"I'm pretty much broke, and even if you did steal the hundred or so dollars, I'm afraid you wouldn't get that far." That reminded me that I needed to somehow handle my schedule better and get in a few hours of work at Jimmy's bar. Not only was my money dwindling, I also needed to send some back home, too, just to help out a little.

Her eyes softened. "I won't steal your money."

I smiled at her and didn't think before speaking. "I know you won't, baby."

I managed to hold her gaze a few seconds longer than our usual before she cleared her throat and turned back to her work.

Maybe *baby* hadn't been the best word choice, but I couldn't take it back now.

"You said you're free between four and eight, right? Do you have a study group at eight?" Maybe I could thank her with a small surprise.

I watched her shoulders stiffen. "Not exactly. Why?"

"I'll think I'll make it back around nine, thought maybe we could watch a movie together or something. I haven't seen you much this week."

I put my palms down on the counter and waited for her answer. It took a while.

"I'm not sure when I'll get back. I...uh...I have a date tonight."

Well then.

"You have a *date*."

Our eyes met for just a second when she looked at me over her shoulder, but she was quick to glance away.

"Yeah. I don't think I'll be too late, but you go to bed pretty early on weekdays, so I'm not sure if you'll still be up when I get back." Her eyes flicked up and then down again. "We can do it another time? This weekend, maybe?"

"I won't be around this weekend. We have an away game."

"Oh. Okay."

Okay? "I guess I'll see you later then. Have fun on your date." *Or not*, I thought, but didn't repeat it to her. "Thank you for helping me out today. I owe you one."

Her lips pressed together and she nodded.

"I have ten minutes before I'm supposed to meet up with my trainer so I'm gonna have to run." Gulping down my orange juice, I started to look around in the drawers for my last protein bar.

I sighed. "Zoe, have you seen my protein bar? I left it on the counter this morning."

"Yeah, I put it in the cupboard next to the bowls, the one next to the fridge."

It'd been weeks since I'd moved in, yet I still didn't know where everything was in the kitchen. I knew where the pots and pans lived, the mugs and glasses, and the spoons and forks, but that was where my knowledge ended, even though I'd already cooked dinner in there once or twice. I usually ate with the team, since we had our own chefs, but if I was home early, I didn't go back out just so I could have dinner with everyone else.

One other thing I'd learned about Zoe was that she hated having things lying around. I wouldn't call her organized, exactly, because I'd seen the state of some of the drawers, but it seemed like as long as the counters were empty and clean, she was fine, which meant if I left something out, she stashed it away as soon as she could get her hands on it.

I opened the cupboard in question and just stared.

"Uh...Zoe?"

"Yeah? It's right there on the first shelf—did you find it?"

I reached up and grabbed my protein bar. Like she'd said, it was right there...among other things.

"I distinctly remember you saying you didn't buy peanut butter M&Ms because you had trouble not eating them all at once." I heard her get up from the floor with a sigh. In a few seconds she was standing next to me, staring at what I was staring at.

"You found them, huh."

"Uh, yeah. They're right there. If you were trying to hide them, you did a pretty shitty job."

"I wasn't *exactly* trying to hide them, but I can't even see them if I'm not standing on my toes—it's not my fault you're freakishly tall."

"I'm not freakishly tall, Flash," I mumbled and looked down at her then back at the countless reddish-orange bags of candy on the shelf. "Is there something you want to tell me?"

"Surprise?" she blurted out like it was a question, drawing my gaze back to her. "I got them for you...as a present...a few presents."

I raised an eyebrow. "Zoe, give it up. There have to be at least twenty-five, thirty bags of peanut butter M&Ms here."

She groaned. "Fine, I lied. I bought them all for me, and if you want to be exact, there are only twenty-three, but I can't eat them."

"Right, twenty-three. And why exactly can you not eat them?"

"I told you: I can't stop."

"Then why the hell did you buy them?"

She sighed again and closed the cupboard as if she couldn't bear to look at them any longer. "Because I can't stop myself from buying them either. I just like to have them around, you know. If I know they're there, it makes it easier to stay away, like if I had a craving I could reach up and get one and everything would be okay, but if I don't have them in the house and it's too late to go out and buy some, then what am I supposed to do? Or what if they're out of peanut butter M&Ms, then what? Does that make sense?"

I just shook my head. "Not really."

"It's like this: it's better to know I have them than not have them, and if I have them, I won't eat them because then they'll all be gone. I like that they're there. Oh, let's look at it like this."

"Let's."

"I bet you eat your favorite food on the plate last, right? Let's say you have meatballs, broccoli, and...rosemary and garlic roasted potatoes. Which one would you leave for last?"

I just blankly stared at her.

"I would leave the roasted potatoes. I'd want to savor them, so I'd leave them to eat last. Get it now?"

"Please tell me you don't have a bag of roasted potatoes tucked away somewhere—and also, for the love of God, don't tell me you occasionally like to take these M&Ms down, line them up on the counter, and just stare at them."

"Of course not! I'm not a weirdo, I just have...some quirks. It's cute to have quirks."

"Well, excuse me for asking. If you did that, I was gonna start worrying about you."

"Don't you have that *one*—or, okay, a few food items you're afraid to eat too quickly because then that will be the end of it and you won't have more? I like fries, too. I can never share fries, and I always get extra even if I don't eat all of them. I just want the option of eating more. Do you get it? If you still don't get it, I'm pretty sure you're the problem here, buddy, not me."

As she looked up at me with hope-filled eyes, I could do nothing but just stare at her.

She bit her lip then started laughing, and two seconds in, a small snort escaped her. She slapped her hand over her face, but it was too late.

The grin I gave her was a little filthy, a little lazy. "You're so fucking fascinating, Zoe Clarke."

What did I get for my compliment? A smack on the arm and an impressive growl.

———

IT WAS around ten when I heard a key turn in the lock and the apartment door slammed open, hitting the column right behind it.

I leaned back in my seat and watched Zoe struggle with taking her bag off her shoulder.

"I've gotta pee! I've gotta pee! I've gotta pee!"

Each time she repeated it, her voice rose higher.

My eyes dropped to the dress she was wearing: black and tight on her upper body, leaving nothing to the imagination as far as the size of her boobs, and looser on her hips—not by much, but still. It ended a few inches above her knees. *Date, right*—she was coming back from her date.

"Miss Clarke!" another voice chimed in. "Miss Clarke, I need you to—"

Holding on to the door and squirming in place, Zoe replied, "I'm sorry, Ms. Hilda, I've gotta pee. I can't. I really really can't. I have to pee."

With that she slammed the door, finally managed to untangle the strap of her bag from her hair, threw it right over her head, and ran straight to the bathroom.

Like I said, I found her fascinating.

A few minutes later she came out of the bathroom, and just when I thought she was heading to her room, she stopped in her tracks. I could've sworn I saw her tilt her chin up and smell the air.

"I smell pizza. Is it pizza? Did you have pizza?"

This time she was running toward me, or more like the pizza box right in front of me, and the expression on her face—priceless. When she finally made it, she didn't waste a second before she tore into the box...only, I'd already eaten pretty much all of it and there was only one slice left.

Again, her face when she realized it was all gone—priceless, and cute as fuck. Turned out she could pull off a mean face better than I expected.

"You ate it all? *This* is all you left me?" she asked slowly, big eyes staring down at the empty box.

I raised an eyebrow. "I was really hungry. Didn't you eat on your date, anyway?" I hadn't meant to mention her date at all, but apparently I was still stuck on that.

She scrunched up her nose and the appalled look on her face disappeared, leaving sad, sad eyes. "He couldn't make it."

My brows drawing together, I checked my watch, just to make sure. "It's a little past ten, Zoe—don't tell me you waited for him for two hours."

She blew out her cheeks and dropped down on the couch behind her.

"He said he might be late but would try to make it." She gave me a half-hearted shrug as if to say it was okay, but her facial expressions were so easy to read. Anyone could see that it wasn't okay.

Worthless son of a bitch.

"You didn't have anything to eat while waiting for him?"

She rubbed her temple. "The restaurant wasn't anywhere near campus, and it was a fancy place. I didn't feel like having anything on their menu—didn't wanna spend over fifty dollars for a few spoonfuls of pasta. Also, I'm not good at eating by myself at restaurants, or anywhere really. It feels like everyone is looking at me and collectively thinking, *Oh, poor girl.* So, short answer to your question: nope, I didn't have anything to eat."

There were a few things I could've gone after in her speech, but I chose to focus on one thing and one thing only while fishing for more. "Your boyfriend is a college student and he can afford fancy restaurants, huh? I guess I can see why you would have trouble ending it."

Just like that, I'd screwed up. I didn't know what had pushed my buttons exactly, but as soon as the words were out of my mouth, I knew I had fucked up—big time.

Her brows inched up to her hairline and she met my eyes—a rare occurrence—then tilted her head.

"Wow."

Placing both her palms on the couch, she pushed herself up. The pizza forgotten, she continued to hold my eyes as she stared down at me.

"Wow, Dylan. I don't expect you to know me in a month, or however many weeks you've been here—hell, we barely see each other some days—but...actually, you know what? Maybe I did. Maybe I did think you'd figure out at least that much. I'm the last person who'd date someone for the amount in his bank account."

Having trouble taking my eyes off of her, I flinched at her words. When she moved to storm past me, I caught her wrist and got up.

She stopped, but she didn't look at me. She didn't even tell me to let go of her.

Her *complicated situation* had officially started to fuck with my head. If only I knew for sure that it wasn't...

"I'm sorry, Zoe. You're right, and I'm an asshole. Of course I know you're not like that. Of course I do." I softened my grip on her wrist and snaked my fingers around hers. "I'm sorry. If it'll make you feel any better, you can insult me too."

She hesitated before sending a quick glance at me. "You really ate the whole thing?" Of all the things she could've said, she went with that.

"You're not gonna bust my balls?"

She slipped her hand out of mine and rubbed her palm on the side of her dress.

"What am I supposed to insult you with? *Gee, your body is so ugly, you're ruining my view every damn morning?* How pathetic does that sound? I don't have anything on you—at least not yet—but I'm pretty sure I'll remember this and say something when the time is right, when you're least expecting it, of course."

I smiled at her. She liked watching me work out in the mornings. I already knew that since she came out and found things to do while I was busy with my sit-ups and push-ups, but hearing it from her confirmed what I'd already guessed. My smile slowly morphed into the biggest grin.

"What now?" she snapped.

"I hope you won't break my heart too much, Zoe Clarke."

"Only as much as you broke mine, thinking I'd be interested in someone because of their bank account."

That wiped the smile clear off my face.

In a rough voice, I said, "I'm an asshole. I deserved that."

Her teeth scraped her bottom lip. Helpless to do anything, I just watched.

Averting her gaze, she took a step away from me. When she looked up, her eyes only made it to my lips. "Look, I'm cranky, a little tired, and maybe just a little hangry thrown in there, too. I'm just gonna go to bed. I have an early class tomorrow, anyway."

"Don't you want the pizza? If nothing else, we can fix the hangry part." Just because that sick bastard had stood her up and hadn't fed her didn't mean I was gonna let her go to bed unhappy.

"The pizza?" She sighed and looked back at the almost empty box. "That doesn't count as *the* pizza, Dylan. It's just *a* slice of pizza. So, I rather not. It'll only make me hungrier for more. I'll see you tomorrow."

Another step away from me.

"I guess that means you're not up to watching a movie with me either."

She only managed half a smile when she looked my way. "Maybe another night. Good night."

"You might wanna check the oven before you leave."

"What? What do you mean?"

"It was supposed to be a thank you for helping me out with

the groceries today, but I'm thinking I owe you an apology now." Finally her eyes met mine, and I tilted my chin toward the kitchen. "Just see if you want it. If you don't, you can get away from me."

A small smile formed on her lips. "Is it pizza? Please say it's pizza. I want it to be pizza so badly. Please say pizza."

I laughed. "I don't know, see for yourself."

Moving toward the kitchen, she threw over her shoulder, "If it's not pizza, I'm gonna be doubly pissed at you, just so you know." She opened the oven and bent down to check inside.

There was a small gasp then she came up with the pizza box in her hand and the biggest smile plastered on her face. "Dylan, it's a whole pizza...just for me?"

I chuckled. "Yeah, you don't have to share."

"It's from that Neapolitan place, and it's still warm, too."

"I just got in about ten minutes before you. I wanted to wait, but I wasn't sure what time you'd be back, and the smell got to me." I tried not to think where she'd been or who she'd been waiting for.

Giving me another one of her sweet-as-fuck smiles, she set the box on the island and opened it. Holding back her wavy dark brown hair with both hands, she leaned down until her nose was almost touching the pizza and inhaled.

The loud groan she let out made my dick surge to life in my pants.

"God, the smell. This is not fair, you know," she said quietly, her face still practically in the pizza. "I'm kind of angry at you, and you got me my absolute favorite thing."

I wouldn't tell her I'd spent the last bit of cash I had on me so I could get us this treat. Whatever was left on my debit card after the grocery shopping she'd done for me was all the money I had until I could pick up some shifts at the bar, which was probably thirty dollars or less. "I told you, I'm an asshole."

"I didn't think you were, actually, but yeah, apparently you are." Closing the box, she picked it up and made her way back to me. "Still, thank you. I was trying to play it cool, but I was really pissed at you for eating an entire large all by yourself."

I laughed. "I'm afraid you weren't that good at playing it cool, Zoe."

"Whatever," she mumbled under her breath as she climbed on the couch. Sitting cross-legged, she carefully placed the box on her lap and opened it. Breathing in deeply, she let it all out, picked up a slice, and looked at me intently. "I'm not good at sharing."

I never would've guessed. "It's okay," I said, chuckling. "I already ate more than I should." I sat my ass back down, right across from her.

One hand curled around the box possessively, she took her first bite and released another groan, this one longer and somehow more erotic than the one before.

"So good. So so good," she mumbled in between chewing.

I couldn't take my eyes off of her. Swallowing, she took another bite, closed her eyes, and chewed as slowly as possible, her lips curling up in the process. It felt wrong to watch her eat. If I'd known her entire face would light up just for pizza, I'd have somehow bought ten more. My eyes drifted down to her throat where I could see the exact moment she swallowed. Then my gaze dipped lower and I watched the swell of her breasts rising and falling with each breath. I was in so much trouble.

"You okay?"

When I looked up, she was looking at me. I shook my head and cleared my throat. "Yeah."

"So are we gonna watch something or not?"

I checked my watch: it was almost eleven.

"I'm sorry," Zoe muttered, putting her slice down. "I know you get up early. You don't have to sit and watch me eat."

"I can watch a movie with you," I told her. How could I leave her? "No doomsday movies, though. Anything but that."

Her smile back in place, she picked up her slice and took another damn bite. "I actually wanted to watch *Geostorm*, but didn't wanna do it alone."

"Yeah, I don't think so. Pick something else."

"I still get to pick?"

"Sure, why not? I'm an asshole, remember? You get to pick the movie." *And I get to know you better*, I thought to myself.

"How about an old-ish movie, like *The Fifth Element* or...*Speed*? Or how about *Lord of the Rings*? Both Kayla and Jared refuse to binge-watch them with me, and that's a movie I'd rather watch with a friend. Definitely one of my favorites." One more bite and she had me licking my lips. Before I could manage to respond, she'd already swallowed and was starting again. "I know we can't binge them tonight, but maybe another time? The only other person who loves it as much as me is in Phoenix, and it's been so long since I watched it."

I cleared my throat. "I thought for sure you'd force *Titanic* or *The Notebook* on me as a punishment."

Licking her fingers, she shook her head. "I like romantic movies, but sometimes they're too sweet. I have to be in the mood for that."

Great. I was her buddy, her friend—nothing romantic about that.

"How about we go for *Fifth Element* then. It's been a while since I watched a Bruce Willis movie. How are we gonna do this? Your laptop or mine?"

"Mine. I think I have that on my account already." She sprang up from the couch, barely keeping her balance as she thrust the pizza box into my hands. "Don't steal," she warned, her expression serious.

Holding back my smile, I gave her a nod.

Just as she took off in a jog, the doorbell rang, stopping her forward movement.

Slowly she turned to me and whispered, "Ms. Hilda? I don't wanna open it. If she wants me to do something, by the time I get back, my pizza will be cold."

Just as quietly, I whispered back, "I already helped her with some heavy boxes today. Let's ignore it—I'll check on her tomorrow." I wouldn't exactly call the old lady sweet, but she was definitely treating me better than she treated Zoe; I'd witnessed that on more than a few occasions.

She bit her lip and glanced at the door.

Before I could get up and nudge her toward her room, someone knocked loud enough to wake the whole damn building.

The noise made Zoe jump, and she looked at me in confusion. Frowning, I got up from my seat.

CHAPTER TEN

DYLAN

"I know you're in there, you asshole! Open the fucking door."

Oh fuck.

"Who is it?" Zoe asked, still whispering.

I sighed and put her pizza on top of mine. Rubbing my neck, I went to open the door before someone called 911 for a noise complaint, or worse, Ms. Hilda decided to come out, if she hadn't already.

I knew it would be pointless, but I still blocked his entrance.

"What the hell are you doing here JP?"

"Hello to you too, you motherfucker."

Great.

I glanced at Zoe over my shoulder and she made a face that clearly said *shit*.

Shit, indeed.

I turned back to my impatient, pissed-off friend. "What do you want?"

He shook his head as if he couldn't believe I'd ask such a question, and then he pushed me back, sweeping right into the apartment and coming face to face with Zoe.

"Oh, what do we have here?"

I exhaled a deep breath and closed the door. At least the dumbass had come alone.

When Zoe said hi, I turned around to find JP circling her like a shark observing its prey before deciding on an attack plan, much like he had years before, actually, though I doubted he'd remember her from that night, not like I did.

"Don't even think about it," I warned him. "What are you doing here, man?"

He quit playing and focused on me.

"What am I doing here? Good question. Wait, I think I have an even better one—what the hell are *you* doing here?"

"I live here."

"I already got that much. You've been coming straight here after splitting with us these last two days."

"Are you fucking crazy? Have you been following me?"

"Excuse the fuck out of me for being worried about you."

"Maybe I should just go to my room so you guys can—"

My eyes landed on Zoe as she started to back away. "You stay," I ordered her.

JP glanced between Zoe and me. "Is this why you've been so tight-lipped about where you're staying? Because you're shacking up with some girl and playing house?"

"Do you *want* me to knock your ass out?"

He raised an eyebrow. "I'd love to see you try, you fucker."

"O-kay. As fun as this is to watch, I'm just gonna take my pizza and—"

"Sit down, Zoe, and eat your pizza. JP will be leaving soon."

Her eyes grew big and her lips twitched. "Aye aye, captain."

As she walked back toward the couch, I scrubbed my hand down my face and sighed. JP was apparently still waiting for an answer, because he was still standing in the same spot, arms crossed over his chest.

"I told you I found a roommate. Why the hell are you worried about it?"

He relaxed his stance and sighed. "Come on, man. Finding a roommate isn't the problem here. You barely speak to the guys unless we're on the field or in a meeting. Do you think they don't notice how distant you've been? You've been ditching us for study groups, and you always get all tongue-tied whenever we ask where you're staying. I get calls from Vicky asking me where you are, and I don't even know if you're talking to her again or if it's just her crazy ass trying something. It's not just you trying to keep a secret about where you're staying for some damn reason. It's our last year—you can't pull this shit now. What the hell is going on with you?"

Out of the corner of my eye, I saw Zoe tuck her legs under her and hug the pizza box to herself as she lifted a slice up to her lips. At least one of us was enjoying the moment. I turned my focus back to JP. I really didn't want to get in trouble with Coach by having JP in the apartment, but since he was already standing in the middle of the living room, I couldn't see how I could avoid it either.

"Nothing is going on with me, JP. What do you expect me to do about the team? I'm not dropping the ball out there, that should be enough. I don't think you'd act any differently if you were in my shoes. Do you honestly believe none of them saw what was going on with those three at that party?"

"*I* was at that party, Dylan, remember? Chris was there too. You think we knew what was going on?" he asked in disbelief.

"No, not you, but don't tell me you believed them when they said it only happened that once. Screw that. I don't even care about it anymore, but don't expect me to trust them any time soon. On the field, we're a team, always, and I'll have their backs, but off the field?" I shook my head and leaned my back against the door. "No, man. I don't have a problem with everyone, but nothing says I have to like those few who I'm sure knew what was going on just because we're playing for the same team. And of course I'm going to ditch your ugly asses to study. You said it yourself, it's our last year. Scouts are there, watching every game. This is it. We either make it or we don't. I gotta give it my all. Instead of being a creep and following me around, you should be studying too since Coach will have your head if your average drops."

"So that's it? That's all of it?"

"What else do you want me to say?"

My friend gave me a cold stare. "How about an apology for making me worry about your stupid ass like a mother hen?"

"You being serious?"

"Yeah. Let's hear it. I had better things to do than follow you around to find out what the hell you were up to, not to mention I didn't know which apartment you disappeared into and had to knock on a shit ton of doors before I found it."

I laughed. "Fine. Sorry. We good?"

"Yeah. It'll do for now."

I pushed off the wall and we did a one-armed hug, thumping each other's back.

"Awww, you guys love each other. Either my eyes are watering or there's a dust storm happening where I'm sitting. I would've never guessed that football players would be this emotional," Zoe said as she popped the last bit of a crust into her mouth, her fingers immediately reaching for another slice.

Amused, I shook my head and sighed. "JP, this is Zoe, my roommate and my new buddy. Zoe, this is JP, my surprisingly emotional teammate."

"Fuck off." After elbowing me in the stomach, JP made his way toward her.

Giving my friend a shy smile, Zoe wiggled her fingers at him. "Hi."

"Do I know you from somewhere?"

Zoe's eyes slid to me then back to JP. "I don't know how you would."

I walked around the couch to sit down. There went my plan of watching a movie with my so-called buddy and spending a quiet night in.

"Do we have a class together or something?"

"Nope."

He turned to me. "Do I know her from somewhere?"

"No, you don't," Zoe repeated, answering for me. I wasn't planning on embarrassing her in front of JP, especially if he didn't remember meeting her two years back, so I didn't correct her.

"Where did you find her, again?"

Zoe narrowed her green eyes at JP's back.

"I told you, I found her online. She was looking for a roommate. Be nice."

JP's eyebrows rose up toward his hairline, but other than giving me a shrug, he didn't say anything. I'd hear about it later; he'd say whatever was on his mind when we were alone.

"Apparently, I need to be nice to you," he said. Leaning down, he lifted the top of the cardboard box, which was still on Zoe's lap. "And it works both ways. I be nice to you, you be nice to me." Zoe looked at JP then back at the four slices of pizza left. How the fuck had she eaten half of it that fast?

Before my friend could lift one of the remaining slices, she slapped the box closed and held it away from him.

"What the fuck?"

Zoe leaned to her left to look around JP and met my eyes—another one of those rare occasions where she forgot she was too shy and avoided them. "I'm sorry, Dylan, I know he is your friend and all, but I really don't want to share. I'm not at all a good sharer."

I laughed. "It's okay, I got it for you. He can buy his own pizza if he's hungry."

She tilted her head back to look up at JP, who was almost as tall as me. "Look, I haven't had anything to eat since noon and I had a shitty night. Even though I'd be willing to give you one slice, I've seen how Dylan eats, and I can guess you're no different. One slice won't be enough for you, and I'm not willing to give you the rest...though, to be fair, if I only had one slice, it probably wouldn't do anything for me either. So, why bother having a slice if it's not gonna do anything for you? If I don't have that one extra slice it'll mean I'll go to bed hungry, which would mean two people going to bed hungry. But, if I get all of these slices, at least one of us will be full."

"You'll go to bed hungry," JP repeated, not as a question, but more like a statement. Zoe hugged the pizza box closer. "What's going on with this one?" he asked, looking at me in confusion.

I smiled, relaxing into my seat for the first time since JP started banging on the door. "Nothing. She just loves pizza, maybe a little more than you and I do."

"You can have his," Zoe added when JP continued to stand over her. I didn't think JP had ever been refused food by any girl.

He opened my nearly empty pizza box, which was still on the coffee table, and frowned down at it. "There's only one slice here."

"See!" Zoe told him. "I said the same thing when I saw it, and just like I told you, one slice means nothing."

Again, JP met my eyes, waiting for an explanation. "What did you say was wrong with her again?"

"Nothing is wrong with her." I had trouble looking away from Zoe as I spoke, and JP obviously picked up on it because his next question made me wanna cause him serious injury, even risking his spot in the next game.

"You're definitely playing house here. Is that why Vicky is in such a tizzy? Does she know about her?"

"If you mention Vicky one more time, I'm gonna kick you out."

Sitting down on the arm of the couch, he started to look around.

"Are you his sugar mama or something?" he asked Zoe when he was done taking in his surroundings. "I'm not judging, girl. To each their own, but how did you afford this place again, D? Even half the rent must cost an arm and a leg."

Zoe's eyes jumped from JP to me. Before I had to come up with a bullshit answer, there was another knock on the door.

JP jumped up. "You kids stay put. I'll get it."

I scrambled up after him. "JP, no." If Coach was at the door, I was screwed.

Out of the corner of my eye, I noticed Zoe doing the same, finally putting the pizza box down. Was she thinking the same thing I was?

JP opened the door, and thank God it was only Chris who walked in. "Come in, come in. Look who I found here." JP gestured toward me.

I groaned and dropped back on the couch, this time taking the seat closer to Zoe instead of going back to the other end. "For your sake, man, I hope he's the only one you told." I tried to meet Zoe's eyes to assure her that they would leave soon—if not, I would kick them out—but she only had eyes for our quarterback.

My brows furrowed and I looked over my shoulder.

"What's going on here?" Chris asked, looking between Zoe and me.

JP slung his arm over Chris's shoulder and made a show of introducing Zoe.

"This young thing over here has been—"

I interrupted him by getting to my feet. "Just finish that sentence, man. Please do it."

Zoe cleared her throat and all eyes turned to her. Her cheeks were flushed, eyes sparkling. For some reason, that image of her didn't sit well with me. Was she getting all worked up over Chris? She certainly hadn't reacted that way to JP. It also looked like she had no trouble meeting Chris's eyes whatsoever.

I furrowed my brows and watched her wipe her hands on her dress. "Hi. I, uh...I'm Zoe. Uh, Zoe Clarke." She threw a quick glance at me, but I didn't think she actually saw me. "I'm Dylan's roommate."

And just like that, I was demoted from friend to roommate.

"Nice to meet you," Chris said, sounding a little unsure.

After a long moment of silence where no one said anything, I sighed and gestured to my left. "Since you two don't look like you're planning to leave any time soon, you might as well sit your asses down."

Chris walked past by me to take me up on my offer, but JP headed toward the kitchen. "Is there anything to eat in this place —other than your girl's precious pizza, that is. I'm starving."

Zoe chose that moment to pick up the pizza box and offer it to Chris. "Would you like to have some pizza?"

JP said exactly what was on my mind: "Are you fucking kidding me?"

CHAPTER ELEVEN

ZOE

I knocked on the door and walked in as soon as I heard a muted, "Come in." When his eyes lifted up and he saw who was in his office, he sighed. "This is not the best time, Zoe. I'll call you later."

Ignoring his words, I took a deep breath, clicked the door shut, and squared my shoulders. "I want to tell him."

I was in Mark's private office, standing as far away from him as possible. Anyone could've told me he didn't want me in there just from his body language and I didn't want to be there either, but I'd sucked it up and made my way over to the athletic administration building as soon as I left the apartment that morning anyway. He was just going to have to deal with me.

"No." Mark looked at me with hard, unyielding eyes. Was he ever planning on telling him? At that moment, it didn't look like he was, but we had a plan and he was going to tell him. He had to. I just couldn't wait any longer.

"I need to tell him," I repeated, my voice coming out stronger this time—at least it sounded stronger to my ears.

He leaned back in his seat and the chair gave a small groan. I barely managed to hold back my flinch.

"Is this because I couldn't make it last night? I'll make it up to you some other time. You know how busy it gets during the season."

He wanted to talk about that? Sure, why not?

"You were the one who invited me out in the first place. You didn't have to make me wait two hours in that restaurant halfway across town if you had no intention of coming, but this isn't about last night. It's not the first time it's happened, and I'm guessing it won't be the last, either. I get that you're busy. It's fine either way."

"You need to remember who you're talking to."

I needed to remember? I wanted to forget all about him.

Mark tapped the pink end of the yellow pencil he had in his hand on one of the papers that were strewn all over his desk and looked down at them, dismissing me.

"I give up. I don't want to do this anymore," I confessed, and his gaze came back to me. Was that relief I was seeing in his eyes? I let out a deep breath and swallowed my disappointment. "If you don't want to see me, if you don't care about getting to know me, that's okay. You don't have to. But, you should know, Chris was at the apartment last night. That's why—"

As soon as the words left my mouth, Mark was up on his feet. He threw the pencil on his desk in a calm manner, just a flick of his wrist, which was not what his body language said at all. Instead of meeting his eyes, I watched the pencil roll off and hit the ground with a small thump. When it stopped moving, I finally found the courage to look up at his face. I straightened my spine and tried my best to look like I wasn't afraid of him or the radiating anger coming off him in waves. Though I had to say, it was the angriest I'd seen him in the last three years. His face was flushed and he bent to put his fists on the table, eyes on me the entire time.

"What did you just say?"

"Chris...he was at the apartment last night, with one of Dylan's friends, JP. I think they were worried about him."

"What did you tell him, Zoe?"

When I'd first come in, Mark hadn't invited me to sit down, so I was still standing in the same spot. My hand tightened on the strap of my bag and the edge of the leather bit into my palm. It felt like the bag was my only protection against him, though in reality, it meant absolutely nothing. I didn't think he'd actually hurt me, but he'd never looked at me like he wanted to end me right then and there either.

Hadn't my dad warned me on multiple occasions to be careful around him?

"What the fuck did you tell him!" thundered Mark when I didn't reply fast enough, and this time, I visibly flinched.

I hated the fact that he had the ability to hurt me. He shouldn't have, I knew that, and the fact that my voice was small when I answered him bothered me even more.

"Nothing," I forced out. "They didn't stay for long."

"Sit down and tell me everything."

Maybe I had made a mistake in mentioning it to him. "I didn't come—"

His palm hit the desk with a sharp crack. "I said sit your ass down and tell me everything!"

My heart hammering, I forced myself to walk with stiff legs and sat on the edge of the chair farthest away from him. A result of the anger I felt toward him, my fingertips bit into my palms the entire time. When I was finished telling him about the night before, making sure to keep the parts about me and Dylan out, he started pacing—angry steps, angry eyes, sharp, angry words.

"He doesn't know about your mom. How many times do—"

"Our mom, you mean," I muttered.

His eyes narrowed at me. "Danielle has never been his mom. We adopted him. His mom is Emily."

It was right on the tip of my tongue to say something, but I decided to let it go. When it came to Mark, I knew it was better to pick my battles. I wanted to reason with him. Technically he was my father and I wished I could manage to call him by that title one day, but every time I thought about doing exactly that, I felt like gagging. This was one of those times.

"Mom called you before she passed away and told you about me. I wasn't the one to call you. *You* said you wanted to meet me, *you* said you wanted to get to know me. *You* were the one who invited me to come here, so I came. I came because I wanted to get to know you too, not just Chris. My freshman year, you said it should be just us for a while, said we should have the time to get to know each other, and I agreed because I was already nervous about how and why—"

"What are you getting at Zoe? I don't have time to go over the last three years."

"Don't put all this on my mom. She was your wife's friend and you both cheated behind her back. She didn't get pregnant on her own, and twice at that. I have no idea how you talked your wife into adopting Chris—I guess maybe she was really desperate to have a kid and forgave you for cheating on her—but I know the lies you told my mom to convince *her* to give him up."

He just stared at me, anger burning in his eyes. I rose from my seat and forced my hands to relax at my sides.

"At first, I thought you liked me," I said in a controlled voice. "I might have been a surprise that came, what, eighteen, nineteen years later, but you acted like you cared about it, cared about learning more about me. I thought we were getting closer. I never assumed I'd be like a daughter to you, but I thought we would have some kind of relationship." I gripped my bag tighter. Why did I think he'd interrupt me to say something to ease my hurt? Surely he could see it with his own eyes, but he said nothing. "Never mind. I already have a dad, right? I couldn't ask for a better one. You don't have to like me, I don't mind that at all"—that was something I no longer cared about—"but I want to get to know Chris. That's what I said from the very beginning. Other than my dad, I have no family. No one. He is my brother, not half-brother. He is my *brother*, and I want the chance to get to know him."

Something must have made it through because his eyes softened, the angry lines on his forehead slowly decreasing, at least I thought so. "We can't tell him about your mother." He sighed. "And Emily doesn't know about you. She won't handle it well if she learns that Chris knows she's not his mother."

My mom had been sleeping with Mark behind his wife's back when she got pregnant with Chris. Just two months before she passed away, she sat me down and told me all about their toxic relationship. She hadn't thought of it as toxic, but that was exactly what it had been. Initially, Mark wanted her to get an abortion, but when my mom refused to do so, Mark came up with a better idea. Since his wife couldn't have a baby because of her health issues, why not adopt the one Danielle was going to have and kill two birds with one stone? My mom didn't know what he had told his wife, but to her, he'd promised to leave the wife when the time was right. Only problem was, the right time never came. A scandal would affect his football career. His coach at the time was his wife's father, and surely he'd have done everything he could to get Mark fired if he learned that he was cheating on his daughter. If she didn't let them adopt the baby, he'd never acknowledge it, never see her again. However, if she did, they'd keep seeing each other behind the wife's back, and when he left her, they'd raise Chris together. I'm not sure if my mom was so naive because of her young age or because of love, but she went along with his plan.

"What do you mean we can't tell him about his mother?"

"I'll only agree to tell him you're his half-sister, and you'll wait for me to tell him, Zoe. You're not going to say one word to him without my knowing. That's the best you'll get from me."

Jesus. Was he actually negotiating with me about this?

"This is his last season, and I'm going to wait till it's over. I can't afford for him to lose his focus and screw up his future over this. If you care about him, you'll wait till the season ends."

I wanted to ask so many questions, but I simply nodded. I'd waited three years to meet him after all; a few more months was nothing.

When he didn't move his eyes off me, I gave him a tight nod and turned around to leave. The air inside the room was becoming stifling.

"One more thing, Zoe."

I stopped with my fingers on the handle.

"I don't want you to be friends with Dylan Reed."

My brows drew together in confusion and I faced him. "What? Why?"

"When I told him he could stay at the apartment, I thought you'd already moved out to live with your friend...what was her name...Kelly."

"Kayla."

He sighed. "Yes, her. Dylan is busy enough so I know he won't be around you, but I still want you to keep your distance since he is one of Chris's friends. I assume you'll be moving out soon anyway. I'm going to talk to Dylan about it, but if Chris or any of my players come around to the apartment again, I want you to stay away. Get out if necessary."

I blinked at him.

Fuck you.

I'd wait till the season was over before I told Chris anything, because it wasn't just my secret to tell and I wouldn't want to mess up his game. Mark would never be a father to me or anything even close to that, but he was Chris's. Beyond that, he was right—it'd do Chris no good if I blurted everything out right in the middle of football season. I was pretty sure that wouldn't make me his favorite person.

All that being said...Mark Wilson was the last person on earth who'd get to choose who I was friends with.

———

"Dad?" I whispered into my phone.

"Who is this stranger calling me 'Dad'?"

I wanted to talk, but I couldn't force the words out.

"Zoe? So you do remember that you have a dad, huh?"

I could only manage a whisper. "Yes, Dad."

His tone changed from playful to worried in a second. "Zoe? Are you there?"

Mumbling something unintelligible, I sniffled and pulled my legs up to my chest. Resting my forehead on my knees, I wiped a tear from my cheek before anyone around me could see I was crying.

My dad sighed into the phone and I closed my eyes tighter. Oh, how I wished he was right next to me and I could just disappear into his hug and never leave his side.

"Tell me what he did," he ordered with a slight edge to his voice.

"How do you know it's him?"

"Who else could manage to make you cry? Even when you were a toddler you didn't cry as much as you have these past few years. Tell me what he did now."

What was it that broke that tight hold when a girl heard her dad's voice, even over the phone, even when he was four hundred miles away? "I don't know what I'm supposed to do anymore, Dad." More hot tears made their way down my cheeks and onto my jeans.

"You're supposed to tell me what's going on, my pretty girl. I can't bear it when you call me crying like this."

"I'm sorry," I mumbled. "Did I interrupt your work?"

"Zoe..." Another long-suffering sigh. "You're never an interruption, and you barely call me as it is. Tell me what's going on so I can help you. That's all I want to do, I promise."

"I know, Dad." I hated how he always felt like he had to be careful when we were talking about this specific subject. I wished we didn't have to talk about it at all.

"Good," he grunted. "So tell me what's been happening and we'll figure it out together, just like we always do, all right?"

Bah. It was like there was a button, and more tears came out.

"I was in his office just a few minutes ago. He yelled at me, but that's not important—God knows it's not the first time—but the things he says...he doesn't even realize how much he is hurting me. He's making me feel like a dirty secret. I feel...wrong."

"Just wait a second—he's been yelling at you? Why is this the first time I'm hearing about this, Zoe? You promised you'd tell me everything. That was our agreement before you left."

I bit down on my lip to hold off on saying anything. I could picture him taking off his glasses and rubbing the bridge of his nose, just like he always did when he felt troubled.

"I don't like him yelling at you, let's get that out of the way first. He doesn't get to do that, do you hear me?"

"Yes."

"And I don't want to hear the words 'dirty secret' out of your mouth ever again. If I do, we'll have a problem. What's wrong with you? You're *my* girl, not his, not in the way that counts, anyway. You're everything I ever wanted to have in a daughter. I couldn't be more proud to be your dad."

"Dad," I groaned. "You're making it worse here." His words were a soothing balm to the fresh wounds Mark had left, and they made me emotional too, just in a different way. I finally raised my head and wiped my nose with the back of my hand.

"Nothing he does or says can make it otherwise. You've never been anything but a joy to me. I don't care if he happens to be your biological father, doesn't mean one thing to me. I raised you better than this, so why are you letting him hurt you?"

I couldn't talk through the lump in my throat, so my dad—my hero in everything—continued for me.

"You tried. *I* know you tried your best to get to know him, but if it's not working…maybe it's time to call it. You gave him the benefit of the doubt and waited for him to tell Chris about you. You did everything he wanted, and you're still doing it, so maybe it's time for you to do what you want, huh?"

"I can't tell him," I croaked out. "I promised Mark today that I wouldn't tell Chris anything before his last season is over, and I hate it because he's right, but he's been manipulating me for years now and I'm just heartbroken."

"Do you realize that's been his excuse for the last three years? And how hard is he trying to get to know you? Because I happen to know how many times he's promised to be somewhere and never showed up."

"He was at the apartment, last night, Dad."

"Who? Mark?"

"No…uh, actually, before I tell you about that…please don't be angry. I didn't tell you this because I wasn't sure how you'd react to me living with a stranger, but—"

"Living with a stranger? What are you talking about?"

"Well…apparently one of Mark's players had some trouble with his roommates and needed a place to stay. I hadn't told

Mark I wasn't moving in with Kayla yet, so...thinking I wouldn't be at the apartment...well, he offered it to Dylan."

Not a sound could be heard from the other end of the line. I'd known he would be pissed, which was one of the reasons I hadn't been calling him as much as I usually did. I hated having to lie to him.

"I've been living with him, with Dylan I mean, this last month, or maybe a bit longer," I rushed out.

Complete silence. Then, "A month, or maybe a bit longer."

Wincing, I tapped my forehead against my knees a few times. "Yeah, but he is a really good guy, Dad." I could've told him about the times I'd met him before he moved in, but I didn't think that would go well at all. Oh, and there was also the time where he held my hand and let me fall asleep on his shoulder when the electricity went out, but again, that wouldn't go over well.

"Zoe...do you *want* me to have a heart attack?"

"I'm serious, Dad. I was expecting him to be this..." Ah, how to explain Dylan to my dad who didn't even know I had a roommate, let alone a roommate who was a football player. "...this completely different person, but he's not." A small smile tipped my lips up. "I mean he *is* different, but in a good way. Actually, I think you'd really like him."

"I want you to move out, Zoe. I'm coming up there tomorrow and we'll find another apartment for you."

It sounded like everything I'd just said had fallen on deaf ears. I let out a heavy sigh. "No, you're not. I can't move out, at least not this year. I've been saving money, but not enough to move out yet."

"Stop being so stubborn and let me help you out. I'll pay your rent."

"No, Dad. I can't ask you to do that. You're still paying off Mom's hospital bills, and I'm not gonna add to that stress."

"You're killing me, here. Do you realize how helpless I'm feeling? You're not letting me do anything about that Mark. You expect me to sit back and be okay while I'm listening to you cry about things you keep from me, and you're not letting me help with your living situation—what the hell am I good for then?"

My eyes bulged. My dad never cursed. I wouldn't really label *hell* as a curse, but coming from his lips, it might as well have been a heated *fuck*.

"Dad...I..."

There was a long exhale. "How could you not tell me you've been living with a boy, Zoe?" Thinking of Dylan as a *boy* made my lips twitch. He was most definitely more than just a *boy*, and he probably had been for a very long time.

"If it was Jared or one of your friends, that would be something else, but a football player? Does he at least have a girlfriend, or maybe a boyfriend? How old did you say he was again?"

"He's a senior, and sorry for crushing your dreams, but I believe he is straight." Yeah, I had no doubt about that. "He is Chris's friend, actually. That's what I was go—"

"Is he the reason you haven't been calling me? I thought you'd been swamped with your classes, but are you and this guy—"

"Nope, you don't even need to finish that sentence. He is too busy to have a girlfriend since he is working hard to go pro, not that I would be interested if he wasn't busy, or that he'd be interested in me, but—"

"You're rambling. You like this boy, don't you?"

"No," I rushed out, a little too quickly. "No, I don't." So why did my voice come out so high-pitched? "We're actually becoming friends. Maybe you'll get to meet him if you come to visit. And yes, my classes are picking up. Assignments and the small shoots I'm doing for other students pretty much take up all my time. I've also been taking stock photos to sell online, you know, styling little scenes and selling them individually. My photography professor is going to let me know if any of her photographer friends need an assistant for any of their shoots, like weddings or things like that, since I'm interested in portraits more than anything else. So, yes, it's been really hectic, and that's the only reason I haven't had the time to call you. I don't want you to worry about me. I can handle it—I've been handling it. Still, I'm being serious when I say I'm going to move out of his apartment next year. I always thought it was the least he could do—letting me stay there, I mean—but yeah, I don't want any strings between us, not anymore. I feel like I owe him something, and I don't like it."

I was too late to realize my last sentence would set him off again.

"You don't owe him a single thing—not one thing, Zoe."

"I know that, I guess, but still, I don't want any strings. If he won't tell Chris by January or February... Anyway, I don't want to talk about Mark anymore. Dylan, on the other hand, I don't want you to worry about. Yes, he is my roommate, but we barely see each other. Trust me, he is even busier than me"—which was a shame—"so you have nothing to worry about. You know I'd tell you if he was making me uncomfortable or if we were seeing each other. I always tell you stuff like that, you know that."

"Would you? Because I've heard more than a few things you've been keeping from me in this phone conversation."

Touché.

Change the subject, Zoe.

"Uh...what I was trying to tell you earlier...last night two of Dylan's teammates came to the apartment. One of them was Chris, and I was there...and I didn't know what to do. I didn't even know where to put my hands. It was so awkward."

"You could've told him."

"Dad, I can't just come out and tell him out of nowhere. Do you forget how I reacted? He'd think I was crazy, and what was I supposed to say, anyway? *Oh, hello, I'm your long-lost sister you never knew you had. So, how have you been? Oh, also, the woman you know as your mom is actually not. Do you want to know about your real mother?* Besides, I might have stared at him a little too much yesterday, so he might already think I'm missing a few screws."

"If only your mom could've gotten in touch with him before she...then you wouldn't have to go through all this. She wanted to see him so much."

I could never tell him my mom was actually more excited about seeing Mark than anything else. She was hopeful, even.

I would never forget the day she told me Ronald Clarke wasn't my real father. She'd broken my heart that day, and if my dad—because whatever she said, he'd always be my dad, because blood doesn't make you family, not always—had been in the room with us, she'd have broken his heart too. Maybe she thought I'd be happy to hear that Mark had been the love of her life, and as good as Ronald had been to her, no one could take Mark's place, the rush of their relationship. Maybe she thought that.

After getting to know the guy, I couldn't have disagreed with her more.

There were a lot of things I was angry at my mom for, but it would hurt my dad if I voiced any of them. He loved her more than she loved either one of us.

I hated lying to him, but I couldn't talk about her. "Dad, I have to go. I have a class in ten, and I need to go find Jared before that, so..."

"Okay. Now that I know all your secrets, promise me you'll call more—and Zoe, no more secrets, okay?"

"Sure. I love you so much, Dad."

His voice was rough when he replied. "I love you, too, baby."

CHAPTER TWELVE

DYLAN

The bar was filled with college students who were out to celebrate the end of midterms. Some of those students were my teammates hell-bent on starting the bye week with a bang. A few of them rounded the pool tables, waiting for their turn, and a few of them were content with watching a heated game of beer pong between a few girls. Others were in front of the TVs watching a rerun of the previous week's games. It felt like the whole team was there. A loud cheer would go off somewhere in the bar and before you could understand which corner it came from, the sound was swallowed up by the loud crowd and the music Jimmy blasted from every corner of the place.

Pulling the lever, I filled a pint and handed it to Chuck, one of the waiters.

"Thanks, man," he yelled over the din before heading back out.

I tried to get in as many hours as humanly possible at Jimmy's place without messing up my training schedule in the process, because bartending helped me pay for everything the football scholarship didn't. Some nights I made enough that I could afford sending some of it back home, without my dad knowing about it, of course. The last thing he wanted was for me to worry about money problems.

Washing a shaker and the few glasses that were piling up behind the bar, I watched JP make his way over to me.

"When is your break again?" he asked, jumping onto a bar stool and eyeing Lindy, one of the other bartenders who was on with me that night.

"Missed me?"

Before he could answer, I made my way toward the two girls who had been waiting for me to come around.

"What can I get you, ladies?"

The blonde, who was wearing a low-cut red dress, leaned over the bar with a flirty smile, handing me the twenty that was tucked between two of her fingers. "Tequila shots, two rounds—and to chase those, I'll take your number."

I grinned and lined up their shots after checking their IDs. "Maybe next time."

I ignored how the redhead looked at me intently as she licked the salt on the back of her hand and making an even bigger show out of sucking one of the lime wedges I'd provided. As soon as they were done with their first round, I filled their second and left them to it.

"Let me know if you need anything else."

JP was still waiting for me when I got back. "You're the stupidest son of a bitch I know, you know that right?"

"So you keep telling me."

"What the hell is wrong with her?"

He tipped his head to the side, and I glanced at the girls, catching the blonde one sending me a wink.

"Nothing is wrong with her, but you know I haven't been a fan of random hookups since freshman year. Why does it surprise you now? Also, doing some random girl is the last thing on my mind right now. Weren't you there when we almost lost the last game to Colorado?"

"The keyword is *almost*. We won, didn't we?" He leaned over the bar and grabbed a handful of peanuts. "And it's more like you don't do *anyone* anymore. When was the last time you got laid?"

"If only you were this interested in—"

My eyes caught something just over JP's shoulder and I trailed off. The soft glow of the yellow and red lights hanging from the ceiling gave the bar a relaxed, welcoming look, and it made it possible for me to recognize Zoe walking in with a guy, her arm wound around his. It hit me like a fucking blow to the stomach.

JP followed my gaze and saw what had my attention. "Ah, that's Zoe isn't it? So, you won't do a random girl, but you'd do her, wouldn't you? I swear to God I've seen her before, but I can't remember where."

"You haven't," I muttered absentmindedly as my brows snapped together. "And we're friends—no one is going to do anyone."

She wasn't holding on to his arm anymore, but I watched her grip the guy's shoulders to get up on her toes and look around over the crowd. When she found what she was looking for, a big smile broke out on her face and she yelled something at the guy right before she started dragging him behind her toward the back of the bar. She must've been looking for her friend, because a girl slid out of a booth closer to the end wall where all the TVs were mounted and met them halfway. There were muted squeals and hugs and kisses. Was this the guy she was dating? I followed her with my eyes all the way to the booth and watched her settle in right next to the dick face.

"From what I can see, looks like she is definitely doing someone. Dude—hey! Did you hear what I said? Earth to Dylan?"

My fingers clutched the rag in my hand to the point where I

could feel my fingernails biting into my palm through the material. I forced myself to look away and focus on JP as every muscle in my body tensed.

"What did you want?" It came out harsher than I'd intended, so I rolled my shoulders to try to relax.

His eyebrow slowly rose up and he leaned back in his seat. Surprisingly, he chose not to push me further.

"I'm waiting for the guys." He paused, his eyes slightly narrowing. "Do we know who the guy is?"

"Probably her boyfriend. I don't know."

"Do we kill him? Or just break his legs as a warning?"

I laughed, but it felt foreign. "Neither. Trust me, he is a better option than what I was afraid of."

"What do you mean?"

Shrugging, I walked away to serve a few newcomers.

Raising his voice, JP kept at me. "So she's dating, huh? That means she really isn't dating you. That's interesting. Did you know about this or is it a surprise?"

I braced myself on the bar with one hand and knocked JP's away with the other when I saw he was reaching for the peanut bowl again. "What's so interesting about it? She's dating—everybody dates."

His shrug "Oh, nothing. Did you know about it?"

"Yeah, she said she had a boyfriend and it was complicated." I gritted my teeth and glared at my friend. "I guess it got uncomplicated. Don't you have something else to do? I'm trying to work here."

"I'm not holding you up. I'm a paying customer just like everyone else in here." He looked over his shoulder, and I couldn't stop myself from looking her way again. Zoe was up and leaning over the table to pull her friend up. All three of them made their way toward the small square section in front of the TVs that most of the customers saw as a makeshift dance floor.

There were maybe seven, ten people already dancing. "Despacito" by Fonsi started up for the thousandth time that night, yet somehow, it'd never sounded as good as it did just then.

"Who are we watching?" I hadn't even noticed Chris and Benji had joined us and were already looking over their shoulders until Benji spoke up. I was never going to live this down, yet that knowledge did nothing to pull my eyes away from the trio I was watching.

"Is that...your roommate?" Chris asked before JP or I could answer.

"In the flesh," JP answered for me.

"Nice ass, man," added Benji, our starting linebacker.

I shot him an irritated look, but his head was still turned away. All three of them were watching it unfold, and there was nothing I could do to stop it without looking like a complete asshole.

Zoe was slowly swaying her hips side to side, and her lips were mouthing the words to the song with Justin Bieber. Her girlfriend didn't look as enthusiastic about being on the dance floor, so Zoe grabbed her hands and forced her to move with her. She laughed and twirled under her friend's lifted arm and managed to pull her farther away from the edges of the tables. When the girl finally started to get into it, laughing along with her, a satisfied Zoe nodded and let go of her hands. Next thing I knew, the guy— her possible boyfriend—lined himself behind her and they started swaying together, all the while singing and smiling. Maybe I didn't like Fonsi and Justin Bieber all that much after all.

Then both girls started to dance around the guy, their fingers walking all over his chest, all three of them singing and laughing. Zoe stopped when she had her back against his chest, the other girl did the same when she was at his back, and then as if they'd timed it, they swayed their hips to the beat in small, barely there movements, mesmerizing everyone watching them—my horny friends weren't the only ones staring. They started to drop down, sliding their bodies all over him. Zoe lifted her hands and that simple white t-shirt that said *Live It Up* on the front rode up, displaying a few inches of the creamy skin of her stomach, not just to me, but to everyone who was watching them. My jaw clenched.

When Benji let out a groan, I hit my palm on the bar, hard enough to get the attention of my teammates and some of the other customers.

Their heads turned to me in surprise. "Can I get you guys something or are you just here for the show?" If my question had come out as a snarl, I had no control over it. "If you're not here to drink, move to one of the tables, or maybe just head out since we're pretty full tonight." JP opened his mouth, but I lifted a finger in his direction. "Don't even think about it."

He raised his hands in surrender but didn't quite manage to wipe the grin off his face. "This song is lit as fuck, that's all I was gonna say."

Chris eyed JP with interest but wisely didn't make any comments before turning his gaze on me. "When is your next break? We need to talk about our training schedule this week."

Benji pushed at Chris, fucking up his balance on the stool. "Dude, are you serious? It's the first day of the bye. Take a day off for fuck's sake."

I had to force my eyes to stay on Chris and not look for Zoe as the damn song finally ended and an old Shakira tune started up. I was too chickenshit to glance her way. I sighed and ran my hand over my head as I exhaled a big breath. "Tomorrow I'm sleeping in, man. I'll be in the weight room at nine AM, but not a second before that."

"So you're sleeping in one extra hour? That's not sleeping in, dude. You guys are crazy. I'm taking a day to myself and sleeping in the whole day. I'd like to think I deserve my beauty sleep."

JP snickered. "As if you have the balls. Coach would kick your ass straight to the end zone the second you showed up late to the meeting."

Benji told JP to shut up with a grumble and turned to me again. "At least tell me you're coming to the party they're having at the frat house."

"When is it? Tomorrow night?" I asked.

"I can't believe I'm friends with you three. How do you not know about tonight's party man?"

"Dylan, three pints—stat!" Chuck yelled out the order then disappeared back into the crowd.

I raised my hands up. "As you can see, I'm not going anywhere. I'll be here every night this week. I need to pick up more hours."

Benji got up with a huge sigh. "Okay, I'm done. You're killing my buzz like no other. I'm leaving." He looked at Chris and JP. "You guys coming or are you gonna hang out with this loser?"

Chris was the first one to follow his lead and get up. "I'd rather have stale beer at the frat than go home tonight. I'm gonna crash at Mandy's place." He rapped his knuckles on the bar top. "I'll meet you in the morning?"

I finished filling the pints and placed them on a tray, ready to be taken out to the floor. "You're on again with Mandy? When the hell did that happen?"

"We're not *on* on, exactly."

"What do you call crashing at her place? Don't tell me you're gonna sleep on her couch when you're there."

He gave me a one-shoulder shrug and his mouth curved into a satisfied smirk. "Just testing the waters to see if it's time to be on again. See you tomorrow, man." The relationship he had with his dad, our coach, was strained at best, and whenever he felt like he needed space, he was never in need of a place to crash.

Chris was the quiet one in our group. He was the team

captain, a good leader out on the field, but when it came to socializing with people, he preferred to stay back. There was always a throng of girls following him like lost puppies, dying to get the quarterback's attention, but he was more like me on that front than JP. However, unlike me, he didn't mind random hookups, but even that only happened during the off-season, not when our future hinged on how we did this season with all the eyes we had on us, not to mention the combine was right around the corner.

"Yeah, see you." Chris followed after Benji, who was chatting with some of our teammates on his way out, leaving me alone with JP. "What?" I asked.

"Just one question."

I sighed. "What is it?"

"Do you like this girl?" He pointed over his shoulder with his thumb.

"We're just friends, JP. Not sure how many times I need to tell you that."

"Yeah, sure. I get that, and friends are good, but..." He hesitated. "Trust me...not trying to get all sappy on your ass, but you deserve to have some fun, man. If not now, when will you? You know what they say: work hard, play harder. If you want her..." Wisely, he left it at that. "Just think about it, that's all I'm saying."

"I guess you tuned out the part where I said she has a boyfriend." I neglected to mention that I was in fact very interested in Zoe Clarke and was only waiting for the right time to make my move, a time when she was unattached and uncomplicated—though maybe I was already too late after all.

"Like I said, we can always get rid of him or break his legs. Either way—"

"Dylan, I could use some help over here!" Lindy sing-songed as she put her hand on my arm and winked at my grinning friend.

"Don't worry about it, okay?" I said to JP. "I'll see you

tomorrow morning. Don't make me come drag your ass out of whichever bed you're planning on falling into tonight."

"I keep telling you, I should be your role model." He sighed. "Yeah, yeah. Fine. See you around. I'm going to find myself a Mandy for the night."

"Don't do anything I wouldn't do."

"Dude, that ship sailed a long time ago."

Putting Zoe out of my mind, I laughed and went to Lindy's side, helping her with the orders.

"You should take your break as soon as it slows down a little," I said loud enough so she could hear me as we worked side by side. "Talk to your little bugger before he goes to sleep." Lindy was a single mom who left her three-year-old at home with her dad when she came to work. She called her son on almost every break instead of smoking or shooting the shit with the waiters and waitresses.

"What time is it?" she asked, her hands busy with shaking a cocktail. Most of the customers at Jimmy's went for cheap beers since the vast majority were college students, but there were a few fancy ones who went for cocktails every now and then.

"It's past nine."

She stopped with the shaking, poured the pink drink into a martini glass, and garnished it with a maraschino cherry. "Yeah, he's probably in bed, waiting for me to call. Thanks, Dylan."

I nodded and just as I was taking another order, my eyes found their way back to Zoe again, still dancing. At least I couldn't spot the dick face anymore, but how long was she gonna dance anyway? Wasn't she tired yet? And wasn't she supposed to be shy? How did she look perfectly fine dancing in front of all these people when she couldn't even look me in the eye for more than a few seconds?

All of a sudden, I noticed a hand sneak around her waist. A

growl escaped my lips and a few of the guys sitting in front of me gave me strange looks. I offered them a chin lift. "What's up?"

They just shook their heads and got back to their loud conversation.

I glanced past them again. What the hell did I expect from my friend? Of course he was there; of course he was talking to Zoe. She smiled at something JP said and took a discreet step back, dislodging his arm without much effort. JP leaned down to say something in her ear and when he was done, he patted her head twice, said something to her girlfriend, and walked away from them. Just as he was about to exit the bar, he turned and hit the door open with his back, giving me a thumbs up and a shit-eating grin right before he disappeared.

It was a done deal—he had basically given me permission to kick his ass the next time we were on the field. He must've known I wouldn't like his hands on my friend...around her waist, touching her, feeling her body.

"Dude!" Lindy shouted from the other end of the bar, and I forced myself to look at her. Making big eyes at me, she motioned toward the mug in my hand, which was currently overflowing with beer.

"Shit!" I shook my hand and cleaned the mug with a rag before handing it off.

"What's wrong with you tonight?" Lindy asked, sidling up to me.

"Nothing."

Trying not to react to the eyes I could feel on me, I finished the order and started on another one. My curiosity got the better of me again, and I glanced Zoe's way. All three of them were watching me. The guy I'd had my eyes on ever since they walked in leaned toward Zoe and got her attention. Either they couldn't hear each other from a few inches away and the dick face had to lean even closer to her ear—which I thought was complete bull-shit—or he didn't like Zoe's attention on me.

Cursing myself for tensing up when I noticed him pull back and tuck a strand of hair behind her ear, I got back to my work.

Not even a few minutes had passed when the guy I'd just served a beer got off the stool, and suddenly I was staring at Zoe's smiling face.

"Hey stranger, what are you doing here?" She looked around. "Are you trying to impress someone?"

There was a small smile on her lips when our eyes met. It took her only a few seconds to hide her gaze from me and get busy with propping her elbows up on the bar. Was she surprised to see me there? Maybe annoyed? Happy? Was the light flush on her cheekbones for me, or was it residue from whatever the hell the dick face had been whispering in her ear? Or maybe she was flushed because of all the dancing she had done. She was still a little breathless, after all.

There was no trace of a smile on *my* lips when I managed to force the words out. "What does it look like?"

She looked confused at my tone and her smile faltered, the corners slowly dipping down as she blinked at me.

"Is everything okay?"

I swallowed my annoyance and rolled my neck before taking a deep breath. All I could smell was alcohol, and underneath it, a whiff of fucking berries.

Keep it cool, man. She didn't do anything.

I exhaled before I opened my mouth to speak again. "I'm sorry. Long day. What do you mean trying to impress someone?"

"You're behind the bar."

I looked down at myself and around me. "Yeah, I work here. That's how bartending works. You stay behind the bar and serve drinks."

"No you don't," she fired back.

"Yeah, that's pretty much it."

"No, I mean, bartending?" She looked taken back. "You're really working right now?"

"Yup. What did you think I was doing?"

Her teeth lightly grazed her bottom lip. I watched her mouth move as she said something, but I was too busy admiring her lips and missed it completely.

"What?"

She leaned forward an inch or two and yelled a little louder. "I said, I thought you were trying to impress someone! You know how attractive bad boys are to girls, and you're a football player on top of that. Basically, double the trouble." She widened her eyes. "And bartenders tend to be—not that *I'm* specifically saying you're hot or anything, but I thought you were just back there—"

Looking over her shoulder, I met the dick face's eyes. Both he and the other girl were watching Zoe and me. It was his own idiocy that he'd let her come to me, so why should I be the one to stay away? She was my roommate, my friend, after all. *Fuck him.*

I leaned on the bar, bringing us closer, and rested my arms right next to hers. Only inches separated us. If she moved, my skin would drag against hers. She stopped rambling and took in the repositioning of my arms. Then, knowingly or unknowingly, she shifted in her seat, moving her delectable little butt from right to left.

"Zoe," I said, my voice lower since we were now closer. "You're rambling again. It's too cute, and it's completely okay if you think of your friend as hot. I think you're hot, too."

My arm brushed hers when Lindy walked behind me and I was forced to move forward another inch. She completely ignored the fact that I'd just called her hot—or maybe she simply thought I was joking—and leaned forward as if she couldn't help herself. The movement was barely perceptible, and I would have bet she hadn't noticed it herself.

"I didn't say you were hot."

"I'm pretty sure you just did."

"No," she said slowly. "I just meant they tend to hire good-looking guys so that—" She let out a breath and changed the subject. "I didn't know you worked on top of everything else you did. Your schedule is crazy. I'm just surprised, that's all."

I raised an eyebrow. "I specifically remember telling you I wasn't rich."

"Yeah, but I didn't think you...I just didn't think, apparently. You know me and my tendency to stereotype football players. Most people usually think they get everything handed to them, and apparently I'm one of those people, but...I like that you're working." She huffed. "You're a really..." She scrunched up her nose then shook her head. "Never mind."

I leaned closer and my forearm grazed hers again. We stayed skin to skin. She couldn't keep her eyes away. I would've loved for her to finish her sentence, but there was something else I wanted to know more.

I turned my head a fraction, bringing my lips closer to her cheek area—the cheek her boyfriend's fingers had brushed only minutes before. "So that's your boyfriend, huh? I don't think he likes that you're over here talking to me." The bastard was still watching, and it was starting to get on my nerves.

Her head snapped up and her eyebrows drew together. "What? Where?"

I pulled back. "Your boyfriend," I repeated, motioning to the guy with my chin. At that moment, his arm was casually draped over the booth and he was chatting with the girl sitting across him instead of staring at us. "The one you've been dancing with since you walked in." I turned my eyes on Zoe. "And I thought you were shy, Zoe—seemed like it since you can't even manage to look into my eyes for more than a few seconds—but that girl dancing up there didn't look all that shy."

Slowly she turned back to me. My muscles were tensing up again. Why was I getting so worked up over her dancing with her fucking boyfriend? It wasn't like I didn't know she had someone, and I should've been happy that it was just a student. I straightened away from Zoe, deciding to actually do the job I was getting paid to do and help Lindy with the customers.

After I served a few, I checked to see if Zoe had left, but she was still sitting there waiting for me, her eyes tracking my movements.

I found myself back in front of her. I was being a dick without meaning to. "Can I get you and...your friends anything?" I asked a little loudly so I wouldn't have to lean in again.

Her frown got deeper and she scooted forward in her seat. Her lips parted, but nothing came out. Then she nodded. "Yeah, I'll have a pint of whatever you have on tap and a Corona, please."

I returned her nod with a curt one and served my roommate. Plunking the pint in front of her, I reached down for a bottle of Corona. Her left hand closed around the handle of the pint and she reached for the bottle with the other.

"Can you carry them yourself or should I have—"

What she said was not what I was expecting to hear at all. "That's not my boyfriend, Dylan. He is my friend, Jared, and just so you know, shy doesn't mean I can't function or dance with my friends or just *be* around people. I only get shy and awkward around certain people, and you happen to be one of them, that's all."

I have no idea if she chose to tell me all that in pretty much one breath with a lowered voice so I might not hear half of it or if she thought she'd be gone before I could piece it together, but thank fuck I got it the first time.

Since her hands were full, she didn't manage to escape as

quickly as she hoped. Before she could hop off the stool, I put my hand on her wrist and stopped her forward movement.

Stuck sitting sideways, she stilled and looked at me.

My hand was still around her wrist, and this time I didn't hesitate to lean in closer and pull her to me at the same time. I paused when my lips were almost touching the shell of her ear. "Say that again?" I asked in a low, deep voice.

Oh, I had heard her perfectly fine the first time, but I still felt the need to hear her say it again.

She tilted her head enough so I could hear her. I stayed exactly where I was, breathing in her scent. "I'm shy around—" she started haltingly.

"Not that part. The one before that."

"Oh, that's Jared. He's not my boyfriend, just Jared, my friend," Zoe repeated. I closed my eyes in relief. When I opened them again, I noticed Zoe's white-knuckle grip on the bottle of Corona. Because of the position we were in, she had no choice but to speak right into my ear where I could feel her warm breath on my skin. "He is my friend, and he also happens to be gay, not that it should matter."

That tight feeling that had suddenly appeared in my stomach like I'd been gut-punched when I saw her touching the dick face loosened at her words. I shouldn't have been happy to hear that; it should've made no difference, but it still did. I wasn't prepared to see her get close to another guy. Knowing about it was evidently different than seeing it with my own eyes. Any other time, maybe it would've been all right, but that night, I didn't like it.

I took a deep breath and closed my eyes. Her berry scent was going to kill me from that close. That first night, when her towel did me a favor and unwound itself, she had smelled like berries, too, and since I was her roommate, I had the privilege—or perhaps the burden—of knowing that it was her body wash and not her shampoo. The smell always lingered after she took a shower, reaching to my room and distracting me to no end.

I'd known from the very beginning that she couldn't just be my friend, even if I'd let her think she could, and seeing her with another guy had just cemented that.

Zoe cleared her throat and pulled back from our little private bubble. Only then did I notice the touch of color on her cheeks. When she spoke, her voice was thick. She was affected by me, by having me close. I knew she was—the sparkle in her eyes, the color on her cheeks, the way she tried to hold her breath gave her away. If not, if I was wrong, I was screwed.

"You look beautiful," I said honestly. "You always look beautiful, but tonight you look happier. I like your smile tonight. I always like it when you smile, Flash," I said sincerely.

At my words, her eyes jumped to mine, surprised, unsure. Her lips twitched then finally tipped up in a shy but beautiful smile. "I like your smile, too...really like it."

Drawing farther back, I let go of her arm and looked at her face. Of course, *she* looked anywhere but my eyes.

"Say hi to your friends for me then. Maybe introduce us before you guys leave? It should slow down here soon enough."

She swallowed and nibbled on her bottom lip. "Are you okay, Dylan? I haven't seen you around lately. We're good, right?"

I had no idea how to behave around her anymore, but we were good. "It's always like this during football season, all the practice hours, training, classes, plus midterms. I was swamped, but things should calm down for a week at least. I'm here at night since it's bye week, but you'll see me around."

"Okay." She smiled and nodded. Just before she attempted to get down, she looked over shoulder at her friends for a few seconds then faced me again. "Later, we can watch a movie maybe? Netflix and chill like the cool kids are doing?"

My brows almost reached my hairline. "Netflix and chill?"

When she realized what she'd said, she looked horrified. "No! I mean, I know what that means, and I didn't mean it that way. I meant literally. We could pick a movie and chill out, not pick a movie and have sex while said movie is playing, not chill in that way, not Netflix and—" She let out a little growl. "Forget about Netflix. Fuck Netflix. The last time we tried, your friends came over and we couldn't, so maybe when you come home tonight we can watch a movie?"

I gave her a small smile, thinking maybe it was wrong of me to enjoy yanking her chain so much. "I'm sorry, Zoe. My shift ends pretty late tonight. Maybe we can do that another time?"

Her smile disappeared from her face. "Yeah, sure. Of course. You're probably meeting up with your friends after this anyway."

I touched her arm again before she could slip away, because apparently I couldn't help myself. "Only because it's Pint Night here, and I'm afraid I'm not going anywhere until last call, which is at two AM."

"Oh. Yeah, that's late. Like you said, maybe another time. See you back at the apartment then?"

"I'll see you at home." I liked it better when we called it home, like she had a few seconds before. "I'd love to meet your friends," I repeated before she could leave.

Her smile came back. "Sure. Actually, I think you already know Kayla—you guys kinda dated—and Jared is a fan, so he'd like that too. We'll come over"—she looked around—"when it's not so crowded. I already took too much of your time, I'm sorry."

What the fuck?

"Wait a second—what did you say? You think I dated your friend?"

"I don't think—I mean, she said you guys..."

I glanced back at the booth with a frown. The one she called Jared was openly staring at us, but this time the girl across from him smiled and waved at me a little sheepishly. I narrowed my eyes, looked at her a little closer, and...yeah, maybe she looked familiar, but I was pretty sure I hadn't dated her.

"I'm pretty sure I didn't date your friend, Zoe." I took another quick look. "What did you say her name was again?"

"Kayla."

"Yeah, you're wrong."

"She said you guys met freshman year—well, she was a freshman, so you were a sophomore."

I squinted and looked harder, trying to remember why she looked familiar. "Was she by any chance a redhead?"

"Yeah. Her boyfriend doesn't like the red, so she dyes it brown now."

A smile spread across my face. "Okay, I remember her." I lifted my hand and waved back at her friend. Focusing back on Zoe, I said, "Though, just to make it clear, we never actually dated, just went out with friends a couple times, that's it. I wouldn't call it dating."

"That's what Kayla said, too. Anyway, it'd be okay if you had dated."

I nodded slowly. "It would be okay, but we didn't."

She tucked her hair behind her ear and looked down at the beer bottle in her hand. I watched her thumb slowly wipe the condensation away.

Back and forth.

Back and forth.

I leaned down so I could meet her eyes. "Stop by before you guys leave, okay? We'll talk. Keep me company. Let me see my friend for a while longer."

"Okay."

I felt relieved.

With a half wave, she hopped off and carried the drinks back to her friends. On her way over there, she turned around once, drinks still held high, eyes sparkling, and gave me the biggest smile—causing my own lips to twitch in amusement—then turned back and kept walking. Kayla took the Corona, and the friend who was definitely not the boyfriend took the beer from her hand before she could sit down and poured it into their mugs.

A loud cheer erupted from the group at the beer pong table, and I remembered that I had a job to do.

The orders had slowed down, so I shouted at Lindy. "I have this. Go take your break."

She groaned and pulled at my shoulder to give me a peck on the cheek as she passed me on her way to the door that led to the kitchen.

I spent a few minutes talking to the guys sitting at the front about how the season was shaping up until Lindy came back.

When I looked over to my right where Zoe's booth was, she was the first to realize they'd been caught staring at me and quickly looked away.

CHAPTER THIRTEEN

DYLAN

Jimmy's was only a few minutes away from the apartment so I made it back around two-thirty AM. The last thing I expected or wanted to see when I started climbing up the stairs was Ms. Hilda.

"Oh, Dylan, I thought you were someone else."

"Is everything okay, Ms. Hilda? It's pretty late to be up."

She waved me off. "I always have trouble sleeping at night. When I heard footsteps, I wanted to see who was coming in at this hour. Miss Clarke has a visitor tonight, you know."

My jaw clenched and I stilled. "A visitor?"

She frowned and looked toward our apartment door. "Yes, her friend. That one likes older boys. You see how late it is, and he is still in there—as if she could fool me by tiptoeing past my door."

Maybe her friends had come back with her? Offering a tight-lipped smile and a quick nod, I took my key from my pocket so I could get in and see it for myself.

"Dylan? Did you say your father was a plumber?" She stopped me before I could make it to the door.

"Yes, he is." I shifted from one foot to the other.

"I have this little problem in the kitchen—do you think you can take a look?"

"Ms. Hilda, I'd love to help, but I'm just coming back from work and I'm wiped. I'm not any good at it, but I'll take a look at it tomorrow for you."

She huffed and lost the semi-pleasant look on her face.

"I'll hold you to that young man."

When I turned the key and stepped inside, I was expecting to see the worst. What I found, however, was a sleeping Zoe balled up on the couch. Other than a lone scented candle burning on the kitchen island, none of the lights were on. After locking the door, I dropped my bag and made my way toward her.

She was sleeping with her hands under her cheek, her legs tucked up to her stomach. Her hair was hanging over her shoulder in a messy braid, covering half of her face.

For a second I'd believed what that nosy old woman had said. For a second I'd been scared of what I'd find when I stepped through the door.

A few seconds ticked by as I watched her sleep, trying to decide what to do. Rubbing my eyes, I kneeled right next to her. She was wearing the same outfit she'd had on earlier, the only difference was that she had changed out of her tight black jeans in favor of leggings.

Hesitating only for a moment, I reached up and closed my hand over her shoulder, gently sliding it down her arm and back up again. "Zoe, wake up." She didn't, not even a stir. "Zoe?" I let go of her shoulder and, as gently as possible, brushed her hair back over her shoulder to see her full face. She looked so peaceful.

Her phone, which was lying face down on the coffee table, pinged with a new text. It wasn't my best moment, but I flipped it over and checked who it was from. I couldn't see the contents of the message, but I saw the sender's name on the screen: Mark Wilson.

My hands formed into fists all on their own. It could've been anything. He was a family friend, after all. He wasn't there; Ms. Hilda had been wrong. She was wrong. Zoe was living in his apartment. It was nothing.

Turning the phone face down, I reached out for Zoe again. "Zoe, you need to wake up." Her eyes fluttered but didn't open fully. She released a small moan and wiggled her hips to settle deeper into the cushions. I brushed the short strands of hair away from her forehead, my fingertips lingering. That did the trick, and her eyes slowly opened.

A small frown filled her face, and she seemed confused to find me next to her.

"Baby, you should go to bed," I whispered.

"Dylan?" Her voice was still groggy with sleep. She rubbed at her eyes and looked around the dark apartment. "What time is it?"

She covered a big yawn with the back of her hand.

"Close to three."

"Oh."

"You want me to help you to your room?"

A quick look, there and gone.

"Oh, no. I'm fine, but thank you."

I rose and she pushed herself up to a sitting position. She still seemed confused.

Pushing my hands into my pockets, I asked, "Are you okay?"

Covering another yawn, she looked up at me. "Yeah, I must've fallen asleep after I got back from the bar."

I nodded. "Well, I'm gonna head to my room." I was only at the mouth of the hallway when she called my name.

"Dylan?"

When I turned around, she was up on her feet, her laptop now closed and clutched against her chest.

"Are you going to bed?"

"Yeah, I'm wiped."

"Oh. Okay. Good night then."

"Is everything all right?"

"Yeah, sure."

"Zoe, what's wrong?"

I watched her fingers curl around her computer, her grip tight. "Nothing. Nothing is wrong. Everything's fine. I just... If you weren't sleepy, I thought maybe we could watch something together? But you're wiped, so it's okay. You did say you were gonna get in late, so I shouldn't have waited, but just in case you're hungry or anything, I got you a cheeseburger from In-N-Out. Jared and I went there after the bar so I thought I should bring you back something since you said cheeseburgers were your favorite. You got me pizza last time, so I thought you could—"

"Zoe, stop." I walked back to her and stopped when the couch was the only thing standing between us. "You fell asleep waiting for me?"

"I..." She lifted her shoulders in a shrug. "I thought maybe you wouldn't be able to sleep when you got back and we could spend some time together maybe—if you wanted to, that is...you know, because we didn't see each other all that much these last few days with midterms and your games, and Jared thought I should maybe get—"

"So, it wasn't you who wanted to buy me a cheeseburger, it was Jared. Remind me to thank him the next time I see him." It wasn't a question, but she took it as one and shook her head.

"Fine, I lied. *I* thought maybe you'd be hungry when you got back. I was trying to be a good friend."

I tilted my head. "Were you watching a movie before you fell asleep?"

She looked away, a little too quickly. "No."

That was a big fat yes if I ever heard one.

I took her in. Even if it was only because she was scared, if she wanted to spend time with me, how could I say no? It wasn't like we spent much time together, and she'd brought me a cheeseburger—it would be a waste to not eat it.

"What are watching?"

The corners of her mouth slowly tilted up, and her smile got so big that she had to bite down on her lip to keep it contained. "You're not sleepy? Tired?"

"I'm tired, but I'm good for another hour or so."

"What do you wanna watch?" She bent down and put her laptop back on the coffee table.

I forced my eyes away from her ass as she tinkered with the thing. "I'll let you choose."

"How about...*Speed*? Or *Eagle Eye*?"

"*Speed*? What was that again?"

"Oh, it's an old-ish movie with Keanu Reeves and Sandra Bullock. *Eagle Eye* has Shia LaBeouf and Michelle Monaghan."

"You have a thing for old movies, huh?"

"Old-*ish* movies. They're not that old. So, which one do you want to watch?"

"I might not be able to make it to the end, but let's go with *Speed* tonight. We'll do *Eagle Eye* next time?"

That smile again. "Sounds good. Okay, you sit down." She came to my side and pushed me around and down on the couch. "I'll go get your cheeseburger and fries."

"What did I do to deserve the fries on top of the cheeseburger?"

She headed toward the kitchen but looked over her shoulder when she spoke. "Who would buy a cheeseburger and not get fries? One isn't complete without the other. I also hope you don't mind sharing because I'm not gonna be able to stay away from the fries. I'm bound to steal a few, but the burger and soda are all yours."

Coming back with a tray, she handed it to me then leaned over her laptop to start the movie.

Giving me a look, she sighed. "You don't have to do this, you know that, right? I don't want to keep you up. I can see you're tired, Dylan."

"I'm fine, Flash. Relax. If I fall asleep, I fall asleep. It's okay. As long as you don't draw a penis on my face, we should be safe."

She laughed. "Promise. Did your teammates do that?"

I patted the seat next to me and she took it without hesitation. "Not to me specifically, but I've seen it done." Pressing play, she started the movie and settled back. I grabbed the cheeseburger, took a big bite, and groaned. "I didn't even realize I was starving, thank you." When she didn't reach for a fry, I offered one to her myself.

She took it from me with the tips of her fingers. "Thank you."

"You can have the Coke, too. I don't do soft drinks."

She took a bite and scrunched up her nose. "I don't do soft drinks, either. That's the only healthy choice I make in my life, I think. I don't care for the taste anyway."

A few minutes into the movie, my food was polished off and Zoe had only stolen a few of my fries. Each time she did, she gave me a shy smile and quickly focused back on the movie playing in front of us.

Fifteen minutes in, I was already fading. When I chanced a look at Zoe, I realized we'd ended up with an empty seat between us. Might as well have been an entire football field. She was curled up into herself, both her feet planted on the couch, chin resting on her knees, arms hugging her legs.

My lips twitched. "Which movie were you watching before?"

Out of the corner of my eye, I could see her considering

whether or not to give me an answer, her teeth nibbling on her bottom lip.

"Come on, tell me."

In the end, she decided against it. "I rather not say."

This time, I laughed and she joined me. It felt good, just...*being* with her.

Before the movie was over, we were both fast asleep on opposite sides of the couch. When I woke up early in the morning, she was sprawled half on top of me and I had my arms wrapped around her, holding her as close as possible. We had both moved in our sleep and met in the middle, apparently.

Never in my life had I held someone through the entire night. Snuggling, yes, but even that only lasted for a short while. I closed my eyes and dropped my head on hers, inhaling her scent and just feeling her chest rise and drop against me. Trying my best not to jolt her, I grabbed the light blanket from the back of the couch and pulled it over us. Zoe shifted, and I froze. Then she snuggled even closer and rubbed her face against my neck, her parted lips grazing my skin.

Awareness flooded my body. All of a sudden, I was wide awake, and so were all my body parts.

I sat on that couch for another thirty minutes, just holding on to her, memorizing how she felt in my arms. When I had to get up and leave, I gently slid out from under her and tucked the blanket more securely around her, hoping it'd keep her warm, though not as warm as I could.

CHAPTER FOURTEEN

ZOE

We had just finished our photography class in the lab and I was packing away my lenses when our professor, Jin Ae, caught my attention and said, "Zoe and Miriam, I need you two to stay behind, please."

When I was done packing up my bag, she was still answering questions from other students.

Miriam met my eye. "You know what this is about?"

I shook my head. "No idea."

"Maybe the assignment?"

I gathered all my equipment up and carried it over to Miriam's station. "Probably."

After everyone left the room, Jin Ae came over to us.

"Okay girls, are you two available to travel for a weekend?"

Miriam and I glanced at each other with a frown. "Ummm, I should be," Miriam replied, still unsure.

Jin Ae looked at me. "And you, Zoe?"

"I'm sorry, I have a job scheduled this weekend, and I don't think I can cancel it." Not if I didn't want to lose the job and the money that would come with it.

"It's not for this weekend. Are you available next weekend?"

I thought about it for a second. "Yeah, I think I can do that. Is it a job you want us to do?"

"No, not a job, exactly. The school paper needs two students to follow the football team around at their away game next weekend. Their usual guys can't make it, so Mr. Taylor asked me if I could recommend anyone."

Football team? Following them? I didn't think that was a good idea at all, and I'd have bet Mark wouldn't think so either.

"That's a great opportunity, thank you so much for asking me!" exclaimed Miriam.

I couldn't exactly share her joy, though she was right—it was a great opportunity. "Uh...what are we supposed to do exactly?" I asked. "To be honest, I'm not sure I'd be any good at sports photography. I've never tried it—too much movement, not to mention I know practically nothing about football."

Even if I wanted to go, I didn't think Mark would appreciate me being around him or around any of his players, Chris in particular.

"This will be great for both of you," Jin Ae continued. "If you have no other objections than not knowing about sports, Zoe, I'd like you to take a chance and accept the assignment. The school paper is planning on writing an article, and I didn't get all the details, but I know they need photos of the players and the coaching staff, and not just when they're on the field. You'll need to be around them for the remainder of the time, too—at the hotel, on the plane, at practice, and I think even at the meetings."

Maybe it would be okay if I asked Mark first, but I'd been avoiding all his calls and texts since our last conversation in his office, so asking him anything wasn't something I was interested in doing.

Miriam was the first to speak up after she clapped her hands twice and did a small jump in place. "Okay. I like the challenge. I won't disappoint you."

Geez. You'd think we'd been invited to photograph the royal wedding with the smile she was beaming—not that photographing however many football players would be bad, especially if I could take a few (or a hundred) shots of Dylan while he was working out and get away with it by saying, *Oh, I'm having a terrible time looking at your half-naked body, but...it's for the paper, so what can I do? I'll just have to suffer through it.*

Jin Ae nodded at Miriam then turned her expectant eyes to me.

"Sure. I'll be there, too. Thank you."

"Good." Turning on her heels, she walked back to her desk to grab her phone. "I told Mr. Taylor I'd let him know after class, and I'll text him your information so he can get in touch to coordinate everything. He'll want to talk to you sometime this week, so make sure to be available so he can let you know exactly what he wants you to do while you're with the team."

"Is it just the two of us or will someone else be going as well?" I asked.

"I think another student will be joining to conduct the interview part of the piece. You'll have to discuss the details with Mr. Taylor when you talk to him."

"Okay, one question: do we know where they're going? For the game I mean."

Jin Ae put her phone away and sat down in front of her laptop. "I think he mentions the location in the email, let me check."

"Good question," Miriam whispered as we waited in the doorway.

"Arizona. It says the game will be in Tucson, Arizona."

"You LUCKY BITCH. If I knew this kind of thing would happen, I'd take up photography too. Can you find out if they need someone to sketch the players? Oil them up? I can do that too—both, if needed."

"I'm pretty sure there are no oils involved, but for you...I'll ask. I wouldn't get my hopes up though."

"Bitch," Jared muttered.

As soon as I'd gotten out of class, I'd called my dad to let him know I'd be seeing him in eight or nine days. When that conversation was over, my next call had been to Kayla because the three of us were supposed to meet for lunch. The moment she answered, I knew she wouldn't make it, which wasn't surprising anymore. So, that left me and Jared.

I stabbed my fork into my salad and gave him a long look. "I don't think it'll be as glamorous as you think it will. I'm gonna have to do my best to stay out of Mark's way."

"So? Just don't tell him you're coming along. Crisis averted."

"Yeah? And how exactly do you suggest I get on the plane without him noticing? Or let's say I managed that—how am I supposed to make sure he doesn't see me at the hotel *or* on the field as I'm trying to photograph his players?"

He took a bite of his sandwich and nodded. "You make a good point."

"Yeah. Still, it wasn't my idea, so it should be okay, and anyway, I promised not to tell Chris anything. If we need to take any one-on-one shots, I'll make sure Miriam covers Chris, that way Mark can't complain any more than he probably already will."

"If he says anything, please don't just sit there and take it."

I dropped my fork and rubbed my forehead. "If he was anybody else, yeah, I would have stopped taking shit from him a long time ago, but he is my..."

"Your dad—yeah, I know."

"I wouldn't call him that exactly."

"I don't know what your mom was thinking when she called to let him know he had a daughter. Didn't she already know what kind of guy he was?"

Yup. I was the surprise Mark never wanted. "She loved him, which is really weird, and bad. Her last few weeks were really bad. I think she just wanted Mark to come visit her, and I was the excuse. She was my mom, and I loved her, but at the same time, I'm so pissed at her, too." I shook my head, still having trouble believing everything she'd told me. "I can't believe she gave up her son like that."

Jared took a swig from his water bottle, his eyes calculating. "I bet it was all Mark talking her into it. We know for sure he is the father, right? Your father, I mean."

"Yeah, unfortunately. He wanted a DNA test after he got the call from my mom."

"Well, still...that doesn't mean he gets to jerk you around."

Picking my fork back up, I ate a few more bites before answering him. "I know it doesn't, and he won't get to anymore. I thought we could have some kind of a relationship, but I'm over it now. It was just about Chris when I first came here. I never thought it'd take him three years or that things would end up this way. Every time I got a wild hair and decided I should just stop Chris on the way to one of his classes, I got scared and Mark got all...*I want to get to know you, Zoe. I want us to get closer.*" I huffed and snorted. "I'm so stupid. Time is up now. Chris is graduating this year. I'm going to wait until the season ends, not because Mark told me to, but because I think that's best for Chris...and maybe the combine, but I don't think I can wait that long. The Mark thing is done though. I'm not answering his calls—we have nothing to talk about."

"Screw him. He's a bastard anyway. Who sleeps with his

wife's friend, gets her pregnant, and then convinces the wife it's a good thing because they can finally have a kid? You're better off."

"Yeah."

My appetite gone, I sipped my orange juice then cleared my throat.

"Let's forget about Mark. What are we going to do about Kayla?"

This time it was Jared's turn to sigh heavily and stop eating. "I called her last night, just a random call to say I missed her, and her shit of a boyfriend answered, told me she was busy and I shouldn't bother her that late. It was only nine o'clock, for goodness' sake. I bet she was right there and the fucker didn't even let her pick up her own phone."

"Do you think she'll break up with him soon? It's been longer than usual this time."

"I damn sure hope so, but..."

"But, she'd probably take him back when he came crawling again...yeah."

"Should we talk to her then? Intervention time?" Jared asked.

"We already did that last year and look what happened—they got back together after a month and now the douche knows we don't want Kayla to be with him, which is why he is making sure she sees us as little as possible." I shook my head and pushed my half-eaten salad away. "She thinks we don't get it, but we do. She's loved him since she was sixteen. She thinks she can change him, and whenever I try to hint at stuff, she gets sad and tells me I don't get it. Of course it doesn't help that the douche manages to be sweet to her every once in a while."

"So, there is nothing we can do—is that what you're getting at?"

"I thought maybe *you* would have a brilliant idea."

Balancing his chair on two legs, Jared swayed back and forth for a few seconds. "Do you want me to seduce him or something? Because if that's what you're getting at..."

"Wh-What?" I sputtered. Uncertain whether he was serious or not, I gave him a horrified look. "You'd do that?"

He laughed at the expression on my face. "Please, I have standards. I don't seduce douchebags, but more importantly, I don't go after a friend's man. If I did, I'd go after Dylan before anyone else."

"Dylan is my friend, not my man."

"Sure, let's go with that. He's your buddy, right? And it was only my ghost who was at the bar last weekend, watching every move you two made. I thought he was gonna jump over that bar and pummel me when he saw me touch your face and tuck your hair behind your ear. He looks sexier when he's brooding—I'd suggest pissing him off more often."

"You did that on purpose?"

"No, but if I'd known he'd react that way, I probably would have. I bet he was losing his shit when we were dancing. Too bad we had no idea he was there."

"Oh, shut up."

"You shut up. And what about you? Miss *he's my buddy that's all*. After you went over, every time he touched your hand or your arm, you lit up like a Christmas tree."

Standing up, I shoved his shoulder, causing him to lose his balance and land back on four legs with a loud thud.

"Hey!"

"You don't want me angry, Jared. I'll make it hurt."

"Oh, bring it on. I'd like to see you try. It'd probably feel more like a tickle but give it a go. I give you permission."

Growling, I went after him before he could run away.

When I made it back home, it was almost nine o'clock. I'd just made a hundred dollars by taking fifteen Instagram photos for a student who had over three hundred thousand followers. She had heard about me and my *services* from one of her blogger friends who I had taken photos of before midterms. Any money that added to my savings account was good, so I tried my best to never turn anyone down, but after the fifth outfit change, I thought maybe I should've charged more. Considering it took us over two hours to get all the shots she wanted, I thought raising my rate was a great idea.

Even though I was pretty much ready to crawl back to the apartment after being out for over thirteen hours, I still made sure I was as quiet as a mouse when I tiptoed pass Ms. Hilda's door.

When I got into the apartment and turned on the lights, it took everything in me not to shriek like a banshee when I saw a big figure sitting on the floor in the living room, right under the windows.

"Dylan? You scared the crap out of me. Why are you sitting in the dark?" I dropped my equipment bag right next to the door and walked toward him, hesitating when I got to the couch and he still hadn't spoken.

He had his elbows propped on his knees, hands dangling between his thighs, and he wasn't looking at me, didn't even meet my eyes.

"Dylan? What's wrong?" I took an involuntary step forward but stopped myself from going farther.

Slowly, his head tilted up and his eyes met mine. Usually, I couldn't hold his gaze for more than a few seconds when he looked straight into my eyes like he was trying to see deep into me, but the way he was looking at me right then...I couldn't look away. I couldn't take my eyes off of him.

He, on the other hand, had no trouble breaking eye contact. "Nothing, Zoe," he said quietly then rested his head on the wall behind him. A few seconds later he let out a long sigh and closed his eyes.

"Obviously that's not the case," I stated softly, thinking something terrible must've happened. He didn't even open his eyes, let alone give me an answer.

Where was the guy who smiled at me left and right and made me feel lightheaded without even knowing what he was doing?

Starting to worry, I went and sat to his left, not within touching distance, but not too far away either. We spent a few minutes sitting side by side in absolute stillness. The only sound that could be heard over the heavy silence was coming from a neighbor's TV, most likely in the apartment below us.

"You can tell me what's going on, Dylan. I'm not a bad listener, and I'm supposed to be—"

His eyes didn't open, but he did finally speak. "If you tell me you're my buddy, Zoe, so help me..."

My knees were up just like his, but I decided to sit cross-legged instead, which brought me closer to his side. "I won't say anything, okay? Just tell me what's going on."

He rolled his head toward me and finally let me look into his eyes.

Slowly, I released the breath I hadn't even realized I was holding. He looked devastated. "What happened?" I whispered, angling my body toward him so I could put my hand on his arm. His gaze followed the movement, and I felt his muscles tighten under my touch. Thinking maybe it wasn't a good idea, that he didn't want me to touch him when he looked ready to bring down the building, I attempted to pull my hand back. But, the second I lifted it, he reached out and took his time lacing our fingers together.

"Is this okay?" he asked, his eyes glued to our intertwined hands. "Am I allowed to do this?"

I swallowed, hard. What was I supposed to say when he

looked so devastated? *No, actually, it's not okay, Dylan, because my brain seems to short-circuit every time you get this close to me.* I didn't think so.

"Is this what buddies do, Zoe?" he continued, his voice harder.

Is he angry at me?

What the hell did I do?

My brows drew together, but I didn't try to pull my hand away—like I said, short-circuit in the brain, and holding his hand had helped before, the night I'd fallen asleep on his shoulder. Maybe he was a hand holder; maybe that was his thing.

He studied my face then made some sort of huffing sound and let our hands drop to the hardwood floor. I tried not to wince.

"Dyl—"

"Don't answer that."

When his head hit the wall behind him yet again, I couldn't hold back my wince.

"It's JP," he said to the ceiling.

"What about him?"

"He got injured."

Didn't college football only happen on the weekends? It was only Thursday.

"When? I didn't know you had a game today."

"No game, just practice. He had a little trouble with his foot in the last game, but he said he was fine. Today one of the guys stepped on it wrong and now he has fucking a Lisfranc injury."

"Lis—what? Is it bad?"

His eyes closed as he released a humorless laugh. "Is it bad? Yeah, it's bad. He is done for the season. We don't even know if he needs surgery yet. If he doesn't, it'll still take him at least five to six weeks to recover, and that's me being a fucking optimist." As an afterthought, he added, "It's a foot injury."

When he roughly scrubbed his face with his free hand, I gave the other one that was still holding mine a small squeeze. It was the wrong move, because it drew his attention back to our hands again.

"If he ends up needing the surgery...how long is the recovery time then?"

He met my eyes and I held my breath. *Oh God...* Jared was right; I loved his smile. I both hated and loved how I couldn't stop myself from smiling back at him, but the look on his face when he was angry...it made me wish I had my camera with me so I could take a shot of him just like that and freeze time for us, a heartbeat I could carry in my pocket that would forever be mine.

"Five to six months," Dylan replied, oblivious to my thoughts. "And even after that, no one can know for certain whether he'll get back to his pre-injury state or not. Doesn't even matter because he won't make it to the combine either way."

For the third time since I'd met him, I couldn't look away from his eyes, and it wasn't because we were having a staring contest. It had nothing to do with that; I just didn't want to. I'm not sure if it was because of the vulnerability I could see in them or if it was the obvious pain and worry, but I couldn't do it.

"Where is he?"

He was frowning at me but still answered my question. "Coach sent him home. He can't bear weight on his leg."

"And when will they know if he'll need the surgery or not?"

"They need to run some tests. We should know more next week."

"Don't you want to be with him?" I asked tentatively.

His frown deepened. "He doesn't want to see anyone. We were supposed to do this thing together. Now, with the timing of his injury, his entire career might be over. This whole goddamn year is—"

His phone must have been sitting next to him because the next thing I knew it was sailing in the air, heading toward the wall right in front of my eyes, until it thankfully came to a stop right after crashing into my equipment bag. If my bag hadn't been in the way, with the force he'd thrown it, it would've been broken into a million pieces.

"I'm sorry, Dylan." I gave his hand another squeeze, and this time he squeezed back. Only problem was, he never loosened his hold. Don't get me wrong, he didn't hurt me or anything, but that extra bit of squeeze caused my already pretty fast heart rate to kick up another notch.

Knowing nothing I could say would change anything or lighten his burden, I kept my mouth shut.

His eyes narrowed at me. "You're not looking away."

A tingle went through my body. "Should I?"

"You shouldn't, but that hasn't stopped you in the past."

Time to change the subject.

"How long have you been sitting here?"

"I don't know...ever since I got back, I guess."

No point in asking what time that was. "Are you hungry?"

"No."

"Are you sure? I make a mean grilled cheese, and I don't do it for just anyone." I gave him a small bump with my shoulder.

"And what makes me special?"

Good job, Zoe. Walked right into that one, didn't you.

"I...uh...you're...you know...you're hungry."

Lame. Lame. Lame.

The longer he looked at me, the easier it was to spot the twitching muscle in his jaw.

"That's not much of an answer to my question. How about this question then? Maybe you'll have a better answer for this one, what do you think?"

I was pretty sure I wouldn't like the question, but... "What's the question?"

"Are you still dating him?"

Where had that come from? "You like pushing me, don't you?" I asked instead of mumbling something meaningless that would only be a lie. I tried to pull my hand away from his so I could walk away. So much for worrying about him.

His hold tightened to the point where my fingers tingled and goose bumps rose up on my arm. Then, just as quickly, it loosened.

"No," he said roughly. "Stay." It took only one word. I stayed until he was ready to let go.

I tried to get comfortable as we sat hand in hand. When he saw I wasn't going anywhere and I wasn't pulling back, his eyes closed and he rested his head against the wall, jaw still tight, teeth still grinding.

I didn't know why, but I had a feeling it had cost him something to ask me to stay.

CHAPTER FIFTEEN

ZOE

I was doing it. I was really doing it.

I was about to board a plane with Mark, Chris, Dylan, and their whole freaking team.

We were supposed to take the same bus to the airport as the team, but both Miriam and the guy who was coming with us for the interviews, Cash, had been late. Instead of braving it and getting on the bus on my own, I'd opted to take an Uber to the airport with them.

As Cash and Miriam chatted away during the ride over, I was worrying about how my sudden appearance would go over. Neither Mark nor Dylan knew I was joining them for the game. I could've and should've told Dylan, but after the week he'd had with what had happened to his friend, I'd barely seen him after the night I'd found him sitting in the dark. Even when I did, he usually went to his room to crash as soon as he walked through the door.

That evening had been the second time we'd held hands for what seemed like hours and didn't even acknowledge it afterward. I wasn't sure if he saw it as a normal thing, but if you asked my heart and the butterflies that seemed to make a home in my stomach, it was very far from a normal occurrence. It didn't help that I could still feel the impression of his hand around mine. If I made a fist, I could almost mimic the exact same pressure I'd felt when his hand had squeezed tight around mine.

Miriam's bag bumped my shin as she wheeled her carry-on bag toward the escalator.

"Shit."

"Oh, I'm sorry, Zoe." She stopped next to me and released a big sigh. "It's lunchtime and I didn't even have breakfast yet. Do you think they'll give out snacks?"

"It's not a commercial flight, so I doubt that."

"You're right, I guess. I'm hoping there is good food at—"

"What are you doing standing around? They're waiting for us. Hurry up," Cash yelled as he passed us in a slow jog. He was wearing a short trench coat even though it was still warm, and he had a wrapped burrito in one hand while he hugged his laptop to his chest, a duffel bag in the other. He was a complete mess.

"I call dibs," Miriam said quietly, leaning toward me.

"What?"

"Cash—I call dibs on him," she repeated before following the guy in question up the stairs.

She could have him, all right.

I took my sweet time getting up those steps, so it was no wonder I was the very last person to board the plane. I hated that the anticipation of Mark's reaction was affecting me to the point that I was on the verge of dragging my feet like a six-year-old.

The plane was filled with chatter and guys...so many guys. Some were standing up, pushing their bags into the overhead bins, some were laughing, some singing.

When I saw that Cash and Miriam were still lingering where the rows of seats started, I considered hiding behind them for a brief moment. If I ducked my head, there was a strong possibility that Mark wouldn't see me, but then Miriam and Cash moved. If I didn't want to run the last few steps that separated us—and I did not—I was doomed to make the walk down the aisle with my head held up high. He'd see me at the hotel anyway, and trying to hide made me feel stupid.

Feeling like I was getting ready to step in front of the firing squad, I squared my shoulders and started following my companions.

I spotted Mark before he could spot me. He was sitting right at the front in a window seat, and he was talking to another guy who I guessed was one of the other coaches. I was just walking past him when Miriam stopped in front of me. In my haste to escape, I bumped into her back, and she gave me a curious look over her shoulder. I mouthed an apology and made sure I had my back to Mark at all times.

My eyes slid to an older guy who had risen up from his aisle seat and put his hand on Cash's shoulder.

"Boys!" he shouted. When the chatter didn't quiet down, he tried again. "Hey!"

All eyes turned to us. The plane went silent, but there was definitely a roar in my ears. I didn't know how many players traveled with the team, but to me, it looked and felt like there were hundreds of eyes on us. I swallowed the huge lump in my throat.

Out of the corner of my eye, I looked at Mark and saw that he was still deep in conversation with his seatmate.

"I want you to meet Cash. He is with the school's paper and will be interviewing some of you." He stopped yelling, turned to Miriam, and in a lower voice, asked her name. After her, it was my turn. I practically leaned all the way over Miriam to give him my name so Mark wouldn't hear me, which was stupid since it was about to be shouted in a matter of seconds.

"And this is Miriam and Zoe. They'll be taking photographs

of you. Be nice to them—and when I say nice, I mean respectful. I don't want to hear a single complaint."

My mouth had gone dry, not only because I could feel Mark's eyes boring into the side of my head as he realized I was on the plane, but also because this was my worst nightmare. Walking through rows and rows of seats where every single eyeball was on you? Yeah, I could already feel the heat on my cheeks.

When we finally started to walk, the chatter on the plane picked up again. On the way to our seats, which were at the very back of the plane, we got a few quiet whistles, a few casual greetings, and a few quiet murmurings about posing nude; as a reaction to the latter, I stepped on Miriam's heels—twice.

We must've been only halfway to our seats when I heard his voice, and something melted in me.

"Zoe?"

I lifted my eyes up for the first time and met Dylan's confused gaze. He was sitting in the middle seat when he called my name, and I watched him slowly take off his black headphones and stand up. Somehow seeing him centered something inside me. An unexpected warmth spread through my body and I was able to release a long breath.

"Hi," I mumbled with a small wave, and when I realized Miriam and Cash were getting farther away from me, I pulled my carry-on behind me and started a jog to catch up. Looking over my shoulder, I made sure to send another quick wave Dylan's way. I felt like a little baby duckling being left behind in the middle of nowhere, so it was important to catch up.

When we finally reached our seats, I was ready to shout hallelujah. After Cash helped us with our bags, he took the window seat. Miriam gave me a pointed look and followed him. I took the aisle seat.

"What's wrong with you? You're acting weird," she whispered into my ear.

I clutched my bag to my stomach and gave her a small shrug. When I lifted my gaze over the seat in front of me, I realized Dylan was still standing up, his back to me. I watched him lean down and say something to his friend. Was it Chris sitting next to him? I hadn't even noticed. In my panicked state, Dylan had been all I could see.

A moment later, he stepped into the aisle and started moving toward the back of the plane...toward me. It took him some time to reach us because he stopped to talk to his friends every now and then on his way.

Eventually, he stopped right next to my seat and I smiled up at him.

"Hey."

"Hi."

"What's going on?"

My smile shifted from small to big. "Nothing."

He laughed and shook his head. Holding on to my armrest, he crouched on his heels.

"You're coming with the team? To photograph us?"

Forgetting all about Miriam and Cash, I turned my body to face him. He was pulling on me like a magnet, it seemed. I went to put my hands next to his, but they were in the way so I kept mine to myself. "Yeah. It's for something the school paper is working on, I think. My photography professor asked us if we could go, so here we are."

His eyes warmed. "Here you are. Why didn't you tell me? Wait." He stood up and lifted the headphones off the head of the guy sitting in the seat across the aisle from me. "Drew, take my seat."

Just like that, the guy jumped up and Dylan took his place.

As he sat down, a flight attendant appeared from behind us.

With a smile fixed on her face, she said, "Seatbelts, please. We'll be taking off in a few minutes."

Nodding, I fastened my seatbelt, and Dylan did the same.

When our eyes met again, I smiled. "Hi."

My heart leapt at the sight of his easy smile, always so open and warm.

"Hi yourself."

"Dylan."

The unexpected voice startled both of us.

"Get back to your seat. I need to talk to you and Chris about a few changes we're going to make," said Mark. I noticed the guy waiting just behind him, the one Dylan had swapped seats with. He looked just as uncomfortable as we did.

Intentionally, I kept my eyes on Dylan's face and watched his brow draw together in confusion.

"Coach, we already have a meeting right after we—"

"Back to your seat, son."

Son.

Was that his way of saying Dylan was off limits too? I couldn't be friends or friendly with the guy he himself had sent to live with me? Sure, when he'd given him the apartment keys, he hadn't expected me to be *in* the apartment, but still, I *was* living with the guy.

Dylan did what he asked and undid his belt to get up, but when his eyes found mine, he was still sporting a scowl. I dragged my eyes back to Mark then pointedly looked away before he could say anything.

IT WAS after we had entered the hotel we'd be staying in for the weekend when I next saw Dylan and Chris. He broke off from his friends when he noticed me standing apart from Miriam and Cash and made his way to my side. He was wearing his black sweatpants, and I could've sworn he had a dozen or more of them in different shades of gray and black, just so he could make a girl go crazy. My personal favorite was the light gray. A tight black t-shirt covered his torso and pulled all the attention to his biceps and chest.

"Which room are you in?" he asked, head tilted, eyes on the envelope in my hand.

"Uh, let me check." I forced my eyes away from his body and opened the envelope I'd picked up from a table where the hotel employees had lined up dozens of them. "Room 412. I'm sharing with Miriam."

He gave me a chin lift. "We're on the same floor. I'm with Chris."

One of his teammates drew his attention by slapping his shoulder so he turned away. I looked around me. Mark was nowhere to be found, but the other coaches were busy trying to wrangle all the guys. Some of them were handing out sheets of paper while others were simply huddled together and talking. My eyes found Chris and when I saw him glancing my way, I forced a smile on my lips, not sure how I was supposed to react. Instead of smiling back like I'd hoped he would, he shook his head and turned back to talk to one of his friends. Feeling more and more alone by the second, I pulled my phone out of the back pocket of my jeans and sent a group text to Jared and Kayla.

Me: *Okay, we landed and made it to the hotel. There are so many people and I know no one other than Dylan. Oh, and Mark is pissed at me. When I say pissed, I mean PISSED! But I ignored him on the plane so be proud of me. I'm only texting you guys because I have no idea what I'm supposed to do and instead of standing in the middle of the lobby looking around like a little fish out of water, I need something to do with my hands. Write back so I can stop talking to myself like a weirdo and have a meaningful conversation with you guys instead. Quick. Quick.*

"Here."

Lifting my head, I saw that Miriam was handing me one of the papers the coaches were handing out.

I reached for it. "Thank you." It was a detailed schedule of what the team was supposed to do and where they were supposed to be at any given moment.

"Cash wants us to take photos of their dinner, just how they interact I think, maybe get a few shots of everyone while they're eating. After that, we're free for tonight. Tomorrow, we'll trail him and do whatever he asks us to do. He said it'll mostly be meetings, warm-ups, and then the game. We'll have a meeting of our own at breakfast and he'll give us more details."

I nodded and looked up from the detailed schedule. "Sounds good. I think I'm going to skip snack time and head up to our room. Are you coming?"

She looked over her shoulder to where Cash was talking with one of the players. "I think I'll stick around."

"Okay then," I murmured to myself when she walked away after a quick wave.

Dragging my teeth along my lip, I looked around again. Half of the players were already gone. I saw a few standing around the elevators and a few walking toward the back of the hotel where I assumed the snacks were waiting, if the sign with the team logo and *Meal Room* written on it was anything to go by. I glanced around to see if I could spot Dylan, but with lobby still being so busy, I'd lost him. Pulling my carry-on behind me, I headed toward the elevators.

My phone pinged with a new message.

I let out a huge breath and filed into the elevator with three other players. Even though they were talking among themselves about the following day's game, I could still feel their curious eyes on me. Ducking my head, I focused on my phone.

While I was hoping it was a text from Kayla or Jared, my

already nervous stomach twisted even more when I saw that it was Mark who had texted me.

Mark: *Which room?*

My fingers hovered over the screen. I was either going to keep ignoring him and try to stay as far away as possible, or I was going to get over it and focus on what I'd come to do. I waited until I was standing in the room before I texted him back. My phone pinged again, but this time it was Jared replying. Feeling the inevitable anxiety creep in, I decided not to write anything back to my friend until Mark found his way to my room, said what he needed to say, and left.

Only ten minutes had passed when I heard the insistent knock on the door. The first thing I did when he stepped in was to tell him that the trip was for one of my classes. I didn't think he was even listening to what I was saying, because he started in on me before the words had even left my mouth. The energy he was giving off was scaring me, but I tried my best to keep my face neutral. After a long rant about the same things I had become all too familiar with, he warned me to 'watch myself' around his boys and strode out.

As soon as the door slammed shut behind him, I took a deep breath and let it all go. I was not going to let him get to me, not anymore.

After sending a quick text to my dad to let him know when he could come pick me up, I worked on some shots I was going to put up as stock photos on a few websites while talking on the phone with Jared. Miriam came up a bit later and eventually announced that she was ready to head down to the team meal room, so I grabbed my bag and my camera then followed her down.

"When will you get back?" she asked once we were in the elevator heading downstairs.

"I'm not sure. Why?"

"Well, the curfew for the team is eleven. Do you think you'll be back before that?"

"I didn't think the curfew was for us. Do I *have* to be back before that?" If I did, that would only give me a few hours with my dad, which wasn't much considering he was driving in from Phoenix just to see me.

"I don't think so. I mean, we can ask Cash to make sure, but I doubt it. I'm only asking because...well, I was wondering if you could send me a quick text before you head up to the room when you're back."

I gave her a quick look just as the elevator doors slid open. "Why?"

"Cash and I will...you know."

"Oh. Yeah, sure. I'll sit around in the lobby until the coast is clear."

She let out a relieved sigh and linked her arm with mine as if we'd been best friends for years. "You would do that? Ah, thank you, Zoe. My roommate is a real killjoy. If she were here, she'd just walk in and interrupt us in the middle of—"

"I don't mind," I cut her off. "I mean, as long as it's not for hours on end, it's okay. I'll grab my laptop before I leave so I can work while I'm waiting."

She squeezed my arm a little tighter. "Oh, you're the best. Thank you. Tomorrow is going to be so much fun. I can't wait."

We walked into a huge room where hotel employees ran around arranging tables and chairs for the players. There were still twenty minutes until the guys would be filtering in, and Cash wanted us to be ready to take shots of them as they piled food onto their plates. If they were happy with the photos we took during the weekend, apparently the team was going to consider using them in their brochures for the next year.

Under Cash's careful watch, it took us fifteen minutes to take the photos then it was our turn to choose from whatever was left

on the open buffet table. I grabbed some mashed potatoes, broccoli, and chicken.

When I hesitated while following Miriam, she touched my
arm. "You coming?"

My eyes were glued to Dylan, who was sitting alone at one of
the tables. Mark had already eaten and left, and I hadn't seen
Chris around after I'd taken a quick shot of him constructing a
steak mountain on his plate. If there was ever a choice between
Dylan and anyone else, I'd always go with my roommate.

"No, you go on. I'll see you later."

One hand holding the strap of my camera, the other
balancing my plate, I pulled out a chair with my foot and sat
across from Dylan.

"Hi," I said softly, offering him a smile as I settled down.

He stopped eating and studied me with angry eyes.

When he didn't say anything back, I started to lose my smile.
After giving me a quick nod, he focused on his food again. Dylan
had been one of the last ones to come in, so while I'd been taking
shots of the players and the coaches who were eating, Dylan was
nowhere to be found.

Picking up my fork, I pushed the broccoli stems around. "Are
you okay?" I asked in a low voice as the silence turned uncomfortable, which had never happened between us before.

He dropped his fork with a clatter and reached for his water
bottle.

Had I done something? I forced myself to swallow down a
piece of broccoli and waited for him to say something.

Seconds passed, but nothing happened. As soon as he
cleaned his plate, he started looking over his shoulders. It was
obvious he didn't want me sitting with him, and I had no idea
why. Feeling a little bit hurt and, truth be told, confused, I
cleared my throat and gathered up my plate so I could leave. "I'm
sorry, I didn't realize I was bothering—"

I was halfway up when he stopped looking around the room and met my eyes. "Was that Coach I saw going into your room earlier?"

I dropped back down in my seat and my plate clattered on the table, drawing the curious eyes of his teammates.

"What?"

"You heard me. I was coming to your room to see if you wanted to hang out, but Coach made it there before me so I didn't bother."

I swallowed hard. How to get out of this one? "And?" It was a lame attempt to play it cool, but I had nothing else.

"And?" His nostrils flaring, he pushed at his plate and leaned over the table. "I didn't know you were close enough to invite him into your *room*." Something he saw in my face made him pause, but unfortunately, it didn't stop him. "I didn't see either of you around for an hour."

My mouth opened and closed as my hands formed into fists under the table. I slid forward in my seat, mimicking his stance.

"An hour? What are you saying, Dylan?"

His eyebrows inched up to his hairline. "I think you know what I'm saying."

I sat back. I did know what he was saying, and why was I so surprised anyway? I'd already expected him to think exactly what he was thinking, but how had I not anticipated the hurt it would cause to actually hear the confirmation?

"He was only in my room for five minutes, Dylan, six *tops*. My dad is driving in from Phoenix to see me, and Mark wanted to know if he was going to make it to the game tomorrow."

My heart sank, and I hated myself a little more for the lie Mark had essentially forced me to tell.

"Your dad is coming," he echoed.

"Yes." I pushed my plate away, grabbed my camera, and stood up. "He should be here any second, so I better go..." I was waiting for him to say something, but it was pointless; he just studied me with his ocean blue eyes as if trying to decipher everything I couldn't say out loud. "Yeah, I'll just leave." And with that clever closing remark, I pulled my eyes away from Dylan's expectant gaze and walked away.

Instead of waiting in the lobby, I sat down outside on the stairs and tried not to think too much about Dylan and how my feelings for him were evolving from just a simple attraction. About an hour had passed when I saw a metallic blue truck coming my way. Quickly, I got up and ran toward it. As soon as my dad's feet hit the ground, I threw myself into his arms and closed my eyes.

"Dad."

His arms rounded my shoulders and he held on just as tight as I did, if not tighter.

"My little baby girl."

My nose was already tingling. "I missed you," I mumbled into his chest. "I missed you so much."

His hand smoothed my hair down and he leaned back to look at my face.

"Zoe? What is this?"

His arms slowly dropped and he held my face in his palms, his thumbs wiping away my silent tears.

"Nothing," I muttered after a pathetic sniffle, again pushing my head into his chest where I knew he would keep me safe.

I had no idea where the tears had come from—well, okay, I knew, but I hadn't been planning on losing it so soon and worrying him. He sighed and burrowed closer, my body rocking with unexpected sobs as I realized how much I had missed him.

We heard a honk behind us, but I was reluctant to let him go, and thankfully, my dad showed no signs of hurrying. He kissed my forehead, brushed my tears away yet again, and nodded once he was sure I was holding it together.

"We'll figure it all out together," he murmured. Walking me back to the passenger side, he helped me up. When I was securely inside, he closed the door and jogged around the car. After lifting a hand in apology to the car behind us, he hopped in.

As I wiped my face with the back of my hand, my eyes caught on someone near the hotel door. He was leaning against one of the columns, arms crossed over his chest, his face unreadable from afar.

It was Dylan.

AROUND ELEVEN THIRTY, my dad dropped me off back at the hotel and we had another tearful goodbye. He was spending the night at a different hotel—he didn't want to come face to face with Mark—so we could spend a few more hours together the next day, but I didn't want him to sit around and wait for me when I didn't even know if I'd have any free time to sneak out.

My mind on anything but Miriam and Cash, I took the elevator all the way up to my room only to find the *Do Not Disturb* sign on the door handle. After the weird exchange with Dylan earlier, I'd completely forgotten to go back up to my room to get my laptop before meeting my dad. Instead of knocking on the door, I went back down to the lobby.

The whole place pretty much looked dead. Other than a few people hanging around the front desk and the occasional hotel guest stumbling in through the door, I was pretty much alone where I sat facing the front doors.

After sending a quick text to Miriam to let her know I was downstairs, I watched puppy videos on Instagram to kill some time.

Just as I was writing out a text to Kayla, another message popped up on my screen.

Dylan: I'm sorry.

I stared at the screen, not sure whether I should answer or not. Answering him meant I'd have to keep lying to him, but then again, it wasn't like I could avoid him forever, or *wanted* to avoid him at all.

Dylan: I'm a complete asshole.

Dylan: Will you open your door if I knock?

My lips stretched into the biggest smile. No, I really didn't want to avoid him at all.

Me: Didn't you have a bed check at eleven?

Dylan: And?

Me: So aren't you supposed to be in bed since it's past eleven?

Dylan: Just because we have a curfew doesn't mean we have to go to sleep at eleven.

Me: But it means you shouldn't leave your room, right?

Dylan: It's okay if you don't want to see me Zoe. You can tell me.

My fingers hesitated. I hit myself in the forehead with the back of the phone a few times before I found the courage to type out what I wanted to say next.

Me: I'd love to see you Dylan. I always like seeing you.

Lame. Lame. Lame.

Dylan: :)

Dylan: Then open your door.

Did I tell him I was actually in the lobby because Miriam was getting busy in the room and risk him getting in trouble with Mark if he decided to come down?

Me: I don't want you to get in trouble, and Miriam is here, too, so...

Dylan: Yeah. Okay, you're right.

Dylan: It's just weird knowing you're here and not seeing you, I guess. I think I'm missing my roommate.

I looked around to check if anyone was watching me. Thankfully, no one was. Pressing on my cheeks with my fingers, I tried to keep my smile in check. Before I could write back that I was missing him too, another text chimed in.

Dylan: *I saw your dad. You cried.*

Me: *I miss him.*

Dylan: *I shouldn't have said what I said at dinner.*

I watched the dots appear and disappear several times.

Me: *It's okay. Just don't do it again.*

When nothing came back for a few seconds, I wrote again.

Me: *I think I'm missing my roommate too.*

Dylan: *Yeah?*

Me: *Yup.*

Me: *Are you in bed? What are you doing?*

Dylan: *Yeah. Chris brought his Xbox with him so we've been playing Madden since dinner, but he's on the phone now.*

Dylan: *And I'm talking to you.*

Oh God. Are we flirting? I really hoped we were flirting. My heart skipping all over the place, I put the phone down in my lap and pressed the backs of my hands to my cheeks to absorb some of the heat, and to stop myself from smiling like a lunatic in the middle of the lobby—though, I was pretty sure it was too late for that.

I must have taken too much time to come up with something clever because before I could reply, I saw the dots jump around again.

Dylan: *Are you in bed?*

Yup. We were flirting.

Abort. Abort.

Me: *Yep.*

So clever, Zoe.

Dylan: *That's good.*

My heart in my throat just from texting with him, I dropped my head back and gazed at the colorful high ceilings.

Just when I was about to write, *Yeah it's comfy*—another terribly clever response—Miriam saved me.

Miriam: *Coast is clear. You can come up!*

Thinking I would for sure come up with something better once I was in my room, I headed toward the elevators.

Dylan: *I think you fell asleep. Sweet dreams, Zoe. I'll see you tomorrow.*

Groaning, I decided not to answer so he could get some sleep and just headed up to my room.

CHAPTER SIXTEEN

ZOE

The entire day was a whirlwind of breakfast, meetings, nap time, meetings, lunch, and then game time. Before I could take in the stadium or the level of noise around me, Cash was ushering me to the sidelines so I could take a few shots of the players warming up before the game.

"Miriam will cover the coaches. You cover the boys."

That was fine with me—more than fine, actually. I did a 360 and gulped when I took in my surroundings.

Dear God.

So *many* eyeballs.

It didn't escape my notice that I'd been saying the same thing a lot since the day before, but there were just so many people... hence so many eyeballs.

"Zoe! Get to it!" Cash yelled as he was walking back to Miriam's side. I swallowed again and nodded.

I was standing a little to the left of the player tunnel, camera in my hand, trying to find the perfect setting, when Dylan, Chris, and a whole slew of guys jogged out.

I felt eyeballs on me all right, not because they couldn't take their eyes off of me or anything like that, but more because I looked lost, like a fish out of water. Only one set of those eyeballs sent a tingle up my spine, and those belonged to Dylan Reed.

With the confidence in the way he walked onto the field, the way his eyes locked on mine over his shoulder right before he joined his friends to stretch and do drills...I was done for. Seeing the perfection of him in that uniform wasn't helping the matters at all.

My camera still in my hands, I watched him disappear into the crowd of his teammates. A few seconds later, I spotted him again, thanks to the big number twelve on the back of his jersey. I kept watching as his biceps bulged under those huge shoulder pads and he lowered himself to the ground, where he and the rest of the team started their pregame warm-up routine with stretches. Was his ass that tight at all times or had he done something to it in the locker room? All I had going for me was that my mouth wasn't hanging open; that was pretty much it.

I was startled enough that I did a little jump when I heard Cash yell my name again.

Right.

Photos.

I was supposed to take photos.

So many coaches and important-looking people milling around, talking, arguing in huddles. Like a little snake, I walked around them and took a shit load of pictures of the boys doing drills on the field, and then I approached Miriam and Cash where they stood away from everyone. If they thought there were too many photos of Dylan Reed, that wasn't my problem.

"You done?" Miriam asked, taking a step away from Cash.

"I think so. I think I got some good shots, but it's my first time doing this, so I'm not sure if they're actually good. I like them though."

She bit down on her bottom lip and looked around. "It's a little overwhelming isn't it?"

That was an understatement.

"There are so many men with cameras around, I have no idea why they needed us."

Miriam shrugged and gave me a small shoulder bump. "Who cares. It's been fun, and don't think I didn't notice you cozying up to Dylan Reed last night in the meal room."

It was right on the tip of my tongue to tell her I wasn't cozying up to anyone and that he was just my roommate, but I managed to keep it in and offered her a smile instead.

Gesturing to Cash with my chin, I whispered, "Looks like that went well for you."

"Oh yeah. Sorry, I fell asleep before you made it up to the room—he pretty much killed me."

I leaned forward a little to take another look at Cash. I could admit he wasn't awful or anything like that. Five nine to Miriam's five five with an okay body—though in comparison to Dylan and all the other players on the field, he was basically skinny—and fingers long enough that you felt obligated to do a double take, he had longish wavy hair that curled around his ears, brown eyes that moved around restlessly, and thin lips pressed into a straight line. Different strokes for different folks, I supposed. There was nothing wrong with his look, but the way he acted like he was working on a story for the Times would start to get on my nerves if I had to spend one more day around him.

Right as I was about to say something else, I felt hands on my waist, and a second later I was flying through the air as I shrieked like a banshee.

"Look what I found," someone sing-songed behind me as I tried my best to grab the hands that were clamped around my middle. Thank God the strap of my camera was wrapped around my wrist, saving it from flying across the field.

Recognizing the voice, I looked over my shoulder and down. "Trevor?"

"That's me," he replied with a grinning face.

"Trevor, what the hell do you th—"

My words turned into another scream when he maneuvered —or more like abruptly flipped—me around until I was holding on to his neck, cradled like a baby in his arms.

"What's up, buttercup?" he asked, his shit-eating grin still in place. I was pretty sure he'd been born with that smile, or another possibility was that he had worked on it in front of a mirror for years until he perfected it. "I've been watching you the last ten minutes. I couldn't believe my eyes."

"Let me down, you idiot," I swore, out of breath.

"I'll do just that once I get you away from enemy lines."

I growled at my childhood friend, but it didn't seem to have the desired effect on him; it never did. Gripping his shoulders for dear life as he sprinted away, I looked over his shoulder and my eyes zeroed in on one person.

Dylan.

All his teammates were filtering into the tunnel to get back to the locker rooms, but he was standing still, one hand holding his helmet by the fingertips, the other on his waist. I wanted to give him a wave or a smile, but he was looking at me in Trevor's arms with a face carved from stone, his jaw set, expression completely closed up.

Something tightened in my chest, squeezing at my heart.

I slapped Trevor's shoulder twice.

"Trevor, stop. Trevor, you have to stop!"

He must've heard the urgency in my tone because we finally came to a halt. Gently, he put me down back on my feet, and my eyes stayed on Dylan the whole time. I watched him take a step toward us, and then another, and another. My heart pounding just from seeing the determination on his face, I couldn't take my eyes off of him. Something was about to happen—or was happening already—and my heart was flipping out on me. Trevor said something to get my attention and touched my shoulder.

My brows snapped together and I murmured a distracted, "What?"

Was Dylan jealous?

When he started a light jog toward us, I felt all the hairs on my arms stand up. I gave Trevor a quick glance.

"Can you give me a minute?"

He glanced back at what I was looking at, and I was already walking to meet Dylan halfway. The need to go to him had come out of nowhere. Maybe it was the way his hard eyes locked onto mine, daring me to look away, or maybe it was something about the controlled way his body was moving. God, he looked so good in his uniform, almost as good as he looked when he worked out in our kitchen half naked...almost. He looked larger than life, bigger and better than anyone else warming up on the field.

Before I had taken four steps, Chris blocked Dylan around the thirty-yard line. He rested his forehead against Dylan's, squeezed his neck, and guided him toward the tunnel. Dylan frowned at him then shook his head once as if coming out of a trance. Then he was nodding and jogging alongside his teammate.

When he disappeared into the tunnel, I turned back to Trevor with a sheepish smile.

He raised an eyebrow, which only added to his signature cocky look. "Did I step on some toes?"

"What? No. What are you even doing here? I thought you were in Boston."

"Yeah, I was, but I transferred here this year. You dating number twelve? That Reed guy?" he asked with a flick of his head toward where Dylan had disappeared to.

"No. He's just my friend."

After giving me a long, thorough look, he spoke again. "If you say so." His big smile back in place, he gave me a playful shove. "Look at you, buttercup. I haven't seen you in two years and this is where I find you? I missed you."

"Don't call me that," I grumbled as I shoved him right back.

"Still so cute. What the hell are you doing here then? Came to watch your boyfriend get his ass handed to him by me?"

"I told you, he's not my boyfriend." I lifted my camera as if that would answer his question. "I'm on an assignment, taking shots of the team." And because I didn't like him talking about Dylan like that, I added, "And don't be so sure whose ass will be getting kicked. They're amazing."

I actually had no idea if they were. All I knew was that Dylan was amazing.

His eyebrows shot up. "Are they now? And did you become a football expert because of a certain someone?"

We heard someone shout his name, and Trevor looked over his shoulder. "Shoot. Okay, I have to get back." Grabbing the heavy camera out of my hand, he lifted it up in the air as if to take a selfie. "Come on, I want a photo of us together. I have a prettier face, and you need something better to look at than those baboons."

"It's off, you idiot." I laughed when he couldn't quite manage to figure out how to work it.

I turned the camera on and let him pull me to his side so he could get a shot of us together. When we heard his name called again, he thrust the camera back into my hands.

"Here, take it. Email me—both the photo and your number. I don't have yours, so you better send it my way." Jogging backward, he kept talking. "Don't forget, Zoe bug. Better yet, I'll email you my number and you can text me."

"Okay!" I yelled back, smiling.

When he was close enough to his coaches, one of them hit him on the back of the head and his grin got bigger.

"Okay!" he yelled one last time, and then he was out of sight.

———————

OUR TEAM WAS WINNING—DYLAN'S team. I didn't know exactly when it'd become *our* team in my mind, but I was swept up in the rush of the game and the magic of being in the stadium. Sure, maybe I didn't get what was happening most of the time, but I was right there with them when everyone was cheering, yelling, or swearing. Even being close to Mark hadn't managed to kill my excitement.

And Dylan...he was a beast. The way he ran away with that ball, his speed, the way he ducked and dodged and rolled and twisted and everything else he did—I was mesmerized just watching him.

It sounds weird to say out loud, but he felt like mine. I knew how he looked in the mornings, knew pretty much every muscle in his upper body. I hadn't touched them or anything like that, but they were burned into my brain. I knew what he liked to have on his pizza, which was very important. Extra cheese, pepperoni, and black olives was his go-to, and he didn't look at me like I was an alien because I liked pineapple on my pizza.

I knew his smiles, and he had a handful of them, each one deadlier than any other smile you could imagine. I knew when he brushed his palm through his short hair that he was stressed, agitated. I knew he liked to hold my hand; I didn't know why, but I knew he liked it. If he was rolling his neck and that muscle in his jaw was working, he was angry and having trouble keeping himself under control. I knew making me blush just with the way he was looking at me amused him, and that usually prompted his amused smile, which never failed to kick my heart rate up. I knew he was the hardest working guy I'd ever seen. I knew he was one of a kind, and I knew with every passing day I wanted him to be mine—not my buddy, but mine, just mine.

Knowing all that about him scared the shit out of me. When it was the last play of the third quarter and the scoreboard showed 31-42, someone else walked out of the tunnel and joined his teammates on the sidelines.

JP Edwards.

My gaze zeroed in on the crutches under his arms, and the smile I had plastered on my face suddenly didn't feel right.

The ref blew the whistle to end the quarter and the team huddled together with their coach. After some helmet slapping, back thumps, and what I assumed were encouraging words, they made it to JP's side. I was watching Dylan the entire time.

Out of breath, he came to a stop in front of his friend and took off his helmet, shoulders tense and high, the black paint under his eyes smeared. Balancing on one foot, JP rubbed the back of his neck and shook his head once. My camera was already in my hands so without second-guessing myself, I lifted it and took a quick shot, not sure what I was looking at, but wanting to capture it. I saw their lips move, but I had no idea what they were talking about. Dylan put a hand on JP's shoulder, and JP shook his head again. Dylan's hand curled around his neck and he dropped his forehead against his friend's.

Click

I zoomed in and took another shot, realizing both their eyes were closed.

JP's hand went around Dylan's neck.

Click

Chris joined their little huddle and dropped his helmet to the ground next to them.

Click

Click

I lowered the camera and looked away. I'd already intruded more than I should've, but I hadn't taken those shots for the assignment. Those were mine. If I was honest, I had taken a lot of shots that were just for me since the game had started.

"I'm gonna grab something to drink. You girls want anything?" Cash asked us. Miriam was busy texting on her phone, but she looked up long enough to shake her head.

"Water would be good," I said, and he moved off toward the team, talking to a few players before heading our way.

When he got back, I couldn't stop myself from asking, "You know what's going on over there?" I tipped my chin toward JP, where at least ten or fifteen of his teammates were surrounding him in a half-circle. I took the water bottle Cash handed me.

"Yeah. Bad news for JP, and the team, really. Apparently he's done for the season. He's gonna need surgery for that foot injury, and his career is probably over if he can't recover fully. It's too bad—he was a hell of a player."

"Just like that?" I asked. "One injury and he's out? Done?"

"Yeah. That's how it goes with sports. You never know when you'll be forced to tap out."

"I didn't see him at the hotel, or on the plane," I managed to say through the rock lodged in my throat. I remembered the anguish and anger on Dylan's face the day I'd found him sitting by himself in the dark. He was gonna be devastated.

"He wanted to be the one to tell his teammates and join them for one last game before all that, so they flew him in today."

The boys ran to the fifty-yard line and the last quarter of the game started. It turned vicious in no time. I'd seen tackles, but after the last quarter, after the news from his friend...if Dylan had been a beast before, he'd turned into the Hulk in no time. I flinched and gasped throughout the entire thing, especially when someone tackled Dylan right after he practically flew into the air and caught the ball. It was brutal, sure, but Dylan always got back up with the ball still in his hands, and I got over it pretty quickly. Trevor hadn't stepped foot on the field for the first half of the game, but he'd been there for the second half. So, when Dylan took Trevor to the ground right at the beginning of the last quarter after Chris threw an interception and Trevor caught it— at least that was what Miriam told me had happened—I was worried he'd broken my childhood friend in half. Trevor eventually pushed himself up, but it took some time.

The rest of the game went the same way—tackles, passes, whistles, cheers, tackles again. The game hadn't even ended and I already had a crick in my shoulder blades from all the tension.

When there were only seconds left, Chris took a few steps back then threw the ball in a perfect arch straight toward Dylan from the forty-five-yard line, and I was up on my feet right along-side Miriam and Cash. It seemed like every player on the field was running toward that damn ball. Sucking in a breath and holding it in, my hands clutched my head and I watched Dylan shoulder bump another player, jump high, and snatch the ball right out of the air with his fingertips. Before I could process the perfect catch, he had the ball tucked under his arm and was off running toward the goal line like the roadrunner from the cartoon.

A player caught up to him from behind and threw himself toward Dylan's back, but as if he had eyes in the back of his head, Dylan swerved right and avoided him by inches. I jumped up and down like a giddy little school girl. "Yes! Yes!" All caught up with the roaring crowd now, I was about to come out of my skin when someone came out of nowhere and tried to block him. Dylan jumped to the side before the guy could do anything, and he ran the last five yards without another player hunting him down. They were too slow for him. My cheeks hurting from smiling so damn hard, I jumped up and down as I watched my buddy score his third touchdown of the night.

He was amazing.

My hands shaking a little, I lifted my camera up, ready to photograph the joy on his perfectly chiseled face if he took his helmet off, but instead of letting his teammates tackle him down like they had before, he dodged every single one of them like they didn't exist for him and ran straight back to the fifty yard line, ignoring every player and non-player pouring onto the field. I followed him with my eyes to see where he was going and watched as he stopped and dropped to one knee in front of JP, who looked like he was having a little trouble standing upright with his crutches. Out of nowhere, Chris appeared right next to Dylan and dropped to his knee as well.

Holding my breath, I lifted my camera a little higher, my fingers itching to capture just a second of their moment. Then, one by one, all the players on the field kneeled in front of their teammate, a few behind Dylan and Chris, a few to their right.

Before the chanting started, I ran toward the mouth of the tunnel, came to a quick stop, and lined up with JP to the left so I could have Dylan right in the middle of my shot. I focused on Dylan's hard, unyielding, sweaty face and took the shot that would become one of my most cherished photos.

When it all stopped, I was still standing in the exact same spot, rooted in place.

Dylan got up and went to his friend. Whispering something in his ear, he carefully pulled JP to himself and they gave each other one of those manly hugs. I was having a really really hard time holding back my tears. When the rest of his team swarmed around their injured teammate, Chris included, Dylan's dark blue eyes met mine, piercing me with his gaze.

As he broke off from the crowd, I slowly lowered my camera and watched him stalk toward me, our eyes never losing contact. He covered the distance between us in no time. When he was standing right in front of me, I stared up at him, just as out of breath as he was, if not more. On top of that, I could feel my hands shaking ever so slightly as I tried not to lose the smile I'd plastered on my face.

Calm your tits, Zoe. It's nothing more than an adrenaline rush. He is still your friend.

"Who is he?" were the first words out of his mouth.

My smile faltered. "What?"

"Number four." I must have looked as clueless as I felt because he waited for an answer from me before continuing. "Trevor Paxton—you were in his arms."

Snorting, I relaxed and my smile tipped my lips up again. I'd been right before—he *was* jealous. Just the realization eased something in my chest. "My friend from Phoenix. We grew up in the same neighborhood, same high school and everything. Strictly friends."

At my words, his shoulders dropped down slightly. "Okay. Okay, that's good."

I nodded in quick jerks and tried not to grin. Yeah, it was good.

His eyes bored into mine and his jaw clenched. "You're not looking away. Why are you not looking away?"

I ignored his words and lost the battle with my lips. I smiled big, teeth and everything. "You were amazing, Dylan, really freaking amazing." Standing in front of me in all those pads, he looked so intimidating, so big.

His frown smoothed out completely and he gave me a boyish smile. "Yeah?"

My eyes dropped to his lips for a few seconds as I took in that beautiful, surprised smile—another one to add to the list.

I wish he was mine, I thought as I lifted my eyes back up.

I smiled even bigger, if that was possible. "Yep."

One of the coaches ran past us, breaking our little huddle.

Dylan grabbed my arm and shuffled me back a few steps until I was almost against the wall, bringing us closer.

"Now I understand all the hype," I continued before he could say anything else. "I feel a little light headed, like I'm a drunk on the game. You guys were amazing." Another winning—or losing, depending on where you stood—smile from me. "I admit, I know practically nothing about football, and I only watch it on TV for twenty minutes tops before I get bored, but it was different being here. I'm not sure you'd call it fun since you're the one being chased and occasionally tackled, but I loved it. I didn't like seeing you get tackled like that, of course, but you know what I mean. It was almost better than watching you work out in the kitchen—almost." I paused to take a breath. I was awestruck, and I didn't mind him seeing that in my face. "I want to do it all over again, right now. You were really great, Dylan."

The deep blue in his eyes sparkled with an emotion I couldn't name. "You said that already, Flash," he murmured, his deep voice sending a thrill through my body.

I swallowed and moved my head up and down, because I was having trouble coming up with more words, and yeah, I had said that already—a few times actually. My brain was telling me it was time to leave before I started rambling.

When Dylan looked over his shoulder toward the field, I looked that way too. A few of his teammates had already started to head for the locker rooms.

"I should let you—"

I stopped speaking when Dylan's gloved hand—his *huge* gloved hand—cupped my cheek and gently tilted my face up. The world around me slowed down, and I stood still. I swear to you, I watched his eyes roam my face in slow motion.

"I like having your eyes on me, Zoe."

I managed to force a nervous smile. His thumb moved on my cheek, rendering me...basically completely helpless.

Forgetting myself, forgetting where we were, I whispered, "I like watching you."

His tongue peeked out and touched his lower lip. "I know."

Oh, Dylan, why did you do that?

"I meant I like watching you—*liked* watching you play tonight. I didn't mean it to sound like I like watching you when you're not playing. I definitely wouldn't watch you if you were just standing there, or I don't know...I wouldn't watch you when you're working out, and I would never watch you if you were—"

"You know why I like watching you?"

The question shut me up pretty quickly, which was probably for the best; who knew what else I would spew out.

"Because I can't take my eyes away from you. Everything else...it all disappears, and..."

And... And...

"And?"

I tried my best not to look eager for his answer—or let's say not *too* eager, because there was no way he couldn't tell I was very interested and invested in hearing what he was about to say.

He let out a heavy breath and decided not to finish that particular sentence. I'd seen it in his eyes, a slight change, there and gone.

Goddammit!

"I don't know what I'm going to do with you, Zoe. You're driving me absolutely fucking crazy. First Jared, and now this Trevor guy."

Come again?

His chest still rising and falling rapidly, he looked like he wanted to say more but just stared into my eyes instead.

When it started to become too much for me—I mean, I'm a puny human, after all—I tried to clear my throat as a prelude to getting the hell away, but something—most probably air—got stuck in my throat and triggered a small coughing fit, forcing his hand to drop away.

"Sorry," I wheezed out when I could breathe again.

More and more players were heading toward the locker rooms. Some of them hit Dylan in the back with comments like, "Good catch, man," and "You did good, bro." Some only offered snickers.

He put a little distance between us, backing away, but his eyes lingered on my lips. "It'll happen soon you know. I wonder if you're ready for it, because we're almost there. I can see it in your eyes, and you're going to lose, Zoe, just like I knew you would."

"What? Almost where? Lose what?"

"The bet," he explained calmly. "You're going to kiss me and lose the bet. You won't be able to help yourself."

Lips tipping up, he grinned at me playfully.

"Oh, I won't, huh? So humble, too."

"Yeah." He shrugged. "So you should give up, uncomplicate the things you needed to uncomplicate. If there is...more I don't know about and you can't do it for some fucked-up reason, tell me. I'll uncomplicate it for you. I like the anticipation of you, Flash, not gonna lie about that, but—"

"Hey, Dylan! You coming or what?" My head moved toward the sound and I saw Chris and JP waiting for my oh-so-humble roommate.

"You go ahead, I'll be right there," he shouted back.

I watched his friends shake their heads and walk away. When I looked back up at Dylan, he was studying me closely. For a brief moment, I wondered if Mark had seen us standing like this, but I didn't give a shit about that, not at that moment, at least. If there were repercussions—such as him yelling at me for no good reason —*well, fuck him.*

"We need to talk, Zoe. Soon, we need to talk and figure things out."

"Uh, figure what out?" I asked, distracted by his moving lips.

"The thing you need to uncomplicate."

I looked up and into his eyes again; there was a storm brewing there.

"It's driving me crazy," he continued.

Like the idiot I am, I just stared at him. What the hell could I have said?

Someone bumped him in the back, causing him to lose his balance and brace his palm on the wall behind me. He mumbled something under his breath and looked over his shoulder before looking down at me.

"It's going to happen."

He was jogging away before I even had a chance to nod or open my mouth.

"I'm telling you, any time now," he yelled one last time before disappearing from my sight.

Seconds later, Mark and his entourage walked past me without even noticing I was standing there. If it had happened when we were back in L.A.—actually, it *had* happened on campus more than a handful of times, and on each and every one of those occasions, I felt like I was nothing but a nuisance when he looked right through me, but this time I couldn't have cared less. He was the least of my worries.

CHAPTER SEVENTEEN

DYLAN

As the weeks passed in a blur, it was getting harder and harder to keep my hands and eyes off of Zoe. With everything going on with JP and his recovery, other than Chris, she was the only person I was interested in spending time with. As much as being friends with her had been a joke to me from that first day she'd jumped on me, very much naked after her towel failed her, she'd actually somehow ended up being exactly that.

My buddy.

My very own buddy...who I wanted to fuck senseless.

Every time her arm accidentally brushed mine as we passed each other in the hallway or in the kitchen, every time she looked up at me and smiled, all those nights we'd sat on opposite ends of the couch and watched a movie on her laptop...every time she came out of her room with sleepy eyes, smooth legs, and that fucking perfect ass I always got an eyeful of when she reached up to grab a bowl from one of the cupboards and pretended not to watch me while I did my morning workout routine right in front of her as she had her breakfast...every time we bumped into each other while heading to the bathroom to brush our teeth, eyes sleepy, voices husky...every time she opened the cupboard that held her precious M&Ms and spent a few seconds staring at them for God knows what reason...every time I caught her tiptoeing into the apartment so Ms. Hilda wouldn't catch her...every time she held my gaze for more than a few seconds...you get where I'm going with this?

It seemed like every time she took a breath, I got hard just watching her chest rise and fall, my hands itching to touch her skin, her lips, her neck, her chin, her hands, her legs, her delectable ass. She was slowly killing me, and from everything I knew about her, she didn't have a single clue what she was doing.

Every time I saw her, I had more and more trouble remembering why I couldn't be with her. While I was going crazy for her, day after day, she was still seeing him. I told myself it wasn't possible, that I was blowing things out of proportion, but all the little clues were there. Just because I hoped I was wrong, hoped it would end any day now, that didn't change the outcome or the facts. She had something going on with Coach, and it was fucking with my head like nothing else ever had in my entire life. I didn't believe their families were friends. I didn't know what to believe, but I didn't believe that. I couldn't imagine Zoe being with him; she wasn't that kind of girl, yet...

On top of everything, I barely had time to do anything. I was either working on a paper or in the weight room, getting my ass kicked by our trainers. It didn't help that I was keeping a secret from Chris, maybe several. Oh, he knew his dad was seeing someone again—he'd told me that just a week before—but they always knew when his dad was having an affair. The thing he didn't know was that the apartment I was staying in was actually his father's, and he didn't know that Zoe was also staying in his father's apartment. He had no idea what it all meant.

Weeks had passed since Zoe had photographed our away game, since I'd seen her with another guy and came close to losing it in front of everyone. We still hadn't sat down and had our talk. Some days I thought she was avoiding me on purpose, some days we just didn't have the time, and some days I wanted to do nothing but sit down next to her on the floor in front of the couch and just have dinner while talking about nothing in particular. Halloween had passed, we had lost and won more away games and home games, and this crazy thing I was starting to feel for her wasn't going anywhere, despite the circumstances.

I no longer gave a damn about how wrong it was to mess with someone else's girl because I couldn't accept the fact that she either really was someone else's girl—if she was, I was the world's biggest fucking idiot for starting to fall for my friend—or she was in a really fucked-up, weird situation with my coach. If that was the case, I was ready to fix it.

The only upside of feeling frustrated to no end when living with the girl I thought should be with me and not some other bastard was that I worked harder than I ever had in my life. All my trainers were impressed. Chris and I were perfectly in sync out on the field, and I was giving it my all. The dream I'd had since I couldn't even remember when was going to become a reality. I was going to make my family proud.

After a heavy workout session with one of the trainers who was helping me get ready for the combine coming up at the end of February, I headed home, hoping I'd get to see Zoe. I knew her schedule by heart, and if she hadn't booked a photography job at the last minute, I knew she'd get home a little after me. Ever since the away game, she tried her best not to be alone with me for too long if she could help it, but we lived in the same damn apartment. She slept literally steps away from me, so there was only so much running away she could manage—not that I actually believed she was trying her best at it.

I considered stopping at her favorite pizza place to surprise her but changed my mind and decided to wait for her to come home then convince her to go out for pizza. In my mind, it sounded like a much better plan.

Only it wasn't.

I realized that once I made it to our floor and found Vicky waiting for me in front of our apartment door.

Standing frozen at the top of the stairs, I thought I'd kill JP if he was the one who'd told her where to find me. Vicky's head snapped up from her phone when she heard my footsteps and she pushed off of the wall.

"Dylan, I—"

"What the hell are you doing here?"

She pushed her phone into her back pocket, took a step toward me, and then stopped.

"I want to talk to you, just this once. Please, Dylan."

I got unstuck and walked past her to unlock the door.

"We have nothing to talk about. You shouldn't have come here, Victoria."

I looked over my shoulder and caught her subtle flinch at my use of her full name.

She raised her hands then dropped them to her sides. "Well, too bad. You're not answering my texts or calls so I'm not moving an inch until you talk to me."

As her voice started to rise steadily, my head flew toward Ms. Hilda's door. Normally, the grumpy woman would've been out that door the second she caught someone coming up the stairs, without fail, but there was no sign of her at the moment, and I wondered if she was watching us through the peephole.

Ignoring Victoria, I opened the door and threw my bag inside before facing her again.

"I have no reason to return your calls, Victoria. It's been months. There is nothing to say."

Having said everything I would say on the subject, I went to close the door in her face, but she was faster and slapped her palm against the surface to stop me. The sound echoed off the walls, and if Ms. Hilda, for some unknown reason, hadn't been aware of what was going on right in front of her doorstep, she definitely would've heard that noise and would soon come out to investigate.

"*I* have things to say," she announced with a lift of her chin as she met my gaze.

"Victoria...leave," I gritted out through clenched teeth, and she was smart enough to notice how close I was to losing it on her. She dropped her angry stance and took a step back, going back to the innocent act.

"I'll leave. I promise, I will. I just want to talk, Dylan, just this once, and then if you don't want to, you'll never see me again. I only want to apologize."

A key rattled, signaling that it was too late to get rid of Victoria without an incident that would take even longer to resolve. Ms. Hilda would be out as soon as she unlocked her door, demanding to know what was going on, and I had no time for that woman.

Out of options, I jerked my head. "Get inside."

Victoria walked in. Just as I clicked the door shut behind her, Ms. Hilda's door groaned open.

Walking past my ex-girlfriend, I headed straight toward the kitchen area. "You have until I hear the next-door neighbor close her door." Pressing my palms on the breakfast bar, I felt it necessary to repeat myself. "I don't need your apology. I will listen, only because you forced me to, but I have nothing to say to you. I thought I'd already made that clear when I caught you getting fucked by my teammates."

"You're still angry—don't you see what that means?" she asked, walking toward me.

"What the fuck do you think it means?" I shot back.

"If you're angry, it means you still care. I know I hurt you,

Dylan. Trust me, you finding me that night, *seeing* me like that... it hurt me more than it hurt you and—"

"Are you fucking kidding me right now?"

"I'm really sorry you had to see that—you have no idea how much—but it was just a one-time thing. I don't even know how it happened. One minute I was waiting for you upstairs and the next I found mys—"

When she rounded the corner to get to my side, I straightened up and walked away.

"You're done."

"Wait, Dylan." She caught up to me and grabbed my arm. "I just wanted to see you to apologize, okay? You didn't even let me do that."

I glanced down at her hand, which was still attached to my arm, and pointedly met her gaze. She let go of me and took a step back.

"You were so busy. First, it was summer classes then it was... We hadn't had sex in two weeks and you were—"

"I was going through fall camp, Victoria. I was barely dragging myself back home at the end of the day."

Her hand landed on my forearm once again and she stepped closer. "I know. I know, and I should've been more understanding. I know that now, but it wasn't like I had planned to—"

We heard a key in the lock, and Victoria leaned to my right to see past me.

"Did you know that a seahorse—the male, by the way, in case you didn't know—gives birth to up to two thousand tiny baby seahorses? Can you imagine? That's two *thousand*. I just watched an Instagram video and it—"

I looked over my shoulder and saw Zoe frozen just inside the open door.

Her eyes jumped between Victoria and me as she cleared her throat. "Hi. I'm sorry, I hope I'm not interrupting."

Like I had started doing every time she walked into the room, I took her in. Her hair look mussed up and I knew she had just taken it down from a messy bun at the nape of her neck; she wanted it out of her face when she was taking photos. She had on those sexy brown boots that made my dick twitch for some goddamned reason, skin-tight black jeans that did more things to my dick than just make it twitch whenever I got an eyeful of her ass in them, and as always, a simple white t-shirt that had something written on it on the front under the wine-colored cardigan she couldn't seem to part ways with lately.

Zoe turned her back to us to take her key from the lock, and my eyes dropped to the curve of her ass. Before I could take my eyes off of that, they both spoke up.

"Do you want me to leave, Dylan? Maybe we can talk later," Victoria whispered next to me.

"I didn't know you had someone over. Maybe I should leave and..." Zoe said over Victoria.

"Yes, leave," I rushed out in a flat voice. With a frown on my face, I watched Zoe's eyes widen as her face crumpled.

"I'm just going to leave this here," she mumbled in a small voice, and by the time I turned around fully to see what the hell she was talking about, she had already dropped her camera bag next to the door and was closing it. The only thing was...she was on the wrong side of the door.

"I think she didn't realize you were talking to me."

Ignoring Victoria's presence, I rushed to the door, but there was no sight of Zoe when I yanked it open, only the sound of her running footsteps.

I closed the door with barely controlled anger and turned to Victoria.

"Get out."

"I didn't know you were seeing someone, Dylan. I'm sorry, I really didn't mean to—"

I glared at her. "Victoria, get out. Please."

"I asked the boys and they told me you weren't seeing anyone. I'm sorry. I know you won't believe me, but I didn't come here to cause trouble. I just wanted—"

"What the hell did you want, Victoria? You said you came to apologize, and you did. Now that you did, you can leave. I don't need to hear you say you're talking to the boys."

She shook her head and lifted her hands up. "Oh, no, I didn't mean it like that. I meant your teammates, not Max and Kyle. I talked to your...other teammates."

It was like she wasn't hearing a word of what I was saying, and I needed her to get the hell out like yesterday.

"I can talk to your girlfriend, explain."

"She is not..." *Mine*, I thought. She wasn't mine yet, but that was going to change. I was done waiting. "She is my friend, and you're not going to say a single word to her."

Either she finally saw how angry and tense I was or she heard it in my voice, because she took a few steps back and looked up at me with sad eyes.

"You're so angry."

"Victoria," I growled, my hand practically shaking the door handle with fury. I needed to go after Zoe, not stand around and indulge my ex.

"I think I should leave."

"You think?" I asked in disbelief.

Closing my eyes, I rolled my shoulders to relax. It didn't help.

Opening the door, I waited for her to walk through. Instead of leaving right away, she stepped out and faced me.

"I just needed you to know I'm sorry, and...I miss you, Dylan. It's college and I made a mistake and—"

"Now I know," I interrupted and closed the door in her face.

Bending down, I took my phone from my bag and dialed Zoe's number.

It rang and rang, but there was no answer. She had it on her, I was sure. Sending her a quick text, I didn't wait for her to get back to me. There was a good chance she had misinterpreted Victoria's presence and was ignoring any calls and texts coming from me.

I kicked my bag and it slid toward the living room.

"Goddammit!"

Rubbing my palm on my head, I called Jimmy.

He answered on the second ring. "Jimmy here. Talk to me."

"Jimmy, I know my shift starts in two hours, but I'm not gonna be able to make it tonight. It's...football stuff."

"You realize it's Saturday, right? I need you here, man."

"I know, and I'm sorry, but it came up pretty last minute. I can't skip this. I promise I'll make it up to you. I wasn't scheduled for tomorrow, but I'll come to help. I'll come in midweek too."

He released a long sigh that blended in with the music in the background. "Fine, fine—but you can't skip out on me tomorrow."

"I won't. I'll be there. Thank you, Jimmy."

My next call was to Chris.

"What's up?"

"Do you have a phone number for the fullback who played our first and second year? You know, the one who got transferred?

"You mean Tony?"

"Yes, that's the one. Do you have it?"

"Let me check. What's going on?"

"I need to ask him something."

"Oh, thanks, that explains a lot. Hold on...okay, I have it."

"Good. Text it to me."

"Are you going to tell me what's going on?"

"Later. Text me."

I headed out before he could text me the number. If I had taken Zoe's friend's number two years ago myself, it would've been easier to find out where she'd gone, but I hadn't. Even if it was a long shot, Tony might have held on to the number of the girl he had dated for almost a year before he transferred, and I was pretty sure that girl would have Kayla's number. It was my only shot. Sure, I could've waited for her to come back to the apartment, but that could take hours, and she'd spend those hours thinking something I didn't want her to think. It wasn't a choice I even considered more than a second.

My phone pinged with a new text at the same time I stepped out of the apartment building.

It was my lucky day. After talking to Tony, I got the phone number of the girl, whose name was apparently Erica. Then I called Erica and asked for Kayla's number.

The voice on the other end of the line answered timidly. "Hello?"

"Kayla?" I asked, not sure if it was the right number or not.

"Umm, yes? Who is this?"

"It's Dylan, Zoe's..." What the hell was I for her? "Zoe's friend—her roommate. I'm sorry for bothering you, but I'm trying to find Zoe and she isn't answering my calls. Do you have any idea where she is?"

"Give me a sec," she whispered.

There was some rustling, a door opening and closing, and then she was on the line again, her voice stronger than it had been before.

"She texted me a few minutes ago. Why do you want to know where she is? Is something going on?"

"No. I just need to see her."

I waited through the silence.

"Okay. I don't know what's going on, but I hope you won't make me regret this."

"Please," I forced out.

"I'm heading to a party at my boyfriend's frat house. She texted me to ask if we could meet so I told her I'd meet her there in an hour so. I don't know where she'll go if she's not home."

"Where is the party?"

CHAPTER EIGHTEEN

DYLAN

When I stepped through the frat house's open door around ten PM, there were already red Solo cups littering the ground and the air reeked of sweat, beer, and the worst mix of perfumes—the staples of college parties. Just a few steps in and I could already see the closely pressed bodies on the dance floor. I pushed past the few people who were standing around the door, casually chatting by screaming at each other over the music, and started to look around. Skipping the dance floor, I searched every inch of the house, including the upstairs rooms. Zoe was nowhere to be found, and neither was her friend, Kayla.

Hoping maybe they just hadn't made it there yet, I did another sweep of the first floor then headed for the basement. Thankfully the music wasn't loud enough to make my ears bleed, but I knew I'd have a headache the next morning.

Frat parties are never a good idea if you're sober and tired through the whole thing.

Spotting a few teammates on my way down, I had to stop to exchange a few pleasantries. When I spotted Zoe sitting on an ugly green couch in the corner near an ongoing beer pong match, I was able to breathe easier and think again. She was sitting next to Kayla, who had her back to me, and they were talking in what seemed like hushed tones—as hushed as they could get in that ruckus with everyone cheering on the beer pong champions.

It was when I was halfway to them that Zoe finally noticed me and our eyes met across the room. Someone touched my shoulder and tried to stop me from getting to her. I turned to the guy with a scowl on my face and he backed off.

"Sorry, dude. Just wanted to say congrats on a fucking awesome game yesterday."

"Thanks," I mumbled and gave him a chin lift, already walking away.

Pushing away the few people standing in my way, I finally reached Zoe.

Without stopping or breaking one of our rare periods of extended eye contact, I leaned down and grabbed her hand in mine, tugging her up with ease.

"Zoe!" Kayla yelped, grabbing her left arm.

"I need to talk to her," I explained before we started playing a round of tug-of-war and Zoe could cut in. I didn't want to give her a way of escape.

After Zoe gave her friend a cautious nod, Kayla reluctantly let her go. I took the half-empty red cup from her free hand and put it in the middle of the beer pong table. Ignoring the groaned protests, I took her toward the staircase, which had a small pocket of privacy directly behind it.

I stepped on something sticky that made me pause, but when I saw that it wasn't puke, I ignored it kept walking. Pulling Zoe next to the wall, where the music was slightly muted, I studied her face. With her big, vulnerable eyes, she looked so unsure. Carefully, she pulled her hand out of mine.

"You left," I started, and I could hear how gruff my voice sounded.

She looked taken back but still answered. "Yes, because you told me to leave."

"No. I told *her* to leave."

"You were looking right into my eyes when you spoke. It's okay, Dylan. You're allowed to have friends over. I shouldn't have... I hope I didn't interrupt—"

I towered over her and she leaned back. "Are you being serious right now?"

Even bigger eyes. "What?"

"You *hope* you didn't interrupt?"

Her brows drew together in confusion. "Yes?"

"Are you playing with me, Zoe? Because I can't believe you can be this clueless. You can't be."

"I'm not doing anything. You're angry with me for some reason, and I think I'm just gonna go back to Kay—"

As she turned away from me, I caught her wrist from behind and pulled her back to my chest. After the initial grunt, she stilled. Thanks to those boots I loved so much, her head reached almost up to my chin.

Tilting my head, I took a deep breath of her sweet scent and tried to calm the hell down. Her shoulders tensed.

"You can't be this clueless," I repeated in a whisper against her ear, catching the slight tremble in her body. Her head twisted, just a small movement. I glanced down to see her hand gripping the edge of her cardigan, so I reached for her fingers and laced them with my own, ignoring how tensely she was holding herself.

"Dylan, I—"

"I just want you to listen to me, just once. That's it, Zoe. That's all." Grasping her other hand, I did the same and wrapped our arms around her stomach. Her left hand squeezed mine in a tight grip, but she didn't yank herself away.

I closed the last few inches separating us by pulling her flush against my chest.

"Dylan, there are peo—"

"It's dark, and no one can see us back here," I muttered in a bitter voice. Her warning helped me remember exactly why I couldn't and shouldn't hold her like this, not even in a dark corner at a party where no one cared about anything but their booze and who they'd get to take to bed or whatever empty surface they could find. "Don't ask me to let go, please. I can't."

She quieted so I gave her middle a squeeze as a thank you and let out a long breath. Resting my forehead on her shoulder, I inhaled deeply. Slowly, as if she was afraid she'd startle me, she rested her temple against the side of my head, and something inside me unraveled, my blood boiling hot.

I couldn't do it. I couldn't stay away anymore.

My fingers tightened around hers to the point that I knew I must've been hurting her, yet we still stood like that for several seconds.

Lifting my head, making sure our temples stayed in contact, I started to explain what she had walked in on before she ran away.

"I came home just a few minutes before you and she was waiting at the door. I told her to leave, but she kept insisting she wanted to talk to me."

Zoe's body stiffened against mine. Having no clue what I was allowed to do, how much I could cross the invisible line that existed between us, I leaned harder against the wall to restrain myself from doing something stupid and limited myself to stroking just over that small dip where her thumb and first finger met.

"Before I could make her leave, I heard Ms. Hilda unlock her door so I had to let her come in. When you got there, she'd only been there for a few minutes."

"Who is she?" she whispered, her head tilted to the side, eyes half closed, her breathing uneven.

I huffed and nuzzled her temple.

"Victoria, my ex. I had nothing to say to her, I swear, and when you came in, she asked if I wanted her to leave at the same time you did. I didn't even think, just said yes. I didn't think you'd misunderstand. I didn't think you'd leave."

There was no reaction for long seconds, but she wasn't walking away either.

"I was going to take you out for pizza before my shift at Jimmy's," I muttered into her ear when the shouts coming from the room rose up and blended with the music.

Her head tilted farther, offering me more as the back of her head dropped to my shoulder.

Fuck.

She muttered something, but I couldn't hear it, so I leaned down until her mouth was right next to my ear.

"I love pizza," she repeated, and I had to close my eyes because her lips had brushed against my skin, nearly rendering me incapacitated.

"I know you do—you only say it every day." I smiled in relief and pressed a lingering kiss on her cheek that surprised the both of us.

Slowly she lifted her head from my shoulder. Reluctantly, I let her hands go and our arms dropped down. I had no idea what the hell I was doing, and I was afraid I was too far gone to stop myself when it came to anything involving Zoe.

Clearing my throat, I continued, and this time I tried to talk louder so I wouldn't have to speak directly into her ear. The closer we stood, the more dangerous it was. "I ran after you, but you were already gone, and I didn't want to leave Victoria in the apartment. I sent her away less than a minute later then came after you."

Turning around to face me, she looked up, straight into my eyes. "How did you know I was going to be here?"

"I called Chris and got the phone number of the guy who dated Kayla's friend back when I met her. Then a couple more calls and I got Kayla's number. She didn't tell you?" She bit her bottom lip and shook her head. Unable to stop myself, I reached up and cupped her cheek, saving her lip by pulling at it with my thumb. "I didn't know where you were, so I had to wait an hour before coming here."

"I went for pizza," she said with a hesitant smile on her lips.

Letting go of her cheek, I dropped my head back on the wall and laughed, relaxing a bit.

"Of course you did," I said when I could look at her again.

She lifted her shoulder and gave me a half shrug. "Food makes me happy, pizza especially."

When neither of us uttered a word, just keeping our eyes on each other, my smile slowly disappeared and I straightened from the wall.

At the same time, the music stopped and there were only shouts and boos.

"Zoe..."

She was quick to look away and gave me her back.

"I don't think Kayla is okay. Something's wrong, and I should get back to—"

I grabbed her hand from behind since it had kept her from leaving the last time.

I couldn't let her go, not just yet. That little pocket of space was ours, providing shelter for us, for what I'd been craving for weeks, and I wasn't ready or willing to let it go so quickly or easily. "Ten minutes," I said. "Just ten more minutes to feel like this."

When I gave her hand a gentle tug, she didn't argue or pull away. In two steps she was back in my arms and I was hugging her to my chest even harder. She didn't seem to mind and I didn't plan on letting go, not for at least another ten minutes.

The way my heart was hammering in my chest, I didn't think I'd ever been so anxious in my life. It was the same kind of thrill as being on the field.

"Dylan," Zoe mumbled when the back of my hand brushed the underside of her boob and her head rested against my shoulder again.

I hugged her tighter.

"Choose me, Zoe." The words rushed out of me before I could stop myself.

Her grip reflexively tightened around my hands at my words as her eyelids closed slowly.

"Leave him," I continued. "I'm right here and I want you, so damn much. I'm not sure how much more I can take. Every time I see you with a guy...I just want to rip his head off for touching you, for looking at you, for being close to you when I can't. The guy from the Tucson game? I've never played that aggressively before. All I wanted to do was take him down. You're driving me crazy, and I've never been so jealous of anyone in my life." I paused. "I need you to let him go, Zoe. Whatever it is that's going on between you two, I don't want to know. Just...I need you to choose me now. I'm the one that's supposed to be with you, not anyone else."

Her back still flushed to my chest, she shifted in my arms enough to look up at me. "Dylan," she whispered, and I watched her lips move, her tongue sneaking out to wet them. "You don't understa—"

I pulled her hair away from her neck, pressed my lips against her skin, and felt the vibration of her groan against my lips.

My body overheated from being so close to her, from having trouble deciding what I wanted to do to her first when we were alone—truly alone, not in a frat house surrounded by drunken idiots. Just thinking of the possibilities made my dick press harder against the fly of my pants.

Seven minutes more. This was mine. Ours.

As N.E.R.D.'s song "She Wants To Move" started in the background, not even realizing what I was doing, I opened my mouth, grazed her skin with my teeth, and gently sucked on her neck, not hard enough to leave a mark, but hard enough to make her lose a little bit of control and let me hear her moan again.

Instead of going in for more like I was desperate to do, I stood still and tried to clear my mind.

What the fuck are you doing, man?

I let go of her and her body stiffened.

"I should apologize for that...it was more than just a friendly kiss...but I can't."

"I don't have a boyfriend," she blurted out, head turned toward me, eyes focused on my chin, arms hugging herself as if she was about to fall apart and was barely holding herself together.

"What did you just say?"

"I don't have a boyfriend," she repeated slowly, this time meeting my gaze.

"It's over? It's done?" I asked in disbelief as something indescribable coursed through my veins.

"I..." She looked away and nodded. "Yes."

Reaching for her hand, I turned her to face me, everything around us turning into a messy blur. I cupped her cheeks and rested my forehead against hers, not breathing. "When?" She opened her mouth to answer, but I cut her off. "Never mind. I don't care."

Nudging her nose with mine, I kissed the edge of her mouth as she let out a harsh breath.

"We need to talk, Dylan. I need to tell you what was going on. I don't want you to think—"

"We'll figure out what to do," I murmured and kissed her cheek.

"What do you—"

"Are you drunk?"

"What? No. You need to listen to—"

"Then kiss me, Zoe."

She pulled back, studying my face as her eyes slowly narrowed. "And lose the bet?" Her eyes dropped to my lips then back up. "You kiss me first," she said, all breathless as her cheeks turned a pretty pink.

She was going to lose the bet.

I slipped my arms around her waist, caging her in, and smiled down at her. I felt light, relieved, exhilarated. "Are you scared?"

"What? Scared of you?" She snorted and then blushed.

My smile grew bigger and I hid my face against her neck. "You're so damn cute, and you're trembling," I whispered in her ear. "Are you scared of kissing me?" A pause so I could press another lingering kiss on her neck. "Or are you scared I'll kiss you?" Lifting my head, I met her big eyes. "I don't give a fuck about the bet, I just need—"

Someone bumped into us and Zoe gasped loudly as she bounced against the wall to her right. She rubbed her shoulder as I pulled her behind me.

"Dude!" shouted a slick-haired fucker, looking at us with half-shut eyes. The girl hanging on to his shoulder giggled behind him.

"Get the fuck out of here," I growled, and his bloodshot eyes widened.

"Take it easy, man. Every room is full. Didn't know someone had already claimed this spot. We'll find another corner."

"Yeah, do that."

When they left, I turned around to find Zoe leaning her forehead against the wall, eyes closed.

Stepping behind her, I rubbed the arm she had bounced off of. "You okay?"

Clearing her throat, she nodded but didn't give me her eyes.

Instead of forcing her to face me, I slid my arms around her and pulled her hands away from the wall. I wasn't ready for her to hide from me. I needed more.

More of her eyes on mine.

More of that shy, shaky smile I loved so much.

More of her touch.

More of her lips, her skin.

"Zoe," I coaxed. Her forehead still pressed against the wall, she was looking down at our hands. My palms were open, her hands resting on top. This time she was the one to curl her fingers around mine and hold on tight.

Lost in our little bubble, I flipped our hands and pressed the backs of hers against the tops of her thighs. With no hesitation at all, I pulled her ass against my rapidly growing erection.

I was watching her so closely, every hitch of her breath, every drowsy blink of her eyes. It was easy to catch the moment she stopped breathing and time stood still.

Then she groaned, a low, sexy sound just for my ears, and it broke the hold I had on myself. I hadn't realized there was no music in the background until that sound ripped through me. As I held her in place, it took everything in me not to grind myself against her ass, or better yet, just take her against the wall.

She pushed her ass back and I dropped my head to her shoulder with a growl.

"Dylan," she moaned, triggering another thrust of my hips. Her skin was burning under my lips as I kissed the little spot right under her ear and felt her shiver.

Removing her hands from mine, she grabbed my forearm with one and placed the other on the wall. I kept my hands on her thighs and pushed both of my thumbs right under the edge of her jeans and her underwear so I could pull her tighter, so we could fuse together and become one bundle of need. She rolled her hips back against me.

"Fuck, Zoe. Don't do that."

I lifted one of my hands and gripped her chin, slowly turning it toward my lips. We were both breathing hard when my mouth touched the edge of hers. She let out a small groan and with another roll of her hips, my dick wanted out and in her.

Just when I was about to claim her lips and lose myself in what was probably going to be the best fucking kiss of my life, someone called her name and we both froze.

Zoe gulped.

Unfortunately for us, we heard the same voice again and had to reluctantly step away from each other.

Instead of turning around like Zoe had done immediately after the second call, I faced the wall and adjusted my dick before looking over my shoulder to see Zoe talking with Kayla. I took a deep breath, willed my heart to slow the fuck down, and turned to casually lean back against the wall. When Zoe came back, I took in her flushed cheeks and parted lips—all because of me, all for me.

"What's wrong?" I asked, my voice all kinds of fucked up, and I realized it was taking a whole lot of effort to keep my hands to myself.

"Something...I'm not sure," she replied, her eyes rising to mine for the first time. "She wants to leave, but Keith isn't listening. Something is wrong with them. I need to go."

I straightened from the wall. "I'll come with you."

Shaking her head, she touched my arm then quickly pulled it back.

"She won't talk to me if you're there. She called an Uber and I'm going to go with her."

"You won't come home?"

"I...I don't know. I'll text you if I can."

Fuck.

"We need to talk, Dylan," she said quietly, voicing exactly what was going through my mind. Yes, we needed to talk, badly, but first, we needed to do other things—quenching the thirst I had for her being the first item on the list.

"Tomorrow. We'll figure everything out tomorrow. If you can come back, call me and I'll come get you."

"You don't have to do that. I'll call an Uber or just walk. It's not that far away from the apartment."

I closed the distance between us and tucked her hair behind her ear so I could kiss her temple. "Call me—I don't want you out on your own so late, definitely not walking."

A quick nod as she stared into my eyes, and then she was walking away from me.

CHAPTER NINETEEN

ZOE

"Hi," I said as I answered my phone. If I sounded a little breathless, it had nothing to do with the fact that I was speed-walking—and occasionally hopping to avoid puddles—to the library to meet Kayla and Jared, and everything to do with who was on the other end of the line.

"Zoe."

I had to close my eyes, not because the rain was picking up, but because of him, because of what he did to me. Was there *anything* better than hearing Dylan's morning voice mumble my name on the phone? I didn't think so—or maybe there was; hearing him mumble my name right against my ear would do it too. In fact, it would do it way better.

"You came home and didn't wake me up," he continued as I tried to recover from what his voice was doing to me. The previous night was still fresh in my mind, and I could still feel his body pressing against mine, how I eager I'd been.

The damn had broken.

"It was pretty late. You looked tired, so I didn't want to wake you up." I'd snuck by and tiptoed to my room after finding him asleep on the couch, but I had thrown a blanket on him...so that counted for something.

Knowing what would happen, what we'd end up doing if I did wake him up had prevented me from continuing where we'd left off.

You might call me a chicken; I call myself smart.

I didn't want to have to lie to him—or depending on what you thought, I didn't want to have to *keep* lying to him. I didn't have a boyfriend; that was what I'd told him, and it was the truth. Sure, I was forcing it a little bit since I'd never had a boyfriend to begin with, but still, I didn't have a boyfriend, and I would tell him the rest—really, I would. As I'd guessed, he thought I had something going on with Mark, and who could've blamed him for coming to that conclusion, for God's sake? It was all on me, and I knew that.

So, in a few hours or so, depending on what Kayla wanted to talk about, I'd call Mark—or better yet, text him—not to ask permission, but just so he wasn't blindsided completely in case Dylan said something to him about it. I'd given him Chris, had let him decide on the best time to tell him, but Dylan was mine. He wouldn't have that. I wouldn't let him decide when or how where Dylan was concerned.

There was also the fact that Chris was Dylan's best friend, and thinking about that had kept me up all night. Would Dylan run and tell Chris who I was? He was his best friend—could I ask him to keep me a secret? Would he? Did I even have the right to ask him?

Needless to say, I had no answers.

But I had Dylan.

I had the ghost of his touch on my neck, on my skin, constantly driving me crazy, and I wanted more. I wanted pretty much everything from him.

"Zoe? Did you hear what I said?"

"Sorry. Can you, maybe, repeat that? My mind just wandered off."

"Your mind just..." A long sigh. "Where are you? You're not running away from what happened last night, are you?"

"No. In fact, I'm offended you'd think that." I huffed out a breath. "I'm meeting Kayla at the library, and after that...well, I have no idea how long it will take—she just sent a text this morning and I'm not sure what's going on, but she wasn't good last night. I didn't want to leave her, but her boyfriend got back pretty drunk with two of his friends so she sent me away. Something's definitely up, and I think she might be breaking up with Keith, though it's happened before and he's always managed to win her back so I'm not so sure if this time will be any different, but then again—"

"Baby." That raspy chuckle pretty much killed me. "Stop. You were saying, after that..."

Baby. Baby. Baby.

I halted and closed my eyes. Twice he'd called me that, and each time the butterflies in my stomach had taken flight.

I cleared my throat and started walking again. "I was saying what?"

Another low chuckle reached my ears and my heart warmed at the sound.

"You said you're meeting Kayla at the library then you got off track after that part."

Right.

"After that, I want to talk to you." I heard a long sigh and then a door close.

"Yeah, talking. We need to do that."

"Where are you?"

"A few minutes behind you, I'm guessing. Have you made it to the library yet? It's raining, so be careful."

I did a 360 and looked around. There were people running

around trying to escape the rain, but that was it. It was Sunday, after all. "I'm not melting away, if that's what you mean by be careful, but what do you mean a few minutes behind?"

"I'm meeting with Chris for a workout. If you're not done with Kayla by the time we're finished in the weight room, I'll come find you at the library."

The sooner, the better, I thought. Being out in public instead of in a private, confined space like the apartment where there were beds and couches and counters and semi-flat surfaces would help.

"Okay. Okay, that sounds good. I'm here so I should...let you go. Say hi to Chris from me? Or not. You don't need to say that. I'm not sure why I said that, don't say hi to Chris."

The silence stretched and I face-palmed myself.

"I'll tell him hi and I'll see you soon. Don't disappear on me." A short pause. "I hope you're ready to lose our bet today."

With that, he hung up.

I would not be the one to lose the bet; he just didn't know how stubborn I was yet.

I shook off my umbrella and texted Mark as I walked into the library.

Me: I have to tell Dylan. I'm going to tell him. I don't care what you say.

As soon as I heard the swoosh sound that indicated the message had been sent, I turned my phone off. I knew he'd call the first chance he got, and I didn't want to argue with him or let him scare me off.

Despite knowing that Mark would lose it, I still managed to hold my smile until I found my friend at the very back of the library, in a study room separated from the main sitting area.

As SOON AS I saw the state Kayla was in, I ran to her side and sat my ass down on the chair next to her. "What happened?" When she kept staring at her hands on the table, I covered them with my own. "You have to tell me what's going on Kayla. Look at you."

She raised her head, and I studied my friend's red, puffy eyes as fresh tears ran down her cheeks.

"Kayla?"

"Thank you for coming so quickly."

"Of course, but...what's wrong, KayKay?"

"I think I need help, Zoe."

I pulled her shaky hands off the table and held on tight. "What happened?" *Will she finally say something? Tell us what's going on?* "Do you want to wait for Jared?"

She shook her head. "I didn't call him. I'm not sure I can say this to him."

"Okay, you're officially scaring me. Say what?"

"Look at me," she hissed angrily, yanking her hands from my hold and wiping her cheeks. "I can't even say it to you. How am I supposed to say it to other people?" Her anger disappeared in a heartbeat and her eyes stayed fixed on the table as the tears picked up speed. With my now empty right hand, I brushed off the new tears and looked around us.

Since it was Sunday, the library wasn't filled with students as it would've been if it had been any other day, not to mention it was still early and the place had just opened up. There were only two more early risers like us, and they were sitting in the main room. We were tucked away in the very corner, closed in by bookshelves and four more tables. You could only spot us if you were standing at the doorway and at the right angle.

"How long have you been sitting here?" I asked when she didn't go on. "Come on, let's go out and get some fresh air."

Her hand tightened in mine and she looked at me with fear-filled eyes. "No. No. We need to stay here. I don't want to see him."

"Keith?" I asked, frowning. I'd known he would be the reason she was upset, but...the look on her face, the way she held herself —everything about her screamed that whatever was wrong between those two was far worse than I'd imagined.

"Yes. I'm sorry, I know I'm not making any sense, but this isn't easy to tell. It isn't easy to... I'm sorry, Zoe. I shouldn't have called you. There's nothing you can do."

"Kayla," I whispered, and her blurry eyes tried to focus on me. "I want to help. Please...I miss my friend. Jared misses you, too. We've barely seen you these last few weeks. I can help. Please let me help so I can have my friend back. Tell me what happened and we'll go from there."

"I don't think I can go back," she said quietly. "Everything I have is back at the apartment, but I don't think I can go back to pack my things."

"That's okay. I can do that for you. I'll go with Jared and pack up your stuff. You can wait for us at my apartment and we'll take care of everything, but that's not important right now. Can you tell me what happened to make you this sad? Did he break up with you? Cheat on you? Is that why you don't want to go back? Did something happen after I left?"

Before Kayla could answer me, there was suddenly someone else in the room with us. "Here you are! For fuck's sake, Kayla, I've been looking everywhere for you. Are you fucking deaf? I've called you thirty times."

My head spun around and I watched Keith stride in with his usual smarmy smile on his face. I glanced back at Kayla with worry, only to see her disappear into herself.

As he rounded the desk and made it to her side, I spoke up before he could say anything else. "Keith, I don't think this is a good time. Something is obviously going on between you two, but this isn't the place to hash it out. Just let me talk to her."

He stared at me with a blank expression for a full twenty seconds or so, pupils dilated to hell. Something was wrong with him, even more than usual.

Was he on something? Was he high?

"Shut up, Zoe—or better yet, get the hell out. This doesn't concern you."

I watched him with my mouth open. Sure, he was a dick, always had been, but I hadn't ever seen him high or heard anything from Kayla about him using drugs. Was this what she'd been hiding from us?

He crouched down next to her, one hand on the chair, the other on the desk, boxing her in. Kayla stiffened even further and leaned her entire upper body toward me so she wouldn't have to touch Keith.

I stood up when he opened his mouth to speak. I had no idea what I thought I'd do, but I sure as hell didn't want him near my friend anymore.

"Keith, I don't know what you're on, but go get sobered up. You can't do this here."

"I'm sorry, babe," he groaned, ignoring my presence. "I thought you were into it, swear to God. I didn't hear you say no. Why didn't you say no if you didn't want it?"

A cold chill ran through my body, freezing the blood in my veins. I had to hold on to my chair to stay upright.

"What did you do?" I asked in a broken voice. "What did you do, Keith?"

Kayla started crying in sobs, her body shaking and shaking. Keith kept muttering to her the whole time. I couldn't hear a single thing he was saying through the roar in my ears. It couldn't be true...shouldn't be.

Livid, I mentally shook myself off so I could think, or at least try to think of what to do. The best I could come up with was pushing Keith away from my beautiful friend so he would stop trying to touch her.

I tried to yell at him, tried to shout at him to get the hell away from her, but my voice wouldn't work and all I could manage was a harsh rasp. "Don't touch her you son of a bitch. Don't touch her."

He clearly wasn't expecting *me* to touch him because he fell right on his ass on the black and red checkered floor when I pushed at his shoulder with all the strength I could muster. Before I could get Kayla out of her chair and away from Keith, he was on me, pushing me away from my friend. Then he kept pushing me again and again until I crashed into the chairs.

"Who do you think you are, you little bitch," he snapped right in my face.

Shocked and enraged out of my mind, I pushed myself up, ready to go after him, but he gave me another shove and managed to knock the breath right out of me before I could do anything.

Then his fingers wrapped around my throat, and I had no choice but to still. With him so close to my face, I could smell the alcohol on his breath.

Kayla finally snapped out of wherever she had disappeared to, jumped up, and tried her best to yank him away by clawing at his arms, but to no avail.

"No, Keith! Stop. Let her go. Please!"

Starting to panic for real, I looked around and realized that the few people in the library couldn't really hear us, and nobody could see what was going on. None of the other students had a direct view of our spot.

His hand around my neck wasn't tight enough to cut off my air completely, but he was getting there, taking his time, enjoying the shock in my eyes. When he pressed harder, I gagged and gasped, my eyes starting to bug out. I put my hands around his wrists to pull him away, tried to kick him to get him to let go, to loosen his hold, but his eyes looked empty, dead.

He pushed his face into mine until we were nose to nose then hissed, "Don't touch me again."

When he was done playing his game, he shoved me away, and the back of my head bounced off the desk with a loud thud. I slid down to my hands and knees and coughed until I couldn't anymore.

When I looked up, Kayla was covering her mouth as she cried silent tears, inconsolable. Keith was cooing to her, touching her hair, caressing her face. The closer he stood to Kayla, the harder her tears slid down her cheeks. He gripped her arm and yanked her to his body, whispering something in her ear.

Reaching for her purse where it sat on the desk, he tried to get her to move with him. I somehow picked myself up and grabbed Kayla's other hand. The last thing I wanted was to play tug-of-war with my friend in between, but there was no way I was letting him take her anywhere.

"Keith, stop," I croaked out, my throat still aching, burning.

"Let her go," he demanded through gritted teeth.

"I can't do that. You're scaring her. You need to leave."

Then Kayla broke my heart by repeating those unacceptable words. "Keith...you raped me. You raped me."

"Shut up!" Keith hissed right next to her. "Shut up so I can think! Look what you made do. I came here to apologize and look what you made me do!"

Keith shoved Kayla and she broke her fall by crashing into a chair and grabbing the desk. He started pacing the length of the wall, blocking our exit. I hugged Kayla and held on to her as she shook in my arms. She wasn't the only one crying anymore.

"I'm sorry, Zoe. I'm so sorry," she kept whispering. My ears were ringing with the ugly truth, and I could barely hear what she was saying, could barely comprehend what had happened.

"Shhh, it's fine. It'll be fine. It's okay. We just need to get away. He won't do anything."

But wouldn't he? He looked fried, high off his ass. I didn't have any experience with drugs, and I didn't like being around people who were out of their minds, but even I could spot that he was way off. Was this his first time taking drugs? What the hell was he even on that had turned him into a complete stranger and a raging lunatic, a psychopath? If he didn't calm down soon, I was afraid he was gonna do something worse to hurt Kayla and me.

Suddenly, he stopped pacing. There was complete silence, and we didn't have time to get away.

"You, get out," he ordered me. "I need to talk to Kayla alone. She is not going to leave me over a misunderstanding."

I stared into his eyes and couldn't see anyone in there, certainly not someone my friend was—had been—in love with. When had things had gone so wrong with them? How could Kayla not tell us?

I tried my best to swallow down my fear, but even that hurt, and my voice was still shaky. "I can't leave her here, Keith," I said, panic swelling in my chest. "She is so scared. You're scaring both of us. Can't you see? You need to calm down and let us leave."

In a quick movement, Keith was on Kayla, pulling her away from me, cupping her cheeks to get her to look at him. He was only inches away from her face. Kayla's right hand held on to my arm and she whimpered when Keith's fingers yanked at her chin. Helpless to do anything, I flinched, feeling my heartbeat in my throat.

"Tell her she doesn't know what she's talking about. You would never be scared of me."

I wasn't sure if I was shaking because Kayla's was trembling or if it was just my body, but it only intensified when Keith shot me a look filled with pure hatred.

"That's why I don't like you and that other one talking to her. You fuck with her head too much."

Pulling at Kayla, he broke the hold my friend had on me and started crowding me, pushing at my shoulders until I was once again backed up against the wall.

He kept cursing at me, spit flying out of his mouth, his voice ugly and wrong and hurtful. "You did this. You're taking her away from me. Get the hell out before I hurt you, Zoe."

On the verge of having a panic attack, I lost my breath when he pinned me against the wall with his palm on my chest.

Kayla tried to come to my aid, but he held her back.

"Don't try me, Zoe. I'm not going to tell you again. Get out."

When he dropped his hand and moved to Kayla's side, I stayed plastered to the wall. I couldn't move. I was stuck. Even if I had the ability to move my limbs, how was I supposed to leave my friend alone with this monster? Would I be able to live with myself if he did something to her?

He already did do something to her, you idiot, I thought. *He already did something to her and you weren't there.*

"I can't move," I admitted honestly, quietly.

He took a step forward, but before he could start in on me, Kayla stepped in front of him, blocking him from advancing farther. She was still trembling, but her tears had dried up.

"Keith—Keith, look at me. You were right, I was wrong. You would never hurt me. You didn't mean to hurt me in front of your friends. I understand that now. I'm sorry. Please, you need to get out of here. You hurt her. You'll get in trouble. Please. *Please leave.*"

In the blink of an eye, he was on her, hugging her, kissing her lips fervently. "There you are. There's my baby. You freaked out because you liked it, didn't you? I would never hurt you, baby. I just wanted us to have fun with my friends. I'm your boyfriend, and you love me—that's not rape."

Feeling sick to my stomach, I covered my mouth with my hand to keep everything in.

"We need to get out of here together," he rushed out. "I'm feeling so good right now. You have no idea babe—if you had listened to me and taken the drugs, you wouldn't be shaking like a leaf right now. I feel on top of the world, baby! Next time it'll be just the two of us, don't worry." Pressing a kiss to her forehead, he pushed Kayla away and crouched down to pick up her bag from the floor.

She looked my way and shook her head.

I couldn't—*wouldn't* let him leave with Kayla. I wouldn't let him touch her again. Before they could walk past me, I blocked them.

"You're not leaving with him, Kayla. Have you lost your mind?"

Just like that, Keith's hands were on me again, and this time he wasn't going easy. My back hit the wall yet again, and this time I saw stars when the back of my head thudded against the wall, the sound echoing in the room.

I tried to breathe, but I couldn't. I clawed at his arms, but it was no use. I couldn't do anything to stop him from choking me.

CHAPTER TWENTY

DYLAN

Even though I knew I shouldn't, I headed toward the library so I could see Zoe before Chris and I began our daily workout. I should've given her space. It wasn't like she was running away from me, but I still wanted to see her, still wanted to make sure everything was okay after the night before, make sure there was no chance of her pulling back from me again.

I was too far in my head, trying to come up with a solution for Zoe and me. For no reason at all, I quickened my steps, and soon I was full-out running. There was just something nagging at me, and I felt the need to see her.

Feeling strange, I ignored the rain and pulled out my phone, trying Zoe again.

Her phone went straight to voicemail.

Was she still at the library? Was she really meeting a friend, or had she lied to me?

The need to find her squeezed something in my chest and I took off toward the library like a bat out of hell.

When I finally made it there, I slowed down to a walk. I

walked straight in only to find that there were hardly any students around.

I could hear people murmuring in the main room so I followed the voices. There were only two students, and both of them were wearing headphones, lost in their work. The voices stopped. Walking in farther, I checked the room on the right then headed for the opposite side. When I pushed in some chairs to pass by, I spotted Zoe's friend through the doorway in the east wing. Then my mind registered Zoe being held against the wall by some guy. Her face was flushed, eyes big, and she was silently gasping for air, her hands unsuccessfully trying to push the guy away.

I ran to them, not giving a damn that I was bulldozing through the desks and chairs in my way.

Her name spilled from my lips, but I didn't think she heard me. Neither of them did.

I stepped through the bookshelves and was on the guy in a few seconds, though it felt like several minutes had passed. I gripped his shirt and yanked him away from Zoe. Startled, he lost his balance and stumbled back. Before I could catch her, Zoe fell to her hands and knees, coughing and crying.

I was down on one knee before her friend could get to her.

"Who the fuck are you?" the guy roared, coming at us, but I ignored him and pushed Zoe's hair away from her face.

"Are you okay? Baby, talk to me—you okay?"

She grabbed my arm and lifted her head, her free hand covering her throat. "Yeah," she gasped, her voice rough and barely audible. She cleared her throat and tried again. "Yeah, I'm okay. I'm fine."

I helped her up and her friend took over.

The guy was still spewing shit, shouting and cursing, but I heard not a single word. My senses dulled and all I could focus on was this fucking bastard who had dared to put his hands on Zoe.

As I walked toward him, I took in his bloodshot eyes, twitching hands, and noticeable restlessness.

In three steps I was on him and none of it mattered. I punched him right in his nose and heard the satisfying crack. Out of the corner of my eye, I saw the girls run out of the small room, but my only focus was on the bastard holding his bloody nose.

Shoving at his shoulders until I had him against the wall under the high windows, I reached for his throat. He managed to kick my legs once, his fingers grasping my shirt.

"How does that feel, you son of a bitch," I whispered, slowly tightening my grip. "Does it feel good?"

He made a pathetic attempt at pushing my face, but he was much smaller than me and I slapped his bloody hand away with no trouble.

So focused on the guy, I didn't notice Zoe hitting my arm until she was begging and shouting at me to let go.

"Dylan, Dylan, please. You'll get into trouble, please stop. Dylan, let him go."

I pushed the guy away in disgust and he groaned, coughing and wheezing, his face a dark red. "My head is pounding. I can't think, I can't think," he said as he moaned, coughing between words. He held his head in his palms and kept mumbling on the ground.

Disgusted, I let Zoe pull me away.

Kayla was back and we had more than a few onlookers, mostly students who had filtered into the library. The desk lady was at the door, a phone clutched in her hand as she spoke to someone hurriedly. Campus police would arrive any second now. Gritting my teeth, I turned to Zoe and cupped her face, trying my best to control my breathing. She looked so scared as her eyes welled with tears, and she already had dried tears on her face. How late had I been? What else had he done?

Fuck.

My hands were trembling. "Are you okay?" I asked, my voice coming out harsher than I'd intended. "Did he do anything else?"

She shook her head and blinked, causing the tears to finally slip out. Looking down at her, I wanted to take it all back and wake up early before she could take a step outside the apartment's door.

When I looked back, the guy was on the ground, hitting the back of his hand against the wall.

He just kept muttering the same thing over and over again: "Kayla, what did you do? What did you do?"

Kayla sat down in one of the chairs and starting sobbing uncontrollably.

Zoe's eyes flashed with anger.

"He raped her, Dylan," she whispered, bringing her attention back to me. "We need to do something. He raped her."

CHAPTER TWENTY-ONE

DYLAN

I t took hours for the cops to let us go. They took Kayla to the hospital, and Zoe begged me to take her to her friend. How could I say no to her ever again?

It was seven PM when we finally walked through the apartment door. Kayla had been taken to the hospital where Jared's mom was a nurse, and once we'd gotten there, Zoe had called Jared. As shocked as he'd been, he was at our side in no time. When it was time to leave the hospital, I couldn't convince Zoe to let Kayla leave with Jared and his mom; it took a private conversation with Jared's mom to make that happen.

Like two strangers, we hadn't spoken a single word to each other on the ride back to the apartment. Ever since we'd made it out of the library, Zoe had been holding it together with a very thin thread that I was pretty sure was about to snap at any second.

"Zoe..." I started when I closed the door and leaned against it. We were finally alone, and she was already moving away from me.

She stopped, and her eyes drifted my way.

"I'm going to take a shower."

I sighed as I watched her shuffle toward the bathroom. The door opened and closed then a few seconds later, I heard the rushing sound of the water.

Feeling tired in my bones, I threw my keys toward the living room, not caring where they landed. I gave her an entire minute, not because I thought she would ever call out to me, but because I needed to make sure she was okay and a minute was as long as I could make myself wait.

Skipping a knock, I opened the door and closed it without a sound. The mirror had already fogged up from the steam, but that wasn't what had my attention. I had already heard Zoe's sobs the second I'd pushed open the door, before I'd even stepped in. Dragging the shower curtain open, I stared down at her curled up body sitting under the stream of water. She was wracked by sobs so badly that for a second I considered taking her back to the hospital just so they could give her something to calm her down, but that would've meant staying away from her and letting other people touch her, and I didn't think I could do that, not that day.

Reaching over my head, I yanked off my shirt, decided to keep my sweatpants on, and stepped in next to her. Crouching down, I put my hands under her arms and lifted her up. Thinking it was going to be hard to force her to accept my help, I was ready to argue with her, but I should've considered the fact that she might actually want me there.

Her clothes were still on, plastered to her trembling body. As I studied her face, I couldn't tell the tears from the water raining down on her. Despite the sadness and anger written all over her face, she looked so damn beautiful. Hands gripping her elbows, she stood motionless in front of me for a few seconds as I tried to come to terms with what I was feeling whenever I looked at her, and then with chattering teeth, she finally spoke. "It—s c—old."

It wasn't—the water was burning hot—but I accepted her

thinly veiled invitation and stepped into her, gently rounding my arms around her. Without any hesitation, she rested her temple against my chest and I felt her arms around me, hugging me back. Then the sobs came back with a vengeance and she broke my heart. At first, I was holding her as gently as possible, my arms just under her shoulders, scared I'd hurt her in some way, but then it all changed. The harder she sobbed, the closer I wanted to get to her. My arms drifted lower as I bent and wrapped them tighter around her waist. When she was standing on her toes and holding on to me as hard as I was holding on to her, I eased my hold and let my hand sneak up over her wet t-shirt to hold the back of her neck.

"It's okay, baby. Cry all you want," I whispered, water dripping from my face. "I'm right here, Zoe. Just hold on to me. I'll be right here. I'll always be here."

I straightened a little, my left hand holding her neck, my right arm tightly wound around her waist. She shuffled closer, still on her tiptoes, almost stepping on my feet. Barely a minute had passed when she clawed at my naked chest and pressed in harder. Both of her arms went over mine and around my neck. If you could've stepped into that bathroom with us, you wouldn't have been able to tell which one of us was holding the other tighter under the water. I bent my knees and gathered her even closer, dropping my head against her shoulder.

I heard her whisper my name and I lost it. Suddenly, I couldn't get air in fast enough. I couldn't bring her close enough, couldn't slow down my heartbeat enough.

"Zoe." I moaned when I was on the verge of crushing her. "Zoe."

We stayed under the water, just like that, holding tight, for God knows how long. I could've stayed locked to her for the rest of my life, but I knew I had to force myself to let her go. I wanted to believe she was just as reluctant to leave my arms.

"Let's get you out of these," I murmured finally.

Piece by piece, I took off her clothing until nothing but her underwear was left, and she let me, holding my shoulders when I bent down to shimmy her jeans off.

We were both a mess, but she was beautiful. Even with all her hair plastered against her cheeks, dripping wet, eyes red, she was still the most beautiful girl I'd ever seen.

When her fingers hesitantly reached for my sweatpants after giving me a quick look, I let her pull them down and stepped out of them myself. Thankfully she didn't reach for my boxers, but I knew she'd noticed the bulge. Biting her lip, she looked up at me shyly. Her hair was stuck to her cheeks so I reached up and pushed it away until all I could feel was her warm skin against my palms.

"You scared the shit out of me, Zoe," I rasped out before gently kissing her cheeks as hot water rained down on us. "Don't you ever do that to me again. Don't you ever put yourself in danger like that." Because of the way I was holding on to her, she barely managed to nod. Breathing hard, I rested my forehead against hers, closed my eyes, and listened to her breathe. I just needed one more minute to hold her in my arms, breathe her in, and calm myself down, and then I could be whoever she needed me to be—her roommate? Her friend? Her everything?

By then, I already knew I was not just her roommate, not just her friend, not just a buddy.

Leaning back, I looked at her throat, at the bruises already forming ugly shapes. I breathed in through my nose and let it all out through my mouth. If I could've gotten my hands on the guy right then, I would've done more damage. I would've broken his neck, and it still wouldn't have been enough. Gently, as gently as possible, I traced her bruises with the tips of my fingers. I knew Zoe's eyes were on me, studying, watching, *seeing*, but I couldn't look at her, not yet. I traced every single bruise, and then every inch of her neck not marred by his touch. I took my time and she let me. Every now and then I'd hear a small gasp escape her mouth and I'd meet her eyes to make sure she was okay. When I knew she was, I'd pick up where I'd left off. Before I was done, she reached for my hand and stopped me. Curling my fingers, she leaned down and kissed my reddened knuckles. My breathing labored, I could do nothing but hug her to me.

Eventually the water started running cold, so I loosened my arms around her and let her go. My muscles screamed at me. "We need to get you out of here or you're gonna get sick," I mumbled, turning the water off. She still hadn't spoken a word to me.

I stepped out before her, grabbed a towel, and wrapped it around my waist. I knew I'd have to take care of my boxer briefs before I left the bathroom, but right then, taking care of Zoe was all that mattered. Reaching for another towel, I held it open and she stepped out of the tub, into my arms again.

I wrapped it around her and rested my chin on her head, trying to warm her up through the towel.

Turning her head, she rested her cheek against my naked chest. "Thank you, Dylan," she whispered, her voice tugging at my heart.

"Always, baby."

CHAPTER TWENTY-TWO

ZOE

I felt like I was just waking up from a coma, not sure where I was, what time it was, what day. I rubbed at my eyes and groaned when I finally got a look at the time on my phone. I hadn't slept for a few days, just six hours. *At least I slept at all*, I thought.

I wished I could say I didn't remember anything from what had happened, that it had just been a bad nightmare, but I did. I did remember, and it made me feel sick to my stomach all over again. I swallowed down the bile rising in my throat and threw my legs over the side of the bed. My eyes finally adjusted to the dark, and thanks to the light still coming off my phone, I realized there were no lights coming in under my door. Just as I could remember everything that had happened early in the morning, I could also remember Dylan carrying me to my bed after he helped me out of the shower and holding me as I cried myself to sleep.

I checked my phone again and noticed a new text message that had come in at nine.

Dylan: *I had to leave for work. I'm sorry, Zoe. After bailing* *on Jimmy yesterday, I couldn't skip today's shift, and I needed the hours. Let me know when you wake up, call or text me.*

Bailing on Jimmy...? Had he skipped work the night before because of me? He said he needed the hours, which meant he needed the money. God, he needed the money, and because I'd fled after seeing him with another girl, he hadn't gone to work. I felt awful, like a little shithead who had gotten jealous over nothing when he... I closed my eyes and let out a deep breath. It was a little past one AM; was he still not back?

I pushed myself off the bed and felt a little dizzy, so I had to stand still for several seconds before I felt steady enough to move. The entire apartment was dark. Being as quiet as possible, I tried Dylan's room after I made sure he wasn't in the living room and prayed I'd find him there.

The moonlight streaming into the small room was enough for me to make out his still form lying on the narrow twin bed.

Something loosened inside of me. He was home. Tears rushed into my eyes and my throat closed up. Not even considering the fact that he probably needed his sleep after the crazy day we'd had, I crawled into his bed. There wasn't enough space, but I thought there was *just* enough to make it work.

He jerked awake and his fingers closed around my upper arms before I could lie down.

"Zoe?" he croaked, sleep heavy in his voice, and then his grip loosened. "Are you okay?"

I would be, knew I'd be fine once I could feel his heartbeat and make sure he was real, make sure he was...everything that he was.

"I can't sleep," I whispered, my own voice sounding scratchy from all the crying I'd done. "And my head hurts a little."

Obviously, it was a lie—not that I was hurting, but that I couldn't sleep. Either way, I didn't feel a single ounce of guilt for being a coward and not saying why I needed to be close to him. I just needed him to hold me in the dark where nothing could come between us—no secrets, no lies. I needed him to make me feel alive, and above all, I wanted to be with him, around him, near him...just with him, any way I could, simple as that.

I'd accepted the fact that no one would ever hug me like he'd hugged me in the shower, and I was fine with that; I'd just have to hold on to him stronger. No one would ever make me feel the things he so easily made me feel with just one of his teasing smiles, so why would I need anyone else? I didn't care if half of me would have to dangle out of that twin bed because he was so big; I was getting in it, and that was that. Before I forced my way in next to him, Dylan shifted to his side and opened the covers.

A wordless invitation.

An offer for me to take the world.

I didn't utter a single word. Facing away because otherwise I'd have to be right in his face, I lay down next to him and closed my eyes in relief. One of his arms went under my neck, the other slowly pulling the covers over us, and as the bed groaned under our weight, I shifted in place until my butt settled against his lower stomach. I stilled because even a very small, really tiny downward movement would bring me in contact with the *thing* between his legs, and I didn't want him to think me being there was about that. I moved away until a third of my torso and my knees were dangling off the bed.

Dylan sighed, a heavy sound in all that loud silence that warmed my skin where my neck met my shoulder and made my eyes go all wonky. Then the arm under my head moved and he tugged me back, curling his elbow as he reached for my shoulder with his hand, trapping me in his embrace. His right forearm moved over my stomach, fingers gently diving under the t-shirt I had haphazardly put on after our shower, sending goose bumps all over my body. He stopped when half of his hand rested under the waistband of my PJs, his skin warming me from inside out.

"You're going to fall off," he whispered.

I was officially in a Dylan cocoon, and I couldn't have felt cozier—*hadn't* ever felt cozier, or happier.

I turned my head a few inches, and he nuzzled my neck with his nose.

"You're okay?" he asked, his voice still gruff. It was perfect, so perfect.

Instead of a verbal answer, I angled my head, moved it up and down, and felt his smiling lips against my skin. If I attempted to speak, I was afraid I'd say more than I was ready to say.

Neither one of us spoke for several minutes. I had no idea what he was thinking, but my mind was working overtime.

Kayla, Mark, Chris—everything and nothing was coming at me at once, and there were two words I repeatedly heard over everything else.

Tell him. Tell him. Tell him.

"Shhh," Dylan murmured, pressing his lips against my neck and lingering. "I can almost hear you thinking. Just go to sleep, baby. I'll watch over you until morning."

And he will, won't he? I thought.

He'd help me breathe after scaring me to death. He'd save me from earthquakes, hold my hand after watching a scary movie, buy me pizza because he knew it'd make me happy, protect me from anything and everything by putting himself in front of the danger. He'd watch over me until morning.

When the lights came on, he'd still be there. After he learned all my secrets, he'd still be there, holding my hand—at least I hoped so.

"He forced her in front of his friends," I said into the darkness. "How do you come back from that?"

"She has her friends. You'll bring her back."

"I don't think I could've been as strong as she was today if it had happened to me. She's loved him since she was sixteen, and he..."

His arms tightened around me, so I reached up to curl my hand around his forearm, holding on.

"You don't have to think about that, not tonight. Go to sleep so you can be there for her tomorrow."

A few minutes passed in silence and I wondered if he'd fallen asleep. "Dylan..."

"Shhh."

"I like your voice," I blurted out quietly.

His voice was so low when he hummed next to my ear. "Mmmm, you do?"

"Yes," I murmured back as I closed my eyes to process that hum. "How was work?"

A short laugh as his chest shook behind me then a warm huff against my skin, making more goose bumps dance on my arms. "Same as always."

That didn't give me a chance to hear his voice all that much, did it?

"You must be so tired."

He grunted, but even though I knew I was being selfish, I wasn't ready to let him go. I guess it hadn't been much of a lie when I'd told him I couldn't sleep.

"When do you have to get up tomorrow?"

"You don't have to worry about that. I won't leave before you wake up again."

"It's not that..." Unconsciously, I started to move my thumb up and down through his arm hair. "Are you going to work out in the living room? Or are you meeting with Chris? Would it be okay if we skipped classes and hung out here after I spend some time with Kayla? But, it's Monday, so you'll have practice. I was just wonde—"

"Zoe," he groaned and tilted his hips up, quieting me pretty efficiently with just one move. My finger stopped moving on his arm. As you can imagine, I could feel the thick, round head of his cock against my ass. "I'm already having a hard time as it is, Flash. If you keep moving your finger like that and talking in that husky voice, I'm not gonna be able to... Just let me hold you like this and go to sleep."

I swallowed and nodded, but a few seconds later, I couldn't help myself. I shimmied my butt then stilled when he groaned and his teeth grazed my neck.

Shifting in the small bed, his hand dragged lower on my stomach, causing me to hold my breath. Lower and lower he went until his palm lay flat over my underwear, just a few inches higher than the center of my body. A second later he pressed his palm against me and shifted higher in the bed at the same time, safely nestling not just the mushroom head but also the thick length of his erection right against me.

"Dylan," I moaned, feeling a little dizzy and maybe a bit drunk on him as I restlessly tried to move my hips. I buried my face against his arm and, still holding his forearm with my left hand, put my right one over his hand on my lower stomach. Flipping his hand, he linked our fingers together and lay still.

I wasn't ready to lay still. I was ready for anything but lying still.

His mouth gently sucked on my neck as his hips moved behind me, once...twice...thrice, just a slow roll of his hips, a barely there movement I might not have been able to feel if my entire body wasn't screaming for him. I whimpered, my whole being electrified by his touch, down to my soul. Never in my life had I felt anything like it.

"I'm so tired, baby." A kiss on my neck and then everything stopped. "And you just went through hell. You need your sleep—I'm not gonna do anything."

"But—" I sputtered, earning myself another soft kiss that caused all kinds of tingles and shivers to go through my body.

"Sleep, baby."

Are you kidding me?

He'd just played Tetris with our bodies and then what? I was supposed to just drift off to sleep?

I wouldn't have thought so, but to my utter shock, I did just that. With his breathing steady and reassuring against my back, I did just that.

CHAPTER TWENTY-THREE

DYLAN

Before I even opened my eyes, before I was even fully awake, I could feel her next to me, not because I'd have known her smell anywhere or because we were still pretty much wrapped around each other in the exact same position we'd fallen asleep in, but because it was *her* that was in my arms.

Not knowing what time it was, I opened my eyes to darkness. Frowning, I moved just an inch or two and tried to reach under the pillow to get my phone without waking Zoe up.

"Dylan?"

Her voice was still husky, still groggy.

"Ssshhh, I'm here. Go back to sleep," I whispered into her neck then finally managed to grab my phone under her head.

The light coming from the phone illuminated us, and I had to blink to see the time on the screen.

"What time is it?" Zoe asked as she shielded her half-closed eyes with the back of her hand.

I turned the phone off and pushed it back under the pillow.

Zoe shifted and turned her head to look at me. I could barely make out her features in the dark, but I could see that her eyes were open and staring into mine.

I ran the backs of my fingers against her cheek. "It's only four thirty."

"So we slept, what, just a little over two hours?"

"Something like that." I let my fingers trail down to her neck and tried to be gentle as I did a quick sweep.

"It felt like more," she whispered in a low voice.

"Does it still hurt?" I whispered back, anger laced through my voice. She swallowed and I felt the movement under my touch.

"It's okay."

I could've killed that sick bastard for putting his hands on her. If she hadn't stopped me, hadn't burrowed herself into my arms, I'm not sure I would've stopped. Feeling helpless, that deep burn in my chest—the same one I had felt at the library when I'd first seen him press Zoe against the bookshelves—started to consume me again, that intense initial shock, the sudden anger.

"Dylan? What's wrong?"

After three maneuvers, she was facing me. At first, she didn't seem to know what to do with her hands, but then she placed her right one on my chest.

"Hey, where did you go?"

I covered her hand with my own and dropped my forehead against hers.

"I don't think I'm gonna be able to go back to sleep. Since I'm already awake, I'll get in a workout. You go back to sleep. You need a few more hours."

I moved to leave but had to stop halfway out of bed when she spoke up.

"I can't go back to sleep either."

"Zoe—"

"I can go back to my bed if you can't sleep because I'm here."

Frowning, I folded myself back into the bed.

"Where did that come from?"

"Why are you leaving?"

"I won't be able to fall asleep, Zoe. I'm still angry. You can go back—"

"To sleep. I heard you already. Are you angry at me?"

"Why would I be angry at you?"

"If you're not, why am I being punished?"

I relaxed and chuckled. "You want me here that bad?"

"Yes."

I hadn't thought she would answer, so when she did, it threw me for a loop. "I...okay. Okay, you got me then."

"Okay. Good. If we're going to be miserable, we might as well do it together."

"That's the only reason?"

She pulled her hand out from under the covers and gave my shoulder a light punch, and then another. Silently, I waited for an answer.

"No," she replied with a sigh. "Dylan, I..."

I reached between us and laced our fingers together. Lifting her chin, she peered up at me.

"I have this...thing for you," she said quietly, letting out a breath as if relieved to say it out loud. Did she think she had been hiding it from me all this time? Did she think I didn't know, didn't feel the same...thing?

After resting our hands on her hip, I leaned down so I could speak into her ear.

"I have a thing for you, too, Flash."

She groaned and tried to let go of my hand, but I held her tighter. "I'm not joking, Dylan. I really have a big thing for you."

"How big?" I asked, having trouble keeping the smile out of my voice. There was another tug on my hand, so this time I let her go.

"I'm trying to tell you how I—"

My hand free, I caught her chin between my thumb and index finger and tilted her head up so she could look into my eyes. There wasn't quite enough light for her to make out my expression, but I was hoping hearing it in my voice would help.

"It was after the second time I saw you, the time you tried to run away from me and crashed into that building. Remember that?"

"I wasn't *trying* to run away fr—by the way, it was just a model. It's not like I ran into an actual bu—"

"I looked for you," I whispered over her. "To be honest, I didn't ask around to try to find you, wouldn't have even known where to start to do that, but I was hoping to see you again. So, I think without even realizing what I was doing, I was searching for you. I remember this time when a girl walked around a corner, holding her books to her chest just like you were doing when you saw me that second time. She was laughing with her friends, and I just stopped walking. Her face was turned so I couldn't see her enough to recognize you, but she had the same hair color"—I tucked Zoe's hair behind her ear—"same pale skin. She stopped me right in my tracks, Zoe, because I thought, *There she is. There she is again.* Then she turned around and she wasn't you. I remember feeling so disappointed. It happened a few times, not to that extent, but I thought I saw you and you were never there."

She took a deep breath and waited for more.

"Now...now I couldn't possibly not recognize you. Now you're everywhere, always on my mind. I close my eyes and I can see you, right there." My focus dropped low as I brushed her bottom lip with my thumb and her lips parted. "Now, I could never mistake you for someone else. Your shy little smile, your big happy smile, the shape of your eyes...you're all I think about, Zoe. When I wake up, I can't wait to work out because I know you'll be up only minutes after me. I'll hear your footsteps, you'll come into the kitchen still half asleep and so beautiful, and then you'll innocently perv on me while acting like you're having breakfast."

She groaned and I laughed.

"Don't be mean to me," she muttered in a serious voice, but the quiet laughter that came after gave her away. "And I wasn't perving on you. I was just..."

"I don't care what you call it. I like it. I like having your eyes on me. I love it even more when you look into my eyes and give me your biggest smile. Every time I see you smiling at me like that, like after the game in Tucson, it feels like you're handing me your world. Even in the dark, I can feel your—"

Before I could finish my sentence, her head shot up and her lips found mine. Not prepared for it, I couldn't soften the kiss, and our teeth clashed. She immediately drew her head back. I knew she was blushing; I didn't need any light to know that. She covered her mouth with her hand.

"I'm sorry. I just—"

This time I didn't wait to hear the rest. As far as I was concerned, even though it had lasted only one second, that brief kiss was the best kiss of my life.

Pulling her hand down, I cupped the back of her head and went in for more. I didn't want to miss out on another second with this girl. Fuck everything. Fuck everyone. None of it mattered. She molded her lips to mine without a second of hesitation. My body moved closer and hers did the same until we were flush against each other. I tilted my head and went in deeper, my tongue tasting every inch. She moaned against me and I felt her fist pulling on my shirt. Our mouths moved in perfect tandem as we pushed and pulled at each other for more.

When we had to breathe, Zoe moaned my name. "Dylan."

Just that single word coming from her lips added fuel to the fire inside me, and I let go of the back of her head to slide my hand down to her waist so I could pull her even closer, even though there wasn't even an inch of empty space separating us. She made no protest, only arched toward me and kissed me again. Our breaths coming in harsh bursts, she whimpered into my mouth and wrapped her arms around my neck.

With difficulty, I stopped kissing her and whispered against her lips. "Too much?"

"No," she said breathlessly. "It's not enough."

With a groan that came from deep within my chest, I bit her bottom lip and pushed my tongue back inside. I shoved my left arm underneath her and pulled her on top of me as I dropped to my back on the tiny bed. She squealed into my mouth but never stopped kissing me. She just planted her hands on either side of my face, threw her leg over my thigh, and kept going. I pulled her hair to one side and shifted my hands from her shoulders to her arms and then to her waist. I pushed her shirt up just enough so I could feel her skin under my hands. She shivered when I grasped her waist as tight as I could without hurting her.

Our breathing still out of control, I opened my eyes when she whispered my name and touched my face with her hand.

"Yeah," I croaked, and then I pushed up just enough so I could take her lips. A second or two was sufficient time for breathing. She kissed me back, just as hard, just as hungry as her tongue tangled with mine.

"Wait," she murmured, her lips moving against mine when we had to break apart to breathe. "Just a second."

I groaned but stopped like she'd asked. I focused on the edge of her lips and neck instead.

One of her legs had dropped between mine when I'd pulled her over me, but she straightened a little, taking her soft skin from my lips, and straddled me, sitting right on top of my dick.

"Shit," I groaned, reaching for her hips. "Maybe that's not a good idea, Flash."

One of her hands was resting on my stomach for balance as

she pushed her hair away from her face with the other.

"What?"

I pulled her hips a little forward so she wouldn't be *right* on top of my already hard-as-a-damn-rock dick and grunted when the rough slide felt better than anything ever had. "That," I repeated gruffly, hoping she'd know what I meant. Now both of her hands were on my stomach and she was still out of breath, just like me.

She pushed her hips back right where they'd been and bit her lip. "Funny, to me that felt like the most amazing idea in the world."

"Yeah?"

"Yes."

I sat up and caught her with one arm before she could fall back. Dragging our bodies higher up in the bed, I settled against the low headboard. My head slumped back against the wall as she squirmed on my lap until she was comfortable.

Pushing my hand back up under her shirt from behind, I grabbed her neck as gently as possible and pulled her down to my mouth. She came eagerly and moaned even louder as I kissed her and she moved her little butt restlessly against my shaft. I couldn't even remember the last time I'd had a dry-hump session, let alone one I enjoyed so damn much.

I flicked open her bra and moved both my hands on her back, letting the material just hang loose as I curled my fingers around her shoulder then stroked her back again.

After a particularly hard grind, I let out a grunt and hit my head on the wall with a heavy thump as I tore my lips away from hers.

"Fuck, Zoe..."

My eyes slowly opened when I felt her breath against my lips. I swallowed and licked my lips, waiting to see what she'd do. The worst part was, she wasn't moving on me anymore.

"Dylan," she whispered before kissing my lips twice. I let her set the pace, and neither one of them lasted more than a few seconds. "My heart beats differently for you. It feels different somehow. I know this probably doesn't make sense, but...it beats louder, wilder when I see you." I ran my hands down to her waist and held on tight. She rested her cheek against my temple and rolled her hips. "And I feel like...how am I supposed to keep it in its place? How am I supposed to get used to seeing that smile on your lips? It breaks my brain. *You* break my brain sometimes—complete mush. Even that first time in the bathroom...though that was just nerves and being horrified, so maybe we can't count that one...but the second time, when I saw you walking toward me, I just got stuck. How could anyone possibly look away—"

I didn't let her finish her words; I couldn't. In seconds I had her on her back and I was hovering over her. It didn't matter how dark it was; I could picture the look on her face. She was burned into my mind. Those big eyes, that flush on her cheeks—I could see it all.

Not wanting to waste another second, I kissed her again, only pausing when I felt her hands pulling at my shirt. One hand right next to her head, I used the other to reach back, pull it over my head, and fling it away. When I looked down, she was struggling with her own shirt.

"Let me," I mumbled then helped her take it off, bra and everything.

I couldn't see her clearly and it frustrated me to no end, but I didn't think I could untangle myself from her long enough to go get the lights. I settled my hips between her wide open legs, my lips against her already swollen ones as I put my palm on her stomach and moved my hand up, up until I could cup her breast. It was more than a handful, and I couldn't wait to get a taste —literally.

I started fucking her with the rest of our clothes on, and every moan, every hitch of her breath pushed me to a level where I knew neither one of us would be satisfied with just what we were doing. I groaned quietly over her little moans. It felt so good to finally be able to touch her like this, to feel her like this. When I was a little rough with her breasts and started rolling her nipple between my fingers while I sucked the other one as hard and deep as I could, she gasped and grabbed my head.

I pressed my length harder against her as I moved with deliberate forward motions. Every rock of our hips pushed her a little higher on the bed.

"That feels so good," she gasped when I was busy kissing her neck and heading for her breasts again. One of her feet was on the bed and she was pushing herself up in time with my forward thrusts as she arched her back.

"Yeah? You're gonna make me come in my pants," I groaned, feeling drunk on her. "I don't remember the last time I did that." I still had my slacks on over my briefs since I'd fallen asleep as soon as I hit the bed, and all she had on was thin pajama bottoms. She could feel every single inch of me dragging against her pussy. Just in case she needed more, I let go of her breast, her nipple for the first time since I'd gotten her half-naked and pushed my hand under her ass, inside her PJs and panties, pulling her more firmly against me and my dick.

"Jesus," she groaned, wrapping one of her legs around mine.

Her head was thrown back, and I watched breathlessly as she climbed to her orgasm right in front of my eyes. I picked up my speed.

"Dylan," she cried in seconds. "Dylan, I'm so close."

My name on her lips dragged me to an edge. "Come on, baby," I murmured into her throat as I left small kisses on her hot skin.

Her legs opened wider under me and I squeezed her butt cheek harder.

"Tell me what you need, Zoe."

"Just you. I just want you."

"I know, Flash. I know. Tell me what you need so I can make you come." Breathing in her sweet fruity scent, I licked a trail on her neck over her bruises and sucked her skin, making sure it wasn't where it would hurt her. She groaned, the sound so low and rough.

"No. No. Stop," she said suddenly, surprising the shit out of me.

"What?" Dazed, I straightened up, putting a few inches between our chests. I stopped moving against her but didn't have enough strength to separate us completely. "What happened? What's wrong?"

Next thing I knew, her hands were on the waist of her PJs and she was trying to wriggle out of them altogether.

Pulling back a little, I asked, "What are you doing?"

"I want to come when you're inside me, Dylan, and I think I might actually die if you're not in me within the next minute or so. No, I'm not being dramatic at all, so come on—lose the pants, get naked."

The last thing I was expecting to do at that moment was laugh, but I did just that.

Zoe managed to wiggle herself halfway out of her PJs but was having trouble untangling her legs because I was still hovering over her. I helped her pull them the rest of the way off and had to steady myself after for a second or two. I ran my hand all the way up to her thighs then down to her ankle. I loved her legs. I'd spent weeks watching those smooth legs and imagining them wrapped around me as I fucked her and she begged me for more.

"I don't think you can do what I want you to do with those pants on, Dylan," she murmured when I just stood on my knees like an idiot and moved my hands all over her. I reached for the hand she was busy clutching the sheets with.

"Just a minute," I murmured then wound her legs around my waist and settled between her naked legs, my shaft pressing and pressing right over her clit. I just wanted to feel her heat. "Get me naked then."

"Shit," she mumbled, her hands moving over my chest and curling around my shoulders. Then they traveled lower as I leaned over her, kissing and sucking her parted lips. Her legs dropped from around me.

I lifted my hips enough so she could lower my pants without trouble then I looked down between us to see the head of my dick make an appearance. If she touched me, she'd feel I was already leaking pre-cum. She pushed a little up and lowered my pants a few inches more, freeing my entire length. It bobbed between us, the tip touching her stomach.

"Now that you took it out, what are you planning on doing?" I asked in a rough voice. I rested my forearms on either side of her face and looked down at her. I could just imagine her biting her lip and looking unsure.

Instead of hearing words, I felt her fingers wrap around my hard, swollen length, nothing unsure about her touch at all. I twitched in her hand and felt her thumb brush the wetness down and around me. My heart hammering in my chest, I moved my hand lower, slid it all the way down, dragging my palm against every inch until I felt her wetness on my fingers, and that was it for me. I was gone.

"Condom," I said, my mind working just enough to remember that we needed condoms—lots of them. "Condoms. I don't have condoms, Zoe."

Her hand stopped moving on me, but she didn't pull it away.

"What?"

I slammed my hand on the bed and dropped my face on her neck. I licked and bit her earlobe before I spoke because I couldn't quite stop myself. "I don't have any condoms."

"I do!" she half yelled, and then her hand wasn't pulling on my dick anymore. "I do. One—I have one."

She let go of my dick, slid out from under me, hesitated, then grabbed the pillow and hugged it to her perfect naked body before jumping up and running out of my room. Seconds later she was back, and I was sitting on the edge of the bed, my fingers itching to touch her, to pull her, to keep her.

"What's up with that?" I managed to ask as I gestured toward the pillow, my dick painfully hard, and even more painfully ready.

I offered her my hand and she took it without hesitation. With my other hand, I grabbed the pillow away and threw it back on the bed.

"Dylan..."

"It's already too dark in here as it is. Don't hide yourself from me, Zoe, not anymore." I gave her a gentle pull and she climbed into my lap.

"Here," she said, handing me the condom after sitting on my thighs. "I just have this one." She paused. "Jared gave it to me, just in case."

"Just in case what?"

She shrugged. "Just in case you and I...As a joke."

"Fucked. Are you too shy to say fuck?"

"Just in case you and I had sex."

"Fuck sounds better to me."

"Fine, fuck then."

I chuckled and kissed her. Her arms slowly wrapped around my neck as she melted against me.

"I want to watch you put it on," she said against my lips.

"Whatever you want, just tell me and it's yours."

She worried her bottom lip between her teeth and tilted her head down to watch me as I worked it over my length as fast as humanly possible.

I lost patience somewhere along the way so I lifted her off my lap and dropped her back on the bed with a bounce right before climbing on top of her. "I need you so bad, Zoe. I can't look at you any longer and not know how it feels to sink into you."

She pulled my head down and went for my lips. Keeping our chests apart, I reached between us and went to feel the wetness between her legs.

"Shit, Zoe," I hissed, resting my forehead against hers. "You're all ready for me, aren't you?"

"I've been trying to tell—"

I pushed two of my fingers inside her and she stilled under me, her legs tense, her fingers digging into the skin of my arms. She was dripping. After a few shallow thrusts, I tugged them out and dragged her wetness over her clit, stroking and swirling. Her hips were restless under me, demanding, her hands still on my skin, her touch searing.

I leaned down and whispered against the shell of her ear. "I need you so bad, Zoe."

"Please...Dylan, please."

I took her at her word and wrapped my hand around the base of my dick so I could slowly slid inside until she had all of me. It took a few seconds and a few sexy grunts and gasps from her as she arched under me, but I was all in and nothing had ever felt so tight, so right, so utterly...mine.

I wanted to fuck her till the morning light streamed in and I could memorize every dip and curve of her skin. Feeling a little dizzy, I pulled out until she had just the wide head inside her then pushed it all the way back in. I dropped back on my forearms and finally started fucking her with a slow rhythm.

A small moan slipped from her lips and I bent down to capture it with my mouth. I wanted all of her moans, all her sighs and gasps. I wanted everything from her.

"I'm going to take everything from you," I whispered against her skin. It was only fair to let her know.

"Good," she answered. Her hands cupped my face, and I could feel her staring straight into my eyes as I moved inside her with hard, shallow strokes. "Great even." Another grunt after a particularly hard thrust. "As long as you give me everything of yourself."

"You already have me, baby."

After that, it was all lost in a frenzy. *I* was lost in her. I grasped one of her legs and pulled it high up around my waist so I could get even deeper. When my movements picked up speed, so did the soft noises she was making. She clutched at my biceps, squeezing and pulling and cursing when I went especially deep and fast. Then she was arching, her breasts protruding, offered to me so sweetly, and I was tasting her.

Grunting.

Breathless.

Gone.

"You're driving me crazy," I gasped, my heart beating like crazy in my chest, having trouble keeping up with us. The sound of our skin slapping with each thrust was the best sound I would ever hear in my life.

"You feel so big inside me," Zoe gasped, bringing my attention from her breasts to her swollen lips.

I slowed down my thrusts and kissed her lazily, sucking on her tongue, dragging my cock out of her as slowly as possible and then pushing it all the way back in.

"Too much?"

Biting her lip, she shook her head.

"Does it feel good?"

"I want to come," was her answer as her fingers closed tighter around my arms. "I want to come on you," she repeated, her voice all hoarse and breathy. I kissed the edge of her lips.

"Tell me. Say it out loud. I want to hear. Does it feel good?"

She put her palm on my cheek before she gave me an answer.

"It feels amazing. It feels like I'm going to explode." A gasp. A moan. "You feel amazing, love it, but I want to come. It...doesn't happen every time for me, but it's so close, I can feel it. I want *you* to make me come. Please make me come on you."

With a challenge like that, what else could I possibly do?

I got up on my knees, dragged her legs over my thighs, and tugged her even closer with my hands on her hips then started fucking her like there was no tomorrow. She pushed herself down on me, her hands braced against the headboard, and I could feel her slowly tightening around me, her legs squeezing, her whimpers louder.

"Zoe," I hissed out. "Zoe, you feel so fucking good around my cock, squeezing me like that. Look at you, all ready to let go and come all over me."

Then her orgasm took over and she tried to pull her legs closed from around me, but I held them open and kept pumping into her until she went straight over and gasped, almost soundlessly, and then she came with her mouth open, her body arched, her breath lost.

Watching her face, watching her breasts move with the force of my thrusts, I knew I couldn't hold back any longer. I was so goddamn deep in her, and she was so goddamn tight that I didn't know if I could ever stop.

My blood hummed in my veins and my spine tingled.

Zoe stopped coming and found her breath as my name spilled from her lips again. She reached up and ran her hands across my chest and stomach, making me shiver. I didn't know how long I could keep moving inside her, but I was getting close to losing my mind.

"I can't," I forced out. She was burning me inside out and I had no idea why I was trying so hard to keep going instead of letting go.

"Don't," she whispered, pulling me down against her skin. We were both covered in sweat, and feeling her boobs pressed against me, her strong heartbeat, her scent, her breathlessness... none of it was helping things at all.

The headboard was hitting the wall with every single thrust, and both Zoe and I were moaning through every second. I felt her tighten around me again and she cried out, coming again, her hips moving, her arms around me, holding on to me. She hid her face in my neck and got incredibly tight and wet around me.

"Look at me," I moaned with urgency. "Zoe, look at me."

Breathless, she dropped her head back on the pillow and our eyes met in the dark. With a groan of my own, I took her lips and buried myself to the hilt, again and again. I kissed her as deeply as I could, our heads moving and tilting, and spilled myself inside of her in a rush like I had never felt before. I came, but it felt different, like it had been ripped out from somewhere deep inside me, like what we did in that damn tiny bed was something much more than just having sex, more like an exorcism.

When I could see and hear again, I found myself still moving inside her gently, slowly sinking in as deep as I could go. I never took my lips off of hers. I kept kissing her until we couldn't anymore. My hands never stopped roaming her skin, memorizing. I could have kissed her like that for hours, for days, years. When it felt like I would die if I kept moving, I dropped half on top of her and tried to catch my breath.

"Fuck. I think you broke me," I muttered into the pillow. "Let's do that again."

She laughed, the soft sound giving me shivers.

I pulled out and stepped away from her to get rid of the condom. When I came back, she was pulling the sheets over herself, hiding again.

Slipping under the covers, I put my hand behind her waist and pulled her flush against my chest as my dick lay half hard, half soft between us.

"Don't hide yourself from me," I said quietly. "Please."

"I'm not," she whispered back.

I brushed her messy hair back away from her face and stared at her for a moment. "Zoe, that was the best thing that's ever happened to me." I pressed a kiss to her swollen lips and when she parted them, I went in for a longer one without hesitation. When we stopped, she sighed and pressed her forehead to my shoulder, right under my chin. I kept going. "It feels like I've been waiting for this to happen all my life, waiting for you to happen."

I caressed her back, up and down, up and down until she looked back up at me.

"That was intense. I've never done that before. The...coming twice thing, I mean. I think I was too wet. Is that even normal?"

"I think it's our normal. Was it too much?" I frowned down at her. "Did I hurt you or something? Your neck?"

She shook her head. "No. No, it's not that. I've just never felt like that, so...crazy. I just wanted you deeper and deeper even though it felt like you were all the way in there...you know."

"Yeah, I know what you mean. I tried to go easier, but it wasn't happening." I kissed her forehead and closed my eyes. "We should get a little more sleep, Flash. Tomorrow is gonna be another tough day for you."

She sighed and snuggled in closer. "I can sleep with you?"

"Just try to get away from me."

She seemed to settle in after that and we fell silent.

I was about to doze off with her in my arms when she spoke up quietly. "Dylan."

Suddenly, I was wide awake. Still, based on her tone, *that* conversation was not one I was ready to have just then, not when I could still feel her tightening and pulsing around my dick.

"Not now," I said shortly.

"I think we—"

"No, not tonight, not after I just had you. We'll talk tomorrow or the day after. Then we'll move out as fast as possible."

"Move out? What are you talk—"

I gave her a squeeze and she stopped. I looked down and met her confused gaze. "We can't stay here, in his apartment. I won't."

Her frown only deepened until understanding dawned on her and she started shaking her head.

"No, Dylan. I mean, yeah, but—"

I kissed her lips, cutting her off, because I couldn't help myself.

"Not tonight. Please."

"But you need to know. There are things—"

"I'll know everything tomorrow or the next day. Just give me one more day, okay? Just us, you and me, no one else. Nothing else between us."

She stared into my eyes for a few more beats then exhaled a burst of air and nodded.

More seconds ticked by and I couldn't fall asleep. I cleared my throat. "By the way, you kissed me. You lost the bet you were so sure you would never lose."

Her head shot up, hitting me under my chin. "I didn't! You kissed me!"

"I don't think so. You went for it first."

"No. That doesn't count. You kissed me first."

I had the biggest grin on my face when I finally fell asleep after arguing with her about who had lost the best. In the end, I'd gotten her, in every sense of the word—only I had no idea none of it would matter the next day, not after the way she broke my heart.

CHAPTER TWENTY-FOUR

ZOE

He was playing with my fingers; I think that was what woke me up initially, that and hearing his voice murmur my name against my skin. It was just a little more than a whisper that suddenly spurred my heart into a fast beat. It was too damn early to get that excited just because you heard someone's hot, sleepy voice.

I opened my eyes with a cheesy grin plastered on my face. One look at that bed and you'd have bet money there was no way two people—especially with one of them being Dylan's size—would fit in there, but we did. We fit perfectly. Sure, his feet and half of the arm that was under my head were off the bed, my legs were tangled with his, and my knees were hanging off the side, too, but who cared? Like I said, we fit perfectly.

"Good morning," he murmured, and I looked back so I could meet his dark blue eyes. He gave me a lazy grin, one I couldn't not reciprocate.

"Good morning."

"Sleep good?"

Still sporting that grin, I nodded, and his smile got bigger. I could feel the heat rushing to my cheeks. My eyes dropped to his lips and I watched the grin turn into the smile I loved the most on him, the one where he smiled with his eyes just as much as he did with his lips. It was warm, genuine, hot. It sounds cheesy, I know, but it was true that it basically took your—okay, maybe it wouldn't take *yours*...it better not...but it took my breath away.

Whoosh.

Gone, just like that.

"Don't move," I said in a rush then threw open the covers, squeaked, and scrambled to pull them back up.

"What's happening?" Dylan asked, looking at me with amusement dancing in his eyes.

I pulled the covers higher. "I...just...let me get the pillow." I didn't give him a chance to even utter a protest or yank it away before I could get to it. I pulled it right out from under him and his head bounced on the mattress. Muttering a quick apology, I hugged it to my chest and carefully exited the bed. He caught my hand before I could straighten up.

"Where are you going?"

"I'll be right back. I just want to get something."

He let me go and I backed out of the room, hoping everything was covered.

When I got what I needed from my bag, I rushed back to him. He was still lying down, using his arm behind his head as a pillow. I took in the muscles, the arms, the chest, the smooth skin, the bulge under the covers—just thinking about his cock made me go all hot inside. You should've seen him; he looked so relaxed, so hot, so...other words I couldn't possibly come up with due to the way he turned my brain to complete mush, but take my word for it, he looked perfect.

Still clutching the pillow to my torso with one hand, holding my camera with the other, I got back in next to him and finally let go of the pillow when I was back under the covers.

"You can't still be shy, Zoe," he said, coming up on his elbow and looking into my eyes with a small frown. "Not after last night."

"It doesn't just go away like that. Give me a break, there's daylight now," I huffed. "But forget about that. I've been dying to take your picture and I—"

"You took pictures of me at the game."

"No, not like that—like this." I put my hand on his chest. "I want to keep this."

"Collecting memories, heartbeats," he murmured, echoing what I'd said to him the first night he'd come to the apartment. Smiling, he pushed a lock of hair behind my ear. "Both of us?"

Excited beyond measure, I bit my lip and eagerly nodded.

He opened his arms and I dove in, deliriously happy to be there.

"Your arm must be dead by now. You should've pulled it away after I fell asleep."

"It's fine," he said distractedly as he gathered me closer.

After I played with the ISO and shutter speed until it was all just right, I exhaled and lifted my Sony A7R II high up over us so we could both fit in the frame. The flip screen didn't flip around so it was going to be a shot in the dark, but I was okay with anything at that moment.

Grinning like crazy, I looked at Dylan, and he smiled. "Ready?" I asked, not giving a damn that I looked like a maniac.

He chuckled and kissed me on the cheek.

That was gold. I took the shot before he even had a chance to back away. Giddy, I turned the camera to check how it looked—*perfect*. I did look a little crazy with that grin on my face, and my eyes were closed, my head tipped toward his head, but it was perfect. His side of the photo was perfect, and I looked out-of-my-mind happy. If you'd seen the photo, you might've thought I was a total loser, but *I* didn't think so.

When Dylan laughed next to me, I knew he didn't think so either.

"So beautiful," he said, and a delicious shiver ran through my body.

Capturing that single moment would've been just fine with me. I was planning on putting my camera down, but Dylan stopped me.

"More."

"Can I?"

"Yeah. Take as many as you want," he said, giving me permission.

I probably took a dozen of the same exact shot of us, but I didn't give a single fuck. They all consisted of Dylan kissing me while I lay on his shoulder, Dylan kissing me while his palm covered my cheek, me laughing as he leaned down and kissed my neck, me looking at Dylan with sparkling eyes as he smiled at me, camera completely forgotten. Then Dylan took it from my hand, which was already shaking from holding it for so long, and after a little fumbling, he started on the next set of the same photos: him kissing the corner of my lips as I finally looked up at the camera, him reaching my lips and finally kissing me as I turned my body to face him, me with my eyes closed as he whispered words into my ear. Then there was a shot of his arm snaking around my neck, one of his defined torso and my waist as he twisted in bed.

Then it was just silence and him and me.

Reaching over me, he placed the camera on the carpeted floor and looked down at me. Sometime during our impromptu little shoot, the covers had revealed my upper body to him and he could see everything he hadn't been able to before.

My heart skipped a beat as we stared at each other. Dylan's expression softened as he studied me.

"Hi, Flash."

I smiled. "Hi, buddy."

He bent his head and laughed. "Right, we're buddies. You're the best buddy I ever had."

"Likewise."

His fingers moved over my bruises, his eyes following along, and I swallowed.

"It kills me that these are here."

I couldn't speak.

Looking at me some more, one of his hands stroked over my waist then down my thigh. When he lifted it up and planted my foot firmly on the bed, it took everything in me not to do a full body shiver. Just like that, I was drenched for him. He lowered his hips on me and I remembered how he'd put his briefs back on when he got up to take care of the condom. Still, the fabric separating us meant nothing; I could feel every inch of his hardness just fine, and in a few more seconds, he'd be able to feel how intensely wet I was for him.

I grabbed his arms, closed my eyes, and let out an involuntary moan when he pressed forward and the head of his cock pushed hard on my clit.

Then I felt his lips dancing on my cheek, over the shell of my ear, on my neck, licking, gently sucking, kissing.

Blindly, I reached between us, pushed his briefs a few inches down, and jerked when his heavy, hot cock lay on my stomach.

Feeling a little crazy, I groaned and turned my head so I could kiss him. He returned my groan with his own when my hand wrapped around him and pulled hard. I swallowed his grunts and jerked him harder. A drop of pre-cum dropped on my stomach, making me gasp and shiver, goose bumps traveling all over my body. Then another drop, and another. I renewed my assault on his mouth by rounding my free hand on his neck and pulling him to me. He angled his head and went deeper, his tongue stroking mine, taking and giving, biting and licking, soothing and kissing.

Then I felt his thumb and forefinger on my chin and he pushed himself away, our lips making a loud smacking sound.

"Please tell me Jared gave you more," he growled, the sound and the tone melting me into the bed even farther.

My eyes only opened halfway and I managed to mutter a low, "What?"

"Condoms?"

I forced my eyes to open a little bit more and my heart sank. "Oh, no."

He groaned and rolled to his side, his cock slipping from my hand in the process.

"Sorry," I mumbled, propping myself on my elbow and looking down at him as he rubbed his hand over his face a few times.

"Then I should get out of this bed—hell, probably the apartment while I'm at it."

I smiled. "Why?"

He gave me a frustrated look, his expression just as dark and tight as his eyes. I lost my smile pretty quick and cleared my throat. Without another word, I got up on my knees, a little breathless and a little unsure, settled next to his legs and swallowed. I wasn't going to ask permission, and he wasn't stopping me. I could feel his eyes burning into my skin. Was it uncool to be so fascinated by a cock? Because apparently, I couldn't take my eyes off of his. The thick shaft, the dark pink head...the way it rested on his hard stomach, that thick vein on the underside...the anticipation of how good he would taste...all of it rushed at me at once and I couldn't wait any longer.

I chanced a glance at Dylan and saw him swallow, saw his throat moving and how set his jaw was.

I reached to take him in my hand, but he stopped me before I could and linked our fingers together.

"Use the other one," he said, that thick, needy voice rushing over me and causing goose bumps to explode all over my skin.

I licked my lips in anticipation. "Okay."

I wanted him in my mouth probably a bit more than even he wanted it. I wasn't a pro at blowjobs per se, but I didn't think I was the worst either. Shaking my head to get rid of all the stupid second-guessing, I grabbed his thick base with my left hand and lowered my mouth over the thick head, rolling my tongue all around it.

Dylan's hips jerked up and he squeezed my hand with his.

"Sorry."

Slowly I moved my hand up and down his length, brushing my thumb over his slit, using his seeping wetness to make it easier. He tried to lie as still as possible.

"Fuck," he hissed, his head sinking into the pillow when I put him in my mouth again. "Zoe, I don't think I'll ever let you out of this bed again."

And he didn't, not until he had to when his phone started ringing over and over. One of his teammates, Benji, was calling to make sure he would make it to practice.

After that, it was a mad rush. I had no idea when we had woken up, but after I made him come all over his stomach and my hands, he reciprocated, and then I got another bonus one. When his friend called and popped our private little bubble, I felt guilty for being so happy when my friend was going through hell.

Fifteen minutes after the phone call, we were both showered, dressed, and ready to go.

"You'll call me when you're coming home?"

"I will."

"You're skipping your classes?"

"Yes, both Jared and I are."

"You'll call if you need anything?"

"I will."

"Text me how she is doing when you get there."

A quick nod from me and I looked away.

He reached up to grab my chin.

"What's wrong?"

I gave him a half shrug. How was I going to explain to him about Mark and Chris? How did you even start a conversation like that?

So...here's the thing, I know you hate liars because you told me that the first night you came here, but I've been lying to you this whole time. Hey, at least it was a white lie, right? I never had a boyfriend, not since you moved in, and your best friend happens to be my long-lost brother, but we're not telling him anything because that's how Mark wants it. Good talk. Bye.

Just like ripping off a band-aid.

To my embarrassment, my eyes burned with unshed tears and I turned away to get to the door before he could see them.

"Nothing. You're going to be late. Come on." I pulled on his hand to tug him out and locked the door.

"Zoe, wait."

He put his hand on my arm, but I was already on the move.

Ms. Hilda's door opened before we could escape. I swore the woman spent half her day—possibly even more—with her ear pressed to the door, lying in wait for her victims.

"Where have you two been? I needed you yesterday and I knocked and knocked on your door. Did you have a party over there? I believe I told you I wouldn't like that when you first got here, Miss Clarke."

If I'd had a to-do list for the day, dealing Ms. Hilda wouldn't have even been the last thing on that list. Very aware of Dylan's presence standing tall and strong behind me, I tilted my head and took a deep breath. "Did you hear music or something, Ms. Hilda?"

"No, but I could have sworn I heard—"

"We didn't have a party, and we're not planning on having a party in the near future either. I would love to help you with whatever you need, but right now I'm late for class and Dylan needs to get to practice, so I'm sorry, but you're gonna have to find someone else to check your drapes. Have a good day, Ms. Hilda."

While she was staring at me with an even deeper frown and an open mouth, I started down the stairs. A second later, Dylan's footsteps followed.

When I stepped outside, I tilted my head up to the bright blue sky and felt a little better with the wind on my face.

"What's going on?" Dylan asked from behind me. Then his arms were around my waist, pulling me back to his chest, his lips pressing the lightest kiss on my neck.

That felt even better than the wind, and I relaxed further.

"Nothing," I answered then tilted my head to the side, shamelessly asking for more. He didn't make me wait. Gripping my chin, he gave me a long, wet kiss, chasing away every bad thought.

"Nothing," I repeated breathlessly when we stopped. I looked up to his dizzying eyes and believed it would all be all right.

———

"Is she asleep?" I asked when Jared walked back into the living room.

He sat on the couch with a huff and held his head in his hands. "Yeah, finally."

I twisted so I could look at him but was stopped short by a little hand tugging on my hair. "Zoe, no, no, no. You're messing it up. You can't move, silly. Now I'm gonna have to start again." There was a cute sigh behind me, dripping with mock annoyance.

"I'm so sorry, Miss Bluebird," I drawled, using the new nickname she'd begged me to use as soon as I'd stepped foot into the apartment. Jared's little sister, Becky, was the cutest little girl, and the smartest, too, just like her brother. "Do I have to pay extra now that you're starting again?"

Her fingers stopped moving in my hair. "I get paid?"

"Well, you're my hairstylist, so I think I should pay, don't you? I mean, you've been working at it for how long now? Half an hour?"

"Yes. Yes, you pay me, okay?"

"Okay, I pay, but you have to make me look pretty, okay?"

"I'm trying. How much are you paying?"

"Ouch," I mouthed to Jared, but he wasn't even paying us any attention. "How much do you want?"

She turned to Jared. "Jar, I'm getting paid today. How much money do I want?"

I grinned a toothless grin and managed to hold my snicker back. Becky always called her big brother Jar or Jer.

After a long negotiation process, we settled on three dollars because she envisioned me with three braids like her toy horsey had and it was gonna be beautiful because she was the best at braids—Jar had said so—and she was gonna buy all the chocolates with her money.

Letting Becky continue to play with my hair, I glanced at Jared's bent head.

"Her parents are coming tomorrow. It'll be good for her to see them," I said quietly.

Agitated, he rubbed his neck and exploded up to his feet. In the three years I'd known him, never once had I seen him as angry as he was that day. He couldn't sit in one place longer than a few minutes.

"Fuck! I could kill him! We should've said something sooner, should—"

Abruptly, chubby little arms wrapped around my neck and

Becky hid her face against my hair. I reached up to stroke her arm reassuringly.

"Jared, sit down," I hissed at him. "Oh, it's okay, Becky. He just got upset."

Hearing my tone, his eyes snapped to me then lowered as he finally remembered that his sister was in the room and sat back down.

"I'm sorry, princess," he murmured, kissing her cheek and coaxing her out of her hiding spot behind my hair. "You're not gonna tell on me for using a bad word, are you?" A few more kisses later, Becky was giggling and all was well in her world again.

I put my hand on his knee until it stopped bouncing and stilled. "She knew we didn't like him, Jared," I started quietly. "This wasn't our fault, and it wasn't Kayla's fault either. She loved him. There is only one person responsible here, and he's gonna get what's coming to him."

"You think his parents won't get that"—he shot a quick look at his sister—"b-a-s-t-a-r-d off faster than you can say his name?"

"It won't be that easy."

He got up and started pacing the room again. "And he hurt you too, for fu—God's sake! Why didn't she call me? Why didn't you call me, for that matter? If I had been at the library with you two—"

"Okay, you're gonna give me whiplash. Please sit down." After the look he gave me, I changed my mind. "Or don't, fine, but be quiet," I grumbled. "She's been like a ghost the entire day, and just when she finally closes her eyes for more than ten minutes, you're gonna wake her up again."

"Talk to me about something else then. I'm gonna lose my mind if I can't smash his face into a pulp."

"Hulk. Smash!" Becky popped in. "What's pulp?"

"Is my hair done, Miss Bluebird? Can I look?"

"I get mirror, you see it. You sit here. Okay, Zoe? You sit and you wait, kay?"

As I helped her off the couch, I nodded. "Sit and wait —got it."

Before she could run away, Jared stopped her with a hand on her arm. "KayKay is sleeping in my room and the door is open, so be quiet when you're looking for that mirror, okay?"

"Is KayKay sick?"

"No, sweetheart. She just has a little headache so she needs her sleep. She'll be fine. After you finish showing Zoe her new hair, you're going straight to bed yourself. It's way past your bedtime."

"Okay Jar. First hair, then bed." Satisfied with her answers, she ran away to her room.

"I should get going, too. It's past nine and I need to get back." As soon as Becky was out of earshot, I blurted it out because I couldn't hold it in anymore. "Also, just in case you want to know, I slept with Dylan, and even if you didn't want to know, now you know. In his bed, with him, last night—well, more like morning, but let's go with last night...and then a little bit in the—"

"Wait, wait, wait—hold up," he sputtered. He was holding his hand up, his eyes blinking and blinking. "You did what?"

"I slept with—"

"Clarify, please. You slept with him in the same bed, or you slept with him, meaning you fucked his brains out? Which one?"

"Well..." I pulled my legs up and hugged them to my chest, lips already curved into a smile. "If we're talking about fucking brains out, it was probably mine that got fucked out."

Still with that shocked expression on his face, he dropped down on the couch next to me.

"I guess that means I can't try to seduce him anymore."

I burst out laughing and had to put my hand over my mouth to keep quiet. Then I sobered and my grin disappeared. "I feel so bad for feeling this happy when Kayla is going through this. I didn't plan for it to..."

"Zoe, if it were left up to you, you'd probably wait ten years before you made a move. I already know there was no planning involved."

"He was so good to me yesterday, Jared. As soon as I walked into the apartment, I just crumpled and he picked up my pieces. And then..." I loved Jared to pieces, and he was one of my best friends, but for some reason I didn't want to share every single detail of what had happened after we made it home. The way he held me, the way he hugged me in the shower, the way we fit so perfectly—it all felt private, like it was just ours, mine and Dylan's.

"Then it happened," Jared finished for me.

"Something like that."

"Now it makes more sense."

"What does that mean?"

Before he could answer, Becky came running in, a small pink mirror in her hand as she whisper-yelled at us. "I found it! Zoe, I found it!"

"Oh, that's a beautiful mirror, Miss Bluebird. Now, let's see what you did to my hair."

After she demanded I put her to bed, I checked my hair more thoroughly in the bathroom mirror and had to spend a few minutes calming everything down.

As I was walking past Jared's room, Kayla called my name.

"Is everything okay? I thought you were sleeping." I walked in and sat on the edge of the bed as she sat up.

"Heard Becky talking to you guys. You're still here?"

"Yeah, just wanted to stay around a bit longer." After a long stretch of silence, I asked, "How are you doing?" I'd been worried I wasn't coming up with the right questions the entire day.

"I'm good." She sighed. "I'm better, let's go with that. You can leave, Zoe. It's late. You don't have to wait around."

"Don't worry about me. I'll leave whenever."

She sighed but nodded. "Mom and Dad are coming tomorrow." This time it was my turn to nod. "I'm not sure if I'm gonna come back here in January, Zoe. I'm not even sure I can handle finals."

I wanted to protest, wanted to say it was the stupidest idea I'd ever heard, but it wasn't. I wanted a chance to spend ten minutes alone in a room with Keith, but I knew it wouldn't undo the hurt my friend was going through.

Keeping my eyes focused on the dark gray bedding, I choked up. "I want to beg you to come back, KayKay, but I know I can't."

"I just don't think I want to...actually, I don't think I *can* is a better answer. I think, and my parents think..."

"I understand, and I want you to do whatever will heal you and make you happy again. You think you'll stay in Texas, then?"

"I'm not sure."

I gave her a quick look and looked down at my fingers playing with the edge of the sheets. "Keith's family lives pretty close to yours though, right?"

She shook her head. "They moved when we came to school here. They're in Seattle now, so he won't come to Texas."

We fell silent.

"Maybe you and Jared can come visit me during summer break."

I dashed away a tear that was trailing down my cheek. "Yes, I think that'd be great. I've never been to Texas." I bit my lip and hesitated for a second. "If there is a trial and Keith—"

"I don't want to talk about him, Zoe."

"Okay. I'm sorry." She was fisting the sheet so I put my hand on top of hers. "I'm sorry."

When Kayla didn't speak, I looked up and saw she was crying too.

"I just can't seem to stop it, you know," she said quietly, her lower lip trembling slightly as she wiped the tears away almost as quickly as they were falling. "It comes and goes. One second I'm just fine, and the next I feel sick to my stomach." She lifted her eyes up to me then looked down at my neck where my bruises were visible even through the foundation I'd applied. "And you've been hurt because of me, too—"

I touched my neck with my fingertips. "What? These? I'm not hurt at all, Kayla. I'm just pissed I didn't get the chance to hurt him myself, so don't even think about that part of it."

So far, her preferred method for how to deal with everything had been to avoid all conversation related to Keith. We weren't going to pry, anyway, and having Becky around provided a buffer. We all laughed at her antics, and it almost felt like any other normal day for three close friends.

"I'm going to miss my best friend," I said. "Have you told Jared yet?"

"I'll talk to him."

That's when Jared's head peeked through the open door. "Did someone say my name? I thought you were sleeping, you little liar." He walked around the bed and sat across from me. "Zoe, your phone is going crazy in your bag. Maybe you should get it."

Frowning, I got up. I'd forgotten all about my phone after sending Dylan a quick text to tell him Kayla was doing okay. I had seen missed calls and notifications after reading Dylan's text when I woke up in the middle of the night, but I'd ignored all of it. The first thing I'd done after Dylan and I parted ways in front of our building was combing through everything Mark had sent. After I'd texted him to say I was going to tell Dylan everything, he'd called countless times, left eight voicemails, and sent a couple texts. I'd deleted all of them without even listening to a word. Though I'd ended up reading his texts, none of them had said anything I wanted to hear, so I'd deleted those too. I was done being a doormat for him, and it was way overdue.

I left Kayla and Jared alone and went to find my phone. It was ringing and I hoped it was Dylan, but unfortunately, it wasn't. Reluctantly, I answered.

"Yes."

After a few seconds of silence, Mark spoke up. "Where are you?"

No, *I was worried about you.* No, *I heard what happened at the library.* No, *Are you okay, Zoe?* No *Is there anything I can do?* No nothing.

But none of it mattered because I'd already talked to my dad. He had already asked the questions a dad was supposed to ask. This man was nothing to me, and it was my own damn fault for thinking things could've been different.

"I'm with my friends," I said coldly.

"Did you tell him? Dylan?"

"Not yet, but I will." I would that night, as soon as I decided how to go about it. At that moment, I realized I wasn't afraid to tell him about Mark and Chris. It was just words, and it would've been easy enough to sit him down and explain from the very beginning. What I was afraid of was how he would react. Would he be angry at me for letting him think there was something going on between me and my biological father? Would whatever was happening between us end before it had even begun? That was what I was afraid of—losing him. God knew I'd have been angry at him for letting me think the worst of him.

"Where are you?" he asked again, and I could tell he was gritting his teeth. "I'll pick you up. We need to talk."

"I'm busy right now."

"Zoe," he thundered through the phone. "You are going to tell me where the hell you are and we are going to talk."

Anger bubbled up inside me. I was pretty close to hating him, not that I'd really loved him before, but at least I hadn't detested him. I had been curious, and I'd wanted a chance to get to know him. The first time we met, I told him how excited I was to meet Chris, how I'd always wanted a brother or sister. He'd gently told me it was too early to tell Chris, saying we should take advantage of the time and get to know each other before we told him because he was still shocked himself. He said he was trying to protect his family, and I got that. Oh, it wasn't the best feeling to know he was trying to protect them from *me*, but at least I'd understood him. As the next three years had passed, I'd slowly come to the realization that Mark wasn't interested in telling Chris anything, at least not the whole truth, and the realization had come three years late.

So, it was time I told him everything I'd kept inside for so long. We were going to have a talk, and this time I was going to be the one doing all the talking. It was probably going to be the last time I ever saw him, too, and I was more than okay with that. I gave him Jared's address, and he told me he'd be there in fifteen.

After sitting with Jared and Kayla for another ten minutes, I promised them I'd come back the next day to meet her parents then headed out to wait for Mark to come pick me up. When I told my friends I was going to talk with him, Jared gave me an alarmed look, but I didn't think anything of it.

I should've. I should've been just as alarmed as he was because I didn't know it then, but right that second, Dylan was waiting for me across the street from the apartment building I'd just walked out of.

My phone beeped with a new text and I looked down to read it as I walked toward the sidewalk.

Dylan: *I missed you.*

When I heard a car, I looked up from the screen and saw Mark's black SUV coming toward me. Without sending a reply, I stuffed the phone in my back pocket and nervously waited for him to come to a stop right in front of me.

As I climbed up into the passenger seat, unbeknownst to me, Dylan took a few steps forward and stared at the car in shock. I didn't know he was waiting across the street so he could walk back to the apartment with me. I didn't know he'd wanted to surprise me.

CHAPTER TWENTY-FIVE

ZOE

Mark unlocked the apartment door and gestured for me to go in first. I hesitated.

"Go, Zoe," he said through gritted teeth.

Since Dylan had moved in, Mark had never once come to the apartment. There had been a handful of times he'd invited me to meet somewhere far away from campus—far away from watchful eyes—but more often than not, he had stood me up. In months, I'd seen him a total of three times, or maybe four. On the most recent occasions, he had barely even looked me in the face. The guy who *acted* like he was interested in getting to know me had disappeared somewhere between my sophomore and junior years, and I was an idiot.

I stepped inside and panicked for a moment as I wondered where Dylan was.

Mark didn't waste any time walking past me into the living room. His posture was rigid, his knuckles already white.

"Tell me what this is all about," he ordered when I was standing close enough.

"What?"

"Don't make me repeat myself, Zoe. Where did this thing about telling Dylan everything come from?"

He couldn't be that blind, could he?

"I like him," I said slowly. "We're more than just friends." Just saying it out loud made my stomach tighten in the best way possible. If I hadn't been staring at Mark's angry face, I'm sure I would've grinned.

"You can't be this stupid."

I swallowed the bitter taste in my mouth and chose not to reply.

"He is Chris's friend, Zoe. He'll tell him everything."

"He won't, but why does it matter? We're going to tell him after the last game anyway." He gave me a look filled with hatred, and I tried to keep my expression neutral. "We *are* going to tell him, right?"

In jerky movements, he ran his hand through his hair and muttered something under his breath as he looked out the window.

I took a step back and the backs of my calves hit the couch, so I sat my ass down.

"Even after the last game, you weren't going to let me tell him, were you? You'll never tell him he has a sister."

Deep down, I'd always known. If not, I was pretty stupid, and I really didn't want to believe I was that stupid. At any time I could've walked up to Chris and struck up a conversation, but I didn't because I was partly afraid of how he'd react. I didn't know him, didn't want to deal with rejection, so I let Mark put it off. Also, I think secretly I wanted to give Mark the benefit of the doubt, wanted *him* to want to be a part of my life. He *was* my biological father after all, and loving what came from you was instinctive, wasn't it? Considering the look on Mark's face, I doubted that was the case with us.

"Why did you even let me come here? To Los Angeles? You don't want me near Chris. You don't want to know me. My freshman year, the way you were with me—was that all a lie? Were you just acting and lying to keep me quiet?"

He turned to face me and smoothed down the edges of his mouth with his fingers. "It's not that simple. There are things you don't know."

"What things?" I asked. Frustrated, I hit the couch cushion with my palm. "Tell me then. I'm so tired of this back and forth between us. We're getting nowhere. What things do I not know? Mom said you wanted me here. She said you wanted to get to know me, she said you were excited. She told you I wanted to meet him, that's the whole reason—*he* is the whole reason I wanted to come here. I didn't come here on a whim. I could've called Chris and gotten it done with, but you said you wanted to see me, meet me. What am I missing here?"

"Your fucking mom lied to you, all right? That's what you're missing. She did nothing but lie to everyone in her life. Even in her grave, she is still fucking with me."

I looked at him in shock. His salt and pepper hair was thick, no signs of thinning, and I remembered feeling so silly for noticing it when I met him. When he met my stunned gaze, I stared back at my own eyes: green mixed in with hazel. What a cruel joke. Before I could even think straight enough to come up with an answer, he kept going.

"Did she tell you we were in love?"

She had, but I didn't answer. He didn't seem to need my participation in the conversation anyway. He never did.

He shook his head and kept breaking my heart, disgust written all over his face.

"We fucked," he snapped, opening his arms in exasperation. "We fucked behind my wife's back, her best friend. That's what we did, Zoe. There was no falling in love, just mindless, careless sex because I was having problems with my wife, because we couldn't have kids, because... It was nothing more than a mistake. After I convinced her to give Chris up, she wanted to go back to the way we were and I didn't. That's it. I lied to her so I could get my son. That's where the story ends. You were just another one of our mistakes. It only happened once or twice after Chris, and then she was pregnant again."

My frown got deeper, and I stood up. "No, you're wrong. You didn't know about me. She didn't tell you she was pregnant."

He gave me a long look and shook his head. "I knew about you. I paid her to end the pregnancy. She took the money, told me it was done, and then moved to New York."

We were standing too close so I took a few steps back and put the couch between us. If I could have, I'd have just walked straight out of L.A. without even a glance back.

"What I didn't know was that she actually lied to me and kept it—that I only learned when she called to tell me about her health issues. She begged me to come see her. When she realized I wasn't going to do that, she told me about you. Maybe she thought that would change my mind, or maybe she thought something else. I have no fucking clue what she was thinking lying to me about ending the pregnancy."

I felt like there was someone sitting on my chest, crushing it. My mom and I had had a lot of issues, and there'd been a lot of anger toward the end because of the things she'd kept from me, but I had come to terms with everything. I'd accepted it. It was her life, after all, and it wasn't like I could go back in time and hope she didn't become a cheater the second time around. I couldn't make her reconsider giving up Chris. I couldn't tell her Mark was a liar and she would be stupid to believe any word out of his mouth. Even that first night she had sat me down on the edge of her sick bed to tell me about my 'real father,' I hadn't felt as helpless as I did standing there in front of Mark.

"Why did you ask me to come here?"

"She wanted you with me."

"I already have a dad, her husband. She wouldn't—"

"You don't get it, do you? Your mom was just trying to get my attention, threatening me with calling Emily and Chris, and she'd already told you everything. You would have come here to find Chris with or without me. At least this way I got to protect my son. At least this way he can focus on his future and not this nonsense."

Just like that, I was done with him. Every painful, forced conversation we'd had since I stepped foot in L.A. made much more sense. Was I sad? Yes, but only because I'd been stupid enough to believe he was interested in getting to know me when really he wanted nothing to do with me.

I realized I was holding myself up, hugging my arms. Dropping my hands to my sides, I straightened my spine and nodded. "Now that I'm caught up on everything, I think I want you to leave."

"This is my apartment."

"And you can have it all to yourself. I'll leave first thing in the morning."

"You're going back to Phoenix?"

He could wish that all day every day, but I wasn't gonna do a single thing to make life easier for him anymore.

I let out a forced laugh, but it came out more like a cough. "I'm sure you'd love that, but no. I have another year and a half of school, and I'm not going anywhere until then. Don't worry though, you won't see me anymore. Neither one of us wants to see the other, so at least we have that in common. It should be a relief to you."

"That's fine," he said, looking at his feet with a frown and nodding to himself. "You can leave L.A. after you graduate."

"I'll leave whenever I want to leave. I don't need your permission to do anything—not anymore."

"Fine, do whatever the hell you want. Just stay away from my family."

I felt nothing, absolutely nothing for this man, and the realization was staggering. I was done listening to him, and *that* definitely felt good, like a weight had been lifted off my shoulders. He wouldn't get to have a say in anything anymore, not who I dated, not who I talked to—nothing.

I chose to stay quiet, and Mark didn't like that. He started walking toward me.

"You're not going to tell Dylan a single thing."

"I'm sorry, but that's not going to work for me. Dylan isn't your family," I said in a controlled voice. Inside I was boiling with anger as my pulse rocketed.

"I'm not playing with you, Zoe. You're not going to tell my son's best friend a single thing."

"I won't lie to him anymore. We're not just friends."

"Who do you think you are? Just months ago, he was fighting with his teammates over another girl. Do you think you mean something? He's an athlete with a promising future ahead of him —he'll find someone else in less than a week."

"No. He thinks I'm sleeping with you, and because of you, I couldn't even correct him. If you think you can stop me from—"

Before the words could leave my mouth, he was right in front of me and there was a loud crack in the room then an intense stinging on my face. It echoed in my ears and my cheek burned with a pain I'd never felt before. I stared at my feet in shock and touched my skin with my fingers when the pain seemed to radiate in pulses. Before I could think, before I even knew how to react, Mark's fingers were grasping my chin and he was forcing me to look at him. My hand dropped to my side and I finally looked up into his familiar eyes. The only difference was that mine were filling with tears while his were overflowing with anger.

"I didn't bring you here so you could fuck the football team. You're just like your mom, aren't you? Just a slut going after football players." He wasn't yelling anymore, but his face and throat were red, and I could feel his spit on my face as he hissed at me. "That's what your mom did before she fell into my bed. God knows how many of my teammates had their fun with her, and the apple doesn't fall too far from the tree, does it, Zoe?" My heart beating in my throat, I kept silent but tried to escape his grip. His fingers only tightened further. "It involves my family, so I am the one who decides, not you—never forget that. You're not going to tell anyone anything. I don't care what Dylan thinks of our relationship. I don't care if he thinks I'm sleeping with some girl he thinks he's interested in. You keep your mouth shut and stay away. If you think you can go behind my back and still talk to Dylan, think again. You breathe a word to him, I'll do whatever I have to do to make sure he won't have a future playing football, starting with the team's last game. I see you anywhere near him, he is out of the game this week, and with all the recruiters watching them—"

Before he could finish his threat, the apartment door opened and I knew Dylan had walked in. For a moment I panicked and tried yet again to move my face away from Mark's grip, but there was no point. I was stuck until Mark decided to let me go after seconds that felt like they lasted years. I turned my head. Dylan looked so calm, just staring at me with his blue eyes as if he wasn't surprised, as if he wasn't hurting.

I just stood there, my eyes caught in his stare. Suddenly the sting on my cheek was gone and the pain I felt in my chest took over.

"I think it's time for you to find another place to stay, Dylan,"

Mark said, and I jerked back, noticing how close we were standing.

A chill rushed through me and I stepped away from Mark, discreetly rubbing the spot on my chin where he had touched me. My stomach in knots, I looked into Dylan's eyes until I couldn't anymore. Would he understand that I'd needed him? That I wanted him to take my hand, link our fingers and take me away? He didn't. The moment I broke eye contact, he spoke up.

"Is it, Zoe?" Dylan asked, and my eyes flew up to his again.

"Dylan—" Mark started.

He raised his voice and spoke over Mark. "I want to hear it from her."

My breath got caught in my throat and I couldn't say a single word. Mark could've held a gun to my head, yet I still wouldn't have been able to say, *Yes, Dylan, I think you should leave.*

With Mark in the room, I couldn't give him the long overdue explanation either, not when I knew one wrong word out of my mouth could cost Dylan his future, one he'd been working toward his whole life. I didn't know if Mark was being truthful with his threat, but I couldn't chance it, not on something that important.

I was so lost in my own thoughts, going over everything, trying to come up with a solution, an answer, I only looked up when I heard the apartment door gently close.

That quiet *click* broke something in me and I couldn't get enough air into my lungs. There wasn't enough air in the world, not after he left, not when I was standing in the same room as Mark. Realizing I was on the verge of having a panic attack, I pressed my hand to my chest in the hopes of slowing down my aching heart and tried to ignore the fact that I was feeling dizzy and hot and cold all at the same time.

After a few minutes of struggling passed and I had it under control enough that I knew I could move, I swallowed everything

I wanted to say to Mark and headed toward my room in the back of the apartment.

"Where are you going?" Mark asked.

I just kept walking.

"I'm talking to you, Zoe!" Mark shouted, raising his voice for the first time, causing me to flinch, yet I still walked away without a backward glance.

My first stop was the bathroom, and that's when I caught a glimpse of myself in the mirror. My face was flushed, my eyes big and lifeless. The left side of my cheek was a darker shade of red than my right, the sting had come back with a vengeance, and there was a bonus ache accompanying it. I wondered if Dylan would have stayed if he'd seen the harsh redness of my skin. I tilted my head up and realized my neck didn't look pretty either with all the bruising.

None of it mattered though. None of what I was seeing hurt worse than the ache in my heart.

I took a deep breath and forced myself to look away. Grabbing a hair tie, I put my hair up in a ponytail and started grabbing everything. Then I went to my bedroom and made neat piles of my clothes on my bed. Dragging my suitcases out, I packed every single thing I owned. It took me fifteen minutes.

Tugging my luggage through the hallway, I stopped next to the door and got my keys out of the pocket of my jacket. I found the two that didn't belong to me and pulled them off of my purple key ring. I looked up and saw that Mark was sitting on the couch, his back to me, shoulders hunched forward as he held his head in his hands.

My dad had sat just like that three and a half years ago when I'd learned that he wasn't my real father. He'd been upset because he thought I'd be angry at him for lying all those years, but how could I? How could I be angry at someone who loved me every single day of my existence even though I wasn't his blood?

Seeing Mark sitting like that...that picture of him bothered me. What had he lost?

Nothing.

It was either walk farther into the apartment and place the keys on the kitchen counter or just drop them and leave. I chose to go with the latter and simply let them drop on the hardwood floor. Not even the sharp sound the metal objects made caused him to flinch or look up.

I stepped outside without uttering a single word, and he did nothing to stop me. He was free at last, I supposed.

Still shell-shocked, I stood in front of the apartment door and tried to think. It was pretty late, but I could call an Uber and get to Jared's place, or I could... It was stupid of me to hesitate—where else would I go?

After grabbing the handle of one of the suitcases, I was reaching for the other when Ms. Hilda opened her door. She was the last human being on earth I wanted to talk to. Well...let's say she was second to last, right before Mark. I ignored her completely and started to move. At first she said nothing, but the silence didn't last long. It never lasted when it came to her.

"Where are you going, Miss Clarke?"

"Ms. Hilda, this is not—"

"I heard everything."

"Good for you. Have a nice life."

I was just about to pass her to reach the stairs, but she stepped in front of me. Before I could dodge her, she got a surprisingly strong grip on my chin and started examining my cheek.

When I drew back, she harrumphed and let go of me.

"You could've told me you weren't his mistress, you know."

I pressed my lips together, and my grip on my bags tightened. "If you'll get out of—"

"Oh, stop it. Get inside. I'm not gonna lose sleep because of you, wondering where you are."

"Please!" I raised my voice. "Get out of my way."

Her eyes narrowed at me and she stood straighter. "Do you want him to come out here? I didn't think so. It's midnight. Where will you go?"

"Ms. Hilda—"

"Oh for heaven's sake, just call me Hilda."

Exasperated and pretty much over my limit for how much crap I could take in one night, I tried again. "I just moved out, as you can see. I'm going to my friend's place. If you could just—"

"You're not doing anything of the sort." Despite my protests, she yanked one of my suitcases from my hand and walked straight into her apartment.

"Ms. Hilda! What are you doing?"

She came back and took the other one. "I know I'm not the easiest neighbor to have, but if you think I'm going to let you leave looking like that, you're wrong, Miss Clarke. Now you either keep standing there and wait for that monster to walk out and see you or you get inside and regroup."

Pinching the bridge of my nose, I took a deep breath and exhaled. When I looked up, I saw her standing in the doorway, waiting for me.

"Just for tonight."

She rolled her eyes. "I'm certainly not offering for you to be my roommate."

Grudgingly, I walked inside. The only reason I was accepting her offer was because I didn't want to burden Kayla with all my drama by going back there in the middle of the night.

Ms. Hilda closed the door behind me.

"I'll make some tea and get you some frozen peas to calm down that cheek of yours. Then we can sit down and have a nice talk and you can tell me what you're planning to do now that you're homeless. I couldn't hear everything so you're gonna have to go over some of it." The look on my face must've said it all because she waved me off and headed toward her kitchen. "Oh, don't worry, I heard most of it, I just have some questions. While I'm in the kitchen, why don't you stop standing next to the door like a harassed broomstick and check the drapes for me?"

The next day couldn't come soon enough, because I'd already figured out what I was going to do.

CHAPTER TWENTY-SIX

ZOE

Finals passed in a blur. I don't think I'd be exaggerating if I told you it was the worst time of my life. Ms. Hilda was her usual overbearing, nosy self, but she'd opened up her home to me and I was grateful for that. Me staying at her apartment for two more days might have had something to do with lying in wait for Dylan so I could catch him when he came back to pick up his things, but I never got the chance because he never showed. After the two days passed, I moved my stuff to Jared's. When Kayla had moved into a hotel with her parents, an air mattress had opened up and it had my name on it. It was temporary, just until I could find a new apartment, and maybe some roommates.

Kayla decided to stay for finals, and her parents never let her out of their sight. It was hard saying goodbye to her, and I'm not ashamed to admit that the three of us had a lengthy cry-fest, but knowing we'd see each other as soon as possible helped lessen the pain. I chose not to tell Kayla what had gone down with Mark, but Jared knew all about it. I was a complete mess, and he was my rock through it all. What hurt the most, though, was knowing it was all my own damn fault. If I had told Dylan everything from the beginning, or at least the moment I knew I wanted him to be mine, I could've avoided all the heartache I had gone through.

But, they always say nothing in life worth having comes easy, and Dylan Reed sure wasn't going to make it easy on me.

It was the last day of finals and I was a bundle of nerves as I stood next to the black Challenger. The last time I'd checked the time on my phone, it'd said eight PM, and I refused to check it again since I knew only a minute or two had passed since then.

I was pacing the length of the car when I saw him coming. I closed my eyes and took a deep breath, my heart going a mile a minute, and I was only seconds away from puking my guts out—not the first impression I wanted to make at all. I cleared my throat in preparation and cracked my knuckles.

This is it.

It was the moment I'd waited years for, and all I seemed to be capable of feeling was horror.

Christopher Wilson slowed his walk when he spotted me and stopped next to his car to give me a quick once-over. I couldn't see his eyes because of the hat he had on, but I was pretty sure he wasn't happy about finding me waiting around for him.

After giving me a long look, he just shook his head, opened his car door, and chucked his backpack inside. I stood frozen, waiting for him to say the first words so I'd know how to proceed, but he didn't do that. He got into his car and was about to slam the door closed when I unfroze and grabbed it.

"I need to talk to you," I said, my heart still thumping wildly in my chest.

He looked up at me, and then I saw his eyes—my mother's eyes. "I don't think I'm the one you should be talking to." He pointedly looked at my hand, which was holding his door open. "Now, if you'd step away, I'd like to leave."

His car was parked just outside campus. I'd done a little stalking and it had taken me a few days to find out where he usually parked it; there was no way I was going through all that again. This was the day I was going to tell him everything. No more delays.

I had no idea what Dylan had told Chris, but it seemed like he knew enough to be upset.

"No," I said, finding my voice.

"Excuse me?"

"This has nothing to do with Dylan. I want to talk to you."

"I swear to God, if this is you coming on to me right—"

"No," I burst out. "God, no. Just ten minutes—I need to talk to you for ten minutes, that's it. I promise I won't bother you again, but I'm not gonna go away until you talk to me."

It was true; I was not planning on bothering him after I said everything I needed to say. If he didn't want anything to do with me, that was just fine. I wasn't going to force him to have a relationship with me, but I was done waiting for the truth to be known.

After a half-hearted invitation, I got in the passenger seat and suffered through a painfully quiet car ride to a diner a few minutes away from campus. I assumed he didn't want anyone to see us together, and when he'd told me to say whatever I needed to say, I'd flat out refused to do it in a car.

I sat in the booth and waited for him to settle across from me.

He took his hat off and placed it on the table, messing with his hair. "I'm listening."

I licked my lips and leaned forward. My hands were shaking in my lap under the table, but I thought I looked pretty zen on the outside, at least I hoped so. "This is not gonna sound good, but I'm gonna try to—"

"Hello, I'm Moira. What can I get you kids?"

I closed my eyes, willing my heart to slow down and not make a mess of everything.

"I'll have a coffee, please," Chris said.

Moira's smiling face turned to me, and the warm smile shifted into a frown. "You feeling all right, honey?"

I managed a nod and had to clear my throat before I spoke. "Can I have some water, please?"

"Of course. I'll be right back with those. Let me know if you need anything else."

When Moira walked away, I looked at Chris again. He was watching me, eyes judging.

After years of waiting, I should've been ready for the talk, but there was still a big part of me that was afraid of rejection, and then there was the rest of me that was done with the whole thing.

I reached into my bag and took out the envelope. Squaring my shoulders, I placed it on the table and smoothed it with my hands.

"Here you go. Coffee for you, and water for you." Moira placed a big mug in front of Chris and a gigantic glass of ice water in front of me. "You let me know if I can get you some tea with honey, okay? And maybe a slice of pie to go with it? It works wonders for me when I'm feeling off."

I gave her a genuine smile and she left us alone.

"I can't help you with Dylan. I have no idea what you did to him, but I'm not going to get—"

"This is not about Dylan. I told you that." I smoothed the envelope again and his eyes dropped to watch me do it.

"Then I have no idea what you want to talk to me about, and I can't really say I feel comfortable sit—"

Fuck it. I decided to just go for it.

"You won't believe me, so I thought bringing this would help." I pushed the envelope toward him and clasped my hands on the table when he reached for it.

"What is it?"

"Open it."

I watched him read the single sheet of paper with bated

breath. With every passing second, his frown got deeper and deeper. After he was done, he pushed away his coffee mug, put his elbows on the table, and leaned toward me, reading it again and again.

"Is this some sick joke?"

Before I could answer, he started reading it again, only this time he was reading it out loud.

"The alleged father, Mark Wilson, is not excluded as the biological father of the child, Zoe Clarke. Based on the genetic testing results obtained...the probability of paternity is 99.9999%."

He glanced up at me.

"He wanted to make sure I was his, so we had it done three years ago."

His brows moved up toward his hairline. "You...had it done three years ago?"

I swallowed. "Yes."

He licked his bottom lip and leaned back, the test result still clutched in his hand. He read it again and again, and I waited patiently. I took a sip of my water and placed it back on the table, getting ready to tell him the rest. What surprised me the most was that I no longer felt like the world was about to end. I also didn't feel light and happy, or anything close to it. Sure, I needed to pee very badly, but that always happened when I got really nervous about something. I was just relieved that it was happening and he finally knew at least fifty percent of it. The rest would be harder to hear and accept, but I wasn't scared to tell him.

When he finally looked at me, I was ready to explain the rest.

"This..." He shook the paper in his hand. "Three years?"

I nodded.

He threw the paper on the table and rose to his feet.

"Chris, I—" I started, surprised that he was leaving. I scrambled to my feet, but he lifted his hand to stop me.

"Give me a minute." He slowly backed away from the table, from me. "Don't leave. I'll be back."

I nodded. "I won't. I have more to say."

Without another word, he walked out of the diner.

Trying to calm down, I patiently folded and stuffed the document back into the envelope then put it back in my bag.

Moira caught my eye and winked. God knows what she thought was going on.

I checked my phone. I sat back and listened to the family sitting behind me for a few minutes. They were talking about which movie they were going to watch that weekend, the little girl trying to convince her brother to go with her choice and the dad and mom weighing in. They sounded happy.

The little bell over the diner door chimed and drew my attention. A second later, Chris slid in across from me again. His face looked slightly flushed, his eyes wide and stunned, though it might have been because of the wind. I didn't ask him where he'd gone, but...

"You didn't call Mark, did you?"

His head tilted as he tried to read me. "No."

"Okay. Thank you." I moved back in my seat a little and reached for my water.

"You said you have more to say. Tell me," he ordered.

I placed the glass back on the table and licked my lips. "I'm not sure where I should start."

"You're my half-sister—start from there."

"Actually..." I winced. "Actually, I'm not."

Over the next few minutes, I told him everything—everything that had been told to me, everything that had happened after I came to Los Angeles. The second I started, I couldn't hold any of it back. He listened without asking a single question.

Chris was rubbing his temple with the fingers of his left hand while the other held the edge of the table in a white-knuckle grip. Once I was done, I kept quiet and watched him try to process everything. He reached for the mug and downed half of the luke-warm coffee in one go.

A few minutes of complete silence had passed when he finally spoke. "Why are you telling me this now? Why would I even believe you?"

"Why would you believe me?" I shrugged and stopped playing with the salt shaker I had latched onto at some point. "This isn't how I imagined it would happen, trust me, and I wasn't the one who wanted to wait. I came here three years ago and I was ready to tell you then. Your father—"

"Don't you mean *our* father?" His voice was harsh, and I hoped his words were not intended to hurt.

I shook my head. "Not really. Sure, he is on paper, but that's about it. He'll never be my dad. He doesn't want anything to do with me, and I'm fine with that. I already have a father, and he is more than enough."

"What do you mean he doesn't want you?"

"He doesn't want to have a relationship with me. After every-thing we've been through—after everything *I've* been through, thanks, but no thanks. I don't want a relationship with him." I paused and looked up. "He wasn't the main reason I wanted to come here in the first place, so it doesn't really matter."

"But you two have been talking this whole time. He was spending time with you."

"Yes, but not really—"

"Does my mom know? Does she know about you? About everything after the adoption?" His voice rose as he sat up a little higher.

"No, not about me. I don't mean to say anything bad about your mom, but from what I can tell, they were basically having an affair right in front of her. I have no idea what was going through her mind, but from what she—from what my mom told me, they stopped speaking after she learned about the affair, but she was completely on board with adopting you. Maybe she already knew about it and when the pregnancy came up, she jumped at the idea because she couldn't have kids? I seriously have no idea, but I do know Mark told my mom they would be together eventually, said he'd leave his wife and they'd raise you together."

I lifted my tense shoulders in a shrug and gazed outside.

After a short pause, I continued. "It sounds so stupid when you say it out loud, doesn't it? After adopting you, why would he go back to her? I've learned firsthand how convincing he can be, so I get it to a degree, but at the same time, I don't. Mom said he told her it wouldn't be good for his career if he had a personal scandal like that, but I don't think she was giving me everything. I still don't understand how she could give you up like that." I winced and averted my eyes. "I'm sorry, I'd rather not go into more detail because it wasn't really fun hearing it the first time. Mom told me their marriage was just for show—I think your mom is his old coach's daughter." I huffed and leaned back. "She was just so in love with him, and so sure he was in love with her, I think she believed anything he said. Don't get me wrong, I'm not putting all the blame on him. I hate that they were cheating on your mom and that's how we came to be."

"And you? How did you happen? How old are you?"

"Twenty-one. You're only a year older," I replied with a small, pathetic smile. "I was the mistake, you see—Mark's mistake at least. Mark wanted my mom to have an abortion, gave her the money to do it, but I think that's when she realized he was never going to leave his wife. Skipping out on the abortion, she moved away." I let out a humorless laugh and raised my hands. "Obviously, since here I am. She got married to my dad, but I think she always held out hope that Mark would return to her. We didn't have the best relationship in the world, so I think I'm just a big *fuck you* to Mark, if that makes any sense."

We fell silent for a few beats.

"I thought Mark didn't know about me—that's what he said in the beginning, and that's what my mom said. Turns out he did, and I just learned about the abortion part. I guess he didn't know she hadn't gotten rid of me."

When the silence grew uncomfortable and Chris just kept gazing outside with his jaw ticking, I looked down at my hands and swallowed thickly before speaking again.

"I feel so selfish right now." I looked up to find his eyes on me, so I looked away. "Like I said, this wasn't how I wanted to tell you."

"What was the plan?"

"The plan? I don't think there was ever a plan. That first year I came, he told me he'd like to have some alone time with me, get to know me before he introduced us. He was also worried about how his wife—your mom—would react...to me, to you learning about it all. I thought that was a good idea, to learn more about you and him before, you know...this happened, but then a year passed and he wanted more time because it was important that you focus on your football career, and I said okay because I didn't know how I'd do it without him. Then this year was your last year and it was even more important for you to focus on football, but then last week every-thing kind of went to hell and I just wanted to get it over with." I paused to take a breath. "I completely understand if you don't want...actually, I won't understand if you don't want anything to do with me, but it's not like I'm going to beg you to have a relationship with me. Mom died, and I was so angry at her because that was soon after I learned that my dad wasn't my biological dad. All I have is my dad. Neither he nor my mom had any other close family, so it's just the two of us. I thought I could have more. I thought I'd love to have a brother, to get to know you."

Chris released a long-suffering sigh and smoothed his hair back with both hands. His jaw was still ticking away and his face looked tight, like he was barely holding it all together. The conversation itself hadn't been as awkward as I'd thought it would be, but our reaction to each other was. Whenever our eyes met, one of us looked away. I didn't know what else to say, or what he'd want to hear.

"This is all too fucking much."

"I'm sorry," I said, meaning it.

"It's not your fault," he countered, surprising me. He shook his head as if he was trying to wake up from a nightmare. "He should've been the one to tell me, and not now. The time to tell me was when he learned about you, and my mom...she won't handle this well. I'm sorry, but I don't think it'd be the best idea to tell her I know everything, and definitely not a good idea to let her know Dad kept sleeping with your...ah...your mom. She has her issues, and this would be too much for her."

"Not my decision, and really, I just wanted to meet you. I just wanted to tell you I existed. I didn't come here to mess with your family." I gave him a shy smile and pulled my hands down to my lap. "Just wanted to meet you, that's all."

He cleared his throat and looked away. My stomach dropped. Maybe he wouldn't want anything to do with me either. I knew that was a possibility, but after the week from hell, I hadn't had much time to think it over, to think about what it would mean if he never wanted to see me again.

"That apartment I came to, that's Dad's, isn't it?"

Licking my lips, I nodded.

Slowly, his brows drew together. "Dylan? Fuck, does Dylan know about all this? He was living there...how did he—"

"No, he doesn't. Your dad gave Dylan the apartment keys

only because he thought I was moving in with my friend, but it didn't happen and he didn't know. Then Dylan came and...it doesn't matter. He had no idea, and he still doesn't know. He thinks I'm sleeping with Mark, and Mark wouldn't even let me tell... I couldn't even—" All of a sudden, my voice broke and I couldn't go on.

Dylan, I thought. *Dylan, Dylan, Dylan...*

Ever since he'd walked out of that apartment, something heavy had settled on my chest, like heartburn but worse, because no amount of apple cider vinegar or lemon juice or baking soda would fix it. My heart was broken, and I was so angry, so damn angry—at myself, at Mark, at my mom...at anything and everything.

So, when Chris asked for more information, I told him everything that had happened the last few weeks, how I'd argued with Mark about telling Dylan, and then everything that had happened back at the apartment that night, how Dylan had left thinking he was correct in his assumptions.

I wasn't surprised when tears started to race down my cheeks as I was went through the stories. It felt like my entire heart was full of tears, and I felt alone. Without him, I felt so alone. I didn't see him in the mornings. I didn't get to (not so) secretly watch him work out. I didn't see him in the evenings. I couldn't watch him when he was working on a paper, focusing all his attention on his work. He worked hard, and he looked sexy while doing it. I didn't get to see his smile, the way he looked at me, the way he smiled at *me*, just for me. I didn't get to see his face that first moment when he walked in after a long day of training and saw me sitting on the floor, retouching photos, didn't get to see how happy he looked to find me there. I didn't get to feel his arms around me, crushing me. I didn't get to hear his voice, nor did I get to eat pizza with him or watch a movie and fall asleep on him, with him.

I wiped off my tears, my face flushing when our waitress

handed me more napkins to clean myself up and asked if she could help with anything. Chris thanked her for me then asked for coffee for himself and tea for me.

When I was no longer a blubbering mess, I apologized to Chris.

"He hit you?" he asked, his tone neutral.

I held the warm mug and acted as nonchalant as possible. "It's fine." I didn't tell him that neither my dad nor my mom had ever hit me.

Two hours had passed, and I was drained—drained of words and tears, of energy and emotions.

"I'm going to be honest with you, Zoe...I have no fucking idea how I'm gonna deal with all this."

"Can I just ask for one thing?"

"Sure."

"You have one more game, December 26th, right?"

"Yeah, the Cactus Bowl."

"Can you not tell Mark, or let him know that you know until after it happens? I don't want him to take it out on Dylan. I wanted to tell you because I was done waiting, and it's not like he is going to do anything to mess with your future even if—when he learns about this. I'm not even sure if he *can* do anything to mess anything up for Dylan, but I just don't want to be the reason for—"

"I can't promise you that."

I met his eyes and nodded. That was understandable, but I didn't think he'd throw his friend under the bus.

The silence after that stretched into minutes and we both sat there, not speaking to each other, just sipping tea and coffee every now and then. When his phone started going off in his pocket, he took it out and shot me a quick look before answering.

"Dad."

I stiffened.

"Yeah. I'll be there."

Just like that, their conversation was over.

"I need to leave," he explained.

"All right. Thank you for listening to me. I don't know what I'm feeling right now, but I hope you don't think the worst of me. I just couldn't wait any longer and as soon as I can—after the game, that is—I want to talk to Dylan and explain things. He blocked me so I can't reach him, but I'm going to talk to him somehow. I thought you needed to know before him."

After that, we had officially reached awkwardland. He insisted on paying the bill then offered to drop me off wherever I needed to go. I told him it wasn't necessary then we just stood in front of his car. Neither one of us knew what should come next.

"I can give you my number," I offered, a little hesitantly. "You don't have to call me or anything if you don't want to, but if you do end up wanting to talk again...about other things...or anything..."

"Yeah, sure."

His response didn't sound promising, but I'd take what I could. After all, I already knew we wouldn't be besties right off the bat, or maybe ever, really.

After he got in his car and left, I stood at the corner and called Jared.

"Did you talk to him? How did it go?" was the first thing out of his mouth as he answered.

"I did, and I'm not sure. At least he listened. We talked for a couple hours and now it's up to him."

"How do you feel? It finally happened, Zoe. I can't believe you talked to your brother."

I felt like something was missing, but I didn't tell Jared that. I assumed I'd feel like something was missing for a while longer. Instead, I told him it had felt invigorating, and I was happy no matter happened next, which was true to some extent.

"Are you coming back here now? Mom made spaghetti and I saved some for you. She has the night shift at the hospital again and Becky is already in bed, so we can talk all night if you want."

My eyes filling with tears, I sniffled into the phone. "Thank you for letting me stay this last week, Jared. I don't even know how to thank your mom, and I just—"

"Oh, come on, sweetheart, don't tell me you're crying. You've thanked us a thousand times already. Becky loves you, and you've been babysitting and playing with her, so trust me, my mom is the one who is thankful to have you around. Did your big, bad brother break my best friend? If he did, I'm gonna kick his ass tomorrow. Just say the word—though I won't touch his face because you guys have some excellent DNA."

My lips stretched into a smile and it felt weird, as if I hadn't laughed or smiled for days.

"I'm not crying, just a little emotional. I think I'm gonna walk back so I can get it together—a little fresh air should help. I feel a little weird after finally telling him everything, and I think I'll grab some pizza on the way if that's okay with you. I'm sorry, but your mom's cooking..."

Jared laughed, and the sound made my lips tip up even more.

"Get two," he ordered. "I'm starving."

"On it."

I started walking with the phone glued to my ear.

"I'm thinking we should get drunk and celebrate tonight. What do you think?"

"Celebrate what?"

"We survived finals—what more do you need as an excuse to get drunk? Also, you talked to your brother, and I'd say that's a good reason, too. We'll get drunk and talk boys."

"My favorite pastime," I muttered. "I can talk about your boys though. That should be fun."

"We'll talk about Dylan."

I sighed and pushed my free hand into my jacket pocket. It wasn't cold, but every time I thought about Dylan, a little shiver worked its way through my body and my heart gave an extra little kick.

"I do like talking about Dylan," I admitted.

"I know you do. We'll talk about how fine he is and what fine friends he has that you're obligated to introduce me to once you two kiss and make up, and then..."

I have no idea how long the walk back lasted, but I did it with my best friend's voice in my ear, and I was finally breathing a little easier.

The feeling only lasted a few hours, until I got in my makeshift bed in Jared's room and dreamed about Dylan.

CHAPTER TWENTY-SEVEN

ZOE

January 1st

Chris: *Did you talk to Dylan?*

　　　Zoe: *No, he blocked me. Why? Did he say something? Did you say something?*

It had been a little over two weeks since I'd told Chris the truth, and while you couldn't exactly say he was treating me like his long-lost sibling, he hadn't completely ignored me either.

We'd only talked twice after the day at the diner, but it was still something. The first time he'd called me, it was just to give me a heads-up that he had talked to Mark, but not his mother; I didn't think he was ever planning on telling her. I appreciated the warning. I'd already gone ahead and blocked Mark while I was staying with Ms. Hilda, but it was good to know what was going on. It had been a three-minute conversation—yes, I'd checked—nothing long, but that didn't stop me from grinning like a fool for an hour after he hung up.

The second time was when I'd sent him a short *Happy New Year* text. He responded asking me what I was doing, and we ended up texting back and forth a few times. It wasn't anything deep, but I was happy. He didn't seem to talk much in general, at least that was the vibe I'd gotten from him when he came to the apartment with JP, so it didn't surprise me when he didn't suddenly turn into a chatterbox with me either. I chattered enough for the both of us anyway. I even managed to get a smiley face from him, which was the highlight of my day. Pathetic, right?

I blamed Dylan.

Okay, fine, not really, but I was missing him like I hadn't seen him in years when it had actually only been a few weeks, and it was easier to blame him for everything since he was the one who'd walked out of that apartment instead of trying to take me away with him. The plan had been for my father to come spend New Year's in L.A., but something came up and he couldn't make it; that was Dylan's fault, too. Then there was the time I couldn't get pizza from my favorite pizza place because their pizza oven wasn't working. What kind of pizza place has a faulty oven? All on Dylan. I'm thinking you can see the pattern there. All I knew about him was that right after the Cactus Bowl, he had headed home to San Francisco to spend the short break with his family.

Chris: *It's a good night to go out. Maybe you'd like to have a drink somewhere.*

I read the text once. Then a second time, slower. Was he asking me to hang out?

"Read this." I handed my phone to Jared, who was working on a sketch on the coffee table. "He's asking me to hang out, right? I'm not reaching or anything?"

Jared gave me an amused look and handed my phone back. "Nope. That's an invite, all right. Write him back."

"You'll come, too?"

He returned his attention to his sketch. "Sure. If you don't mind me flirting with your brother, count me in."

When he gave me a hopeful look, I grinned.

"Yeah, maybe not this time."

He chuckled and threw one of his pens at me.

"You little cockblocker."

A little excited and a lot nervous, I texted back.

Me: *I'd love to. Where do you want to meet?*

Chris: *Uh...not with me. I think you should go by yourself.*

At first, I didn't get it, and I felt like crap, but after reading it a few times, my heart started beating faster and I jumped up from the couch, my laptop almost meeting an untimely end.

"What's happening? What is it?" Jared asked when I bounced in place like a lunatic, one hand over my mouth, the other clutching my phone to my chest.

"I think Dylan is back," I shrieked as quietly as possible, so I wouldn't wake Becky. "Chris just told me I should go have a drink somewhere by myself. I think Dylan is at the bar. He's back!"

Having trouble containing the bouncing, I let Jared steer me into his room. "Didn't you already go to the bar to look for him though?"

"I did, but maybe he's back now?"

"I thought you were angry at him."

"I am. I'm so so angry at him."

"Why are you still bouncing?"

"Because I can't wait to kick his ass."

Jared put his hands on my shoulders and steadied me. Apart from my flushed face and the grin I was sporting, I must've looked pretty normal. "You good?" he asked.

I took a deep breath and exhaled. "Yeah. What am I going to wear?"

"You sure you're good? You're still trying to bounce. Stop it." He pressed harder on my shoulders.

"I'm excited, let me bounce a little—and now I have to pee.

Find me something to wear, okay? I need to leave ASAP because I'm not sure if he's working or is just there with Chris. I need to get there before he leaves." I stopped in the doorway and glanced back. "He's back, Jared."

My best friend's face relaxed and he smiled back at me. "I know, sweetheart. Go pee, and then you can go kick his ass."

I STOOD across the street from Jimmy's and tried to contain everything I was feeling. Excitement, dread, panic, happiness, hope, anger—you name it, I was feeling it. After hugging Jared and promising I'd keep him updated on whether or not he'd have to come pick up my pieces, I'd left, and the closer my Uber had gotten to the bar, the harder and louder my heartbeats had gotten.

So, I chose to stand there like a weirdo to give myself a few minutes to collect myself. When I was walking across the street, a couple stumbled out of the bar, heads low as they whispered, hand in hand. For a split second, my stomach dropped and I froze in the middle of the street, because I could've sworn I was seeing Dylan with another girl—but then the girl smiled up at the guy and the guy backed off enough that I could see he actually looked nothing like Dylan.

A car blasted its horn and I hurried across the street.

Before pushing open the heavy door, I closed my eyes and inhaled fresh air. With one final mental push, I was inside.

You wouldn't believe how loud and clear I could hear my heart pounding in my ears, how I couldn't hear anything but my own freak-out. The bar was full as it always was; it didn't matter a bit that it was a Monday. A guy bumped into me as he was heading outside then I forced myself to take a few steps in and look around to see if I could find Dylan or Chris.

I was wearing one of my favorite white tees, black jeans,

black boots, and a thin jacket on top, only because Jared had forced me to. I was burning up with stress.

Then I saw him, and suddenly I didn't know how to breathe, what to do with myself...I didn't know anything. I swallowed and took a step toward the bar where he was talking to another bartender. Head angled down, lips stretched into a small smile, he looked larger than life to me.

I swear my heart skipped a beat—maybe a few—as I got closer to him. I have no idea how I managed to put one foot in front of the other, but it could've been that I was floating. All the bar stools were taken, so I waited...and waited, patiently, never taking my eyes off of him. If he'd just look up and a little to the left, he'd find me standing right there, but he didn't, and it made it easier for me to creep on him as he poured drinks.

When a girl jumped down from one of the stools, a little away from Dylan, I rushed to it before anyone else could take it. I hoisted myself up, placed my hands on the bar top, and then took them down. I squared my shoulders, sat up straighter, and pressed my hands against my stomach to calm the butterflies rioting in there.

Everything was fuzzy around me. Dylan was all I could focus on, and a massive earthquake could have gone off at that moment, yet I still wouldn't have taken my eyes off of him. My heart had missed beating like this, for him, only for him.

"Can I get you something?"

Jumping in my seat, I tried hard to focus on the bartender who had spoken to me. I remembered seeing her the last time I was there, but I couldn't come up with a name. Had I even heard her name? Frowning a little, I leaned forward.

"Uh, yes. Thank you," I whispered. "Beer. Whatever is on tap, please."

"I'm gonna need to see an ID."

I reached into my back pocket and handed it to her. When I

glanced Dylan's way, I got caught up in his gaze, and I stopped breathing altogether.

How necessary was air anyway? Pretty overrated, if you asked me.

I watched his jaw harden, his mouth become a straight line. We couldn't look away from each other. He looked pissed off, maybe rightly so, and I didn't know what he saw when he looked at me. I had thought I was prepared to storm in and yell at him, but in reality, I wasn't prepared to see him at all.

My emotions were at war. I'd missed him so much—*so* much —yet I couldn't do anything about it...not until we talked, until he gave me a chance to talk, though I wasn't going to leave it up to him.

Then Dylan was walking toward me and I was already breathless.

The moment he made it to where I was sitting, he reached for the beer the bartender had already placed right in front of me, right next to my ID. I hadn't even noticed it. Guessing what he was about to do from his angry strides and ticking jaw, I reached for my beer before he could, sloshing it on the bar top in the process.

I could feel my legs shaking when he put his palms on the counter and leaned forward. I had a moment of hesitation on what to do—lean forward, wrap my arms around his neck, and hold on for dear life like a monkey and hope he'd find it cute or get away from the anger I could see blazing in his eyes? I leaned away, holding the beer mug protectively against my chest.

"Leave."

One word—he gave me one word, and I felt the hurt deep down in my chest. I could only manage to shake my head from side to side.

"Zoe, leave."

I hated how harsh my name sounded coming from his lips, but I found my voice anyway. "No."

Nothing could make me leave that bar without talking to him.

He gave me a long, dark look, and I held my breath. Then he leaned back and straightened, walking away without another word as if I wasn't even worth another second of his time.

I spent ten minutes sipping and nursing that beer, ten minutes, and he didn't even give me a single opening to say anything, staying as far away as possible.

"Dylan!" the female bartender yelled, and I flinched. His eyes moved over me as if I didn't exist. "I need to take my break—cover for me?"

He gave her a sharp nod then spoke to the other guy who was handling the bar taps. A few seconds later, the guy was covering the customers where I was sitting, because Dylan didn't want to be near me.

Starting to get more pissed off with every passing second, I downed the rest of my beer to the sounds of Drake and asked for another one from my new bartender.

Only, instead of getting me a fresh one, he put a shot of tequila, a slice of lime, and a salt shaker in front of me.

"On the house," he said with a smile.

CHAPTER TWENTY-EIGHT

DYLAN

I watched Brian place a shot in front of Zoe and had to physically hold on to something to stop myself from going over there and breaking his nose. Zoe grabbed the shot glass and smiled at Brian before swallowing the drink in one gulp. Scrunching her face, she reached for the lime and sucked on it.

I looked away from her—because that was my only viable option—and watched Brian's reaction. The bastard was smiling down at her, leaning in, talking and talking and talking.

Zoe didn't seem to respond to him, but that wasn't stopping Brian from flirting. For a second, I thought about going over there and telling Brian she was into older men, but I decided to ignore them. It hurt—*physically* hurt to look at her, and that pissed me off even more. I'd been so angry the moment I'd heard her voice asking for a drink, and then even angrier when I saw the look on her face as her eyes met mine.

A few minutes passed—or maybe just a few seconds—and I had to look again. This time Brian was placing another beer in front of her, ignoring another customer who was waiting to place an order.

Slamming two bottles of beer on the tray that was waiting to be filled with orders, I stalked toward them. If she had flirted with him...if she had smiled at him, laughed with him, talked with him, looked at him—done *anything*, I don't think I'd have felt as much anger as I did. I think I'd have felt relief more than anything.

"You can get back to your orders, Brian," I ordered, my tone bordering on murderous, and instead of waiting around to see what he was doing, I helped the waiting customers. Brian fell silent, and Zoe's eyes followed my every move.

"I can cover for Lindy, man," Brian insisted, not so wisely.

Brian had started as the new bartender only two weeks before, so he was supposed to listen to whatever I said. If he didn't, I would make him.

"Get back to your spot. Handle the orders." When it looked like he was about to protest yet again, I took a small step toward him, my temper flaring. We were standing right in front of Zoe, and I leaned forward so only he could hear me. "It's not quiet enough for you to play around, Brian, and stay the hell away from her. Get back to your work or get the fuck out of here." I leaned back. "You understand me?"

His brows inched up toward his hairline and he raised both hands in surrender, backing away.

Ignoring Zoe, I poured a whiskey for one customer and got two beers for another. Even though I didn't want to, I could still see her out of the corner of my eye, could see how quickly she was gulping down her beer.

All of a sudden, I couldn't bear to have her around. I couldn't get away from her perfume, that fucking sweet berry scent. I couldn't look away and not remember how good it'd felt to feel her soft skin, to have her underneath me, how responsive she was to my touch, how her eyes had sparkled when I'd run to her side after the game in Tucson, how good it'd felt when she looked into my eyes for more than a few brief seconds...her blue panties, her wet hair, her wounded eyes...her arms around me, holding on... how excited she got when she was eating pizza, how she called the damn thing a *love circle*...her fucking shy smile, her orgasms...

All of it played like a fucking movie in my head.

Anger burned through my insides.

"You're done," I said, coming to stand in front of her. "I want you to leave."

I looked straight into her eyes, and she returned my gaze without a flinch. I couldn't tell if she was already drunk or not, couldn't tell what game she was playing at.

"I'm not going anywhere, not before you talk to me."

"What gave you the idea that we have anything to talk about? If you want me to call Coach to pick you up, let me know."

Her eyes flashed with an emotion I couldn't pinpoint, and she sat up straighter in her seat. "If you want me to leave, you're gonna have to drag me out of here."

I braced my hands on the bar top and watched her.

"Don't try me. I have nothing I want to say to you."

Her eyes narrowed and she leaned forward. "Then just listen to me."

I quirked an eyebrow. "Not interested in that either, buddy."

This time her eyes flashed with anger, and for some fucked-up reason, it thrilled me. My heart rate picked up and I gripped the wooden edge so I wouldn't reach out to her and take her lips.

"I won't leave this spot until you give me five minutes, and you will give me at least that much, *buddy*," she spat.

"Suit yourself." I walked away.

A minute later, Lindy came back in from her break and took over.

Ten minutes passed.

Then fifteen.

Then thirty.

With every second she kept sitting on that damn bar stool, I got closer and closer to losing my shit in front of everyone. When it reached a point where I couldn't take it anymore, I snapped the rag I had in my hand and tossed it away. Getting out from behind the bar, I walked to her side. By the time I was there, she was already standing up, waiting.

"I'm not leaving, Dylan."

"Yes, you are. I'll listen to whatever it is you need to say just so you can get out of my sight."

Grabbing her arm just above the elbow, I pulled her behind the bar.

"I'm taking ten," I shouted to Lindy as I opened a door that took us into the small kitchen then led her out into the dimly lit back alley.

The metal door slammed shut behind us, and I let go of Zoe as if her skin had burned mine then put some distance between us.

"Start so I can be done with you already."

She stayed silent, so I looked at her. Her eyes seemed to be filling with tears. I tried to ignore what I was feeling and stayed put.

"I'm so angry at you," she said quietly, finally.

"Excuse me?"

"I'm so damn angry at you!" she repeated, her voice clear and strong.

"Yeah?" I crossed my arms over my chest. "For what? Because I didn't play along with whatever fucked-up game you were playing at? Because I walked in on you with him and interrupted you two? How dare I, right?"

Her eyes narrowed as she leaned toward me. "I'm angry at you because you blocked me! I'm angry at you because you never even let me talk to you." Then she straightened and she was no longer leaning forward. "I thought I was your friend, Dylan. If nothing else, I thought I was at least that."

I snorted and laughed. "My friend? Were you thinking of your friend when you got into his car and left with him? Or right before I walked in on you two?"

"What are you talking about?" She frowned. "What car?"

"Don't even try to lie to me, Zoe. If you're here to tell me he just came to the apartment on his own and I misunderstood everything, save your breath. I was waiting for you in front of Jared's apartment. I was right there when you ignored my text and climbed into his car."

She licked her lips, stared at me for a moment, and then said, "You're going to feel like a complete idiot and you don't even know it."

"I doubt it. If you're done, I need to go back inside."

She shook her head and bit her bottom lip, drawing my gaze to her mouth. She reached behind her and took something out of her back pocket. Unfolding a piece of paper, she closed the distance between us.

Three steps—that was all it took.

"Here." She slapped the paper against my chest, and I watched it flutter to the ground.

When I flicked my gaze up, she looked unsure. Her chest was rising and falling rapidly. Someone slammed a door shut in the building next to us and the sound boomed in the alley, causing her to jump.

"Pick it up," Zoe demanded, but I didn't move. Her shoulders slumped and the fight seemed to have leaked out of her. "Read it, Dylan."

A few seconds passed and I had to stand still when I saw her eyes start to fill with tears.

"You're an idiot, Dylan Reed!" she shouted, and all I could hear was the hitch in her breath. All I could see was that heart-broken look on her face.

She turned around to leave, and I crouched down to retrieve

the paper that looked like it had seen better days. I unfolded it two times and straightened up. With every word I read, my heart rate picked up. The second I understood what I was looking at, I groaned, let the paper fall to the ground again, and went after Zoe.

I hadn't even noticed or heard the back door opening and closing, but I was the only one standing in that alley. I yanked the door open and caught up to her as she was walking through the kitchen. Her hands were fisted at her sides as she reached the door that would take her into the bar and away from me. I ignored everyone in the kitchen—which was a total of three people—grabbed her shoulder and spun her around.

I was breathing as hard as if I had just run ninety yards for a touchdown. When my gaze met her tearful one, I was almost afraid to speak. She looked so hopeful, so sad, and so damn beautiful.

"Zoe," I whispered.

Then the tears started coming down faster and I couldn't not touch her anymore. I couldn't not hold her, and I couldn't not keep her. I leaned down enough to wrap my arms under hers and hugged her. When her arms encircled my neck and she rested her head on my shoulder, her sobs became louder. I put my arms right under her butt, hoisted her up, and wrapped her legs around me. Her hold on my neck tightened and she pushed her face into my neck, still crying.

Ignoring the looks, I walked us back out to the alley and pushed her back against the door as soon as it shut.

I couldn't feel my arms from the tight hold I had on her and I had no fucking idea how my legs kept us up, but I had no complaints about any of it.

When she lifted her face from my neck and held my face between her hands, I just stared at her, dumbfounded.

"It's true?" I asked, needing to hear it from her lips and not just see it on a piece of paper.

She nodded.

"Let me hear you say it."

"He is my biological father." She swallowed and I watched her throat move, still having a hard time believing she was telling the truth.

"All this time...you let me think..."

She tilted my head up and looked into my eyes. She still had tears in hers. "I was going to tell you, Dylan, I swear to you. That's why he was there, why he picked me up from Jared's place —to talk to me. I told him I was going to tell you about him right before I walked into the library that day, and then everything else happened and I just pushed it back. But, I was going to tell you. I swear to you, I was. I can show you my text to him. I can tell you everything."

I looked down to her shivering lips and couldn't help myself anymore.

You need water to live, can only survive without it for three to five days, and it'd been so much longer since I'd had my fill of her, since I'd tasted her. I'd barely survived.

Our lips crashed and she let out a quiet whimper the second my tongue touched hers. It was the messiest kiss of my life and yet maybe one of the best. Our teeth bumped, our tongues tangled, and still, I couldn't get enough of her. I let go of her legs and pushed myself more firmly against her body, crushing her between the door and myself.

My hands free, I cradled her face and tilted her head to the side so I could get more, and she gave me everything—absolutely everything. Pushing her arms between mine, she wrapped her arms around my neck again and let me lead.

When we stopped, we were both breathing hard, as if we had

just finished a marathon, and I wouldn't have had it any other way. This girl...she took my breath away.

Resting my forehead against hers, I licked my lips. We were standing so close, I tasted hers too.

"I missed you," she whispered. "I missed you so much, you have no idea."

"I think I do," I said, just as quietly. The whole world had disappeared, and it was just us. "You're just mine, then?" I asked, just to have another confirmation.

She pulled her head back a little to look into my eyes. "You're my best buddy—who else's would I be?"

I kissed her again, slower this time, sipping instead of chugging. Still, I didn't think I'd ever get my fill of her.

"I'm so angry at you," she whispered in between my kisses. "Still so angry."

"Why?" I bumped my nose to hers and she ducked her head to kiss me, licking my lips when she was done. I dipped one of my hands down and put it on her butt, pulling her a little lower. When she felt how hard and ready I was for her, she closed her eyes, bit her lip, and groaned, trying to move her body against me. I stilled her and kissed her neck, licking and sucking as I rolled my hips.

"How could you just leave like that?" she asked in a gasp when she could find the words.

I stopped moving against her and my hold on her tightened again. My gaze took in her flushed face and met her glazed eyes.

"How could you not come after me?" I croaked.

"I'm an idiot. What's your excuse?"

I smiled and let my forehead drop to her shoulder.

"You've called me an idiot a few times tonight, so I'm guessing I'm your other half, just as big of an idiot, if not bigger."

"Then we're perfect for each other, huh?"

"We *are* best buddies, aren't we?"

Her grin took me by surprise, and I found myself lost in another kiss until the door behind us was pushed open and I had to carry her weight to protect her.

Lindy's head poked out from the opening and she winced when she saw us.

"Sorry to interrupt, Dylan, but I could really use you out there. Brian isn't really the biggest help at the moment, so if you..."

I cleared my throat. "Yeah. Just give me another minute, okay? I'll be right there."

She nodded and offered me a small grin. "Yeah, sure."

When it was just us again, I slowly let Zoe's feet touch the ground, and she tried to fix her clothing. When she looked up, I exhaled and grabbed her face to press a kiss to her swollen, dark pink lips. She smiled up at me, and my chest felt heavy.

"We still need to talk, Zoe. I need to know everything."

She lost a little bit of her smile but nodded.

"Where are you living?"

A quick shrug. "I've been staying with Jared for now. I'll need to find a place or a roommate after the semester starts."

"I'm staying with Benji. He moved in with another guy and I've been sleeping on their couch. You're not going back to your friend's tonight," I stated.

Still smiling big, she shook her head. "I won't."

"And you're waiting until I close up. You're sitting right in front of me until then."

"I am. I won't move—I won't even look away."

CHAPTER TWENTY-NINE

ZOE

After every single customer had trickled out, then everyone in the kitchen, every waitress and bartender, it was just me and Dylan alone in the place. It looked so big with everyone gone, so quiet, every table empty with the chairs turned up. Dylan had already turned the lights off, all but the small decorative lights that hung above the mirror behind all the alcohol. I thought it was romantic. I was still sitting in the exact spot Dylan had planted me in, on the same stool, and I was wide awake. The only time I'd looked away from him for more than a few seconds was when I texted to Jared to let him know I wasn't coming back and everything was okay again.

I looked up when I sensed Dylan coming down the stairs he'd told me led up to his boss's office. My breath caught in my throat and my heart lurched. He was the best-looking guy in the world, at least he was in my eyes, and I'm pretty sure you'd agree with me if you saw him. His eyes never wavered, and I never looked away. He was wearing black slacks and a simple long-sleeved, dark gray t-shirt that had the bar's logo on his right pec. He looked incredible, ready to be devoured. Basically, he looked and tasted better than pizza.

He also looked like someone I'd never thought could be mine. He was the kind of guy who would get you pregnant just from looking at him for too long. When he made it to my side, he picked me up as if I weighed nothing and sat me down on the bar. I immediately put my palms down to steady myself then he opened my legs and sat between them on my empty stool. His hands moved up and down on my thighs, leaving goose bumps and shivers in their wake.

Having trouble stopping myself, I leaned down, put my hands on his shoulders, and kissed him, just a small, gentle kiss he easily turned into something more, leaving me breathless.

When he pulled back, I just stared at him with the biggest grin on my face. It was like seeing him for the first time and falling for him all over again. He was the dream, the one you always wanted to end up with, the other half of your soul, if you believed in that kind of thing. I was willing to bet Dylan Reed would check every single box every single woman had on their must-have list, and yet there he was, standing in front of me, smiling at me with a crooked grin.

"What? What's that look for?" he asked, his hands moving again, more insistently this time around.

I laughed. "What look?"

He just kept staring into my eyes, and I melted a little more with every passing second.

"No one has ever looked at me like that before, you know," I admitted, having a little trouble holding his gaze.

He moved closer—arms resting on my thighs, hands around my waist—and my eyes closed on their own. "Like what?" I felt him kiss the edge of my lips, then my cheek.

"Like...that," I repeated lamely in a whisper against his lips.

He smiled then brushed a soft kiss right next to my ear. "Can you be a little more specific?"

"Nope."

I felt his chuckle deep in my bones more than merely hearing it. "Okay."

Then he kissed me. Our lips molded together, gently, nothing more than a whisper in the night, up until he spoke.

"You should keep me then. No one else can look at you the way I do."

"That's not what I said, was it?" I protested with a small smile of my own, and I opened my eyes to find him gazing up at me. My heart soared. "So cocky," I whispered.

His thumb moved over my lip, but he didn't look away from my eyes. "Keep me, Flash. I'm a good catch."

I grinned, my heart skipping all over the place. "You know what? I think I will."

His smile got bigger, and I felt out of my mind with happiness.

Hands still around my waist, he stood up. I held his face between my palms and rested my forehead against his. "I'm happy again," I offered out of nowhere.

"Were you miserable without me?"

I thought it was just a throwaway question, didn't think he expected me to give him an honest answer because he reached for my mouth again, but I pulled back before he could drown me in him.

"I *was* miserable, Dylan. I couldn't sleep, couldn't talk to you. Then when I could, after the last game, I couldn't find you. You blocked me," I accused him. "Not that I can blame you, but I guess I still will. I missed you. I missed you like I've never missed anyone in my life." I put my palm on my heart and tried to ease the ache. "I have this ache, right here, and every morning I woke up these last two weeks, I would have this moment, that first second after I opened my eyes, where I thought, *Get up, Zoe, get up and see Dylan. Get up and go to his bed. Get up and have breakfast with him—he's waiting for you in the kitchen.* Then I'd realize I couldn't do any of that."

Dylan looked at me, either taking in my words or deciding how to respond, or both. I wondered if I'd revealed too much of my feelings, not that I'd have cared if I had.

"I missed you more than I had any right to miss you, and it ate at me," he said before the silence could become awkward. "I was so pissed at myself because I couldn't even hate you. Do you realize how hard it was for me to work with him, knowing he got you and I didn't? How hard it still is? You thought of me the moment you woke up, and I thought of nothing but you ever since. I hated that you'd do that to me, that you'd lie to me that way. When I saw you get in his car, I didn't believe it, you know. I was sure you'd explain it, but when I came home and found you two...so close, and him touching you..."

"Can I tell you everything now?"

"Yeah, you have to, and please don't leave anything out."

"I won't," I promised, and knowing that everything would be okay after, that he'd still be standing right in front of me, I told him everything. I started from the very beginning, that first moment my mom told me about Mark and Chris, and finished with how I'd talked to Chris just days after he'd walked in on me and Mark arguing.

"I wanted to find you the next day, and I even called you, but you'd already blocked me. The more I thought about it, the more scared I got that he'd do something to mess with you on the field. The threat was there, and I have no idea if he'd have the power to do it. I wasn't giving up on you, but I didn't think running to you right after I left was the best idea either. I gave myself time, until the game, knowing I'd tell you after the Cactus Bowl—that I was sure of."

For the amount of time it took me to tell him everything, we sat in the exact same position: him right between my legs, touching me, constantly touching me. When I had trouble voicing something, he'd squeezed my waist, reminding me he was there, right there with me. At one point, his hands pushed under my shirt and we were skin to skin. He distracted me countless times but would nudge me to keep going because he was taking in every word I was saying.

His face was tilted down as he listened to me with his focus on his hands, drawing lazy circles on my skin under my shirt, as if he couldn't help himself.

"That's why I don't want you to go to him or tell him anything about this, Dylan."

He looked up at me. "You can't ask me to do that, Zoe."

"I just did. That's why I came here—I couldn't not tell you, but I don't want the whole wait to be for nothing."

"I'm not going to stay away from you until draft day, Flash. You can get that out of your head right now. Now that I know everything, nothing you say can keep me away from you."

Smiling, I leaned down, pressed a kiss to his lips, and pulled back.

"I wasn't planning on doing anything remotely close to that, even on the off chance that you didn't want me anymore."

Then he was the one leaning forward and capturing my lips, his tongue doing things that left me in awe. When he drew back, his eyes were clear.

"What do you want then?"

"I saw how hard you worked to get where you are—just living with you for a few months was enough for me to see that. I'm not gonna be the reason for even the possibility that—"

"What are you asking of me?"

"Just don't make it obvious that you know, that's all."

He gripped my waist in his hands and my body jolted.

"I can't have you sleeping somewhere else, Flash. I can't go another day without waking up to you wrapped around me. We'll find a small apartment and move in together. I know I only have a few months until the draft, and after that—"

Not even trying to contain my smile, I might have shouted my response a bit louder than I was aiming for. "Yes. Yes. Yes!" With the way I was acting, you'd have thought he'd asked me to marry him.

It was the worry in his face that smoothed out first—as if he'd really thought I could pass up the chance to wake up to him for however long—and then he laughed with me.

I couldn't stop touching him, couldn't stop looking into his eyes. "Okay, don't freak out, but I'm falling for you so hard, Dylan Reed—complete free fall. I'll probably land pretty soon, too."

His smile turned playful and he stood up.

"Land where?"

I pushed at his shoulder as his hands started shifting higher underneath my shirt, making me hyper aware of how close we were standing, how affected I was by his touch.

"You know what I mean." For the first time in a while, I avoided his eyes. "And I want you to fall for me too. I want it so badly—so badly, Dylan. I want to be someone important to you, want to be the kind of someone you are to me, someone you can't live without. And fine, maybe I'm a little weird—that's a big maybe—but I want you to...like the fact that I'm weird, and want me—"

"That's easy, Flash. You're my best friend, like I told you you'd be, and I already love your brand of weird. I'll never forget seeing those neatly stacked M&Ms in the kitchen, and the love you have for pizza? That's a whole other level of weirdness."

I groaned and pushed my face into his neck.

"Everyone loves pizza—that's not weird."

"Not as much as you do, though."

Dylan slowly dragged his hands back down, and every inch of

skin on my body buzzed with awareness. Then his hands were cupping my face and he was pulling me away from his neck to look into my eyes.

"I'll catch you when you land, Flash. Just don't take too much time, because I'm already there, impatiently waiting for you."

I blinked. "You can't make a joke about something like that, Dylan."

"Who said I'm joking? You happened in a heartbeat Zoe, I had no chance."

Did that mean what I thought it meant? Then his lips were on mine and I was kissing him as if our lives depended on it, and all thoughts evaporated from my mind. His hands let go of my face as I wrapped my arms around his neck to get closer and let out a surprised squeak when he pulled me down to his lap.

"Shit," I cursed, reaching back to grab the edge of the bar top. "Dylan, I'm heavy. You can't—"

"I can do anything I want to you now."

Did he think that was a threat?

His brows drew together. "Wait, Chris? He never mentioned anything to me."

I pursed my lips and shook my head. "We've only talked twice since I told him, but he texted me to let me know you were here, so maybe..." A small shrug. "Maybe we'll talk more. Up to him."

"So I'm banging my best friend's sister, huh? I like it."

He grinned, and I grinned back.

"I don't feel any banging happening, but if you say—"

The words died in my mouth as we kissed again and I was carried...away...somewhere.

When a door opened and closed, and my back hit a wall, our lips still connected, I opened my eyes to see where we were. We could've walked for hours and I wouldn't have noticed. Apparently, he'd only carried me up the stairs I'd seen earlier; we were in Jimmy's office. I registered the mostly empty mahogany desk, small old-school safe, tall file cabinet, and couch. It wasn't big in the slightest, but it did look pretty comfy, and I was more than happy to spend the night on it with Dylan. Since it was so small, it meant I'd get to creep even closer to him.

When Dylan nipped my lips, I lost all focus again and there was just us. When he carried me away from the wall, he didn't take me to the couch like I expected him to. Nope, he took me to the desk and dropped my ass right on it.

Before I had a chance to open my mouth or even catch my breath, he was taking off my shirt. For a really short moment, I wanted to hide myself from him, but instead, I reached for the hem of his shirt and peeled it off of him. Giving my breasts—which were hiding in my favorite light blue bra—a quick look, he groaned and pulled my legs open, stepping right in between. He put his palms on the desk on either side of my hips, caging me in, and brought his face down to mine to kiss me. I had to lean back and hold on to him to return his out-of-control kiss. He only stopped when my back touched the wooden surface.

"I didn't even get a chance to learn what turns you on," he murmured right before sucking and gently biting the skin on my neck.

"I don't think you need to learn anything," I rushed out, my voice coming out all choppy. "You're pretty much killing me, so I'd say it's working, and you just looking at me seems to get me going, so..."

He laughed, and the sound vibrated on my skin. "You telling me you're wet for me?"

His hands gripped my waist and slid me downward in one quick movement. I gasped and laughed, holding on to his shoulders. Then I felt his thick, hard cock against the seam of my jeans and lost it completely. Biting his neck, I let out the most wanton moan. I wiggled and pushed myself down as hard as I could as his fingers tightened their grip on my waist to keep me still. Letting go of my hold on his shoulders, I reached between us and tried to unzip his jeans. When it didn't get me anywhere, I pulled back from the kiss and hit my head pretty hard on the desk.

"Shit. Shit. Shit."

He had the audacity to laugh.

"Easy, baby," he whispered, one of his hands gently tangling in my hair and smoothing the pain away. "You want me?"

I couldn't have wanted him *more*, and I *really* didn't think I could speak at that moment, so I just nodded. We stared into each other's eyes, not moving, and whatever he saw in my face made him shake his head and smile down at me. His cheeks looked flushed, his lips swollen—because of me. He took a deep breath as I held mine. His already dark blue eyes were darker, like the night sky, and I couldn't remember ever seeing anything more perfect.

"I wish I could capture this moment," I whispered. "You... just looking at me the way you do."

"You'll have all the time in the world to do anything you want to do to me, Zoe. Trust me."

When I licked my lips, his hands finally moved down and he started to take off his pants. I did the same, wiggling and trying to get rid of them as quickly as possible. I knocked a few files off the desk, but neither of us seemed to care.

"Let me," Dylan said, and he took my pants off in a second, my panties sliding off with them.

I didn't think I could wait any longer, so I sat up and went for his lips again. He helped me by leaning down and wrapping his arms around me. I thought he was feeling just like I was, like he couldn't get close enough.

I squeezed my hand between our bodies and wrapped my hand around his cock. When one hand wasn't satisfying enough, I used the other one too. He wrenched his lips away and hissed into my ear when I rolled my thumb over the plump head.

"I want to taste you," I moaned, my voice low.

"It kills me to say this, but not right now."

I felt his fingers between my legs, parting me, pushing in, and I couldn't even remember what we'd been talking about.

At one point he must have flicked open my bra because when he urged me to lie back, there was nothing but the cool surface of the wood against my skin. I shivered and watched him pluck the loose undergarment off of me. When his mouth closed in on one nipple, first licking and then sucking, I didn't know what to do with my hands, so I just lifted them above my head and held on to the edge of the desk, arching my back and offering more. He gave the same treatment to the other one, making me squirm and pant under him.

Then he was right there, pushing his cock into me, straightening up and watching where we connected with a reverence I couldn't explain. My ears ringing, blood roaring through my veins, I opened my mouth to gasp, but I was so overwhelmed by his size and by having him again that nothing came out. A split second later, another gasp, and then I groaned, feeling him slowly work himself inside, stretching me wide open.

"You have no idea how much I missed you, Flash. Missed being inside you. Feeling you work my cock. Fucking you."

My body shivered, and I smiled.

Then he stopped, and I had to force my eyes open.

"Wh-What? No, don't stop."

Still halfway in me, he dropped his forehead right in the middle of my chest, his warm breath on my cool skin causing me to shiver under him.

"Condom—I forgot the condom."

"Shit. Get one, please."

One of his hands moved on my thigh, caressing, pulling me deeper into madness.

"I don't have one, Flash. Goddammit, I don't have one on me." His hips moved as if he couldn't help himself, pressing into me, going deeper, and we both groaned.

"You realize that you're failing at this college thing, right? What college student doesn't carry around condoms?"

"Smartass," he murmured with a smile to his voice, then we both groaned.

It was on the tip of my tongue to say, *I don't care, just please fuck me*, but he spoke first.

"I haven't been with anyone else since you," he murmured, his tongue finding my nipple and swirling around it. "I've never been with anyone without a condom, and I promise I'm clean."

Relief washed through me and I pulled him up to my lips.

"I'm on the pill," I whispered against his parted lips right before taking a deep breath and kissing him. He moved just an inch, causing my body to twitch in pleasure. "Please, fuck me, Dylan." I panted, gasped. "Please." I didn't mind begging—not at all.

Thank God that was all it took. He slowly pushed the last few inches into me, swallowing down my groans with his mouth.

"That's it...just a little more."

When I tried to ease his thickness off a little by rolling my hips against him, he straightened and held on to my waist, watching with such an intensity. I opened my legs wider, putting my feet up on the edge of the desk. Meeting my eyes, he pulled almost all the way out then thrust back in, causing me to bow up.

He put his hand on my stomach and stroked my body into delirium, all the way up to my throat and then down again. Tipping my head back, all I could do was feel his fullness inside me and try not to lose it too early.

I was plenty wet, but it took a few minutes to get used to him.

When I looked at him, my eyes barely open, I saw him watching himself gently thrust in and out of me. I chose to watch his abdominal muscles, the way they contracted and released. I watched the way his strong shoulders rolled with his thrusts, the way his arms flexed, how fascinated he looked, lost, yet found.

When he lifted his gaze and found me watching him, his pace quickened. Reaching for my hand, he pulled me flush to his chest and slipped his tongue into my mouth. I spread my legs wider and wrapped my legs around his waist, wanting and needing more.

"I'm clean, too," I whispered breathlessly when he let me breathe for a second. My mind was all jumbled up. Was I too late to say that?

"Good," he murmured and hearing his voice did something to me. He moved his hands under my butt and somehow managed to spread me open wider, manipulating my body in ways I wasn't prepared for. My butt hurt from his grip, but I didn't mind the pain; it only fueled what was coming. Suddenly, everything faded away and all I could hear was the rush and roar in my ears. Every nerve ending in my body screamed, and it was all too overwhelming.

"Dylan," I moaned, half whimpering. "Dylan, right there—faster, yes. Please."

"Right here?" he asked, fucking me harder. "Are you going to come on my cock? Do you want me to give it to you harder?"

I was seconds away from sweet death, and I only wanted more. My answer was a gasp and an arch of my spine.

"Yeah, that's it, baby. I'm going to fuck your sweet pussy every day until my last breath, Zoe," he murmured before biting my neck and sucking my skin, and that was all it took for me to get pulled under by an intense orgasm. He kept fucking me through it, his thighs hitting my wide open legs with the loudest smacking sound as my world turned upside down in his arms.

My breath hitched as he pressed two fingers right against my clit. "Come on, Zoe. Let me have everything." My toes curled, my eyes rolled back in my head, and I completely froze. Every muscle in my body tensed as pleasure surged through me. I'm not sure how many seconds I lasted without breathing, but when it was over, I couldn't breathe quickly enough. I gripped his hard, unyielding biceps and groaned as loudly as I could as he slowed yet somehow deepened his thrusts.

"Shit, Zoe," he murmured, and before I was ready for it, he pulled out, pushed me down with a hand on my stomach, and came all over me in thick spurts. I was fascinated by the way his hand moved on his cock. His hold was tighter than I would've dared to squeeze, and he drew out every single drop. I felt a wet line slide down the side of my waist, tickling me.

My body bucked in response and I tipped my head back, closing my eyes.

"Stick a fork in me—I'm done."

I heard a tired chuckle then felt hands moving on the tops of my thighs.

"You should see the way you look right now." His words came out just a little more than a whisper, and each one was a caress on my naked skin.

I closed my eyes and stretched. "Let's do that again," I said with a dopey smile on my face. "I don't have the strength to open my eyes, but I can totally do that again."

This time his chuckle was louder, and it made me shiver all over.

Dylan cleaned me up then kissed me for a full minute. I was over the moon. He helped me dress and then I watched him pull on his own clothes. We managed the impossible and lay down on the couch together. It was worse than his narrow bed in the apartment, yet it couldn't have been more perfect in my eyes.

"I can't wait to fuck you in a normal bed." His voice was all sexy and drowsy, and I'm not ashamed to admit that I wouldn't have said no to another go, but he looked so sleepy, so tired.

I kissed him, just a gentle sweep of my lips, and his closed eyes opened to find me.

"I don't want to miss you like that again. You make fun of me for saying it, but you're my buddy, my best friend. I don't want to let you go, no matter what."

"I'm not going anywhere, baby. It's just us from now on."

"Just us." I exhaled, the words giving me life, and then I hesitated. It wasn't the time, but... "But, you won't be here next year, and if—"

"Don't even finish that sentence, Zoe. We'll figure everything out when the time comes, but believe me when I say I have no intention of letting you go. Just let me sleep with you in my arms and we'll take it one step at a time tomorrow, okay?"

I snuggled in closer and closed my eyes, breathing in his scent.

Just when I was about to drift off, right in that between space, his voice brought me back to the room.

"I'm going to hate myself for even asking this, but what's your number?"

I opened my eyes halfway, my brows drawing together in confusion.

"What? What number?"

"How many guys have you slept with?"

"Dylan..." I groaned. "I don't think that's—"

"Tell me."

I sighed. "Three."

"Three," he repeated, his body tense around me.

"It's not that many, and I definitely don't want to hear yo—"

His body tensed further behind me. "Not that many?" he asked incredulously. His fingers pulsed around my wrist. "That's three too many." I felt him rest his forehead against the back of my head. "I wish I could've been your first. I know I probably sound like a caveman saying that, but even picturing you near another man makes the blood boil in my veins. I can't stand to picture you in someone else's bed, lying just like this." He pulled me closer. "Just me from now on—I'll be the only one touching you, kissing you, holding you, fucking you."

"You won't hear any complaints from me on that," I returned after a few seconds passed and his body gradually thawed.

That night, I got the best sleep after weeks of being miserable, and I was pretty sure Dylan did too.

CHAPTER THIRTY

DYLAN

A few months later...

It was the big day—draft day. I'd woken up before the sunrise in the hotel room we were staying at in Arlington, Texas, where the draft would be held. My dad, my mom, Amelia, Mason, my agent—everyone was there to support me. Well, all but one. The one person that was missing had just landed fifteen minutes ago, and I was getting restless and impatient waiting for her at the airport.

When she still hadn't come out, I headed for a shop to grab a bottle of water. I wasn't sure if my excitement was because I was about to see Zoe or because of the big day—probably a mixture of both—and even though it sounded ridiculous to miss her so much since it'd only been a handful days since I'd left her back in Los Angeles in the shitty little apartment we shared with another student, I'd already accepted that everything was different with her.

I'd never been a jealous person in my life, not to the extent that I was with Zoe, and while sometimes the intensity of my feelings for her scared the shit out of me, I wouldn't have had it any other way. If it meant I'd feel like a Neanderthal trying to keep her away from every person who had a dick between their legs, I'd make my peace with it. As far as I knew, she had no complaints either, which might have had something to do with the fact that I kissed her senseless every time she was about to complain, but we'll never know for sure.

As I waited in line to pay for my water, someone poked me in the shoulder. I turned around and there she was, smiling, glowing, bouncing on her feet, hands covering her mouth.

My lips stretched into a big grin.

"Where did you come from?"

Instead of answering, she squealed and wrapped her arms around me. Chuckling, I returned her hug and held her tighter. After a long moment, she looked up at me and smiled.

"I missed you."

"Yeah?"

"You have no idea."

Seeing how happy she was, I felt a little more centered. "Where have you been? I was going crazy without you," I admitted into her ear then kissed her until I had to stop and pay when it was my turn in line.

Grabbing her carry-on, I linked our hands together, and we walked out of the airport, talking the entire way. As we waited for our Uber to come, she leaned back against me and I wrapped my arms just under her breasts, resting my chin on the top of her head.

"I think I'm starting to freak out, and look"—she raised her palms—"my hands are sweating."

"Why are you freaking out again?"

"I'm about to meet your parents, Dylan, and your brother, and your sister. What if they don't like me? What if they don't like what I'm wearing? What if they think I have no right to be here? I want to be there with you, but if it's going to be awkward for them, maybe I should wait back at the hotel with your brother and sister? But I don't want to do that either..."

I gave her a squeeze and sighed. "Zoe, you're not going to leave my side for a minute, and my parents will love you—they already do from everything I've told them about you. Amelia is even more shy than you are, so she'll probably be quiet, but she's sweet. You'll love her."

She grumbled a little under her breath but didn't protest after that.

Only because I thought I should distract her, I pushed my hips forward so she could feel how hard I was for her then pressed a lingering kiss right under her ear.

Her body went rigid and her hands gripped my forearms tighter.

"That's not fair," she whispered, resting her head back on my shoulder.

I licked my lips and pressed another kiss on her neck. "What's that?"

She wiggled her butt and groaned. We'd been going at each other like rabbits for months.

"I missed you," I whispered.

"Do we even have time for that?" she whispered back.

I sighed and pulled back. "I don't think so, not until after tonight."

"Not even five minutes?"

I gently bit her earlobe and absorbed the way her body shivered. "You're adorable. Does that feel like something you can take care of in just five minutes?"

There was a soft slap on my arm. "*You're* adorable."

I laughed, finally feeling complete after days of not seeing her. "Why do you make it sound like an insult? Of course I'm adorable."

Our car showed up and we held hands through the entire car ride back to the hotel where my family was waiting for us. We'd become one of those obnoxious couples everyone hated who had to touch each other at all times. I loved it.

"Are you scared?" Zoe asked when we were a few minutes away from the hotel. "About tonight."

"Scared, no, but I am excited. I want to get it over with so we'll know where we have to move." I tried to act casual and started playing with her fingers. We hadn't had that talk yet. For me, it wasn't necessary—I wanted her with me no matter what—but I didn't know how she was feeling about it. I knew she wanted to move to New York because of her photography work, and one of the teams that had wanted to talk to me and my agent was the Giants—along with several other teams that were nowhere near the northeast—but I didn't want to tell her anything until it was certain. Unfortunately, nothing was certain when it came to the NFL. You could feel pretty good about yourself, confident that you'd be picked in the first round—maybe even in the top ten—and then out of nowhere you could end up going in the third round, *if* you got picked up at all.

I had no idea where I'd end up or how long I'd have to wait.

"We, huh?"

I stiffened in my seat and stopped playing with her hand. She picked up from where I'd left off, linking and unlinking our hands.

"Flash?" I prompted when nothing else came from her lips.

"Hmmm?"

"You didn't answer."

"Sorry, did you ask something?"

All of a sudden, the car was parking in front of the hotel and we had to get out. I put her carry-on bag on the ground and waited. She got out too and stood in front of me.

"Zoe..."

"What?"

I tilted my head and waited.

"What! You never asked me. We got so busy trying to find a place to live, and then there was the combine. How am I supposed to know whether you want me there or not? Plus, I have one more year, and maybe you—"

I let go of the handle of her carry-on and cradled her face in my hands. She was still trying to talk when I slipped my tongue into her mouth and kissed her senseless right there in front of the strangers walking in and out of the hotel.

"I always want you with me—don't you know that by now? It's been months." I groaned against her lips, my breathing already heavy, my heart racing. "I've always wanted you, Zoe Clarke."

"I wasn't sure."

I rested my brows against hers and let her arms snake around my shoulders.

"I'll go wherever you are, probably the day I graduate, Dylan Reed. You're the best roommate I've ever had, and I won't let go that easily."

I let out the breath I hadn't even realized I was holding and pulled her body flat against mine.

Someone cleared their throat pretty loudly, but neither one of us cared about it enough to break apart.

Then I heard my mom's voice.

"Dylan, I'd like to see your girlfriend, please. Stop mauling her face."

Before my mom was even finished with her sentence, Zoe had pushed me away with unexpected force and her face was already turning that beautiful shade of pink I loved so much. She licked her lips and when that wasn't enough, she swiped them with the back of her hand a few times, her face flushing even brighter.

"Mrs. Reed, it's so nice to meet you."

My mom looked at my grinning face and shook her head. Then she was in front of Zoe and pulling her into her arms. "Just Lauren. I've been dying to meet you. I'm so happy you could take a few days off and meet us here."

When my mom let her go, she was still flushed, but instead of that mortified look on her face, she was smiling softly.

"And look at you," my mom gushed, cupping Zoe's face. "Gosh, you're gorgeous. Look at her eyes, Dylan. She is beautiful."

Zoe sent me a helpless look and I laughed, reaching for her hand.

"I know, Mom. That's why I'm keeping her—so I'll have something nice to look at for the rest of my life.. What are you doing out here? The rest of the gang still at the restaurant?"

Finally she let go of Zoe and turned to me. Pulling my face down, she kissed my cheek.

"I couldn't sit down and wait, and, I admit"—she sent Zoe a quick wink—"I wanted to see Zoe before everyone else. Now she is here and everything is so perfect. I'm so proud of you, Dylan. We're so excited."

I groaned. "Lauren Reed, if you start crying again, so help me—"

"No crying, not yet. Oh, okay. Maybe a little bit of crying." She quickly brushed away her tears. "Come on, let's take Zoe inside so she can meet everyone before you disappear for those interviews."

With one of my hands suffering a death grip in Zoe's, I grabbed the handle of her luggage with my free hand and took two of my favorite women inside.

THE LIGHTS AT THE STADIUM, the hushed conversations, the camera guys walking around the tables—all the people around us were starting to get to me. I felt Zoe's hand on my leg, stopping me from bouncing it against the table.

The show was about to start in less than ten minutes.

"You, okay?" she asked, leaning toward me, her eyes worried.

I grabbed her hand under the table and held on. "Everything's good."

She didn't look like she believed me, but her touch calmed me down just enough.

My parents were talking with my agent when I felt a hand close on my shoulder.

"What's up, man?" Chris greeted me with a huge grin on his face when I twisted in my seat to look back.

I rose and we gave each other a quick hug.

"I called you on the way here, wasn't sure you'd make it."

He sighed and played with his tie. "Just a little late, that's all." When Zoe pushed her chair back and joined us, Chris leaned down and kissed her cheek.

She was beaming up at him.

"Hi, Zoe."

"Hey. I texted you earlier to wish you luck, wasn't sure I'd get to talk to you here."

"I called you, but I guess you can't hear a thing with everything going on."

Zoe stood beside me as her eyes skittered around, no doubt looking to see if Mark was around.

"He's not here," Chris commented before I could say anything.

Zoe's frown deepened. "This is the biggest day of your life, how could h—"

Chris turned to me. "You didn't tell her?"

"Didn't come up," I replied, avoiding Zoe's curious gaze as I absentmindedly stroked her back.

Their interaction was still awkward at best, nowhere near a normal sibling relationship, but I knew Chris wanted that... maybe not as much as Zoe wanted it, at least not yet, but I knew he was trying to get there.

A camera guy started to film us as he passed by, and Zoe inched closer to my side. "Tell me what?"

As Chris started to tell her how he'd basically forced Mark's hand to make him resign from the team, Zoe's fingers gripped my forearm tighter and tighter.

"It was either that or I was going to tell my mom I knew about the adoption. In his own weird, sick way, he cares about her...I think." Chris must've seen the look on Zoe's face because he shook his head and gave her the rest of the story. "It's not just you, Zoe. He was messing around with students...girls. He was going to get himself into trouble eventually."

We weren't giving her the whole story, but I'd already spoken to Chris and he'd promised me he wouldn't tell her how I'd broken his father's nose soon after he was no longer our official coach. You see, Zoe had forgotten to tell me what had happened in the apartment right before I'd walked in that night. I'd learned about it only because Chris had made an offhand comment, thinking she'd already told me.

I slid my arm around Zoe's waist and pulled her to my side just as they announced that the event was about to begin.

After promising to meet up after the night was over, we had to say goodbye so Chris could go to the table they had him seated at.

"It's gonna be a long night," Zoe murmured beside me, wringing her hands in her lap.

"How do you feel?" I asked into her ear.

She looked up at me. "About what?"

"Your dad."

"He is not my dad," she replied automatically. "I don't feel anything." She shrugged. "I don't care one way or another, and he is the last person I want to talk about tonight." She reached up to touch my cheek. "Tonight is all about you." Her smile got bigger. "You made it, Dylan. All those shifts at the bar, all those morning workouts—which I enjoyed immensely, thank you very much—studying your ass off to graduate early...*all* your hard work, and look where you are. I'm so proud of you."

Turning my head, I pressed a kiss to her palm. "Not yet, Flash. We don't know anything yet. I have no idea where we're gonna end up."

"Oh, come on. I read some of the predictions—someone will snatch you up in the first round. Your NFL combine was legendary."

I laughed. "Yeah? What do you know about it?"

"Nothing, but I know whichever team gets you will have one hell of a season next year with you on their side."

I laughed harder and drew the attention of my parents. I nuzzled her neck. "You crack me up, Flash."

She pushed me back. "You just keep making fun of me, buddy. I predict you'll be in the top five."

My eyes widened. I pushed a lock of hair behind her ear and my smile softened. "Top five, huh?"

The commissioner was on the stage, and all the players sitting around us fell silent.

"Welcome to the NFL draft!"

The night began as he put the Cleveland Browns on the clock and the waiting game started. The table we were sharing with another player and his family got a lot quieter after that, and my dad changed seats with my agent, Scott, to sit next to me. My mom was next to Zoe and they were whispering discreetly.

The minutes ticked by, and with the first pick, the Cleveland Browns selected a quarterback from Oklahoma.

"For the overall second pick, the New York Giants are now on the clock."

I closed my eyes and ran both of my hands over my head. I was so ready to find out what my future held.

Zoe touched my arm and I looked at her. "It's going to be great. You got this," she whispered, our heads tilted down, side by side.

Eight minutes passed.

"You have an idea which team will pick you?" my dad asked.

"No idea, Dad. If I don't get picked...if I start dropping too much, my chances will get only lower."

He thumped my back two times and shook his head. I could see how nervous and restless he was, but he was doing his best to not show it. We watched the commissioner walk back on stage, and all chatter quieted.

"With the second pick of the 2018 NFL draft, the New York Giants select Dylan Reed, wide receiver..."

It took me a second or two to process what I was hearing, what I was seeing on the screen. My dad, my mom, and Zoe were all standing, but I couldn't hear a single thing because of the blood roaring in my ears.

I covered my head with my hands and slowly got up.

Both of my parents were crying, but I was still in shock. My dad was the first one to pull me into his arms. Everyone was clapping around us, and I felt my dad's chest rapidly rising and falling with his silent tears. He pulled back and looked at me, his hands holding my face. He gently patted my cheek twice then let me go. My mom was standing right next to him, her eyes bright and wide and beautiful as always.

"Look at you," she said, her voice broken but still strong and proud. "Look at my beautiful boy."

When she let me go, I turned around.

She was standing right there, waiting for me, and that's when I smiled. That's when sound started to trickle back in, and she still just stood there, tears running down her cheeks. I went to her because I couldn't look at her and not touch, not hold. Leaning down, I wrapped my arms around her waist, and she stood on her tiptoes to hug me back. I could feel her frantic heartbeats, her pulse beating wildly. Then we started laughing, my own eyes misted with unshed tears.

When they told me I needed to go to the stage, Zoe pulled back and smiled. "Go, go, go."

Everything that came after happened in slow motion, yet I still had trouble keeping up. Chris stopped me on my way and hugged me. I was still surprised...elated, shocked, honored, humbled. Then I was on stage and I could see myself on the big screen as the fans cheered. I took my new jersey with my name on it and smiled for the photographs. I'd made it.

I'd fucking made it.

I had everything I'd ever wanted and more.

As soon as I was off the stage, my phone rang, and I listened to my new coach welcoming me to the team. I don't remember everything he said to me, but I remember repeating a lot of the same things: "Yes, sir." "I won't disappoint you, sir." "I appreciate it, sir."

It was surreal for sure, but it was also bittersweet. As soon as I hung up with my new coach, JP's call came in. He hadn't recovered back to his old self and the trainers didn't think he had a future playing anymore, but he'd taken everything better than I would've if I were in his position. Still, I planned to try my best to help him in any way I could. We would always be a team.

When I made it back to the table, I found Chris and Zoe standing together, smiling and talking. As soon as I got back, I went another round with my mom and dad, and listened to them talk, still just as speechless as I'd been on the call with my coach. I couldn't wait to get back to the hotel and see Mason and Amelia's faces when they heard I was the second fucking overall pick. Mason was going to lose it.

Then it was just Zoe and me, resting our foreheads against each other and just breathing as I held her face in my hands. I tried to clear her tears with my thumbs, but I couldn't keep up.

"We did it."

She put her hands on my chest. "*You* did it, Dylan. This is all you and you're amazing."

"No. These last few months...you've been amazing, and it's New York, baby! It's where you wanted to live."

"I'll live anywhere with you, Dylan. I'll go wherever you are."

"Come with me." Grabbing her hand, I dragged her behind me, dodging cameras and even more people. Breathless, she ran after me to keep up. If I could've kept my hands to myself for a little while, we would have heard that Chris had been picked by the Chicago Bears.

I stopped when we reached the bathrooms and pulled her in behind me, locking the door immediately.

I took a deep breath before I turned around to stare at her. She was leaning back against the sink, her beautiful smile soft and inviting.

"I can give you everything you want now. I know I couldn't do much until now, but Flash, trust me, you'll—"

"Shut up. I just want you, Dylan. Nothing else matters. We'll figure everything out together, right?" I swallowed thickly. "Though I have to say, I can't wait to see you wearing more suits from now on. You look so handsome."

"You like it? You like me like this, Zoe?"

I went to her before she could answer and grabbed her waist to hoist her up. She locked her arms around my neck and hid her face in my throat, pulling me closer. I rested my head against her temple, just breathing, just the two of us, away from everything and all the noise.

"I love you. I've loved you for so long, I don't even know when it started anymore," she said quietly, so much emotion in her voice.

I drew back and looked into her watery eyes.

"You don't know? The first time you saw me, you were grinning at my dick."

She snorted then groaned to cover it up. "I did not fall in love with your dick, Dylan."

"I think you did, but let's go with your version. It's a package deal anyway." I started to drag her dress up her thighs and she let me. Wiggling her butt, she even let me remove her panties. Widening her legs, I yanked her toward me until we were perfectly aligned and I could feel her heat against my slacks. I didn't even care if she gave me a wet spot. She moved closer, her arms already pulling me to her. "You could hardly look away," I mumbled against her mouth, her breath already mingling with mine.

She took my lips in a heated kiss, her tongue pushing between them and demanding I give her what she liked. I kissed her and let her slowly unzip me with her sneaky fingers.

"Do you believe in love at first sight?"

"Not really," she panted.

"I didn't either, but then why would my eyes look for you in a crowd when I didn't even know your name? Why would my pulse jump whenever I saw someone I thought was you?"

Moaning, her eyes closed and she played with my cock, making me hiss.

"You want me inside you?"

She nodded. "Always."

I held my cock in my hand and parted her lips before slowly pushing in. She was slick with arousal, tight and ready for me, as always. My breaths were coming in harsh spurts when I gave her all my length, and her legs trembled around me.

"Will it always feel like this?" she asked, her eyes already unfocused, body restless.

"Always."

"I love you so much," she whispered. "I don't know what to do with it all."

"I love you too, Flash. On and off the field, you're my hardest fall. No one has ever compared, and no one ever will. It was always going to be you for me."

EPILOGUE

"Oh," Zoe gasped as her body tensed for a quick second then relaxed against my chest. I circled my arms around her waist before she could get away from me. "It's you. I didn't hear you come in."

"Were you expecting someone else?"

I stared down at her as her head fell back against my chest and she looked up at me. "Nope."

"Good answer." I leaned down and dropped a quick kiss on her forehead.

When our eyes met, she smiled at me, and my arms involuntarily tightened around her. Years had passed since she'd first told me she loved me, and I still couldn't get enough of seeing how much she loved me in her eyes without her having to say it.

"You don't get to use that smile on me," I said, my heart warming just at the sight of that sweet expression on her face.

"What? Why?"

"I still haven't forgotten about John, Flash. You still haven't made up for that."

She snorted and her smile got bigger. I loved it, loved seeing her face light up, seeing her eyes sparkle when she looked at me with such open, endless love.

"He gave me his wife's phone number. You were there, right next to me."

"Yeah and thank God I was. I've never seen you smile that big at someone other than me or your dad."

"Oh, shut up." Her arms started running over my forearms, caressing, seducing without even noticing what she was doing. "I was just trying to be nice."

"You don't have to be nice to my teammates. Be nice to your husband."

"I'm always nice to my husband, and that teammate just gave me his wife's number so we could talk about a cute little shoot I'll do for them when their baby is born."

Husband—every time the word left her mouth, my chest puffed up, and I couldn't help but feel proud. She was mine, my Flash, and I was the luckiest bastard to walk this earth.

Leaning down, I ran my nose along her neck and breathed in her scent. "Still doesn't change the fact that you smiled at him like that. Admit it—I know you checked his ass out."

"Are you kidding me? Have you seen your own ass in those tight pants? I mean, of course you have, but...do you know what I mean? It's just hard to take your eyes away when someone walks right in front of you. I didn't know where else to look."

I stopped and lifted my head from her neck. "That's not funny at all, Zoe."

She laughed. Her body shook in my arms as she turned and pulled my head down for a quick kiss. "Then don't ask me funny questions. Now go away so I can finish cooking, and don't open the fridge—you don't get to see the cakes."

There was no way she could get rid of me that easily. Instead of getting out of her hair, I pushed her back against the kitchen island and trapped her between my arms.

"I like where I am."

I tried to go for another kiss, but she arched away from me. "Everyone will be here soon and nothing is ready yet."

"Relax. Everything is ready. I can barely walk into the living room with all the balloons," I murmured against her throat.

"How was your workout?"

We were off-season, but that didn't mean I wasn't training. I was working every day to stay at the top and be the best I could. After New York, we had moved once, but it'd been three years with the new team and I was happy with the move. I'd be happy as long as I played, and that was the truth. We were happy.

I ignored Zoe's question and sucked the skin on her neck to make her go crazy.

"Dylan," she groaned, her tone a dead giveaway as to how close she was to giving in to me, but then again, she always gave in to me.

I stole another kiss, this one longer and filthier as I tasted every inch of her mouth and took her breath away. By the time I gave her a break, she was already standing on her tiptoes and reaching up for seconds.

Her eyes still closed, she swallowed hard and licked her lips. I pushed my hands under her silk shirt and caressed her back, smiling when I felt goose bumps break out over her skin.

"Did you get the Nutella?" she murmured.

I buried my face in her neck and grazed her skin with my teeth. "All four of them."

"And did you get all the Reese's, too? And M&Ms?"

I let my hands travel all the way up her back and couldn't hold back my grin when she shivered and tried to plaster the lower part of her body against mine. I gave her what we both desperately needed—always—and lifted her up on the counter, pushed her skirt higher on her thighs, and pulled her legs around me until I could feel the heat radiating from her core through my pants.

"I got everything. Do we have enough time?"

"They—"

Before my beautiful wife could give me an answer, we heard footsteps rushing toward us, then my gorgeous little girl appeared around the corner. Her eyes got bigger when she saw me and her little feet quickened.

"Daddy!" she shrieked, arms open, ready for me to catch her. "Snuggles!"

Zoe unwrapped her legs from my back and I took a step back from her. The little monster aiming for me was the only thing that could distract me from my wife.

I crouched down and caught my little baby, Sophia, in my arms. "Oooff," I groaned when she crashed into me and wrapped her arms around my neck.

"Daddy," she whispered as she laid her face on my shoulder, and my heart just melted. I straightened and saw Zoe watching us with a smile on her face. I couldn't get enough of them, never would, not till the day I died. Leaning toward her, I gave Zoe a small kiss on her lips as she closed her legs and focused on our daughter.

"I missed you like crazy," she whispered when she was done hugging me and looked at my face.

"I know, I missed you like crazy, too."

"It's only been a few hours you two," Zoe said, cutting into our usual lovefest as she jumped down from the counter. I'd have to wait until everyone went to bed before I gave her *all* my attention.

Small hands turned my head, and I looked into my daughter's happy little face, her clear blue eyes just like mine.

"Mommy is jealous," she whispered loudly, and Zoe snorted.

"I know, she is always jealous of us."

Sophia nodded eagerly then a grin touched her face. "Your face looks happy, Daddy. Is it because it's my birthday?"

"It's my birthday, too, you know," I replied. While my baby was a little mini version of Zoe with all her quirks and looks, she had been born on my birthday—the best present Zoe could ever give me.

"Happy birthday, Daddy. But your face is happy because it's my birthday, right?"

I laughed. "Yeah, I think that's why my face is happy."

"See, told ya. Did you buy my Riri's?"

"Yes, I got your Reese's."

"My Nutella?"

"Got that, too."

"Show me."

She was the bossiest little thing in the house, and I loved her for it.

"Let's check them out." I winked at Zoe as she stood barefoot next to the stove and stirred the meat sauce for the lasagna she was preparing. She shook her head, but I knew how much she enjoyed seeing me with Sophia. Marriage hadn't killed our love or sex life—not at all. We still couldn't keep our hands off of each other, and I hoped it'd stay that way till we were wrinkly and old.

I took Sophia to the counter and showed her everything I'd gotten one by one. To say both my daughter and wife had a sweet tooth would have been an understatement.

"Good, good. You did good, Daddy. Now put them all in my closet so I can see them every day."

I threw my head back and laughed. She was the funniest little thing, repeating everything she heard from the adults around her, and just like her mommy, she loved gazing at her prized possessions.

"Where is your grandpa, Soph?" Zoe asked, and she turned her attention to her mom.

"Outside."

"Yeah? What's he doing outside?"

She lifted her little shoulder in a shrug until it touched her ear. "I dunno."

"Sophia?"

"My favorite ball went missing and he is helping me look for it."

My chest shook with silent laughter. "Did you hide it, Soph?"

She turned her big, innocent eyes to me and gave another shrug. "I dunno."

Gently, I put her down and righted her frilly white birthday dress. "Come on, go get Grandpa Ron—everyone will be here soon."

"For my birthday, right?"

"Yes, everyone is coming to see you. Now go get him."

Happy with everything she was hearing, she dashed out of the kitchen after giving Zoe's leg a quick hug and a quick "Love you, Mommy," all the while yelling for her grandpa.

"Granpa, everyone is coming! We're gonna have cakes and I'm gonna get pressies!"

I went back to Zoe and she shrieked when my hands went up toward her boobs. She slapped my arms and forced my hands out of her shirt.

"My dad is coming inside, what are you doing?"

"You weren't worried about your dad a minute ago."

"Yeah, because I knew they were outside. Now Sophia will get him in faster than you can give me a kiss."

Ignoring her protests, I hugged her and rested my chin on top of her head. "We could've gotten pizza—why are you cooking so much food?"

"Don't say pizza. I want one so bad. Everyone will stay for the weekend, so we'll order some tomorrow, and your dad loves my lasagna."

"And you love him."

"Well...yeah..."

I pressed a kiss against her cheek. She loved my family, and they loved her in return. My mom had taken her side on more than a few occasions, and I couldn't have been prouder of my parents with the way they had welcomed her into the fold.

"Did they land? Did they call you? Amelia texted me before they boarded, but I haven't checked my phone since then."

"They did. I just talked to them before coming inside. They're waiting for JP and his wife then they'll head here together." I reached forward and stole a piece of cheese before she could stop me. "JP will probably land at any moment."

"Is he happy now?" Zoe asked before turning off the stove.

"Yeah, he's happy with the assistant coaching job for his old high school, and we have more ideas. It'll be okay." My best friend had struggled with the outcome of his injury, but he'd never given up on anything in his life. A shift of career wasn't going to change that. *Just a different road now*, he'd said. *Just a different dream.* "When is Chris coming?"

"He should be here any minute, and Kayla should be here not too long after him."

"Good." I nuzzled her neck. "Are you happy to live just an hour away from your friend? She's doing better, right?"

She tilted her head to give me more access and dropped the wooden spoon on the counter.

"Yeah," she murmured. "She's not dating seriously, not after that Tyron guy, but she is at least dating. Dylan, my dad is gonna come inside any minute—Dylan! Don't do that."

"I can hear them, and Soph is asking him what pressies he got her." I chuckled and gently bit Zoe's neck as she melted into me. "Just in case you didn't know, we're raising a monster. I don't want her to grow up. This size is perfect."

"You're just now noticing that? Mmmm, that feels good. Jared can't make it by the way. He's busy with work, but he said he'd call you later."

I nodded and kept brushing small kisses on her skin.

The doorbell rang and we both froze. A second later we could hear Sophia's shriek as she ran through the house to get the door.

"Uncle Chrissy is here!"

Zoe chuckled. "*Chrissy*—he's gonna get you back for that, you know," she mumbled as we reluctantly let go of each other.

I sighed and yelled at my daughter. "You're not allowed to answer the door, Soph! Wait for me."

"Hurry up, Daddy. Hurry up, hurry up, hurry up!"

I saw Ronald come into the kitchen with a smile on his face and left Zoe with him so I could go open the door for my best friend, Sophia's Uncle Chrissy.

Zoe and Chris's relationship had definitely evolved. They were much closer than they had been six years before during those first few months after he learned about everything, but it had taken them a long time to get where they were. There were still moments where you could see them holding back, but Zoe was happy she got to see him as often as she did since we were playing for the same team and were pretty much unbeatable.

And Sophia...well, Chris was her favorite human in the world, and we were pretty sure her feelings were reciprocated, which was probably why he came to our house for dinner three or four times a week.

As I walked through the corridor that held my talented wife's beautiful photographs and made it to the front door, Sophia was talking to her favorite uncle through the door.

"I missed you, Uncle Chrissy. Where were you? Did you bring my presents with you? It's my birthday today."

Laughing, I opened the door and Sophia threw herself at Chris, shouting joyfully when he lifted her up in his arms.

"Who is this beautiful girl?" Chris asked, and my daughter beamed at my best friend.

"It's me, silly."

Chris drowned her in kisses and her laughter echoed throughout our house, as it continued to do for the rest of the day.

———

IT WAS eleven PM and my parents had gone to sleep when I found Zoe sitting on our bed.

"Where did you disappear to?" I asked as I opened the door wider and stepped inside.

She looked at me over her shoulder and smiled. "I'll be down in a minute. Where is Sophia?"

I grinned. "Sleeping in Chris's lap." I sat down beside her and grasped her hand in mine. "Is everything okay? Did Chris say something about...?"

"What? No, no. They haven't talked in years, if that's what you're asking. As far as I know, he only talks to his mom, and they've divorced, although—I don't want to talk about him. You don't have to ask anymore."

"Okay, Flash, whatever you want. Are you just tired then? You barely sat down today."

She sighed and rested her shoulder against mine, eyes on our hands.

"It's a good tired. It was the best day." She glanced at me and our eyes met as she whispered, "Happy birthday, Dylan. Don't think I forgot you. I'll give you your present after everyone goes to sleep."

"Thank you, Flash." My smiling lips touched hers and we broke apart too soon for my liking. "What are you doing in here?"

"I came up to get my laptop. I was gonna show Kayla the shoot I did for that couple I mentioned at dinner. And the other two I decided to send out to the gallery in New York. I just sat down for a minute."

"You okay?"

She touched my cheek and smiled. "Yes."

"Are you happy, Zoe?"

She laughed. "It's your birthday—I should be the one asking you that."

I just continued with my questioning. "Do I make you happy? Does our life make you happy?"

Her brows drew together and then she was climbing onto my lap, holding my face in her hands.

"Where is this coming from?"

"Just want to make sure."

Her hands moved to my shoulders and she settled down more comfortably on top of me, earning a small grunt and groan from me.

"I never thought I could be this happy," she whispered.

"Do I give you everything you want?"

"Yes, you idiot, and so much more. I would've been happy with just you—"

I cut her off. "Deliriously happy."

"Yes, deliriously happy, but look at everything you've given me. I love our family so much. I love *you* so much, Dylan Reed. I'm so happy I barged in on you in that bathroom and saw your glorious cock."

"Glorious, yes—good word choice." We laughed together as I caressed her back. "And your little family loves you back, especially me. *I* love you the most, baby. I'm your biggest fan.

However, you missed our breakfast this morning, so clearly I've been worrying. I could barely do my push-ups without your eyes on me. Don't make it a habit, my little pervert."

My dick was already hardening under her, and with the smile she gave me, I lost the battle.

"I was getting our daughter ready."

"And that's the only reason I didn't come get you so you could stare at me."

Holding my neck, she rested her forehead against mine, our lips almost touching.

"Am I too weird for you? You always make fun of my quirks."

"Quirks? Oh, is that what we're calling them now?"

I held her butt in my palms and pulled her a little forward then pushed a little back. Thanks to her short skirt, she could feel all of me. Her eyes closed on their own and she bit her bottom lip.

"I'm stuck with you so...I guess I'll make do?" I smirked and she chuckled.

Ever since the first day I met her, she'd never seen her own perfect, but that was okay. I wasn't planning on going anywhere; I'd be right next to her to show her every day for the rest of our lives.

It's hard to explain what draws you to a person, what it is about them that makes them so special that you give them your heart. I believe it's all about who you are together, how you are together. It's simple, what I feel for her—simple, and the most powerful thing in the world.

We chose each other, and we'd keep choosing each other long after we took our last breaths on this earth.

Zoe Clarke was my forever, the love of my life, and I was hers.

THE END.

ACKNOWLEDGMENTS

There is so much that goes into writing a book and with this one there were a few people I can never thank enough because without their support and help, I don't think I could've finished it.

Erin...You've been there for me from the very beginning and I think you will be in every single one of my thank you notes. I'm not sure how you feel about that, but I'm not sorry. You're my rock. You're seriously an amazing friend to me and I'm so lucky to have you. You listen to my non-stop ramblings and still help me when I'm stuck. I can't imagine doing this without you. Thank you for not getting rid of me. Thank you for holding my hand when I'm having a rough time. Are you ready to do it all over again with the new one? I really hope so because I don't think I'll ever be able to do this without you.

Beth and Shelly-My Delta Beta Squad. You two...first of all-thank you for being there when no else was around. This book wouldn't be what it is without you two. It takes a village to write a new book, and you're the residents of my entire village. You're also kind of stuck with me to be honest, so there is that. I probably will never find the right words that will convey how grateful I am that you decided that it was a good idea to be my friend, so I'm not gonna try and make a mess of it. I know for sure that I wouldn't be writing this right now if I didn't have your help to perfect Dylan and Zoe's love story. And it's not only that you were my only beta readers either (though your comments throughout the book gave me life), it's the daily support you give me, the encouragements, the friendship, the voice messages, the smiles... I'm so lucky to have you two. So unbelievably lucky. Thank you for being there for me when I needed it the most.

A huge thank you to Caitlin Nelson. You make my books readable and somehow even better. I don't know what I would've done if you hadn't taken me back after my long hiatus. Thank you so much for being the best editor.

Ellie McLove, thank you for squeezing me in at the last minute. You're amazing.

Nina, thank you for all you've done. I hope this is just the beginning for us. I promise not to hoard all the teasers.

And my readers...do you still remember me? I missed you so much. If you don't know, I went through some health problems which is why I couldn't release a new novel for almost two years. And while Dylan and Zoe kept me company through that rough time, the one thing that made me sad was that you guys were going to forget all about me. I hope you didn't. I hope this was good for you. I hope Dylan worth the wait. For me he was. I hope that you have a smile on your face right now.

Bloggers. you are AMAZING. Thank you so much for all the love you have shown for Dylan and Zoe's cover. I really hope you enjoyed their story and you too have a smile on your face right now. I hope that Dylan and Zoe wasn't a disappointment. I appreciate everything you're doing for me and my book.